WHISPER
IN THE NIGHT

ALSO BY BRANDON MASSEY

WHISPERS IN THE NIGHT

Edited by
BRANDON MASSEY

KENSINGTON PUBLISHING CORP.
http://www.kensingtonbooks.com

DAFINA BOOKS are published by

Kensington Publishing Corp.
119 West 40th Street
New York, NY 10018

All Kensington Titles, Imprints, and Distributed Lines are available at special quantity discounts for bulk purchases for sales promotions, premiums, fund-raising, and educational or institutional use. Special book excerpts or customized printings can also be created to fit specific needs. For details, write or phone the office of the Kensington special sales manager: Kensington Publishing Corp., 119 West 40th Street, New York, NY 10018, attn: Special Sales Department. Phone: 1-800-221-2647.

Dafina Books and the Dafina logo Reg. U.S. Pat. & TM Off.

ISBN-13: 978-0-7582-1742-4
ISBN-10: 0-7582-1742-0
First Dafina Trade Paperback Edition: July 2007
First Dafina Mass Market Edition: September 2014

eISBN-13: 978-1-61773-609-4
eISBN-10: 1-61773-609-0
Kensington Electronic Edition: September 2014

10 9 8 7 6 5 4 3 2 1

Printed in the United States of America

CONTENTS

INTRODUCTION

Well, well, well. Here we are again. And as the old saying goes, the third time's the charm.

If you're a newbie to the *Dark Dreams* series, here's a quick overview of what it's all about: a collection of horror and suspense short fiction, following no particular theme, with all of the stories written exclusively by black writers, established, upcoming, and those seeing their work in print for the first time ever.

In the three years since the first volume in the series was published, we've seen, happily, more horror/suspense fiction by black writers on bookstore shelves, much of it produced by *Dark Dreams* alumni. Tananarive Due, L.A. Banks, and Robert Fleming have given us memorable novels and short story collections. Evie Rhodes has been growing an audience, with works such as *Expired* and *Criss Cross*. Gregory Townes earned much-deserved acclaim for *The Tribe*, his self-published debut. Speaking of self-published horror novels by black writers, in fact, there are a *ton* of them, and it will be interesting to see how many find their way inside a major publisher's catalog in the near future.

All of this is good. Many eyes have been opened in the past few years; people are beginning to see that black writers really *can* write horror stories. But there is still much work to be done. Personally, I'm looking forward to the day when I'm not referred to as the Black Stephen King or Dean Koontz; I'm looking forward to the day when I can give a speech to a group of readers and don't have to justify why I write the stories that I do.

More important: I'm looking forward to the day when *any* black writer can pen a tale of horror and suspense, and can discuss it with readers without apologies or undue explanation, without being likened to being merely a black version of a white author, without being viewed with suspicion or even fear.

Bottom line—I'm looking forward to seeing genuine *respect* accorded to the brothers and sisters who choose to write in this oft-maligned field. The *Dark Dreams* series is a collective effort by those of us who love the genre to nurture that love in others, too. A grand ambition, to be sure. The only way for us to achieve it is to deliver stories that challenge, thrill, educate, entertain, and delight readers.

The first two *Dark Dreams* books broke new ground in the genre; I truly believe that in this, the third volume, we may have the finest stories yet. This is no easy feat, considering how well received the first two books have been. If you've been following the series from the beginning, you'll notice that many of the writers from the previous collections have appeared yet again in this one. There's a reason for this, and it's quite simple: time and again, they've given me the best stories.

The celebrated Tananarive Due, for example, has participated in all three anthologies. "Danger Word," her story in the first book, which she cowrote with her husband, Steven Barnes, was an apocalyptic zombie tale; her second story, "Upstairs," was a gripping tale of psychological "real world" horror about a little girl who has a secret relationship with a serial killer hiding out in her family's attic. And her entry here, "Summer," is another grabber, a story about a young mother struggling to raise her infant daughter one sweltering summer on the swamp—when her child-rearing troubles are suddenly eased by an otherworldly visitor. . . .

Other three-time contributors include Christopher Chambers, back with "Mr. Bones," a story set in the days of black minstrels on the chitlin circuit—and brought into modern times with a chilling, thought-provoking twist. L.R. Giles uses the recent megachurch phenomenon as the background of his "Power and Purpose," an aptly titled piece about a gifted psychic who may be the only one able to save a popular preacher. Anthony Beal returns with "And Death Rode With Him," a puzzling—and ultimately revealing—story about a bar in the Southwest desert, where the drinks are bad and the patrons never seem to leave. Rickey Windell George, always reliable for a shocker of a tale, will knock you out with "Hell Is for Children," a grisly account of a mother doing her best to raise her child under the most trying of circumstances (only readers with strong stomachs should dare to read this one).

Lawana James-Holland is back with a signature story of history and horror in "Flight," following the adventures of a black man living with Native Americans in the frontier days—when mystical beasts possibly roamed the land. In "Rip Crew," B. Gordon Doyle uses the hard-hitting language and culture of the streets to pull us into a shadowy world inhabited by violent gangs and bizarre sex cults. Chesya Burke questions how far one should go to save a wayward sister in "My Sister's Keeper." And Terence Taylor resurrects the still-fresh tragedy of Hurricane Katrina to inform his unforgettable "WET PAIN," a story of racism, friendship . . . and malevolent entities that feed on human misery.

Those are the members of the "three-time" team. But we've also got writers returning for a second tour of dark dreaming duty. In "The Wasp," Robert Fleming tells the story of a woman who tries to use the legal system to escape her abusive husband—and when it fails and even turns on her, as a last resort she takes a most extreme way out. Maurice Broaddus plumbs questions of God and the Devil in "Nurse's Requiem," as a young Christian man works at a deteriorating nursing home in a quest to prove his faith. Michael Boatman takes another break from his acting work to demonstrate again that he's a multitalented artist, in the satiric zombie tale "Hadley Shimmerhorn: American Icon."

But *Dark Dreams* isn't just about prior contributors coming back to entertain us and challenge us anew; it's also a venue for new voices and first-timers to the series. Wrath James White, known in the horror small-press community for his searing visions of terror, hits a home run with "Scab," a stunning story of a dark-skinned black man tragically haunted by the mocking, derisive voices of his youth, when it wasn't considered "in" to have a dark complexion. Lexi Davis dishes up a load of laughs in "Are You My Daddy?" about a young man who just can't get away from the responsibility of serving as a child's father—a kid gifted in ways that'll make your head spin.

With "Dream Girl," Dameon Edwards, in his first major publication, explores the question that black women seeking a black man continually ask, "Where are all the good brothers?" According to this unusual story, they just might be hanging out at the strip clubs—with a girl from their dreams who materializes from thin air. . . . Tenea Johnson delves into a fascinating racial issue in "The Taken," about a pro-black group that abducts a number of affluent white adults—and stows them on a ship, in a reenactment of the infamous and harrowing Middle Passage that brought millions of Africans to America.

Newcomer Tish Jackson shows a deft touch for tongue-in-cheek comedy and horror in "The Love of a Zombie Is Everlasting," perhaps the most original zombie story I've yet to read. And Randy Walker gives us a fresh twist on the obsessive-compulsive, weirdo writer idea with "To Get Bread and Butter," about an author who makes *Monk* (a TV show featuring a famously eccentric detective) look positively normal by comparison.

There's a startling breadth of work here. If you have a taste for the imaginative, the suspenseful, the horrific, or the just plain bizarre, you'll find something (hopefully, *much*) that you'll enjoy.

And remember, you'd better keep that night-light on . . .

Summer

Tananarive Due

During the baby's nap time, a housefly buzzed past the new screen somehow and landed on Danielle's wrist while she was reading *Us Weekly* on the back porch. With the Okeepechee swamp so close, mosquitoes and flies take over Graceville in summer.

"Well, I'll be damned," she said.

Most flies zipped off at the first movement. Not this one. The fly sat still when Danielle shook her wrist. Repulsion came over her as she noticed the fly's spindly legs and shiny coppery green helmet staring back at her, so she rolled up the magazine and gave it a swat. The fly never seemed to notice Angelina Jolie's face coming. Unusual for a fly, with all those eyes seeing from so many directions. But there it was, dead on the porch floorboards.

Anyone who says they wouldn't hurt a fly is lying, Danielle thought.

She didn't suspect the fly was a sign until a week later, when it happened again—this time she was in the bathroom clipping her toenails on top of the closed toilet seat, not in her bedroom, where she might disturb Lola during her nap. A fly landed on Danielle's big toe and stayed put.

Danielle conjured Grandmother's voice in her memory—as she often did when she noticed the quiet things Grandmother used to tell her about. Grandmother had passed three summers ago after a stroke in her garden, and now that she was gone, Danielle had a thousand and one questions for her. The lost questions hurt the most. *Anything can happen once,* Grandmother used to say. *When it happens twice—listen. The third time may be too late.*

It was true about men, and Danielle suspected it was true about the flies, too.

Once the second fly was dead—again, almost as if it had made peace with leaving this world on the sole of her slipper—Danielle wondered what the flies meant. Was someone trying to send her a message? A warning? Whatever it was, she was sure it was something bad.

Being in the U.S. Army Reserves, her husband, Kyle, didn't like to look for omens. He only laughed when she talked about Grandmother's beliefs, not that Kyle was around in the summer to talk to about anything. His training was in summers so it wouldn't interfere with his job as county school bus supervisor. Last year, he'd been gone only a couple of weeks, but this time he was spending two long months at Fort Irwin in California. He was in training exercises, so the only way to reach him was in a real emergency, through the Red Cross. She hadn't spoken to him in three weeks.

Kyle had been in training so long, the war had almost come and gone. But he still might get deployed.

He'd reminded her of that right before he left, as if she'd made a promise she and Lola could do fine without him. What would she do if she became one of those Iraq wives? Life was hard enough in summer already, without death hanging over her head, too.

With Grandmother gone from this earth and Kyle in California, Danielle had never been so lonely. She felt loneliest in the bathroom. Maybe the small space was too much like a prison cell. But she didn't fight the feeling. Her loneliness felt comfortable, familiar. She wouldn't have minded sitting with the sting awhile, feeling sorry for herself, staring at the dead fly on the black and white tile. Wondering what its message had been.

But there wasn't enough time for that. Lola was awake, already angry and howling.

Long before the bodies were found, Grandmother always said the Okeepechee swampland was touched by wrong. Old Man McCormack sold his family's land to developers last fall, and Caterpillar trucks were digging a man-made lake in the soggy ground when they uncovered the bones. And not just a few bones, either. The government people and researchers were still digging, but Danielle had heard there were three bodies, at last count. And not a quarter mile from her front door!

Grandmother had told her the swampland had secrets. Lately, Danielle tried to recall more clearly what Grandmother's other prophecies had been, but all she remembered was Grandmother's earthy laughter. Danielle barely had time to fix herself a bowl of cereal in the mornings, so she didn't have the luxury of Grandmother's habits: mixing powders, lighting candles, and sitting still to wait. But Danielle believed in the swampland's secrets.

All her life, she'd known Graceville was a hard place to live, and it was worse on the swamp side. Everyone knew that. People died of cancer and lovers drove each other to misery all over Graceville, but the biggest tragedies were clustered on the swamp side— not downtown, and not in the development called The Farms where no one did any farming. When she was in elementary school, her classmate LaToya's father went crazy. He came home from work one day and shot up everyone in the house; first LaToya, then her little brothers (even the baby), and her mother. When they were all dead, he put the gun in his mouth and pulled the trigger—which Danielle wished he'd done at the start. That had made the national news.

Sad stories had always watered Graceville's back-yard vegetable gardens. Danielle's parents used to tell her stories about how awful poverty was, back when sharecropping was the only job for those who weren't bound to be teachers, and most of their generation's tragedies had money at their core. That wasn't so true these days, no matter what her parents said. Even people on the swamp side of Graceville had better jobs and bigger houses than they used to. They just didn't seem to build their lives any better.

Danielle had never expected to raise a baby in Graceville, or live in her late grandmother's house with an Atlanta-born husband who should know better. The thought of Atlanta only six hours north nearly drove her crazy some days. But Kyle Darren Richardson was practical enough for the both of them. Coolheaded. That was probably why the military liked him enough to invest so much training. *Do you know how much houses cost in Atlanta? We'll save for a few more years, and then we'll go. Once my training is done, we'll never be hurting for money, and we'll live on a base in Germany somewhere. Then you can kiss Graceville good-bye.*

In summer, with Kyle gone, she was almost sure she was just another fool who never had the sense to get out of Graceville. Ever since high school, she'd seen her classmates with babies slung to their hips, or married to the first boy who told them they were pretty, and she'd sworn, *Not me.* All of those old friends—each and every one—had their plans, too. Once upon a time.

Danielle wasn't sure if she was patient and wise, or if she was a tragedy unfolding slowly, one hot summer day at a time.

Lola cried harder when she saw her in the doorway. Lola's angry brown-red jowls were smudged with dried flour and old mucus. Sometimes Lola was not pretty at all.

Danielle leaned over the crib. "Go back to sleep, Lola. What's the matter now?"

As Danielle lifted Lola beneath her armpits, the baby grabbed big fistfuls of Danielle's cheeks and squeezed with all her might. Then she shrieked and dug in her nails. Hard. Her eyes screwed tight, her face burning with a mighty mission.

Danielle cried out, almost dropping all twenty pounds of Lola straight to the floor. Danielle wrapped her arm more tightly around Lola's waist while the baby writhed, just before Lola would have slipped. The baby's legs banged against the crib's railings, but Danielle knew her wailing was only for show. Lola was thirteen months old and a liar already.

"*No.*" Danielle said, keeping silent the *you little shit bag.* "*Very* bad, Lola."

Lola shot out a pudgy hand, hoping for another chance at her mother's face, and Danielle bucked back, almost fast enough to make her miss. But Lola's finger caught the small hoop of the gold earring in Danielle's right earlobe and pulled, hard. The earring's catch held at first, and Danielle cried out as pain tore through. Danielle expected to see droplets of blood on the floor, but she only saw the flash of gold as the earring fell.

Lola's crying stopped short, replaced by laughter and a triumphant grin.

Anyone who says they wouldn't hurt a fly is lying.

If Lola were a grown person who had just done the same thing, Danielle would have knocked her through a window. Rubbing her ear, she understood the term *seeing red*, because her eyes flushed with crimson anger. Danielle almost didn't trust herself to lay a hand on the child in her current state, but if she didn't Lola's behavior would never improve. She grabbed Lola's fat arm firmly, the way her mother had said she should, and fixed her gaze.

"*No.*" Danielle said. "Trying to hurt Mommy is *not* funny."

Lola laughed so hard, it brought tears to her eyes. Lola enjoyed hurting her. Not all the time, but some-times. Danielle was sure of it.

Danielle's mother said she was welcome to bring Lola over for a few hours whenever she needed time to herself, but Mom's joints were so bad that she could hardly pull herself out of her chair. Mom had never been the same since she broke her hip. She couldn't keep up with Lola, the way the child darted and dashed everywhere, pulling over and knocking down everything her hands could reach. Besides, Danielle didn't like what she saw in her mother's eyes when she brought Lola over for more than a few minutes: *Jesus, help, she can't even control her own child.*

Danielle glanced at the Winnie the Pooh clock on the dresser. Only two o'clock. The whole day stretched to fill with just her and the baby. Danielle wanted to cry, too.

Kyle told her maybe she had postpartum depression like the celebrity women she read about. But her family had picked cotton and tobacco until two generations ago, and if they could tolerate that heat and work and deprivation without pills and therapy, Danielle doubted her constitution was as fragile as people who pretended to be someone else for a living.

Lola could be hateful, that was all. That was the truth nobody wanted to hear.

Danielle had tried to conceive for two years, and she would always love her daughter—but she didn't like Lola much in summer. Lola had always been a fussy baby, but she was worse when Kyle was gone. Kyle's baritone voice could snap Lola back to her sweeter nature. Nothing Danielle did could.

"She still a handful, huh, Danny?"

"That's one word."

Odetta Mayfield was the only cousin Danielle got along with. She was ten years older, so they hadn't started talking until Grandmother's funeral, and they'd become friends the past two years. The funeral had been a reunion, helping Danielle sew together pieces of her family. Odetta's husband had been in the army during the first Iraq war and come back with a girl-friend. They had divorced long ago and her son was a freshman at Florida State, so Odetta came by the house three or four times a week. Odetta had no one else to talk to, and neither did she. If not for her cousin and her mother, Danielle might be a hermit in summer.

Odetta bounced Lola on her knee while the baby drank placidly from a bottle filled with apple juice. Seeing them together in the white wicker rocker, their features so similar, Danielle wanted to beg her cousin to take the baby home with her. Just for a night or two.

"Did she leave a mark on my face?"

"Can't see nothing from here," Odetta said. But Danielle could feel two small welts rising alongside her right cheekbone. She dabbed her face with the damp kitchen towel beside the pitcher of sugar-free lemonade they had decided to try for a while. The drink tasted like chemicals.

"People talk about boys, but sometimes girls are just as bad, or worse," Odetta said. "We went through the same mess with Rashan. It passes."

Danielle only grunted. She didn't want to talk about Lola anymore. "Anything new from McCormack's place?" she asked, a sure way to change the subject. Odetta worked as a clerk at City Hall, so she had a reason to be in everybody's business.

"Girl, it's seven bodies. *Seven.*"

Seven bodies left unaccounted for, rotting in swampland? The idea made Danielle's skin feel cold. Mass graves always reminded her of the Holocaust, a lesson that had shocked her in seventh grade. She'd never looked at the world the same way after that, just like when Grandmother first told her about slavery.

"My mother still talks about the civil rights days, the summer those college kids tried to register sharecroppers on McCormack's land. He set those dogs loose on them," Danielle said.

"Unnnnnhhhhh-hnnnnhhhhh . . ." Odetta said, drawing out the indictment. "Sure did. That's the first thing everybody thought. But the experts from Tallahassee say the bones are older than forty-odd years. More like a hundred."

"Even so, how are seven people gonna be buried out on that family's land? There weren't any Indians living there. Shoot, that land's been McCormack Farm since slavery. I bet those bones are from slave times and they just don't wanna say. Or something like Rosewood, with a bunch of folks killed and people kept it quiet."

"Unnnhhhh-hhnnnnnhhh," Odetta said. She had thought of that, too. "We may never know what happened to those people, but one thing we *do* know— keep off that land."

"That's what Grandmother said, from way back. When I was a kid."

"I know. Mama, too. Only a fool would buy one of those plots."

The McCormack Farm was less than a mile from Danielle's grandmother's house, along the unpaved red clay road the city called State Route 191, but which everyone else called Tobacco Road. Tobacco had been the McCormacks' business until the 1970s. *Another curse to boot*, Danielle thought. She drove past the McCormacks' faded wooden gate every time she went into town, and the gaudy billboard advertising LOTS FOR SALE—AS LOW AS $150,000. The mammoth, ramshackle tobacco barn stood beside the roadway for no other reason than to remind everyone of where the

McCormack money had come from. Danielle's grand-
father had sharecropped for the McCormacks, and family lore said her relatives had once been their slaves.

"How old's this baby?" Odetta said suddenly. "A year?"

"Thirteen months."

Lola had only been a month old last summer, when
Kyle went off to training. But Danielle didn't want to
talk about Lola now. She had enjoyed forgetting all
about her.

"Your grandmama never told you nothing about
summer and babies?"

Danielle stared at her cousin, whose eyes were
slightly small for her face. "You lost me."

"Just be careful, is all. Especially in July. Summer
solstice. Lola may seem strong to you, but you gotta
pay special attention to any baby under two. It's always
the young ones. And now that those bones have been
unburied, you need to keep an eye out."

"What are you talking about, girl?"

"I'm surprised your grandmama would let you raise
a baby in her house. When your mama was young, she
moved in with her cousin Geraldine. She never told
you that? Lived in their basement until your mama was
two."

The story sounded vaguely familiar, but Grandmother had died soon after Danielle married Kyle,
when Danielle had still been convinced she'd be moving to Atlanta within six months. She hadn't even been
pregnant then. Not yet. She and Kyle hadn't planned on
a baby until they had more money put together. If not
for Lola, they might be living in Atlanta right now.

"What do you mean? Is the water bad?" Now
Danielle felt alarmed.

Odetta shook her head. "Leeches."

Danielle remembered the flies. Now she could expect leeches, too? "You mean those nasty things people put on their skin to suck out poison?" A whole army of leeches could crawl under the back door, with that half-inch gap that always let the breezes through. "Those worms?"

"Not that kind," Odetta said. "Swamp leeches are different. It's just a name Mama used to call them by. You could call them lots of things. Mostly people call them demons, I guess."

Danielle would have thought she'd heard wrong, except that Odetta had a sense of humor. She had Danielle cracking up at Grandmother's funeral, of all places, when Odetta whispered to point out how everyone who gave remembrances called Grandmother by a different surname. Grandmother had been married four times. *When I knew Mrs. Jenkins . . . When I knew Mrs. Roberts . . .* And on down the line. Once Odetta pointed it out, Danielle had to pretend to be sobbing to stifle her giggles. That laughter was the only light that day.

"What did you put in that lemonade after I fixed it? I know you're not sitting there talkin' 'bout demons in the swamp like some old voodoo lady," Danielle said.

Odetta looked embarrassed, rubbing the back of her neck. "I don't know nothin' 'bout no voodoo, but just ask folks. Nobody has young children near the swamp in summer, or there's trouble to follow. Cece's baby got crib death. But usually it just lasts the summer. The babies change, but by fall they change back."

"Change into *what*?" Danielle said, still trying to decide if Odetta was playing.

Odetta shrugged. "I don't know. Something else. *Somebody* else. You watch this baby real close, hear?

Anything happens, ask me to take her by Uncle June's. He's my granddaddy's brother, and he knows what to do. He says it's like those spirits flock to the swamp in summer, the way fish spawn. And they leech on to the young ones. That's why Mama calls them leeches."

Danielle almost asked about the flies she had seen, but she caught herself. What was she thinking about? Grandmother might have kept her candles lit, but this was plain crazy talk. *The minute you start letting family close to you, turns out they're bent on recruiting you for the funny farm, too.* No wonder Kyle was so happy living so far from Atlanta and his relatives. He might never want to go back home.

"Don't look at me like that," Odetta said, grunting as she handed Lola back, almost as if to punish her. Danielle watched the sweetness seep from Lola's face, replaced by the mocking glare she saved only for her mother. If Odetta hadn't been sitting here watching, Danielle would have glared right back.

"I got to get home and see my stories. Just remember what I said. Watch over this girl."

The swamp leeches can have her, Danielle thought. God as her witness, that was the exact thought in her mind.

Just to be on the safe side—and because she knew Grandmother would hound her in her dreams otherwise—Danielle brought Lola's crib into her bedroom so the baby wouldn't be alone at night. Danielle hadn't let the baby sleep in the master bedroom since she was four months old, and Lola never had liked the nursery. Now Lola fussed less at bedtime and Danielle rediscovered how much she enjoyed the sound of another person breathing near her at night.

The strange thing didn't happen until nearly a week after Odetta's visit, when Danielle had all but forgotten the flies and Odetta's story about leeches. A loud noise overhead woke her one night. It sounded like a boot clomping on the rooftop.

Danielle opened her eyes, staring at the shadow of the telephone pole outside on her ceiling. Her bedroom always captured the light from the single streetlamp on this end of Tobacco Road. Sometimes her eyes played tricks on her and made her think she could see shadows moving. *But shadows don't make noise*, Danielle thought.

Kyle would have sprung from bed to get his rifle out of the closet. But Kyle wasn't here, and Danielle didn't know the first thing about the rifle, so she lay there and stared above her. That hadn't sounded like breathing wood or any of the old house's other aches and pains. *Someone is on the roof.* That was plain.

Not a rat. Not a raccoon. Not an owl. The only thing big enough to make that noise was a deer, and she'd stopped believing in creatures with hooves flying to the roof when she was eight. The clomping sound came again, and this time it was directly above her.

Danielle imagined she saw a large shadow on the ceiling above her, as if something was bleeding through. *Imagined*, because she couldn't be sure. But it seemed to be more than just the darkness. It was a long, large black space, perfectly still. Waiting. Danielle's heart galloped, and she couldn't quite catch her breath.

The thing on the rooftop made up its mind about what to do next.

The shadow glided, and Danielle heard three purposeful strides on the rooftop above the mass. The sound was moving away from her bed—*toward the baby's crib*. The baby was still asleep, breathing in slow, heavy bursts. Danielle could hear Lola over the noise.

Too late, Danielle realized what she should have done: She should have jumped up, grabbed the baby, and run out of the room as fast as she could. It wouldn't have hurt to grab her Bible from inside her nightstand drawer while she was at it. But Danielle had done none of that, so she only lay there in helpless horror while a shadow-thing marched toward her baby girl.

As soon as the last clambering step sounded above—*CLOMP*—the baby let out a loud gasp.

The rooftop went silent, and the baby's breathing was normal again. Well, almost. Lola's breathing was more shallow than it had been before, more hurried, but it was the steady breath of sleep.

After listening in the dark for five more minutes, feeling muscle cramps from lying so still beneath her blanket, Danielle began to wonder if the horrific sound on the rooftop had been in her imagination. After all, Lola woke up if she sneezed too close to her door—so wouldn't the baby have heard that racket and started wailing right away? Suddenly, it seemed all too plausible that the sound *had* been from a raccoon or an owl. Just magnified in the darkness, that was all.

Served her right for letting family too close to her. Just crazy talk and nightmares.

But although she didn't hear another peep from the rooftop—and Lola's breathing was as steady as clockwork running only slightly fast—Danielle couldn't get back to sleep that night. She lay awake, listening to her baby breathe.

The next thing Danielle knew, sunlight was bright in her bedroom.

Lola woke up at six o'clock every morning no matter how late she went to bed, so Danielle hadn't lingered in bed long enough for the sun to get this bright all summer. Danielle looked at her alarm clock: It was ten o'clock! Midmorning. All at once, Danielle remembered the racket on the rooftop and her baby's little gasp. She fully expected to find Lola dead.

But Lola was sitting up in a corner of the crib, legs folded under her Indian style, patiently waiting. She wasn't whining, cooing, babbling, or whimpering. The baby was just staring and waiting for her to wake up.

Danielle felt a surge of warmth and relief, a calm feeling she wished she could have every morning. "Well, look at Mommy's big girl!" Danielle said, propping herself up on her elbows.

The baby sat straighter, and her mouth peeled back into a wide grin as she leaned forward, toward Danielle. Her eyes hung on Danielle, not missing a single movement or detail. She looked like a model baby on the diaper package, too good to be true.

And Danielle knew, just that fast. Something was wrong with the baby.

This isn't Lola, she thought. She would swear on her grave that she knew right away.

There were a hundred and one reasons. First, Lola started her days in a bad mood, crying until she got her *baa-baa*. The new sleeping arrangement hadn't changed that. And Lola never sat that way, Indian style like a Girl Scout around a campfire. The pose didn't look right on her.

Danielle went through the usual motions—seeing if Lola's eyes would follow her index finger (they did, like a cat's), testing her appetite (Lola drank a full bottle and ate a banana), and checking Lola's temperature (exactly 98.6). Apparently, Lola was fine.

Danielle's heart slowed down from its gallop and she laughed at herself, laying Lola down flat on the wicker changing table. The baby didn't fuss or wriggle, her eyes still following Danielle's every movement with a contented smile.

But when Danielle opened the flaps of the Pampers Cruisers and the soiled diaper fell away between Lola's chunky thighs, something dark and slick lay there in its folds. Danielle's first glance told her that Lola had gotten her bowel movement out of the way early—until the mess in her diaper *shuddered*.

It was five inches long, and thin, the color of the shadow that had been on her ceiling. The unnamable thing came toward Danielle, slumping over the diaper's elastic border to the table surface. Then, moving more quickly with its body hunched like a caterpillar, the thing flung itself to the floor. *A swamp leech.* A smell wafted up from its wake like soggy, rotting flesh.

For the next hour, while Lola lay in silence on the changing table, Danielle could hardly stop screaming, standing high on top of her bed.

Danielle didn't remember calling Odetta from the portable phone on her nightstand, but the phone was in her hand. The next thing she knew, Odetta was standing in her bedroom doorway, waving a bath towel like a matador, trying to coax her off the bed. Danielle tried to warn Odetta not to touch the baby, but Odetta didn't listen. Odetta finished changing Lola's diaper and took her out of the room. The next time Danielle saw Lola, she was dressed up in her purple overalls, sitting in the car seat like they were on their way to lunch at Cracker Barrel.

"We're going to Uncle June's," Odetta said, guiding Danielle into the car.

Danielle didn't remember the drive, except that she could feel Lola watching her in the rearview mirror the whole way. Danielle was sure she would faint if she tried to look back.

Uncle June lived at the corner of Live Oak and Glory Road, near the woods. He was waiting outside his front door with a mug, wearing his pajama pants and nothing else. A smallish, overfed white dog sat beside him. Odetta kept saying Uncle June could help her, he would know *just* what to do, but the man standing outside the house at the end of the block looked like Fred Sanford in his junkyard. His overgrown grass was covered with dead cars.

Odetta opened the car door, unbuckled Lola from her car seat, and hoisted the baby into her arms. As if it were an everyday thing. Then she opened Danielle's car door and took her hand, helping her remember how to come to her feet.

"Just like with Ruby's boy in ninety-seven," Odetta told Uncle June, slightly breathless.

Uncle June just waved them in, opening his door. The dog glared back at Lola, but turned around and trotted into the house, where it made itself scarce.

"Let's put her in the bathtub, in case another one comes out of her," Odetta said.

"Won't be, but do what you want." Uncle June sounded sleepy.

Lola sat placidly in the center of the bathtub while the warm water came up to her waist. Her legs were crossed the way they had been in her crib. Danielle couldn't stare at her too long before she was sure a madwoman's wail would begin sliding from her throat. She looked away.

Danielle gasped when she saw a long blue bathrobe hanging on a hook on back of the bathroom door. It looked like a man floating behind her. And the mirror on the medicine cabinet was askew, swinging to and fro, making her reflection shudder the way her mind was shuddering. Danielle wondered how she hadn't fainted already.

"I told you," Uncle June said, and Danielle realized some time must have gone by. Uncle June had been standing before, but now he was sitting on top of the closed toilet lid, reading a well-worn copy of *The Man Who Said I Am*. "Won't never be but one o' them things."

When the water splashed in the tub, they all looked down at Lola. Danielle didn't look away this time; she just felt her body coil, ready for whatever was next.

Lola's face was moony, upturned toward Danielle with the same intense gaze she had followed her with all morning. But the water around her still looked clear. No more leeches. Lola had only changed position slightly, one of the rare times she had moved at all.

"That thing I saw . . ." Danielle whispered. Her fingers were trembling, but not as much as they had been up until then. "Was it a demon?"

Uncle June shook his head. "What you saw . . . the leech . . . that ain't it. Just a sign it's visiting. Evidence. They crawl for dark as fast as they can. Slide through cracks. No one's been able to find one, the way they scoot. Probably 'cause most folks head in the other direction."

"It's under my bed," Danielle said.

"Not anymore, it's not. It's halfway back to the swamp by now."

Danielle shivered for what seemed like a full minute. Her body was rejecting the memory of the thing she had found in her baby's diaper. She waited for her shivering to pass, until she realized it wouldn't pass any time soon. She would have to get used to it.

Lola, in the tub, wrapped her arms around herself with a studious expression as she stared up at Danielle. Lola was still smiling softly, as if she was going out of her way not to alarm her, but her creased eyebrows looked like a grown woman's. On any other day, Lola would be splashing water out of the tub, or else sliding against the slick porcelain with shrieks of glee. This creature with Lola's face might be a child, but it wasn't hers. Water wasn't novel anymore.

"If that isn't Lola . . . then where is she?" Danielle said, against the ball of mud in her throat.

"Lola's still in there, I expect," Uncle June said. "Dottie Stephens's baby was touched by it for a month . . . but come fall, it was like nothing happened. And Dottie's baby is a doctor now."

"Unnnnh-hnnnh . . ." Odetta said with an encouraging smile.

Danielle's heart cracked. A month!

"Course, you don't have to wait that long," Uncle June said. He stood up, lifted the toilet lid, and spat into the bowl. "I've got a remedy. They'll eat anything you put in front of them, so it won't be hard. Put about six drops on a peanut butter cracker, or whatever you have, but no more than six. Give it to her at midnight. That's when they come and go."

"And it won't hurt Lola?" Danielle said.

"Might give her the runs." Uncle June sat again.

"Lola's gonna' be fine, Danny," Odetta said, squeezing her hand.

Kyle's nickname for her was Danny, too. She should call Kyle to tell him, she realized. But how could she explain this emergency to the Red Cross?

"What if . . . I don't give her the remedy? What would happen?" God only knew what was in that so-called remedy. What if she accidentally killed Lola trying to chase away the demon?

Uncle June shrugged. "Anybody's guess. It might stay in there a week. Maybe two. Maybe a month. But it'll be gone by the end of summer. I know that."

"Summer's the only time," Odetta said.

Danielle stared at Lola's face again. The baby's eyes danced with delight when Danielle looked at her, and the joy startled Danielle. The baby seemed like Lola again, except that she was looking at her with the love she saved for Kyle.

"So how many is it now, Odetta? At McCormack's place?" Uncle June said. He had moved on, making conversation. Unlike Danielle, he was not suffering the worst day of his life.

"Six. Turns out they'd counted one too many. Still . . ."

Uncle June sighed, grieved. He wiped his brow with a washcloth. "That's a goddamn shame." The way he said it caught Danielle's ear, as if he'd lost a good friend a hundred years ago who had just been brought out to light.

"Nobody has to wait on *C.S.I.* experts to tell us it's black folks," Odetta said.

Uncle June nodded, sighing. "That whole family ought to be run out of town."

Six dead bodies on McCormack Farm. Six of Graceville's secrets finally unburied.

The other one, in the bathtub, had just been born.

"*Tel*-e-vi-sion."

Lola repeated the word with perfect diction. "*Tel*-evision."

All morning, while Danielle had sat wrapped up in Uncle June's blue bathrobe on the sofa with a mug of peppermint tea she had yet to sip from, Odetta had passed the time by propping Lola up in a dining room chair and identifying items in the room.

Lola pointed at the bookcase, which Uncle June had crammed top to bottom.

"Bookcase," Odetta said.

"*Bookcase*," the Lola-thing said. She pointed up at the chandelier, which was only a skeleton, missing all of its bulbs.

"Chan-de-lier," Odetta said.

"*Chandelier*."

Danielle shivered with each new word. Before today, Lola's few words were gummy and indistinct, never more than two syllables. But Lola was different now.

Odetta laughed, shaking her head. "You hear that, Danny? Ruby's baby did this, too. Like damn parrots. But they won't say anything unless you say it first."

The baby pointed at a maroon-colored book on the arm of Uncle June's couch.

"Ho-ly Bi-ble," Odetta said.

"*Ho-ly Bi-ble*."

At that, honest to God, Danielle almost laughed. Then she shrank farther into a ball, trying to sink into the couch's worn fabric and make herself go away.

Lola gazed over at Danielle, the steady smile gone. The baby looked concerned. *Mommy?* That's what the baby's face seemed to say.

"Your mama's tired," Odetta said.

Tears sprang to the baby's eyes. Suddenly, Lola was a portrait of misery.

"Don't worry, she'll be all right after tomorrow," Odetta said.

All misery vanished. The baby smiled again, shining her big brown eyes on Danielle. Just like Odetta's joke on the day of Grandmother's funeral, that smile was Danielle's only light.

"Ain't that something else?" Odetta whispered. "Maybe this ain't Lola, but they seem to come here knowing they're supposed to love their mamas."

No, it sure isn't Lola, Danielle thought ruefully.

A deep voice behind Danielle startled her. "Gotta go to work," Uncle June said, and the door slammed shut behind him. Danielle had forgotten Uncle June was in the house.

"He never gave me the remedy," Danielle said, remembering.

"Later on, we'll carry Lola with us over to his gas station. It's just up the street. Besides, I'm hungry. Uncle June's got the best burgers under his warmer."

Some people could eat their way through any situation, Danielle thought.

After a time, Odetta turned on the television set, and the room became still. The only noise was from the guests on *Oprah* and a quick snarl from Uncle June's dog as he slunk past Lola's high chair. Lola didn't even notice the dog. Her eyes were still on Danielle, even when Danielle dozed for minutes at a time. Whenever Danielle woke up, Lola was still staring.

"What do they do?" Danielle asked finally. "Why are they here?"

"Damned if I know," Odetta said. "They don't do much of anything, except smile and try to learn things. Ruby said after she got over her fright, she was sorry to see it go."

"Then how do you know they're demons?"

"Demon ain't my word. I just call them leeches. What scares people is, they're unnatural. You don't ask 'em to come, and they take your babies away for a while. Now, it's true about that crib death, but Cece can't say for sure what caused it. Might've happened anyway." Odetta shrugged, her eyes still on the television screen. "They don't cry. They eat whatever you give 'em. And after that first nasty diaper, Uncle June says they hardly make any mess, maybe a trickle now and then. I bet there's some folks who see it as a blessing in disguise, even if they'd never say so. Lola, can you say *blessing*?"

"*Bles-sing*," Lola said, and grinned.

Danielle had never been more exhausted. "I need a nap," she said.

"Go on, girl. Lie down, and I'll get you a blanket. You could sleep all day if you want. This thing won't make no noise."

And it was true. Once their conversation stopped, the Lola-thing sat in the high chair looking just like

Lola, except that she never once whined or cried, or even opened her mouth. She just gazed at Danielle as if she thought Danielle was the most magnificent creature on Earth. That smile from Lola was the last thing Danielle saw before she tumbled into sleep.

Uncle June had owned the Handi Gas at the corner of Live Oak and Highway 9 for at least twenty-five years, and it smelled like it hadn't had a good cleaning in that long, filled with the stink of old fruit and motor oil. But business was good. All the pumps outside were taken, and there were five or six customers crammed inside, browsing for snacks or waiting in line for the register. The light was so dim Danielle could barely make out the shelves of products that took up a half dozen rows, hardly leaving room to walk.

Uncle June was busy, and he didn't acknowledge them when they walked in. Odetta went straight for the hamburgers wrapped in shiny foil inside the glass display case by the cash register.

"You want one, girl?" Odetta called.

Danielle shook her head. The thought of food made her feel sick. She had ended up with the stroller, even though Odetta had promised her she wouldn't have to get too close to Lola. But Danielle found she didn't mind too much. Being at Handi Mart with the truckers and locals buying their lunch and conducting their business almost made Danielle forget her situation. As she pushed the stroller aimlessly down aisle after aisle, hypnotized by the brightly colored labels, she kept expecting to feel Lola kicking her feet, squirming in the stroller or screaming at the top of her lungs. Her usual antics.

Instead, Lola sat primly with her hands folded in her lap, her head turning right and left as she took in everything around her. Odetta had spent the rest of the morning braiding Lola's hair, entwining the plaits with pretty lilac-colored bows alongside the well-oiled grooves of her brown scalp. Despite her best efforts, Danielle had never learned how to do much with Lola's hair. Mom hadn't known much about hair, either. This was the best Lola had looked in ages.

"I'll get to you in a minute," Uncle June called to Danielle as the stroller ambled past the register line. "I know what you're here for."

"Take your time," someone said, and she realized *she* had said it. Calm as could be.

Although Odetta was kin to Uncle June, she had to stand in line like any other customer. She'd helped herself to two burgers, a large bag of Doritos, and a Diet Coke from the fountain in back. *It's no wonder she was still carrying her baby weight eighteen years later*, Danielle thought. With nothing left to do, Danielle stood beside her cousin to wait.

"Well, ain't you cute as a button?" a white woman said ahead of them, gazing back at Lola in the stroller. The woman was wearing an ostrich feather hat and looked like she was dressed for church. Was it Sunday? Danielle couldn't remember.

"*But-ton*," Lola said, the first sound she'd made in two hours.

The woman smiled down at Lola. Danielle almost warned her not to get too close.

"Thank you," Danielle said. Lola didn't get many compliments, not with her behavior.

"How old is she?" the woman asked.

"Thirteen months," Danielle said, although it was a

lie. As far as she knew, the thing in Lola's stroller was as old as the swamp itself.

"Lovely," the woman said. She turned away when Uncle June asked her pump number.

And Lola *was* lovely today, thanks to Odetta. There was no denying it. Maybe that was why Danielle could touch her stroller without feeling queasy, or getting goose bumps. The nasty thing that had crawled out of Lola's diaper that morning was beginning to seem like a bad dream.

"One minute," Uncle June said when it was their turn in line. He vanished through a swinging door to the back room. As the door swung to and fro, Danielle saw a mess of boxes in the dank space, and she caught a whiff of mildew and ammonia. Danielle felt her heart speed up. Her fingers tightened around the stroller handles.

"You sure you don't want your own burger? These are mine," Odetta said.

Danielle only shook her head. A fly landed on one of the ribbons on Lola's head.

Uncle June came back with a brown iodine bottle with a black dropper. He set the bottle on the counter next to Odetta's hamburgers. "Remedy's free. Odetta, you owe me five-fifty."

While Odetta rifled through her overstuffed pocketbook, Uncle June leaned over, folded his hands, and stared Danielle straight in the eye. His eyes looked slightly bloodshot, and she wondered if he had been drinking that morning.

"Remember what I said," Uncle June told her in a low voice, so the man in the Harley Davidson T-shirt behind them wouldn't hear. "Six drops. No more, no less. At midnight. Then you'll have your baby back."

Danielle nodded, clasping the bottle tightly in her hand. She had questions about what was in the remedy, or how he'd come to concoct it, but she couldn't make her mouth work. She couldn't even bring herself to thank him.

Another fly circled, landing on the counter, and Uncle June killed it with his red flyswatter without blinking. He wiped it off the counter with a grimy handkerchief, his eyes already looking beyond Danielle toward the next customer.

"Won't be long now, Danny," Odetta said.

Danielle nodded again.

Odetta opened the gas station's glass door for her, and Danielle followed with the stroller. She was looking forward to another nap. Hell, she might sleep all day today, while she had the chance. She hadn't had a good night's sleep since Kyle had been gone.

Danielle almost ran down an old white man in a rumpled black Sunday suit who was trying to come in as they walked out. "Sorry—" Danielle began, but she stopped when she saw his face.

Danielle and her neighbor had never exchanged a word in all these years, but there had been no escaping his face when he ran for Town Council in ninety-nine and plastered his campaign posters all over the supermarkets. He was Old Man McCormack, even though his face was so furrowed with lines that he looked like he could be his own father. He was also very small, walking with a stoop. The top of his head barely came up to Danielle's shoulder.

Odetta froze, staring at him with a stupefied expression, but McCormack didn't notice Odetta. His eyes were fixed on the stroller, down at the baby.

He smiled a mouthful of bright dentures at Lola.

"Just like a little angel," McCormack said. Some of his wrinkles smoothed over when he smiled, as if a great burden had been lifted from his face. He gently swatted away a fly that had been resting on the tip of Lola's nose. Danielle didn't know how long the fly had been there.

"*Lit-tle an-gel*," Lola said.

McCormack's smile faded as he raised his head to look at Danielle, as if he expected to find himself staring into a harsh light. His face became tight, like hardening concrete.

"Afternoon, ma'am," he said. His voice was rough, scraped from deep in his throat. And his eyes flitted away from hers in an instant, afraid to rest on hers too long.

But Danielle had glimpsed his runny eyes long enough to see what he was carrying. She could see it in his stooping shoulders, in his shuffling walk. She felt sorry for him.

"Afternoon, Mr. McCormack," she said.

He paused, as if he was shocked she had been so civil. His face seemed to melt.

"You and your pretty little girl have a good summer, hear?" he said with a grateful smile.

"Yessir, I think we will," Danielle said. "You have a good summer, too."

Despite the way Odetta gaped at her, Danielle wasn't in the mood to pass judgment today. Everyone had something hidden in their past, or in their hearts, they wouldn't want dug out. Maybe the McCormack family would have to answer to God for those bodies buried on their land, or maybe they wouldn't. Maybe Danielle would give Lola six drops of Uncle June's remedy at midnight tonight, or maybe she wouldn't.

She and this old man deserved a little peace, that was all.

Just for the summer.

Danielle rubbed the top of Lola's head, gently massaging her neatly braided scalp. Her tiny visitor in the stroller turned to grin up at her with shining, adoring eyes.

Scab

Wrath James White

The lithe and sensuous cinnamon-skinned black woman whose desk lay directly across from Malik's cubicle was staring at him again. Malik could feel her eyes crawling over him like maggots on a fresh corpse. He knew what she was thinking.

Tar baby, mud duck, black scab, black dog, nigger, jungle bunny, ugly, dirty, filthy, African!

He'd heard it all before, not from some racist red-necks but from his own people, every day of his life for as long as he could remember. He was getting tired of it. Sick and tired. As a teenager, he'd used every skin-lightening cream on the shelves and he'd done nothing more than given himself a severe case of acne and several chemical burns that had blistered and left scars.

He turned his head to catch her staring and she smiled at him, holding his gaze. Malik turned quickly away. He knew she was just trying to fuck with him.

Malik's self-esteem had been formed in the early eighties when he was just reaching puberty and Michael Jackson, Prince, and Ray Parker Jr. were the symbols of black male sexuality. Effete, sallow-toned, androgynous beings, whose voices lilted like castrated tenors and whose racial composition was as ambiguous as their sexuality. Malik was the very antithesis of that cultural aesthetic, being the color of liquid night, with thick African features, and a large muscular body that held no suggestion of femininity. By eighties pop-cultural standards he was pure ugly, a bete noire destined for solitude and depression.

The fact that the modern aesthetic now favored his complexion and physique was not lost on him. He had been amazed when he first began to see models and actors with skin as dark as his, thick lips, wide noses, and shaved heads. He'd been even more amazed when a black woman had come up to him and called him beautiful for the first time in his life. But more than a decade later, he still found it hard to believe them, and harder still to forgive them and impossible to forget. The cruel mocking voices of his youth haunted him without relent.

"You so black that if you went to night school they'd mark you absent!"

"I bet when you step out of a car the oil light goes on."

The echoes redoubled. They ricocheted around Malik's skull, building up momentum and making him feel like his head was about to rattle apart. His chest started to feel tight; he felt himself starting to hyperventilate just as he had back in junior high school when the walls would close in and suffocate him as he watched the curly-haired, caramel-skinned crowd lord over their darker brethren, insulting them every chance they got and teaching them to hate themselves for not having more European features.

Malik looked back across the room at the beautiful

office assistant and saw one of the greatest tormentors
of his youth leering at him with that cruel smirk as her
mind worked feverishly to concoct the next put-down.
Her name was Kelly. Her cocoa-brown visage swam
into view, transposed over the office girl's features. A
vicious sneer twisted her lips as they moved to form
that vituperative storm of insults Malik had come to
expect from her.

*"Ewww! You so black you look like you've been
dipped in shit. You could stick your finger in hot water
and make coffee. Ya black scab!"*

The irony was that she was just a shade or two
lighter than him. Definitely not the coveted high-
yellow complexion favored at that time. But she was
not alone. Jennifer Hart, who was the color of butter-
milk, added her voice to the choir.

*"He's so black that if you tossed him in a volcano
for about a million years he'd come out a diamond!"*

Between the two of them they had driven him to two
suicide attempts and numerous elaborate murder/
suicide schemes that he'd plotted out to the last detail
but had never put into action. He still heard their thir-
teen- and fourteen-year-old voices in his head, even
though reason told him that the girls would be well into
their thirties by now. He heard them whenever he
looked at a beautiful cappuccino-colored woman like
the one staring at him from the next cubicle. The one
smiling seductively, as if she might actually be interested in a black scab like him.

*"She's too pretty for you, ya ugly mud duck! You
think a pretty little redbone like that would touch
a spook like you? She's looking for Denzel, not Dar-
rell . . . or Malik."*

No. He didn't think she would want him. All she would do was make fun of him and his African ancestry. She would call him a spear-chucker behind his back, when all the girls were gathered around the coffeemaker gossiping in the morning. She'd tell them how disgusting it would be to kiss his big lips. How his hair felt like Brillo. And how his thick arms and chest made him look like an ape. Then she'd laugh just like Kelly and Jennifer had. She'd laugh and laugh until Malik would have no choice but to kill her.

He caught her looking at him again, and once again she did not turn away when he looked back. She held his gaze and smiled, batting her eyelashes flirtatiously, waiting for him to say something. She twirled a pencil in her left hand and touched it to the corner of her mouth, nibbling the end of it as she tilted her head and let her eyes slide slowly down his body and then back up again. He could almost feel the heat of her smoldering stare warming him as it traveled over his flesh, turning him on despite Kelly's and Jennifer's combined voices interpreting every gesture she made into a diatribe of racial slurs.

"You big, black, Mighty Joe Young–looking ape!"

Malik winced as if he'd been slapped as the woman continued to stare at him. He was still turned on, but now he was getting angry as well.

How dare that bitch make me feel like this? he thought. *Why is she fuckin' with me? Why can't she just leave me the fuck alone?*

He whirled around in his chair, turning his back on her and trying without success to go back to his work. He stared at the screen, but all the letters and numbers were running together into some indecipherable stew.

He could still feel her eyes on him, like intimate caresses touching him everywhere. He wanted to get up and choke the life out of her.

Malik had always made it a point to steer clear of women like the beautiful tan-skinned woman in the next cubicle. The majority of his romantic conquests had been with white women or women with skin as dark as or darker than his, though even they sometimes made him uneasy. Not all of the girls who'd teased him back in high school had been light-skinned. Even the ones with skin the same color as his had looked down on him, as if his onyx complexion made him somehow subhuman. Usually when he went after black women they were African or West Indian, or even darker-skinned Cubans and Puerto Ricans. With American girls there was always the fear that some honey-complexioned gigolo with hazel eyes and wavy hair would come and take her away from him.

One of the other office girls had now joined the girl in the next cubicle. Her skin was smooth and flawless and the color of milk chocolate. Her hair was thick and wooly, though neat and well kept the way his had been before he'd gotten tired of fussing with it and shaved it all off. Her nose was wide with nostrils flared like a wild beast scenting a fresh kill and her lips were full and thick. The very same features he'd been ashamed of all his life she wore with beauty and grace. On her that woolly Afro looked stylish and trendy, that wide nose wild and exotic, those full lips sensuous and sexual. He knew that there were women out there who looked at him the same way. But they were usually not black women.

The two women were smiling and whispering and now they were both staring at him. Malik wanted to melt into the floor. He felt as if he were in an interrogation room under bright lights. He knew everything they were saying about him. He could read their lips even with his back turned. He could hear them in his head. See them laughing and pointing at him in his mind's eye, tearing him apart piece by piece until there was barely enough left of him to flush down the toilet.

"You shit-colored black scab!"

His mother had tried to teach him to be proud of his African heritage.

"Your skin is dark because your bloodline isn't diluted. You can trace your ancestry all the way to the slave ships and even back to the motherland. You're a thoroughbred, a pedigree, the descendant of kings and queens and great warriors! You should be proud of your black skin. Those half-breed mulatto kids are just jealous because they're mutts. You just tell them, the blacker the berry, the sweeter the juice."

Malik got up and stormed away from his desk with Kelly and Jennifer screaming in his head and the two office assistants boring their eyes into his back. He had to get some fresh air.

Walking briskly past rows and rows of identical cubicles in which the other office drones toiled, Malik began to calm down. The voices in his head began to slowly abate. He hurled himself into an elevator and rode it downstairs to the lobby, then dashed out onto the teeming city streets, into the flow of pedestrian traffic. He leaned against a light pole and inhaled deeply several times, finding himself inexplicably wishing he had a cigarette even though he'd never smoked a day in his life. The voices were quieter now, but they were still there whispering hateful things to him. It had been a long time since they had come on this strong and Malik knew the reason for their re-newed vigor: that damned office assistant with the Halle Berry smile and complexion. Despite his anger, he could not ignore the fact that he'd been immensely attracted to her, and Kelly and Jennifer had known it too. That's why they had attacked him.

Those fucking bitches! Why can't they just leave me alone?

Malik gnashed his teeth together, the squeaky grind-ing sound drowning out the sonorous echoes in his skull. He whirled suddenly and almost jumped out into the street, pinwheeling his arms to stay on the curb as a cab rushed toward him, his eyes fixed in horror at the beautiful light-skinned office assistant who'd just placed her hand on his shoulder. She reached out for him again to help him regain his footing, pulling him back onto the sidewalk.

"I'm so sorry," she said. "I didn't mean to frighten you."

"You almost killed me!"

She continued smiling at him despite the bristling rage and hate boiling off him in waves. She was obliv-ious. *She probably expects the world to love her*, Malik thought as he struggled to calm his galloping heart-beat.

"I just wanted to introduce myself," she said.

"Why?" Malik found himself backing away from her in horror as if she were something dangerous that might attack him. The woman took a step closer with every step he took in retreat until he was once again teetering on the edge of the curb.

"What do you want?" he asked.

"My name is Danika." She held out her hand and

Malik had to take it to keep from falling off the curb into traffic.

"I'm Malik."

"I know. The girls in the office already told me about you." She swept her eyes down to his feet and back up to his eyes again, and once again his body tingled everywhere her gaze landed.

"What did they tell you about me?"

"They said that you only date white girls."

"What? That's stupid. I date plenty of black girls. I date all kinds of girls."

"Then why haven't you asked me out? How come every time I look at you, you look like you want to run away? Do you think I'm ugly or something or are you just scared of me?"

Why is she doing this? "I'm not afraid of you and you know you aren't ugly."

"Then what's the problem?"

"Why would you want to go out with me?"

"Why? Look at you! You're gorgeous!"

Malik paused and looked closely at Danika's face to see if she was serious, hunting for any sign that she was putting him on or patronizing him.

"What, do you have some kind of bet with your friends or something?" he asked. "Is that what this is about?"

"Look, I just think you're fine as hell and I'd like to get to know you. But if you're not interested, I ain't going to beg you. A sista does have her pride. If you prefer those white girls, then that's just your loss."

She turned on her heel and started walking back into the building.

"Danika?"

"Hmmm?"

"How about tonight?"

The date was going well. Malik was surprised by how much he and Danika had in common. Even the voices in his head were silent for once. Malik was enjoying himself. Each time Danika laughed he laughed with her. She reached out and took his hand as she told him about how her grandparents had to flee the South sixty years ago with the KKK hard at their heels because her grandmother had married a black man. She told him how much she hated being called "high yella" or "redbone" as if she were some other race than black and how she hated being called a mulatto most of all because it sounded so much like "mutt," which she'd also been called on a few occasions. Malik kept his own stories to himself, listening instead, staring at her tiny brown hand in his and wondering what he'd ever been afraid of.

"What about your parents?" he asked. "Were they both black?"

"My mom, like I said, was half black and half white and my dad was Puerto Rican."

"So what do you consider yourself, then?"

"Well, Puerto Ricans have black blood in them too so I just call myself black. It gets too complicated otherwise."

She smiled and Malik smiled with her. The waiter brought their food and they ate their meal of Cornish game hens stuffed with wild rice and cranberries in small bites in between conversation, sipping white zinfandel and never once breaking eye contact.

When the check came, they both agreed not to let

the night end. They went to a nightclub down the street and sat at the bar, drinking and talking. A Marvin Gaye song came on and they went out on the dance floor, hugging each other closely and swaying to the beat. He kissed her lightly on the lips as they danced to "Purple Rain" and she kissed him back deeply and passionately as the song ended.

An hour later, she was nestled close to him with his arm around her shoulders and her head on his chest as he hailed a cab.

"Where to?" the cabbie asked.

They looked at each other and Danika smiled again when Malik gave the taxi driver his home address.

"So, why did you act so weird around me at the office? I've been there a week and you never even looked at me."

"Oh, I looked at you. I just didn't know why you were always looking at me. It made me nervous."

"What? Did you think I was some kind of crazy stalker or serial killer or something?"

Malik chuckled. "Something like that."

"I'm sorry. I didn't mean to freak you out. I just wanted to get with you, so I was trying to let you know I was interested."

"Girls like you aren't normally interested in brothas like me."

"What do you mean, girls like me?"

Malik paused. He knew what he meant, but knew that it would offend her if he said it. "Sistas as pretty as you don't normally dig me. I mean, I know a lot of white girls are into my look, but you know how they are. Once they decide they're into brothas they ain't too choosy."

"Don't tell me you've got self-esteem issues? You? I

would never have guessed that. I mean, with a body like yours I'd think you could get any woman you want. I was worried that I didn't look good enough for you."

"You're the most beautiful woman I've ever seen."

He reached out and stroked his fingers through her thick curly brown hair, staring at her staggeringly beautiful face in amazement, amazed that she was actually attracted to him.

"Is that why you spend so much time working on this magnificent body of yours? You really don't believe you're handsome?"

She ran her tiny brown hands over his muscular chest as they huddled together in the back of the taxi. She slid them over his shoulders and up his neck, cupping his face in her palms. "I think you're the most handsome man I've ever seen."

They were still kissing when they paid the taxi fare and stepped out onto the sidewalk in front of Malik's house. Malik was in heaven. It almost felt as if he was falling in love, on the first date, and with a woman whose skin was the color of cinnamon pastry. The whole thing made Malik as nervous as it did happy. It had been hours since he'd heard Kelly's or Jennifer's voices in his head. As much as it was a relief, it was also a source of worry. They had never gone away on their own like that, not without medication, or without Malik giving in to them and giving them what they wanted, and there was no way Malik was going to do that, and he hadn't taken his medication in weeks. Still, he hadn't heard those shrill scathing voices spilling their relentless stream of vitriol since he'd agreed to the date with Danika. Desperately, he hoped that meeting her had somehow ended their hold on him, which made him panic at the thought of her leaving him now or ever.

"Come inside for a while."

"*This* is your house?"

It was a large single story with decorative stone all around the front entrance, a long driveway covered in stamped concrete that continued up the walkway to the front door. The front yard was desert landscaped with large palm trees and big shrubs of rosemary and sage. It was over two thousand square feet squatting on a lot that was about a fifth of an acre.

"I got lucky on this one. I bought it before the market went nuts. I only paid a hundred and eighty for it six years ago."

"Wow. My house is half this size and I paid three hundred for it. I had to take an interest-only loan out and pray that the thing appreciates in five years so I can refinance. You did get lucky."

"Come on in."

He opened the door and they stepped into the foyer. They were in each other's arms kissing passionately before the door was closed. They undressed in a hurry, desperate for each other. Malik lifted her slim delicate body into his arms and carried her to the bedroom still kissing her passionately, their tongues dueling, lips bruising against each other. He laid her on the bed and kissed his way slowly up her thighs, pausing between them to taste her sweet musk, sending a quiver through her and stealing the breath from her lungs. He kissed his way up her stomach, kissed and sucked each nipple, flicking his tongue across them and making her moan, before returning to her lips. She was trembling all over when he finally entered her. She matched his rhythm as their flesh entwined in urgent thrusts, slowly at first and then with greater and greater urgency, building to a mutual orgasm that shook them both. They collapsed into each other's arms, catching their breath before making love once more. Their bodies complemented each other's perfectly. They made love without inhibitions, not holding anything back, exploring every inch of each other's bodies, getting to know all the spots that drove each other wild.

The night was half over when they lay spooned against each other, breathing heavily with sweat and semen drying into the sheets.

"You still think I only like white women?" Malik kissed the back of her neck gently.

"Oh, you definitely know how to appreciate a sista."

He laughed. "I'll be right back."

Malik got up from the bed. His legs felt as if they were made of Jell-o. He staggered into the bathroom and closed the door behind him, grabbing on to the sink to steady himself. He was just about to turn on the lights when he heard them.

"That bitch must be crazy fucking a big black scab like you. That nasty trifling ho! If you won't kill that bitch, then we will."

Malik knew why he hadn't heard the voices in his head all day. Jennifer and Kelly weren't in his head anymore. They were right there in his bathroom.

He turned his head and watched as the two small shadows crept from his shower stall, forming the tiny teenaged bodies of the two girls who'd tormented him since grade school. They hadn't changed in almost twenty years. Kelly still wore her ruffled shirts with the Izod sweater and tight Gloria Vanderbilt jeans. Her hair was permed and straightened and hung down to her hips. Jennifer was dressed almost identically except her hair was Jeri Curled and she wore a denim jacket with Prince and Michael Jackson buttons pinned all over it and one lace glove. They both were carrying knives.

"We're going to cut that disgusting bitch's heart out."

They kept fading in and out of the night. One second they were featureless silhouettes, shadows moving within the darkness, and the next their features were sharp and clear, knives glinting in the moonlight.

"You can't be here," he said. "This isn't possible!"

Malik groped for his medication, shattering the mirror on the medicine cabinet as he ripped the door open and fumbled inside for the little prescription bottle.

"Are you okay in there?" Danika asked.

"We're going to kill that bitch. She shouldn't have touched you. You've contaminated her now with your filthy black African hands. You were probably just a mercy fuck anyway. She just felt sorry for you. You were her good deed for the day. A charity fuck."

"Ewwww! That's so nasty! How could she do that with you?"

"She said I was handsome."

"You're not handsome!"

"She said you were handsome! Ewwww!"

Malik found the bottle of antipsychotics and struggled with the childproof cap. He removed the cap just as Kelly stepped forward and slashed his wrist with the knife, fading back into the night after delivering the blow. Malik screamed as Jennifer lashed out and slashed the other wrist.

"We should just kill you. You're the one always bringing these whores here and forcing them to have sex with you, making them stoop to your level."

"Malik? Are you okay in there?"

Danika knocked lightly on the bathroom door.

"No, let's kill her. She makes us look bad. She makes this filthy black nigger think he's good enough to be with us. He's so black he sweats oil."

"Yeah, let's kill that high-yellow bitch!"

Jennifer reached for the doorknob and began to open it. Malik rammed into it, slamming it shut, and the two girls turned on him and began slashing at him, cutting up his forearms as he struggled to defend himself. He struck at them with his fists, but his arms passed harmlessly through the darkness as the two girls faded in and out of the shadows.

On the other side of the door Danika had heard enough. Something was wrong. Fear gripped her as she heard Malik in the bathroom arguing and fighting with someone who shouldn't be there, arguing about killing her. Just minutes ago she had been lying in his arms, thinking to herself how easy it would be to fall in love with this man. Now she was afraid that he was some type of psycho.

Danika hit 911 on her cell phone and left the line open as she rushed to gather her clothes. Whatever was going on in the bathroom was growing more and more violent. It sounded as if Malik was in pain. She was just about to run out of the house when something in Malik's voice made her stop. Maybe someone or something was really in there with him?

"Run, Danika! Get out of here!"

"Filthy black ape, black scab. You shit-colored African jungle bunny!"

Malik was covered in cuts and slashes when he came staggering out of the bathroom carrying a knife in each hand.

Danika watched him slash at the air and then slice his own forehead. Blood rained down his face and dripped from the wounds in his neck, chest, and forearms. Danika screamed as she watched Malik's face twist and contort, morphing between rage and terror as whatever demons he was struggling with made war within him . . . and he was heading right toward her . . . swinging the knives.

Danika ran. She didn't know where she was going. The house was big and she could not find her way to the front door in the dark, so she opened the first door she came to and ducked inside. It was the garage.

There were big metal canisters that looked like oil drums scattered here and there inside the garage, and Danika tried to tell herself that she had just seen too many horror films when she started to speculate on what might be inside. She began feeling along the wall for the switch to open the garage door, afraid to turn on the light for fear that Malik might find her again. There was no switch. She'd have to open the door manually.

"That half-white bitch shouldn't have been slummin' around with your big gorilla-lookin' ass. Ya black spook! You so black I can't see you at night until you smile."

"He's so black he could hide in a coal bin."

The voices coming from the house were sounding less and less like Malik and more and more like someone else. Like children's voices in stereo. It sounded as if he was possessed. There were more sounds of struggle as glass shattered and something heavy fell over with a thud. She heard Malik scream again and wondered if whatever was inside his head had slashed one of those knives across his throat and ended his suffering. But then she heard the voices again.

"We know that nasty redbone bitch is still here. We're going to find her. We'll kill her and then we'll finish you off too."

"Nooooo!"

Malik screamed again and Danika stopped halfway to the garage door when she heard him sob and whimper. He was in pain. Those evil voices were torturing him.

"Leave him alone!" Danika yelled.

The garage door rose and Malik was standing there in the driveway, a knife in one hand, and the moonlight behind him, silhouetting his form.

"I said, leave him alone."

She didn't know what she was doing. She didn't know what she was saying. All she knew was that she had to help. It might be the only way to save her own life as well as Malik's.

"You filthy slut! You'll fuck anything if you'll fuck this filthy black scab."

"He looks like he's been dipped in shit."

The voices no longer sounded anything like Malik. His lips didn't even move when they spoke. They were the voices of spiteful children. Conceited little girls who thought it was fun to ridicule anyone they believed to be less than them.

"You're wrong," Danika said. "He's beautiful."

"He's a nasty black ape!"

"He's a beautiful black man! You girls are behind the times. Black is beautiful now. Those light-skinned pretty boys are so eighties. Women want real men these days, and the bigger and blacker the better."

"She's lying! Nobody wants you. You're just a big ugly black African!"

Malik was still standing there on the driveway holding the knife. His mouth still did not appear to be moving even as insults poured out of him. There were shadows hovering around him. As Danika looked she thought she could almost make out the silhouettes of two young girls. She even imagined she could see their faces twisted into smirks of superiority.

"They're wrong," she said. "I wouldn't have come home with you tonight if that was true. I—I thought I was falling in love with you. We might have fallen in love together if these little bitches hadn't gotten in the way."

Malik turned and looked right at the two shadows standing by his side. He had raised his knife to slash into them when the two police officers tackled him, knocking him into the garage right into the barrels. Three of them fell over and one of the lids came off. Danika screamed as a woman's torso tumbled out of the barrel followed by its head. The disembodied head spun as it tumbled across the garage floor, turning toward her. Even though the woman was dead, Danika could tell that she had been very beautiful, with long curly brown hair, light cappuccino-colored skin, and hazel eyes just like her own.

Danika turned to the other barrels and began knocking them over. One after another, curly-haired, tan-skinned heads tumbled out onto the garage floor. Danika looked from one face to the next as more police officers crowded into the garage.

"Are you okay, ma'am? Jesus Christ! Are those real? We need a coroner over here. Somebody call CSU! It's

a fucking bloodbath in here! We've got bodies everywhere!"

Danika pried her eyes away from the lifeless faces
lying on the garage floor and back up to the garage entrance where the two shadows were still standing there,
smirking in superiority, unnoticed by everyone except
her and Malik. She looked back down at Malik as what
looked like half a dozen cops piled on top of him,
twisting his arms behind his back and handcuffing
him, their fear making them use more force than nec-
essary as they tried to restrain him. Malik stopped
struggling and looked up into her eyes even as her vision started to fade and everything began to go black.

"Why?" she asked him. "How could you do this?"

"I'm sorry, Danika. I didn't want to hurt you. Some
wounds don't heal. Some wounds never heal."

Danika fainted, thinking about scabs that continued
to rip open and bleed decades after the wounds that
caused them. The girls had called Malik a black scab.
In a way, they had been right.

And Death Rode with Him

Anthony Beal

An ass-kicking in a glass. That's what you got on any night Browder was pouring drinks at Paradise Pub. To my thinking, that's a mighty fanciful name for a dark little shit-kicker's alehouse out in the Baja Desert, but that's what they call the place. Browder could make a weapons-grade cocktail out of fucking amaretto and grenadine. And one sip would knock you to your goddamned knees. Don't know how he done it. Ain't sure I wants to know.

The stool at the north end of the bar near the toilets belonged to Zadora, the seer. Brown, handsome lady of fifty, maybe fifty-five years breathing, always draped in silk rainbows. She had these salt-n'-pepper braids down the middle of her back look like creeping vines. I ain't ever seen a night when she wasn't sitting over there shuffling her damn tarot cards in between sips of Stout. Sometimes, they got drunk enough, rummies would ask her to tell their fortunes. Sometimes, if her glass was empty or she'd done run out of Swisher

Sweets, she'd accept a donation of smokes or hooch, and be their patron saint for a spell. Most nights found her doing the same as the rest of Paradise's regulars: chasing their demons to the bottoms of pint glasses and ale bottles, and demanding quick refills, hoping to drown the fuckers for good.

At the room's south end, two stools down from the seat belonging to me, you could walk in here any night and find Old Man Solomon—"Old Man," Browder calls him, and the guy ain't seen three summers more'n I have—suckin' on fistfuls of stale peanuts and watching for visions in the cups of black coffee he always ordered. Black coffee. S'all he ever ordered anymore. Ain't seen that poor bastard touch a drop of whiskey since the night he claimed he seen his dead wife's face smile up at him from a steaming cup of joe. He ordered it while sitting in this very same pub on that very same stool. Think he makes it his business to occupy that same seat and order the same thing night after night hoping for a second vision. And night after night, I've sat here sucking down bad beer like unwanted medicine and watched Old Man Solomon hobble home disappointed. I feel for the guy, but how you gon' console someone so hell-bent on grieving?

The room's only television had been mounted from the ceiling behind the bar. Only thing ever played on it was some regional news broadcast I ain't never seen before. I don't watch a lot of TV, and I'm not sure whether my TV gets channel sixty-six, but that's the channel the TV's always set on here. You can always recognize folks who ain't never been in here before, 'cause the first thing they ask for after a drink is whether Browder can turn the channel to whatever boxing match or soccer game they know is on. Browder always claims channel sixty-six's the only station the thing can pick up way out here in the desert. First-timers don't always look prepared to believe him when he say that, but Browder's a seven-foot-tall, shaved-headed, Aryan-lookin' motherfucker with a goatee and a faceful of tattoos. He got arms on him look about as thick as a circus strongman's thighs, too, so I ain't never seen nobody even think about arguin' with the dude. He say that's the only channel it pick up, folks just let it go.

Tonight, I'd only been here for about an hour or so before in walked my man, Carter. I didn't know whether Carter was his first name or his last. All I know is from the night we first met each other here, he stuck his hand in mine and told me to call him "Carter," so that's what I call him. Tonight, he looked strange when he come in, though. Had the look of a man who done just stepped out onto a tree limb and heard a *crack*.

I gave him a nod when he looked up and seen me sitting where I always do, but I noticed he ain't come over to me right away. He just stood there blocking the doorway and staring at me real frightened like; look like he was scared he was gon' catch something contagious if he came too close to me, or like I was on fire and he had done soaked his clothes in gasoline 'fore he come in. Felt like a full five minutes before he worked up the nerve to come over and see about having a drink. Some folks might say I shoulda gone over to see what had set him jittering, but instead I stayed on my stool sipping black-labeled salvation the whole time he spent making up his mind whether to piss or go blind. The way I figured it, I hadn't never brought none of my troubles in here and laid 'em at his feet, so I fucking well wasn't volunteering to sort out whatever pile of shit he'd stepped in that was responsible for the look in his eyes. Nice guy, sure, but ask Carter for the time, he'd tell you how to build a fucking clock.

He finally come over and pulled hisself up onto the stool my foot shoved toward him. I ain't ever knowed Carter to throw back anything harder than Stout, but tonight he ordered up a double shot of gin as chaser to a whiskey on the rocks. After that, he just sat there staring down at his size twelves like somebody'd done clued him in on the exact date and time of his death and had told him he was gon' win the lottery the day before it went down.

I asked him how things are going, speaking more out of courtesy than any desire to know what ailed him tonight. I asked this after letting maybe a full minute stretch between us without conversation. When he finally spoke, something in his voice set me questioning whether or not I was a religious man.

"Can I count on you?" he asked me, his eyes still enamored with them gum-soled gunboats hugging his feet. By this point in the evening, I'd poured enough whiskey down my throat to have drowned at least three of my five senses, so it was his turn to sit there with a drunk and gawking old man for a spell.

Browder come along about that time and set Carter's drinks on the bar. By the time he left us, I'd remembered where I kept my tongue.

"Depends on what you want to count on me for," I told Carter. I ain't never heard nothing resembling good news follow a question the likes of what he was asking me. I knew I damn well better hear his whole tale before pledging him my allegiance.

"I want to know if I can count on you to listen to something I ain't repeated out loud to nobody for fear of the rubber room they'd sling my ass in if I did. I need to know you ain't gon' chalk what I tell you up to my being a drunk in a place that lends itself to all kinds of local legendry."

I knowed more than a few of the tales people told about this place. In these parts, you couldn't swing a dead cat without hitting somebody whose cousin's brother's roommate's fuckin' proctologist had a story 'bout something happening to them in this very room. Everything from haunted urinals in the shitter to folks having shared drinks with the Devil in the wee hours of the morning.

The oldest story I know 'bout the Paradise Pub says it's a cursed place, and that that's why Indian Road 7734 what leads out to it don't appear on no map you'll ever lay eyes on. Lot of folks say you can't go looking for the pub, that it don't take nobody inside it that it don't want, but that it reveals itself every once in a blue moon to folks who deserve to be here. They say the ground beneath it was hexed generations ago by Indians living here who was angry over the white man putting so many of their men in early graves and their women in brothels. Don't know if I buy the whole curse bit, but I can see how them Indians would be pissed at having their entire way of life kicked down around their ears. At any rate, Carter seemed to think I was likely to dismiss whatever he was gon' tell me for another such story.

"Well, I'm listening, so go ahead and talk if you need to talk," I said.

"In a minute," Carter told me, making his chaser

disappear. "First, you see the dude behind me having his fortune read at the other end of the bar?"

I looked past Carter, toward the opposite end of the bar where Zadora sat lighting up another cigarette and turning over tarot cards. The mountain sitting beside her in the army jacket didn't look as old as the socks I had on, but from where I sat, he looked 'bout as wide as Carter and me laid together head to foot.

"I see him. He ain't altogether hard to miss. What about him?"

"Not here. Outside," Carter said, hinting toward the door.

I didn't relish giving up my stool, but curiosity had a hold of me. I found myself polishing off my glass of melted ice cubes and following him through the pub's only door.

He brought me outside into an airless night so quiet you could hear a rat piss on cotton. I followed him around the back of the building to the shadows, where folks liked to park their cars and fire up doobies in the dark.

"All right," I said, once we'd backed as far as we could into the blackness. "Everything about you tonight has me figuring you're in some kind of trouble. Am I wrong?"

"You ain't wrong," he told me, "and I ain't in it by myself. Can't say I'm sorry about that last part, neither."

"Well, you gon' tell me what it's all about, or not?" I already missed the presence of a sweaty, on-the-rocks tumbler in my palm. My patience was a candle burning at both ends.

"All right, all right. So, that big dude in there letting

Zadora's card-shuffling ability hash out his future for him, you've seen him in here before, right?"

I ain't never had much to say to the twenty-something in the army drabs, but I knowed him to be a regular. He hadn't never caused no trouble that I ever seen. Most nights, you'd walk in and find him hugging the wallpaper between the jukebox and the restroom, and burning up clove cigarettes like smoking them was the only thing keeping him alive.

"What about him?" I wanted to know. I won't never forget what Carter said to me in reply. Them words is burned onto my goddamned brain. They'd be burned onto yours too, if you'd been standing in my shoes that night.

"He dead, Lou. I know he dead 'cause I killed him last night."

All I could do was stand there still trying to decide whether or not religion was a stranger to me, and trying to keep the word "bullshit" from slipping through my lips.

Don't know what made Carter think he was going to drop a bomb like that on me without some kind of clarification to go along with it. He should have damn well known what my next question would be, but the son of a bitch made me ask it anyway.

"The fuck you mean, he dead? How can he be dead when he's in there right now having his fortune told and stinking up the joint with them damn clove cigarettes?"

"I know, man. I know I sound like a lunatic, but you know me, Lou. You know that no matter what I might sound like right now, I ain't crazy. And I'm telling you I killed that son of a bitch."

I decided then and there that he was crazy. I was standing alone a hundred miles out in the Baja in the dark with a crazy man.

"Well, I'd tell you he don't look so dead to me, and then I suppose we could have an argument, but we won't. Instead, why don't you start over from the beginning?" I would come to regret saying those words.

"Before we do, I got another question for you," Carter said. His speaking tone had taken on a lunatic's sheen that unnerved me. I didn't know how many more of his questions I was prepared to hear.

He took my hand in his and pressed it between his palms. I don't know whether he was the one shaking or whether it was me, but I could feel the tremors working their way up my wrist in that dark place behind the pub where moonlight didn't dare to reach. They scrabbled up my forearm, and at the rate our conversation was going, they weren't going to stop till they reached my toenails.

"Do you remember the very first time you ever set foot in the Paradise Pub?"

Something dark was bubbling up from inside Carter; something that seemed to take hold of him and didn't seem intent on letting him go any time soon. I'd estimate that I probably outweigh Carter by a solid forty pounds and stand three inches taller than him, but I don't mind admitting that at that moment, he scared the fuck out of me.

What scared me more was that I found his question impossible to answer. Of course, a stubborn bastard like me would die before admitting such a thing, so I tried to rationalize it to myself.

If there's one thing I learned in all my years, it's the

number-one reason that hesitation can be a hazard. Hesitation is dangerous 'cause it betrays fear, and sometimes fear is a pheromone. This was one of those times. Carter must have smelled it, the way he lunged in to swallow up the silence as I stood ruminating. "Can't recollect it, can you? Bet you can't. I bet you fuckin' can't!"

It pissed me off that he was right.

"Hell, I been coming here for so long. At our age, there's got to be a million places I drink at where I don't remember the first time I ever went there."

This seemed admission enough for him. "That's another thing," he practically shouted, making me shush his ass in the darkness. For a man who'd seemed to have privacy concerns about speaking with me, his mannerisms was growing more conspicuous with every word he said. Sweating like a whore in church, he went on, "You say there's a ton of places you drink at besides this one. So when the last time you been to one of them instead of coming here? Huh? When?"

"Man, what the hell you driving at with these questions?" It was all I could think of to say, since I damned sure couldn't recall having gone anywhere else to drink except Paradise Pub in a month of Sundays. I didn't want him to know my memory was dust, of course. And if he knew the reason why I couldn't recall anything removed from this creepy little alehouse out in the middle of nowhere, I felt terrified all at once of him telling me.

"Lou, just answer the question. Humor me. It'll all come together in a minute, I swear it will. Just bear with me and answer the goddamned question. Do you remember the last time you went anywhere other than here? Last time you had a really good meal? A really satisfying night's sleep?"

"No, I don't," I sighed, searching in vain for my shoes where they hid inside the darkness pooled around my feet. They were as lost as I felt.

"I didn't think you could," he told me, softening his voice the way a doctor does who's fixin' to give a child patient a needle. "You don't recall 'cause you're here every night, ain't you? You're here every night just like me, just like too damn many of the folks inside this joint right now."

"You said something a few minutes ago about getting to the point," I reminded him.

"Yeah, I did," he answered, "and here it is. I was as clearheaded last night when I killed that big fat motherfucker inside as I am talking to you right now."

"And how clearheaded is that?" I asked. I was fighting like mad to hang on to my last little scrap of objective rationale, but Carter would prove to be a better grappler than I was. He seemed hell-bent on snatching it away from me.

"I killed him and I knew what I was doing and I did it anyways. There was something I just had to know for myself. And tonight when I come in here, sure as we're standing here, I found his ass sitting inside laughing like nothing had happened. And that's when I knowed what I come to tell you tonight."

"Which is?"

"We're dead, Lou. We dead and we done gone to the Devil. You, me, everybody inside that fucking bar. Dead."

Crazy.

Crazy as a shit-house rat.

"Listen, man, if you and that kid had some form of altercation, that's one thing—"

"We ain't had no fuckin' 'altercation,' man! I'm telling you I murdered that motherfucker! I pressed the muzzle of this here pistol"—he dragged the Colt Diamondback that I knew he always carried out of his belt and shoved it up under my nose—"against his doughy fucking temple and splattered his brains all over the goddamned sand. And I did that because of what I seen one night prior."

I thought about saying I didn't want to hear any more, but it was too late to stop listening now.

His words shook as he talked. "Two nights ago, I was just getting in my car, fixin' to leave for the night, when I seen two of the regulars slip out the bathroom window and take off running into the desert. They didn't know I seen 'em. It was that cute little blond trick what's always callin' us old-timers 'granddaddy,' and that pot-smoking white boy always got his hair tied back in a ponytail. The way they kept looking over their shoulders at the place, you'd have thought the Devil himself was on their heels."

I knew who he was talking about. I remembered back when they was new faces. They started showing up here not long after a bus rolled on Route 2, injuring two dozen people and killing three. I remembered them 'cause they looked too damn young to be regulars in a place like this. I recalled that the big dude in the army drabs started coming here 'round the same time.

"What about them?" I asked.

"I saw them get killed by some damn *things* that I don't know what they was," he told me.

"What kind of *things*? Coyotes? Wolves?" I heard

the questions dive off the tip of my tongue before I'd realized they were in my mouth.

"Man, didn't I just say I don't know what they was? They was some kind of monsters or something. They was big, too. *Big* big, and blacker than night and they scuttled around on all fours faster than my eyes could follow them. The way they jumped all over those kids, they never had a chance."

"The kids talk to each other before they took off running? They say anything that might account for what they was running from?"

When he answered me, Carter's voice sounded like there were ghosts living in it. "All I heard was her keep telling him it was their only chance. She talked like they was risking their lives if they ran and dead for sure if they stayed. Then those monsters come out of the dark like they was made of it and tore them kids to pieces. I swear my insides could *feel* the sound of them jaws, like bear traps snapping shut on arms and legs and throats. That fucked my shit up, man."

Maybe it was the drink in me, or maybe it was the sudden chill growing in the air, but I found myself believing him. That probably only meant I was as loony as he was, but my disbelief was eroding nonetheless.

"What'd you do when you seen that?" I asked him.

"Didn't do nothing. Any man my age who think he gon' outrun a pack of animals that caught prey young and spry enough to be his grandkids is a damn fool. I was too scared to do anything but wait for them to come rip my skin off. But they didn't, maybe 'cause they seen I wasn't trying to escape."

Carter might have been a damned surgeon when it came to spinning a good yarn, but I had to stop him here. He'd slipped a word into that last sentence that bugged me.

"Escape? Escape from what? From who?" I asked. He let the question hang out there in the dead air and twist a little before speaking again.

"If you can stand there and ask me that, then you ain't been listening. Anyway, I watched the things disappear back into the blackness they come out of without paying me no mind. When they was gone, I threw my car in gear and tore the hell out of there. The thing is, I don't remember ever getting home."

"What?"

"I'm serious, Lou, and I'm fucking scared, I don't mind telling you. I got onto Road 7734, the very same road we're looking at now"—he jabbed a finger toward the front of the pub and the uncharted dirt-and-gravel road—"and watched the Paradise Pub fade into my rearview mirror. Then within five minutes, I found myself driving up the road leading to it. I could see it through the fucking windshield. How is that possible? How the fuck is that possible on a road straight as a fucking arrow, Lou?"

"It ain't possible," I told him, suddenly needing to sit down. "It ain't possible."

It wasn't. Indian Road 7734, that alleged phantom service road that only reveals itself to the deserving, is a solitary, southward-heading straightaway. It's got as much curve or loop to it as a number-two pencil. Ain't no way in hell a body could possibly have ridden it in a circle, I don't give a damn how drunk they are.

Carter kept on selling. "So the next night, last night, I come in and the first thing I see is those two kids, drinking, laughing, having a grand old time. Not a mark on either of them to suggest that they'd been minced not twenty-four hours prior. It was like the night before had never happened. So I made sure I didn't touch a drop of beer or liquor. I lured that big dude outside and shot him in the head. I had to fucking know, Lou. I had to see if it'd work a second time. And tonight, he's in there right now, probably drinking himself dumb as me."

I'd heard enough. I told him I'd prove to him that things couldn't be what he thought they was. I'd get in his car with him and we'd take that drive home together. I could leave my car here for a night without worrying about it. Anybody stole that piece of shit, they'd bring it back before they got ten feet with it. Probably bring it back with a dollar stuck in the glove box.

I followed Carter around the corner of the building to his car, a slightly newer piece of shit than mine was. We climbed in and gave the rattling vehicle a couple of minutes to warm up.

"I hope you're prepared for what you about to experience," he told me, as he piloted his car onto the dirt road.

An ass-kicking in a glass. That's what you got on any night Browder was pouring drinks at Paradise Pub. To my thinkin', that's a mighty fanciful name for a dark, little shit-kicker's alehouse out here in the Baja Desert, but that's what they call the place. Browder could make a weapons-grade cocktail out of fucking amaretto and grenadine.

The sound of tires crunching on gravel was the only one to break the silence as we pulled up in front of the pub. I swung my legs out of Carter's crappy ride and drew a deep breath as I stood up. Inside, I took my usual place two seats down from Old Man Solomon. "Old Man," Browder calls him, and the guy ain't seen three summers more than I have. As always, the night found him staring into a cup of coffee with tears in his eyes. He didn't acknowledge me when I bid him good evening, and I really hadn't expected him to. Sometimes you said things just to be neighborly.

On the television, a channel sixty-six newscaster was covering another car accident out on Route 2. That's all there seemed to be on the tube anymore. It looked like a bad one, too: three cars, drunk drivers, no survivors. Fucked-up business.

"Well?" Carter said, draining his first drink of the evening in one gulp.

"Well what?"

"You don't remember, do you?"

"What you talking about, man?"

"Think. Tell me the last thing you remember."

Last thing I remembered was getting into his ride last night and falling asleep. Next thing I knowed, we were pulling up in front of the Paradise Pub. I told him as much.

"Let's go outside," I told Carter, emptying my glass.

We tucked ourselves into the shadows behind the pub. Something felt familiar, felt right about this. Carter lit up a smoke and said to me, "You remember anything I said to you last night?"

"Some," I told him. "Got some holes in my recollection, though."

"I told you about how I killed that big army-jacketed

dude, how I'd seen other patrons die here and reappear at the bar the next night, happy as can be."

"Yeah, I got that," I told him, as I noted for the first time the absence of a single star sharing the night sky with a full moon. "But where the fuck are we? How the hell'd we get here?" The words were barely out of my mouth before I was sorry I asked.

"I guess if either of us knew that, we wouldn't still be here, right?" I added quickly.

I turned to walk back inside when I heard Carter's voice behind me. "Wanna know something? Under proper circumstances, I could get used to it here."

Seems like when he told me that, the sky got a little blacker. I felt the bottom drop out of my stomach the way a roller-coaster rider does right before the car plummets over its highest peak.

"I have to think that's your ass talking, 'cause your mouth knows better," I replied. We hadn't had nearly enough to drink yet for him to be coming at me with that kind of crap.

I heard the pub's front door come open then. A couple of drunken denim-and-flannel shit-kickers come stumbling out of the place, having apparently reached the point in their evening where it was time to drop their pants in the dark and test which of them had the quicker gag reflex.

Carter's eyes looked oddly shiny in the darkness behind the pub. I backed away from him, and was relieved to see he was too concerned with making his point to pursue me. That didn't mean my retreat had escaped his notice, though.

"Slow down and think on it a minute. We're the only ones who know, Lou. We're the only ones who know we're in hell. Ain't you given a thought to what that means?"

"All I'm thinking about is getting the fuck out of here, wherever 'here' is. I ain't had much time to consider indulging every depraved little fucking fantasy my subconscious has to offer me."

"Well," Carter said as he drew his pistol and studiously perforated the scalps of the two denim-and-flannel fuckers, "maybe you should."

Felt like something in the left side of my chest ripped in two when I seen that. I couldn't breathe. A luminous shade of red rose into the blackness of the night sky as I reeled. I saw the heavens turn the color of turbid blood, like a backlit canopy of black sackcloth with hell's inferno glowing behind it. I looked for Carter as my knees gave way. Actually made eye contact with him for a brief moment before I started to slide. My last thought as the ground rose to greet me was that I had to be hallucinating. Couldn't find no other explanation for his eyes suddenly going missing from a face so moldered that it was sliding off his skull in hunks of gray-black meat that splattered his shoes with black blood and pus.

An ass-kicking in a glass. That's what you got on any night Browder was pouring drinks at Paradise Pub.

I found myself sitting in my usual seat. The stool at the north end of the bar near the toilets had the seer perched on top of it. Her deck of tarot cards was spread out atop the bar where she sat reading a rummy his fortune. My thoughts turned to Carter, and I didn't know whether to feel better or worse to find myself remembering more and more with each new moon. The one thing I still couldn't remember was going home between visits to the pub, and the worst part of that was that I found it didn't concern me so much.

I'd lost track of how long I'd been here. A week? A year? Did it even matter anymore? Most nights, I just sat here trying not to wonder how many times I'd relived the same night's activities. I tried not to wonder what sin I'd committed in order to end up here, or how many of my fellow patrons here sat wrestling with the same question.

Tonight, for the first time, I got Old Man Solomon talking a little. I tried to take his mind off those damned coffee cups that keep his face so long. Had I known where the conversation would lead us, I might not have pursued it.

"I see your friend has figured things out," he said quietly after we'd exchanged a few amenities. I felt equal parts offended that he'd called Carter my "friend" and fearful over what he might be alluding to. Carter was changing in ways that made me want to spike his drinks with a little holy water. Whatever he was becoming, he damn sure wasn't my friend, not no more.

When I didn't answer, he told me, "You know what I mean. There's nothing to be gained by playing dumb, am I right?"

I watched Carter from my stool where he stood laughing and chatting up some dude in a leather biker jacket. I noticed Carter wasn't drinking beer tonight. Hadn't heard him order nothing but cola all night. I wondered what that was about.

"Nobody's playing with you, old man," I said. Damn Browder had *me* calling Solomon "old" now.

"Have it your way," he said, returning his attention to the cup of coffee set before him. "A word to the wise is sufficient, or so it's said."

"If you've got something to say to me, then say it," I told him. I wasn't about to be baited.

"I'm saying that I know what it is to want someone to stop the world so you can get off. But the devil of it is that once the world stops for you, it's hell to start up again. Can't be done, most times."

"That what happened to you? Is that what happened to all of us here?" I asked him.

He shrugged, retreating. "I can only speak for myself. We tell our own tales here, Lou. It is 'Lou,' isn't it?" His eyes followed Browder to the far end of the bar.

I nodded as a terrible dawning burned my mind.

Old Man Solomon leaned close to me and whispered, "A word to the wise. The coffee here isn't the best by any means, but there aren't any demons in the pot."

I would have settled for knowledge of where the hell I was and what the story was with the place. I didn't feel ready to know everything Carter apparently knew. He was getting too damn bold, and I didn't like it. The way he saw it, he told me, it was all he could do not to lose his last few shreds of sanity. The way I saw it, his last shred of sanity flew over the cuckoo's nest the minute he killed his first victim. The topic had evolved into one of those things that friends who want to stay friends just don't talk about.

I reminded myself he wasn't a friend anymore as a crash rang out. Carter had emptied his drinking glass and busted it over the head of the biker he was talking to. The bandanna-clad man went down and didn't move. Blood like burgundy sauce spread over the floorboards to halo his head. No one reacted.

"Carter, man, what the fuck you think you doing?" I shouted at him, getting to my feet.

Fixing me in place with a look I ain't never seen on a man who had more than ten seconds of life left in him, he answered, "I'm learning in death how to live."

I replied, "I don't know about Indian curses or what in hell's going on round here, but ain't nobody dead except maybe for that dude lying at your feet." I don't know what made me think he'd buy what I was selling. *I* didn't even buy it.

"Sometimes, Lou, dying is the highest, truest form of living. I've often wondered whether the dead imitate the living, whether everybody we've ever loved and lost are still kicking around somewhere, carrying out the same habits and mannerisms they did when they was alive. I know now that they do, 'cause I'm one of them. And like it or not, so's you."

He'd finally struck me speechless. All I could do was gape at him and wonder whether it hurt to go insane.

"Let me teach you how to live," he told me.

Time slowed down as he remembered the pistol in his belt, swung it up fluidly to align it with my right eye socket, and blasted away the rear portion of my skull.

An ass-kicking in a glass. That's what you got on any night Browder was pouring drinks at Paradise Pub. But I'd had enough for tonight. I was headed home.

Climbing into my car, I recalled a conversation I'd had with the seer. I'd figured on finding someone other than crazy fucking Carter to talk to tonight. I figured on that not long after heading into the men's room to take a whiz and finding him crouching in the room's only stall with his dick embedded in the frothing, gore-caked eye socket of some sweaty redhead prone to selling blow jobs in that very same bathroom after she'd had a couple of highballs.

If you coulda seen the grin on that fucker's face when he looked up and seen me watching him, you'd know why I left early tonight.

Drive home seemed to take twice as long as usual. Night driving around these parts always felt like driving through a mausoleum. Desert was so damn sterile and soundless. It sucked to be the poor bastard driving through the Baja at night with a busted car stereo. Music tended to kill some of the monotony of my drive, which varied between forty minutes and an hour, depending on road conditions. Tonight, when I turned the stereo on, I found Nick Cave wailin' "Your Funeral . . . My Trial" at me like I'd pissed him off. Since my choices seemed to be that or static, I let him yell at me while I drove.

And drove.

I knowed something was wrong after missing the exit that I usually take to get home. When I say I missed it, I don't mean I'd passed it. I knowed I hadn't. What I mean is that it wasn't where I knowed it was supposed to be. I'd half convinced myself that I must have fell asleep at the wheel and passed right by the son of a bitch until I caught sight of a little glimmer on the horizon. Figuring it might be a gas station or a sheriff's depot where I could catch my bearings and figure out where I'd made my mistake, I made up my mind to pull over when I reached it.

And the nearer I got to it, the more convinced I grew that ol' Nick was ridin' with me, and that I'd indeed made my way onto his shit list for reasons as yet unknown to me.

I was coming up on the Paradise Pub.

"You can't tell me you ain't curious," Carter told me, seating himself beside me once I'd come back inside. On the TV, photographs of people who'd died in some drunk driving accident flickered. Their vacant eyes set me trembling. A nice-looking black couple, a mildly overweight but gorgeous Latina, and her brother. None of them had survived.

"I can't tell you nothing if you done already made up your mind that you ain't listening," came my reply.

"It won't let you leave, Lou. Remember those stories about a curse on the land that we always thought was bullshit? Well, I think it's time we wrap our brains around the fact that they ain't."

I ordered up a cup of black coffee, prompting Browder to eye me for a curiosity before going to get it. The coffee machine sat at the other end of the bar near Zadora's stool. Overhead, coverage of the car accident continued to unfold.

"Looks like the place will be seeing some new faces soon enough," she told Browder, tipping her chin at the screen in a gesture that I didn't understand, but would soon come to. He said something in reply that I couldn't hear because Carter spoke to me at the same moment.

"I'll let you kill me if you want, Lou. I'll sit still for it one time. You gotta experience it."

"Get the fuck out of here," I spat, succeeding only in making him laugh till his eyes watered.

"I wish I could, man. Goddamn if I don't," he said.

"I can't believe you're fucking serious," Carter told me the next night, climbing into the passenger seat with me. I couldn't believe he was actually coming along. Don't know what had made me invite him anyway. He seemed all too content here.

"Oh, I'm heart-attack serious," I told him, firing up my car's engine. "We are shaking this fucking mob scene tonight."

I turned the car onto 7734, heading opposite the direction I'd traveled in some nights ago. If I couldn't find my way home, then I'd get us back to Route 2 and consider my options once we got there.

"You think we can just motor out of hell like a couple of bored tourists? Don't you understand that we're *home*? We're home, Lou."

Not five minutes on the road and he was getting on my nerves already. "If you buy that, then what the fuck did you say yes for when I invited you?"

"I came along so I could prove to your ignorant ass that the reason we can't leave is that we're right where we belong," he told me. "Now stop the car."

The muzzle of his Diamondback kissed the side of my throat.

"I ain't gon' ask you but one time," he said, leaning on the gun, making its presence painful against my neck.

I was sick of a lot of things in that moment, but mostly of him. "Fuck you and that gun. You claim you've already shot me in the face and killed me a few nights ago. What more you think you gon' do to me?"

"Pull the fuck over or we'll kick off every night for the rest of fucking eternity with me putting a bullet up your ass. They won't 'kill' you, but they'll hurt like a bastard. Every. Fucking. Night."

Our bluffs waltzed with each other for another second before mine got sumo heaved off the table. I pulled to the side of the road. "Satisfied?" I asked him, making a mental note to bust his ass later and pray the old memory would hang on to it.

"Almost," he said, grinning like a death's-head with only the dashboard lights to illuminate his features. "Get out."

I stepped out of the car.

He leveled the gun on my groin and shot me.

"You'll thank me for this, brother," he told me before driving away smiling and leaving me writhing around on the roadside. If the scent of my blood released into the air didn't set the creatures he'd talked about on me, then the piece of hollering I was putting on surely would.

And did.

The nightmare creatures from Carter's tale came out of the darkness of the night as if woven from it. Black hulking things with leather for skin and hellfire in their throats.

The creatures filled my ears with sound as they exposed my entrails to moonlight and fed on them. Bones cracking like glass rods. Bear traps snapping shut. Screams of the dead.

* * *

An ass-kicking the following night behind a pub in a moonlit desert. That's what Carter got 'cause that's what he deserved.

When I came to myself, I was standing over Carter with blood on my fists and in my hair that didn't belong to me. I dropped to my knees, bringing my two-hundred-thirty-odd pounds down hard in the pit of his stomach. My hands found his throat. My thumbs dug into his larynx as I squeezed. I did this without knowing the reason for it, but something in his smirk refused to let me feel bad about it. Every breath I drew convinced me further that the bastard had it coming and that if I ever remembered what he'd done to deserve this, then he'd *really* be in some trouble.

"I'm proud of you, brother man," he gurgled, smiling before going limp in my arms.

It should have bothered me that I'd just murdered the murderer who I'd chastised for being what I had become. Instead, I felt great.

God help me, I felt fucking great.

"All right, you convinced me," I told him the next night when he sauntered into the pub smiling "I told you so's" at me. "I want to give it a try. I want to kill somebody tonight."

"Hot damn, now you're talking, Lou," he laughed, clapping me on the back as Browder set a couple of lagers in front of us. I thanked Browder, but I didn't drink the bitch. I wasn't drinking nothing else in this fucking place until I tested out a theory. I hoped Carter would polish his off, though, since the round was on me. If my plan worked like I hoped it would, it was the last round I'd be buying for quite some time.

"Yeah. I mean, there ain't shit else to do up in this motherfucker, so I'll play it your way for a while," I said, hoping he was buying my line of bull and wouldn't smell the shit on my breath until it was too late.

"It grabs hold of you, don't it?" Carter said. "Told you I knew what I was talkin' about."

I lifted my glass in salute.

"Let me hold your pistol a minute," I murmured, locking my eyes on a patron across the room who I knew Carter would take for my mark. He practically leered at me as he handed it over, eager to see me walk the walk.

Sucker.

I stood up, turned to face the bar and its bottled demons, and made a wish.

I trained the gun on the bottles behind the bar. I opened up on the top shelf stuff first. The blue label. The gold label. The imported spirits. Colored flasks burst into sparkle dust, slopped expensive vodkas and brandies all over the counter, the floor, the ice bins. Fractured bottle fragments leapt into the air. The sickening sweetness of rums and tequilas and liqueurs wafted around me as each pull of the trigger blew apart the bottles that housed them, raining glass shards over every inch of floor and countertop.

I'd succeeded in getting Browder's attention. He rushed toward me with graveyards for eyes.

"Are you looking to die, old man?" he asked me, frothing with rage at my impact on his inventory.

"You have no idea," I told him.

"Tough," he said.

My mama used to tell me that if wishes were horses, beggars could ride. Her words came screaming back to me as I watched a wave of Browder's skillet-sized palm prompt every glass shard and every drop of spilled liquor to leap back into place.

If I'd blinked I would have missed it; the flash reverse motion of exploded glass vessels reconstituting like jigsaw puzzles assembled by phantom hands. I cussed at the sight of the full, intact bottles sitting unbroken as you please upon the tiers of the bar behind him.

"Do you honestly think you're the first of the insects I collect ever to attempt what you just did?" he said. His mouth had a way of smiling without letting the rest of his face in on the act.

Carter's gun hadn't helped me worth a damn, but I kept it between Browder and me anyway. I felt less naked with it there. "What the hell is this place?" I demanded, no longer doubting my knowledge of the answer to the question, but fearing to know what I knew. "Where am I?"

"It's like the man said," he told me, nodding at Carter. "You're home."

"I tried to tell him," Carter assured the bartender, who seemed to be gaining height by the second.

"Bullshit," I declared, unsure which of them I was addressing.

Browder said, "Listen, old man. I'd say I was sorry for your loss, if I truly were. Truth is, though, that you deserve to be here as much as any of these other losers."

I ain't never been the kind of man to let a face-to-face insult stand. I figured it was time to die with my boots on, so I stepped up to the bar and hoisted myself up on my palms as close to his nose as I could. "The fuck did I do to deserve your ugly fucking mug pouring me that piss-spiked sewage you call beer night after night without end?"

"What, indeed," Browder said, snatching up a nearby newspaper kept on hand for drunks who read while they boozed and hurling it into my arms. "Even a befuddled old sot should be able to add two plus two."

I took his statement as my cue to turn to page four and found a black-and-white photo of a little girl named Emily at the top of the page. She was black, 'bout six years old. A couple of cottony-looking pigtails framed her little apple of a face. She had a smile on her that I couldn't help returning even though it was just a photo. It was the last smile that would ever touch my face.

Emily had my last name.

The article accompanying the photo cited my name as the driver of the vehicle that had killed us both when it plunged into a ravine on our way to the house where her mother and her new husband lived. According to the article, I'd had three times the legal amount of alcohol in my system.

I needed to sit down and scream my way through the tears that followed the revelation, so that's what I did. I'd had a daughter. I'd had a daughter whom I'd killed and a wife, and had apparently fucked up the latter relationship so severely that she'd moved on. And my punishment was to have to choose every night for the rest of eternity. Either sit here and let the memories drive me as mad as Carter, or drink them dead.

Old Man Solomon came to rest a hand on my shoulder and told me, "My wife, Loretta was her name. Four-car pileup. Could have been avoided if I hadn't fled after accidentally running down a mother and child. I hung on for three weeks on life support. Everyone else died instantly."

The pub door opened. When I looked up and seen the pretty Latin girl from the accident on the television earlier walk in, I nearly died. Apparently, it wouldn't be the first time.

Solomon said, "I don't want to forget my Loretta. Guess I'm not like most folks. Most folks who end up here want to forget their sins. They all want to forget eventually."

He hobbled away as Browder returned to offer me a cup of black-labeled anesthesia.

I watched a stronger man than myself make his way to the restroom, and I ordered up an ass-kicking in a glass.

Are You My Daddy?

Lexi Davis

"Are you my daddy?"

"*Hey-ll* no." I grabbed my pants and jumped away from it—I mean, the kid. Shamir acted like nothing was going on.

"You didn't tell me you had a, *uh—uh*—one of those!" I pointed.

Shamir got out of bed, naked and indecent, and put on her robe like it wasn't nothing. "You didn't ask."

"The hell I didn't." I swung my legs around to the opposite side of the bed and scooted into my pants, trying to get away from his big spotlight eyes that searched me up and down like he was on the kiddy LAPD squad. "I *told* you, no *kids*. I got too much going on. Kids are complications. I can't even kick it with a woman who has kids, and I for damn sure don't want none of my own."

"But, Chris, that's Nehemiah. He's *special*."

"Special?" I stood with my back against the closet, my mouth all twisted up to show my pissivity.

I looked at the kid. A kid was a kid. This one had the

biggest dang eyes I'd ever seen—like that *Boondocks* cartoon boy. Hair like him, too—a lopsided, oversized Afro. Other than that, Nehemiah—or whatever she claimed his name was—was just another little snotty-nosed brat.

"Where's his daddy? *MIA*?"

Shamir nodded.

"Can I call you *Daddy*?" the little thing standing at the edge of the bed asked me.

"Aw, heelll—" I couldn't even find the words. I jumped back and banged my butt into the closet doors.

I turned my back to it and whipped on my shoes. I couldn't believe this mess—something out of *The Twilight Zone* or some messed-up stuff like that. And I could tell right off the bat something wasn't right about this kid. She called him special. More like *spooky* if you ask me, especially with the strange way he looked at me with those big old eyes.

I ignored the kid's crazy-ass request about him calling me "daddy" and laid into Shamir, who was combing her hair like this was no big deal.

"We've been kicking it for two whole months. You never said nothing about a—" I turned to point at it again, but it'd jumped from the door and blindsided me on my left. I whipped around and kept my eye on him. Obviously, he was a sneaky little SOB. He kept his eye on me, too. I couldn't tell if he was smiling or laughing at my ass.

Shamir said, "I didn't think it mattered. Chris, you and I get along so good together."

"It *matters*. We got along good because you didn't have a—uh." I turned to point, but the boy was gone.

He yelled from the other side of me, "A kid!" completing my sentence like I needed help.

I backed away again and stubbed my toe on the bed. "Damn! Stop jumping up on me like that, you sneaky little midget!"

"If you'd just give Neh a chance—" Shamir started, but I stopped her quick with that line.

"I'm going to give you a chance to see the back of my head."

I snatched up my wallet and the keys to my ride and got ghost, but before I could make it out the front door, that little bugger had run up on me again. He even beat me to the door.

"What the—How'd you do that?"

He had the nerve to grab my shirttail and try to yank me down.

"I *said*, can I call you *Daddy*?" He poked his bottom lip out with an attitude, like I owed him an answer.

I leaned down to his level. I removed my shirttail from his sticky little peanut butter grip and looked down at my brand-new white Sean John button-up shirt. Brown sticky stains were smeared all over it. *Damn it.* I looked into those big old magnifier eyes of his.

"Look here, you little peanut-butter-smelling, magnifier-eyed, big-headed little skunk. The only thing you can call me is Mr. Invisible Man 'cause you ain't never gonna see me again. Peace out!"

I walked out and slammed the door behind me. He opened the door and hollered at my back. "You coming back tonight? I got checkers. You like checkers?"

I kept walking, didn't look back. I walked to the curb where I'd parked my ride. I got in, started it up, and shook my head. I couldn't believe this shit. I'd kicked it with that girl for two whole months. She never said nothing about no kid. Sometimes we'd kick it at my condo, but most times we hung at her house since her neighbors weren't as close and we could get loud. I'd never seen a toy, a bicycle, a pair of Spider-man briefs—nothing that would clue me in that she had a kid.

I drove back to my place, still shaking my head. Her body was tight, too. Old girl could bounce a basketball off her abs. No stretch marks. Nothing.

I got home, jumped in the shower, and kept thinking. She didn't act like a mother, neither. She never had to get home early. Never said a thing about finding a babysitter. I'd call her, she'd say what's up? I'd say let's go and we'd roll to the beach, a movie, dinner, a club. We even did two weekends in Vegas at a moment's notice. I didn't get it. How could she have a kid right under my nose the whole time and I not know it?

I got out the shower and kept thinking about it. The sex. Whoa! No way could she be somebody's mother. Nobody's "mama" was supposed to do it like that. Old girl was a freak.

Naked and wet, I picked up the phone and called her. "You lying. That ain't your child."

"Yes, it is."

"You made me think you didn't have one. You deceived me," I said, self-righteously indignant.

"You deceived me, too."

"I ain't lied about nothing."

"You said you could last a whole hour."

"Shut up." I hung up the phone. This was serious and she was trying to change the subject.

I didn't have time for this. I got dressed, checked my suit, and slipped my Rolex on my wrist. I rushed out the door. I had things to do. I was Chris "Crisp Dollar" Duckett, owner and CEO of the premier Los Angeles music promotion company, not to mention bachelor extraordinaire. Hard, lean, and mean, that's how I did things. Ask anybody. They'd tell you. And don't believe that lie about not lasting an hour. The girl was out of her mind. She lost track of time. Believe that.

I had a meeting with Nelly's people that morning. I was making power moves, shaking it up and baking things, and as usual, things were going my way . . . until my secretary beeped in.

I pushed the intercom button. "What's up? You know I'm in a meeting."

"Yes, but, Mr. Ducket, I think you need to come out to the lobby."

"I don't need—" I calmed myself. "This had better be important." I got up and apologized to the people in my office. "Excuse me for a sec."

I stepped outside my office, walked down the hall, and opened the lobby door. My secretary and a bunch of other people were standing around a water fountain watching somebody perform.

I walked over there. A little midget wearing sunglasses was standing on top of the water fountain, his pants sagging below his Spider-roo underwear. *Nehemiah?*

He was blowing up a karaoke microphone hooked up to an amplifier, rapping and impersonating artists I've promoted—Bow Wow. Lil' Flip. Twista. Ludacris. D4L. And the little sucker was good, too.

I squeezed through the crowd as he started his Lil' Jon impersonation. He deepened his voice, picked up a drink, pulled on his cap, and put in his silver teeth, the whole nine.

"Whaaat? Whaaat? Yeaahh!"

The little punk had mad talent, especially to be only five years old. I ain't never seen nothing like it.

He had a cardboard sign at his feet: CHRIS DUCKETT DON'T WANNA BE MY DADDY: HELP A LIL' BASTARD OUT. People were breaking off large bills and tossing them into his bucket.

He spotted me in the crowd and lowered his dark sunglasses. He raised one bushy eyebrow over the top and hooked his big bug eye on me.

He pointed at me. "There my daddy is right there!"

People turned around and started hissing at me.

"I *ain't* your daddy."

He yelled back, "That ain't what Dana said."

"Who the hell is *Dana*?"

"D.N.A.!" Nehemiah started crying. Not a little boo-hoo-hoo, but big old nasty blubbering snotty nose wet wailing like somebody had stolen his candy and smacked him upside his head.

A lady hauled off and clocked me with her Gucci bag. "How could you forsake a little kid like that?"

Another one poked me in my back. "You men like making babies but then don't want to take care of them."

Another one shoved me. "Dogs! All of you!"

"He's lying!" I pushed my way through the crowd, grabbed the cardboard sign, and tore it up. "This ain't my kid!"

Nehemiah kept crying louder and even started blubbering into the mic, turning the whole water fountain performance into a riot scene. That lil' bastard really knew how to work a crowd. He moved his little balled-up hands away from his wet eyes long enough to shoot me a smile that nobody could see but me. Could have sworn I saw some fangs on those little teeth.

"You little sucker—" I grabbed his ankle. He kicked me with his other sneaker. I cocked back and was about to smack him when two big, buff, Suge Knight–looking brothers stepped forward.

"What you thinking about doing?" the one with the prison tats snarled at me.

I wasn't scared.

Hell. Yes, I was. I let go of Nehemiah's ankle. "I'm thinking about taking him to his mother. That's all, my brotha."

I backed up and smiled, but threw Nehemiah an *I'm-gonna-kick-your-short-little-ass* look.

Nehemiah dried up his tears, leaped off the fountain, and jumped into me, grabbing me around my neck. "Daddy! Daddy!"

The crowd applauded.

The lady with the Gucci bag patted me on my shoulder. "That's right. Be responsible. Do the right thing. You know you're that kid's daddy. Look at his head. It's big, just like yours."

I grabbed Nehemiah by the neck. The big guy with the prison tats leaned forward. I smiled, lovingly, and removed my hands from Nehemiah's neck.

"C'mon!" I shoved the kid out the front door with me. I stomped through the parking lot to my ride. He struggled to keep up.

"Where we going?"

"I'm taking you to your mama," I threatened him, thinking he'd cry at the prospect of a butt whipping.

He shrugged. "Aw, that ain't nothing but a chicken wing."

Obviously, Shamir wasn't beating his behind enough.

I kept walking fast. "How'd you get out here? You ain't old enough to catch a bus."

Nehemiah's dirty little white sneakers did a flurry and he caught stride with me into the parking lot, even passed me. The kid was fast for his age.

He puffed out his little chest. "I don't need a bus, fool."

Fool? I bent down to pop him, but he hollered and the buff dude came outside the building. I patted him on his head, threw him into the back of my ride, and pulled off.

I headed down Wilshire. He crawled from the backseat to the front. "I'm hungry! Look! Burger King."

Burger King was up ahead on the right. He demanded that I pull over and feed him, like that was my job. I stayed in the far left lane and raised my eyebrow at him. His big old round Martian eyes looked at me like he dared me to pass up Burger King.

I said, "You'd better stick your head out the window, open your mouth, and try to inhale, because that's as close as you're gonna get to eating a hamburger in my car."

He lowered one of his bushy eyebrows, narrowed those big old eyes, and glared at me, like he was going to do something.

"What? Am I supposed to be scared or something?"

All of a sudden, the wheel of my ride jerked hard to the right. My car shot across two lanes and cut in front of an MTA bus. The bus slammed on its brakes and skidded. It blasted its horn and came within inches of my back bumper. Every passenger on the bus along with the bus driver yelled and cussed at me through the window. I tried to brake and swerve, but my ride jetted up into the Burger King parking lot, bounced over the curb, sideswiped the drive-through sign, and came to a skidding halt in front of the plastic Burger King talking head. My window rolled down by itself.

The plastic head said, "Have it your way at Burger King. May I take your order?"

I caught my breath and said the first thing that popped into my head. "Oh, *shit*!"

The plastic head said, "That's not on our menu. Try up the street at McDonald's. I hear they serve nothing but *oh, shit* burgers."

Nehemiah started cracking up. He crawled over me, stuck his head out the window, and started talking to the plastic king head like they knew each other from way back.

"Whassup, King Homie? Whatchu got cooking today?"

The head said, "Hey, Neh, what's up, partna? Where you been?"

"Just hanging low, you know how it go."

Cars behind me started blowing their horns. I couldn't even drive off because my ride wouldn't move. And I still felt like I was about to shit my pants.

"What'd you do to my car?" I tried to push Neh off me.

"Wait, Negro. I ain't ordered yet."

Nehemiah ordered two of everything on the menu. He turned to me. "You hungry?"

"No! I ain't hungry."

He said to the plastic king, "Give my daddy a Whopper."

When he said *whopper* he stomped his sneaker down in my lap and crushed my balls. I muffled about twenty curse words and threw him back into the passenger seat. I balled up my fist. He pointed at the plastic king. "They got a camera in his eye."

I checked myself, muttered a few more four-letter words, and drove up to the window. Three teenage girls ran to the service window, handed me the food, and blew kisses at Nehemiah.

"He's sooo cute." They looked at me. "Ooh, is this your daddy?"

Nehemiah giggled and lied, proudly. "Yeah."

"I'm *not* his daddy. Look, I just want to get out of here. How much for the food?"

"For cute little Neh, it's on the house." They blew him more kisses. He batted his big old eyelashes down over his big old eyes.

I screeched off. Halfway down the block, the smell of that Whopper started tearing up my stomach and hunger pains hit me so hard, I almost couldn't drive. "Give me a damn bite."

He threw a Whopper at me. "Told you you was hungry." The little arrogant squirt laughed like he had some kind of control over me. I hated that, but I tore into that burger like a hungry pit bull. Dang, it was good.

I got to Shamir's beauty shop, threw my ride into Park, and cut off the engine. "Sit your dwarf behind here while I go get your mama."

I locked all the doors, rolled up the windows, and activated my car alarm. I was mad. No, pissed. This kid was messing up my whole day.

I stomped into the shop. Shamir was doing a nearly bald-headed lady's hair. I grabbed her hand as she was applying the hot curlers.

"How you gonna let your badass kid run all around

the city while you go to work without getting a baby-sitter?"

Shamir almost burned me with the hot curling iron. I took it away from her and set it down. Her customer complained. I told her, "Shut up, turn around, and mind your own bald-headed business."

Shamir made excuses for her parental negligence. "Neh don't like babysitters. They can't really control him."

"That ain't no excuse. He needs that butt tapped to get him in line. Come get him or else I'm going to—" Before I could finish my threat, my car alarm started blasting.

I ran outside. Shamir followed me. When we got to my ride, the alarm was blasting but the car was empty. No kid. My rear window was busted out.

"What the—I know he didn't—" I looked inside my car. My CD player was missing. "Aw, hell nah—" I flipped open my cell phone. "I'm calling the police."

Shamir grabbed my arm. "But he's just a kid."

"Nah, he ain't. He's a little demonic—" Just then, a squad car rolled by and I flagged it down. The cop got out.

"I've just been jacked and I know who did it." I started giving him a description. "He's about three feet tall, big lopsided Afro, big eyes like two black flying saucers."

"A midget jacked you?"

"Nah. Not a midget."

"An alien?"

"Nah, worse. A *kid*! About five years old with a weird, spaced-out look about him."

The cop cocked his head to the side like I was crazy. "*Five* years old?"

"Yeah, that's right. It's her son." I pointed to Shamir. "Go on, tell the cop about your little spooky Bebe kid."

Shamir shrugged innocently.

The cop said, "I don't have time to play games with you, mister."

"I'm not playing. There's something wrong with that kid. I locked him up inside my car, rolled up all the windows and—"

"What did you just say?" The officer's eyes got suspicious. He placed his hand on his gun belt like he was about to arrest me. "You locked a kid inside your car on a hot day like this?"

I backed up. " Nah, I didn't really say I—"

"Do you realize I could take you in on a felony for that?"

"I didn't actually—"

The cop reached for his handcuffs. Just then, we heard a loud bang on top of my car. Nehemiah dropped down from the tree where he'd been hiding. His sneakers put a dent in my hood.

The cop asked, "Is this the kid you locked inside your car?"

I looked at Nehemiah. "Uh—"

The cop opened his handcuffs, pointed at me, and asked Nehemiah, "Did this man right here lock you in that car, little fella?"

Nehemiah said to the cop, "Let me get this straight. If I say yes, you gonna haul his ass off to jail?"

The cop nodded.

Shamir said, "Neh, be nice."

Nehemiah looked at me. "You coming to my house to play checkers?"

I remained silent. He waited for my answer. I couldn't

tell if that smirk on his face meant he was being nice or if he was laughing at my ass.

I looked at the cop, looked at the handcuffs. I put on a fake smile and lied, "Yeah, little man. We gonna play checkers."

Nehemiah told the cop, "No, he didn't lock me in the car. He's my *daddy*!"

The cop looked at me. "You're lucky I'm not arresting you. But you seriously need some parenting classes." The cop got into his squad car and left.

I didn't say another word to the kid or his mama. I got into my busted car and started it up.

Nehemiah ran up to my door. "Hey, where you going?"

I gave him the middle finger and drove off.

I ran my hand down over my tired face. Lack of sleep and those big spooky eyes on that weird kid had me on edge. I didn't feel like going back to my office. I knew they were going to ask me a whole lot of questions I didn't feel like answering.

I went back to my place. I called around to auto repair shops and arranged to get my window fixed, get new rims, and have a new CD player put in. I couldn't drive around in a busted car with no music. I had a reputation to uphold.

By the time I got my ride fixed, it was late. I needed a drink. I wanted to forget all about that fine-ass Shamir—the female I'd wasted two whole months kicking it with only to find out she not only had a kid, but had Rosemary's baby boy. Bebe's kids ain't got nothing on that little alien. I flipped open my PDA and went through my "unused" numbers. I always kept a reserve for emergencies just like this.

I called Rachel, a cutie I'd met two weeks ago at a

CD release party. I put on my deep Mack Daddy voice and laid down some game real proper on her.

"I been thinking about you for two weeks, girl." They fell for that line every time. I arranged a date and told her I'd pick her up at seven.

I pulled up to Rachel's place at eight-thirty looking too good for her to complain. Besides, how many single, fine, designer suit–wearing young brothers with serious bank roll and no baby-mama drama were pulling up in a style like mine to take her out?

Rachel greeted me at the door looking fresh out of the oven, hot and ready to bite. I stepped back and took in the view. I shook my head and bit my bottom lip. "Hmm, hmm. You are looking too good to me, Shamir—"

"What did you call me?"

I opened my mouth to say "Rachel" again, but it came out "Shamir."

"Shamir? My name is *not* Shamir."

"I know your name." I pressed my lips together and tried to say her name, but something twisted my tongue again and I said, "Shamir."

Damn!

She yanked down her tight minidress over her shiny thighs, pointed her finger in my face and read me the riot act. "You have the nerve to come knocking on my door calling me by some other woman's name after I got all dressed up for you!"

"Wait. I—"

She slammed the door in my face. I knocked again. She hollered from the other side of the door, "What's *my* name?"

I tried to holler back, "Rachel," but it came out "Shaaa-mirrr!"

What the freak was going on with my tongue?

Rachel opened the door again, but this time she threw a bag full of white flour into my face, then slammed the door again. I spat out flour and tried to wipe the white stuff off my brand-new designer dark blue suit but ended up smearing it more.

I don't believe this. I was ticked off, but I couldn't blame the girl for being mad. I'd tried to say Rachel, but it kept coming out Shamir.

I turned to leave, feeling like a dumb-ass black Casper the Friendly Ghost, blinking and trying to brush flour out of my eye.

I thought I saw something scurry past my foot.

"Ah!" I jumped. The flour in my eye made my vision blurry and I couldn't be sure, but the thing looked like a big-ass rat with a tiny Afro.

I looked again and didn't see anything. I hurried to the elevator.

I got in and started to push the button. Instead of buttons, I thought I saw two big round black eyes.

"Aw, man!" I jerked my hand back and banged my back against the opposite side of the elevator.

I wiped my eyes and looked at the buttons again. The round black eyes were gone and the buttons looked normal. I knew some freaky shit was going on, but I didn't know how or why or what it was about.

"I've got to get outta here," I said to myself.

I got to the lobby. Instead of the black-and-white tile that was there when I came in, the floor was red and black—like a giant checkers board. I jumped across the squares and left.

I trotted to my car, took a water bottle from my trunk, and rinsed my eyes. My whole day had been messed up. I decided I'd call my boys and maybe hang out, shoot some pool, toss back a brew, and do something to get my head right. But everywhere I looked, I saw those big black saucer-shaped eyes staring back at me.

As I reached for my phone, it rang. An unlisted number. I answered. It was Shamir.

"I'm hanging up."

"No, wait. Chris, I want to apologize."

I went silent, left her hanging.

She went on, "I was wrong. I should have told you I had a son. But we were so good together. We can't just end it like this, not without a good-bye. Come over. Let me make it up to you. Let me show you how sorry I am."

Make-up sex? Every muscle in my body wanted to hang up on her lying behind for tricking me—except one, and it was already standing at attention. I shifted my belt buckle. Kid or no kid, that woman's sex was off the hook and well worth the gas money it took to get there. But she'd lied to me. Women don't lie to Chris Duckett and get away with it. I bit my lip and contemplated.

"Is the kid there?" It's amazing how a man's pride gets overruled by his horniness every time.

"No. I took Nehemiah to the babysitter."

Bingo! Exactly what I wanted to hear, but I played it cool. "I may roll by later."

I hung up. I swung by the 24-Hour Mini Mart and picked up some ginseng. Don't get me wrong. I wasn't getting back with Shamir. I had a strict no-kids policy for the women I dated and I intended to stick to it, but I had a feeling that break-up sex with her was going to be off the chain.

I pulled up to her house. It was late, around half past

booty call time. She lived in a bad area on a hill over-looking the city. But I wasn't as worried about thugs as I was about that spooky-ass snot-nose kid of hers. That little alien gangsta made my briefs creep up into my butt.

I looked around for any signs or clues that the 'fro-haired brat was still around. The house looked dark and quiet. Shamir greeted me at the door in a sexy, sheer lingerie piece that I could see straight through to the promised land.

I brushed past her.

"Where are you going?" she asked.

"I'm checking the house." I didn't see any signs of it, but I couldn't take any chances. Shamir might be lying again. I looked in every room, every closet, the bathroom, the shower, the laundry room, out in the garage, and even the backyard. No sign of the kid.

"Okay, let's get busy." I swooped her up and took her into the bedroom. She kept apologizing for not telling me she had a kid, but all I could hear was her body talking to me. That woman was fine and had a body like whoa!

She nibbled my ear. "I want this to be special tonight."

"Oh, it will," I said while I tried to bite off her nightie with my teeth. I was already naked.

"Wait, Chris." Her voice was soft and sexy. "Lay back, boo. Put your hands up and relax." She moved my hands up over my head, turned off the lights, and scooted down my body.

"Oh yeah. Now, see, that's what I'm talking about right there."

She turned me over on my stomach, came back up, and squeezed my wrists. I heard something go *click-*

click and the sound of metal clamping to the bedpost. She'd handcuffed me.

I tried to pull away, struggled, and turned my head to look back at her. "Hold up, woman. What kind of freaky sh—"

"Relax, Chris. Keep an open mind. You're going to enjoy this."

She placed the key to the handcuff on the nightstand next to the bed. She pulled a wet towel from her nightstand and started slapping it across my butt. *Whap! Whap!*

"Woman! Stop it. I'm not into no sick sex!" I craned my neck around in the dark.

She stopped. In a purry, sexy, innocent, girlish voice, she asked, "What? You don't like it?"

My body was tingling where she'd spanked me and I was as hard as Gibraltar. I hesitated. "Well, it was starting to feel kinda good. Go ahead. But slow down, and not so hard."

I turned back over and tried to keep an open mind. I felt her crawl back up on the bed, but after two more *whaps*, it didn't feel like a wet towel anymore. It felt more like a tiny sneaker kicking my ass.

"What the—"

I turned back around in the dark. Instead of Shamir in a sexy negligee, I made out the dark outline of a lop-sided Afro and a big old pair of eyes looking down at me. Nehemiah was standing up on the bed.

"Aw, hell no!"

Nehemiah turned on the light. "You promised we'd play checkers."

I tried to yank the handcuffs hard enough to break the bedpost, but it wouldn't budge. "Boy, does it look like I'm trying to play checkers right now?"

I looked around the dark room for Shamir, cussing, frowning, kicking, and trying to get out of the cuffs. "Get off me, man!"

Stuff had gone from kinky to downright spooky. And all this Stephen King bullshit was really starting to piss me off. "Where the *hell* did your mama go?"

"I dunno. She'll be back." He sounded sad.

I was naked, horny, pissed, and freaked the hell out so I really didn't give a frig. "Reach me that key!"

Nehemiah looked at the key. His eyes brightened. "We gonna play checkers now?"

"Get the key, unlock these handcuffs, and I'll think about it." *Yeah, right.*

He got the key and unlocked me. I grabbed my clothes and threw them on. I felt like kicking my own dumb ass for getting tricked again.

"We gonna play checkers now?"

"Hell no! I'm leaving."

"When you coming back?"

"Never."

"You don't wanna be my daddy?" Nehemiah's face crumbled into a mess of tears, but I couldn't help him. I stopped and turned around in the hallway.

"Look, kid. I'm *not* your daddy. I ain't never gonna be your daddy. I don't know where that cat is, but I bet he ain't coming back 'cause there's some weird shit going on here with you and your mama. Something ain't right so I'm getting ghost, too. As for checkers, I *hate* the game. Sorry. Peace out."

I slammed the door. He started sobbing so loud I could hear him through the door. I thought I heard him say something like "You are my daddy and you are coming back!" *Yeah, right.*

The cold night air smacked me in my face. I trotted

to my ride. Shamir's car was still parked in the driveway. *That trick*, I muttered to myself. Obviously, she was somewhere hiding and playing games while she turned her demon child loose on me. I didn't have time for that.

I started my ride, threw it in gear, and floored the pedal. The car moved ten feet and stopped. The engine died.

"What the—"

I turned the key in the ignition again and again. Nothing. I got out, looked under the hood. Something thick, brown, and sticky was smeared over the engine. It was shoved inside all the spark plugs and even oozing out the oil tank. I touched it. I smelled it. Peanut freakin' butter!

I looked back at the house. The place was dark except for Nehemiah sitting in a window with the light shining behind his big lopsided Afro. Even in his silhouette, I could see those big bug eyes looking at me.

I got back into my car and opened my cell phone. I'd call a buddy or the auto club to come get me, whichever was faster, because I just wanted to get the hell out of there. My cell phone said: No signal. *Damn Cingular!* It smelled funny. I opened the back of it. Brown sticky goo oozed out. More friggin' peanut butter.

I looked back at the house. Nehemiah opened the door and waved for me to come back. *Yeah, right. Screw you.*

I got out of my car, gave him the finger, and took off trotting in the opposite direction. I'd go to one of Shamir's neighbors' houses and ask to use their phone. I took two steps and heard a growling sound. It was dark. All the streetlights had been busted out, probably by some bad little neighborhood kids like Nehemiah. He was probably the leader of a kiddy street gang called the Lil' Spooks. I could barely see the sidewalk. I stamped my feet thinking that growl probably came from a stray dog. The thing growled back and if it was a dog, it was the *X-Files* kind. I did a quick turn and jumped back into my ride.

Screw it. I was on a hill. I decided I'd coast my car back down the hill to the main street, then flag down a car. Nehemiah was still in the window watching me. I threw my car into neutral, released the emergency brake, and started steering it backward, coasting.

I made it about five feet before I hit something in the road. Whatever it was got jammed underneath my back wheels and it stopped the car. Damn! If it was the *X-Files* dog, then I'd killed it. Good.

I tried to look out my back window but I couldn't see anything. I didn't want to get out of my car to see what it was, but I had no choice. Little Spook Boy was still watching me from the house. I took a deep breath and looked around to make sure the coast was clear.

As soon as I put my hand on the door to open it, something popped up at my window right in front of my face.

"Holy *shit*!"

It was Nehemiah. His face was pressed so close to the window his breath formed a fog. His eyes were big like bowling balls and stared straight through the window at me.

I jumped back. "Back off me, freak boy!"

I slammed the lock down and edged over into the passenger seat. Slowly, the driver's-side window started rolling down by itself. I hollered again, "This ain't right. What the—"

The window cracked opened only about three inches and stopped. Nehemiah looked at me, his face all weird and spaced out. He slowly reached his tiny hand through the crack and slid his arm inside. It seemed longer than it should have been. He reached down and popped up the lock, unlocking the door from the inside.

He opened my door. We stared at each other.

Finally, he said, "You wanna come play checkers now?"

I was like, *You must be outta your freakin' little mind!* But I didn't say that; I only thought it.

On the surface, I tried to keep my cool, but it was hard. I knew my ass was in a jam and my balls were quivering. I'd stepped into some weird shit and I needed to figure out how to get out.

I needed to get to a phone. They had one inside. What else was I going to do?

I swallowed and answered him. "Yeah. I'll play checkers now."

He backed away from the door and nodded. "C'mon."

I followed Nehemiah back into the house. My plan was to act cool like I was going to play checkers and when I got a chance, hit the little sucker in his big head, knock him out, grab the phone, and call 911 . . . or something like that.

When I got inside, I saw that Nehemiah had set up the checkers board on the table. He even had cookies and milk on each side of the game board and two chairs set up—a little one for him and a big one for me. I sat down in the big one and watched him. He watched me.

"Your move," he said. A tiny smirk drew up the edge of his chapped little lips around his elf-size mouth. I didn't know if he was smiling at me or laughing at my ass.

I went to move my black checker. As soon as I touched it, all of his red checkers stood on edge and spun around real fast like twirling coins, all by themselves. *What kind of—*

I knocked over my glass of milk.

He reached for it. I stopped him. "No, it's cool," I said.

We sat still. He watched me. I watched him. We watched each other, waiting for the next move.

I made it. I picked up my glass. "I'll go pour me some more," I said. He looked at my hands. They were shaking. I played it off. I said, real cool, "I'll be right back." *Yeah, right.*

I got up and strutted calmly to the kitchen.

As soon as I got around the corner, I grabbed the kitchen phone off its cradle, ran out the other side of the kitchen, sprinted down the hallway, and ducked into the bathroom. I locked the door and dialed 911. The operator answered.

"Nine-one-one Emergency. What's your emergency?"

I started whining like a little girl. "A kid with some big freakin' eyes spanked me with a wet towel, then put peanut butter in my car, and now he's holding me hostage and making me play checkers—"

Click.

The operator hung up on me.

Think, Chris, man! Get a grip and use your head! I couldn't tell them all that—even though it was the *truth*. I had to think of something to say that would not only make them take me seriously, but would also get the police to rush out to the bad neighborhood in the middle of the night.

I called back.

The operator answered. "Nine-one-one. What's your emergency?"

I said, "Quick! Send a squad car. I just saw O.J. Simpson running down the street with a knife chasing a white woman."

There was silence on the other end. I knew I was wrong for that, but it's the only thing I could think of to get the LAPD out quick, fast, and in a hurry.

"Hello? Did you hear what I said? I said, *O.J.*—"

The person on the other end started giggling, and then laughing like a child. He said, "You so funny, Daddy."

Nehemiah!

I dropped the phone. Nehemiah knocked on the bathroom door.

"Go away, you little freak." I kicked the door to try to scare him away. I hurt my foot.

I looked down. Brown, thick, sticky goo oozed beneath the door and started sliding into the bathroom. *Nah! This ain't happening.* It formed a puddle and started bubbling up like gumbo. It rose three feet high into the air and Nehemiah jumped out.

I tried to holler but choked on my own spit. "Eeck-kka!"

Coughing and gagging, I turned and tried to jump into the shower, but when I jerked the shower curtain back, Nehemiah was standing in the bathtub.

I turned back around and shot out of the bathroom. I ran down the hall and darted into Shamir's bedroom. I locked the door, blocked it off with a chair, and looked for something to swing at the little monster.

I remembered Shamir kept a baseball bat under the bed. I dropped down, reached under the bed, and felt something furry. An Afro. I looked. Nehemiah's big black eyes were looking back at me.

"Ahh!"

I fell backward, jumped back up, and sprang to my feet. I pulled on the bedroom door but couldn't get out. It was jammed. Brown sticky muck was all around the door's edges, sealing it shut like glue.

I turned around and faced the little demon. I balled up my fist. I'd had enough. Screw child protective laws, I was getting ready to kick his tiny dwarf ass. But then he crawled from under the bed and levitated up to my eye level. And I knew that if he could float up in midair like that, then he could kick my ass, too. I lost it. I started crying.

"Why you messin' with me, man? I didn't do nothing to you."

"Why you messin' with my mama?" he said with attitude.

"You're just a kid. You're too young to understand."

"Too young, my ass!" He floated around me, looking me up and down. "You horny dudes are all alike."

"Huh?"

"You come in here, you do the nasty with my mama, and then leave. Just like my daddy did."

"I'm not your daddy."

"You just like him!"

"I didn't get your mama pregnant, then leave."

"But you got what you want from my mama! Now you wanna leave. Can't stick around, not even to play checkers. You selfish son of a bitch!"

"Hey, wait a minute now."

"No, you wait." Nehemiah balled up his fist. I flinched. "And what about my mama?"

"What about her?"

"When y'all leave, you make my mama feel bad and look bad."

"Your mama don't look bad."

"That's what you think."

Nehemiah moved over and knocked on the closet door. It opened. Out came a woman in an old dirty bathrobe. She had curlers in her hair, wore raggedy slippers, and was overweight. She was hunched over and hiding her face.

"Shamir? Is that you?" I asked.

Shamir self-consciously pulled at her floppy robe and touched her uncombed hair, embarrassed. She nodded. "This is how I really look, Chris."

"*Da-yum*, what happened to you, woman?"

Nehemiah threw his head back and yelled at me, blowing out a hurricane of peanut butter–smelling wind. "You dickheads did this to my mama!"

Nehemiah jumped in front of her and started spinning around like crazy, just like the Tasmanian Devil. I wanted to run but my feet failed me. He made a dusty cloud around Shamir. It circled her and I couldn't see her. When the dust lifted and the air cleared, Shamir looked hot again—young, thin, hard body, hair done, dressed in a sexy, sheer negligee.

Shamir smiled at Nehemiah, who finally stopped spinning. "See? I told you he was *special*."

I stood there wanting to run and wanting to piss on myself all at the same time. This wasn't real. It couldn't be. This little boy with the big saucer eyes really was special, and I thought about asking him who he was, where he came from, and how he did that. But then I decided, *Screw it!* I picked up a brass lamp and threw it like a fastball directly at Nehemiah's big head.

That little demon child reached out his hand and

caught the lamp with his tiny little fingers in midair. Quick as a lizard, he hurled the lamp straight back at me. It cracked me upside my head and knocked my ass out cold.

When I woke up, I was lying spread-eagle on the bed, my face up and my arms and legs handcuffed to the bedposts.

Nehemiah was standing on top of my chest, his dirty little white sneakers grinding into my rib cage. My vision was blurry and I struggled to breathe. For a little squirt, he was heavy.

He looked down at me. He held up his sticky little brown hands. Globs of peanut butter dripped from them. "Tell this turkey about the peanut butter, Mama."

Shamir came close to the bed, her sexy negligee open, teasing me. "Nehemiah's peanut butter is no ordinary peanut butter. It's homemade."

"Yep. I use special nuts." An evil little smirk perched on his small mouth.

I got nervous—*more* nervous. "What's that supposed to mean?"

Nehemiah made a quick grabbing motion at my zipper. I flinched. He didn't touch me but jerked his hand like he was pulling something off. At that same moment, a thousand screams and pain-filled moans burst through the room like thunder. I jerked my head around to see, but couldn't see nothing.

"What the freak is that noise?"

Shamir looked apologetic. "Those are the screams from the other guys I dated, who left."

"They didn't want to be my daddy, either," Nehemiah said. "So I made sure they wouldn't be *nobody's* daddy."

Nehemiah clasped something inside his small fingers. He opened his hands. I looked. Two round bloody nuts were inside. He tossed them like marbles to Shamir. She caught them and put them in this big jar filled with dozens of them, and closed the lid. The label said: NEH'S PNUTS.

"I like making pea-*nut* butter." Nehemiah laughed like the bogeyman.

I panicked. Fear seized my chest. Nehemiah ground his dirty white sneakers into my skin and rode my pumping chest like a roller coaster.

He smiled, laughing at my ass, and lowered his big shiny black eyes down to my face, staring at me so close our noses touched. I felt his little fingers circle around my nuts. He squeezed a bit, his little fist tightening around my package.

"I'm gonna ask you one more time. You wanna be my daddy?"

Shamir and I were married two days later. Not the young, hot Shamir, but the trapped-in-the-closet, overweight, curlers-in-the-hair Shamir. I quit my job as a music promoter and opened a drive-through-only Burger King down the street. We had a *real* talking plastic king—not a fake one with a microphone hooked up in the back.

Shamir had eight or twelve more babies for me. I'm not sure exactly how many because I stopped counting at six. They were all boys. Though they were mine, they all looked exactly like Nehemiah—big head, lopsided Afros, and eyes as big as bowling balls. Every day we sat inside the Burger King and played checkers. We ate cookies and milk, too.

Every night, they all gathered around me, looked up

at me with those big black saucer eyes, and asked the same question, "Are you our daddy?"

And just like Nehemiah, they were all *special*. That's why I always answered them the same way, "Hell yes. I'm your daddy!"

To Get Bread and Butter

Randy Walker

Bananas. Beef. Beer. Bread. Butter. I only shop for B's on the first Tuesday of the month.

Olson's Supermarket is located exactly 0.8 miles down Main Street from my two-bedroom town house, and it is nearly eleven o'clock at night on Tuesday, February 7. I will make it to Olson's at eleven o'clock exactly, park on the side of the building in a space usually unoccupied, and walk eight yards to the entrance of the store, where I will take the second shopping cart, gently sliding the first cart to the side. I will then proceed to the produce section located on the far right side of the store, working my way across each aisle to the next item on the list. It just so happens that each of my items is alphabetized and corresponds with the various aisles that progress toward the left side of the store. I buy bananas first and butter last, and it just so happens that butter and bread are on opposite sides of the same aisle. This system has worked for me for the last seven years, and I find it very comforting.

Rising from the sofa, I put on my lucky red Adidas

warm-up jacket and lace up my matching red tennis shoes. I am now ready to go.

I step outside the back of my town house and begin walking toward my black Jeep Cherokee when I hear a voice call out in my direction.

"Raphael, hold on for a moment."

As I turn my head, I see my neighbor, Gus, walking slowly in my direction. I continue walking toward my Jeep, slowing just a little so that he might see that I have somewhere to be.

"Raphael," he says again, a bit winded from his attempt to move his slothful mass more quickly toward me.

As I open the door to my vehicle, I respond, "Yes, Gus. How are you doing?"

"Oh, I'm fine. Just wanted to let you know that I read your last book, the one about that treasure hunter."

"Thanks. I'm glad that you bought one of my books." I lift my leg to enter the vehicle.

"Well, actually, I didn't buy it. I'm reading my girl-friend's copy." He reaches in his back pocket and pulls out a dog-eared, mass-market paperback. It appears to be held together by a large, bone-colored rubber band, and I scarcely recognize it as a book at all. As I look at it, my stomach turns. I can't believe that someone would handle my book so poorly. I mean, does this guy even have a clue of how much goes into writing a book for a person to just go and dog it out like that?

I nod at Gus, attempting to excuse myself. I look down at my watch and see that it is 10:55 p.m. I have exactly five minutes to get to the grocery store. As I reach to close the door, Gus runs around to the side of my vehicle and says, "So, maybe you could sign this book for her—or me, since I'm your neighbor."

I reach in my pocket to find one of the three ball-point black pens I keep there. He hands me the mass of pages, and I remove the rubber band. "What's your girlfriend's name, Gus?"

"Shelia. But make sure you put my name down there too, and say something about us being neighbors. That would be really cool."

I hurriedly scribble "to Shelia and Gus, the best neighbors" and hand it back to him.

"Gee, thanks," Gus says. "So, how's the new book coming?"

I glance down at my watch again. I have a little over three minutes to make it to the store. "Gus, you'll have to excuse me. I have to go now."

"Okay. We'll talk later," he says, but I barely hear him as I am already closing the door and starting the Jeep.

It's people like Gus who drive me completely crazy! I was once married to a woman for all of three months before we had to file for divorce. Truthfully, I'm surprised we lasted that long. (I guess that's what happens when you marry someone you meet on the Internet.) We cited irreconcilable differences, but the truth was that she couldn't deal with my need to maintain a certain type of order around me at all times, and I couldn't deal with her always threatening to mess up that order every time I looked up. She called me an obsessive-compulsive asshole. I called her a sloppy gold-digging bitch. To me, order promotes productivity, and with my occupation, I need a lot of order. Personally, I don't understand how anyone would want to go about his daily routine without some kind of structure.

Still bothered by Gus's slowing me down, I whip out of the parking lot with my foot pressed down on the gas, heading down Main Street. Ahead, I see the stop-light starting to change to yellow. I push down on the gas, and as the light turns red I zoom through, nearly clipping a guy walking out into the middle of the street wearing dark colors. Can you believe that? Walking out in the street with dark colors on at night? What in the world was *he* thinking?

I arrive at my usual parking spot at exactly eleven, my heart still racing from the panic of nearly arriving late. I take a moment to catch my breath, but I can't wait too long because I have to be in the checkout line by eleven-thirty, back home after that, and have every-thing completely put away by midnight. It has to be that way because I go to bed at midnight every night so that I can wake up at six o'clock in the morning to do my ten pages for whatever book I'm working on.

I lock my door and walk briskly toward the entrance of the store, and as I enter I reach for the second shop-ping cart. I'm still thinking about the fact that I almost didn't make it on time because of Gus and that guy out in the middle of the road. Oh well, no harm, no foul.

I recenter myself.

Bananas. Beef. Beer. Bread. Butter.

I push my cart over to aisle one, produce. Because I allow myself exactly thirty minutes to grocery-shop for these items, I can take my time and find the absolute best products on the shelves. Tonight as I stand by the bananas, I move the ones on the top out of the way quickly. Too many hands have probably touched those. I find some greenish yellow bananas that look to be very firm. They will ripen well over the next two or three days. Grabbing a plastic bag and tearing along the perforated edges, I slide the bundle of bananas inside, twisting the bag three complete revolutions to seal it. I place them in the cart and continue on toward the end of the aisle.

Beef is along the back wall, and while I could easily jump across the store to grab items, I tend to push my cart past each aisle, curious to see who else does their shopping this late at night. Often it is college students or people getting off work from factory jobs. But as I pass aisle two, I notice that it is empty. No one getting pasta, rice, or spaghetti sauce tonight, I imagine.

I continue pushing my cart, and as I pass aisle three I notice a couple of teenagers making out by the canned soup. At the end of the aisle, near the front of the store, is a dark-skinned, bearded old man facing in my general direction. He looks vaguely familiar, but I can't seem to place him. I divert my attention back to the next item on my list, beef.

Reaching the refrigerated meat area, I sort through various packages of meat, looking for the leanest and finest cuts. Again, I find what I am looking for in a matter of minutes, and I am off in search of the next item.

Next is beer. Aisle seven.

As I pass aisle five, I glance down it. I see the old man again, this time standing next to the coffee section, looking toward my end of the aisle. He looks at me and nods. I nod back. His frumpy, blue Members' Only-style jacket is zipped tightly over his bulging stomach, and his large ears look as if they could have been slapped onto the side of his dark, hairy face. His beard is bushy and runs into the thickness of his nappy gray hair, leaving only his nose and eyes visible. I push on to the next aisle.

Standing closer up the aisle, I see the man again, this time next to the potato chips. I stop for a moment, shaking my head. Only then does it occur to me that this guy might be following me. Is he a fan or a person with too much time on his hands? Maybe I'm still shaken up about nearly arriving late and I'm imagining this whole thing. The man, however, pulls down a bag of chips from the shelf and looks in my direction again, nodding. It is only at this point that I realize that he doesn't have a shopping cart or basket. I nod uneasily in his direction and continue pushing on.

I enter aisle seven for my Budweiser (if it were my M day, it would be Miller). There again, standing roughly ten feet down the aisle, is the old man reaching for a case of sodas. I grab a six-pack and pretend not to see him. To nod at him a third time would be extremely awkward. None of this makes sense to me. All I know is that this man is making me deeply uncomfortable, but I have to stick to my list because time is of the essence. Both the bread and the butter are two aisles over, so I push my cart back up the aisle to the back of the store and make a left.

Passing aisle eight, I see the old man again. This time he is much closer. I stop my cart dead in its tracks, and before I realize it my heart is now racing. The man looks up from the magazine he is holding and nods at me. This time he smiles, peeling back his thick, cracked lips to reveal dingy brown teeth.

I quickly back up my things to the previous aisle, and glance down it to find the same man there, but possibly farther away. I back up another three aisles and the man is still there, farther and farther toward the other end of the aisle. By the time I make it back to the produce section, the man is nowhere to be found.

I glance at my watch. It is 11:20 p.m. I have exactly ten minutes to get my bread and butter and make it to the checkout line. Although the grocery store is open twenty-four hours a day, I find it much easier to stay on my schedule. Already I am in danger of being thrown off, but I sense that once I get to the last aisle, I can make up for lost time and still get to the checkout before eleven-thirty.

For a brief moment, I ponder taking the items that I have already picked up to the checkout, but I can't do that. I either get everything, or I get nothing. And getting nothing is not an option because I shop for my C's tomorrow at three o'clock p.m. It would destroy my entire schedule for the month if I left here tonight empty-handed.

I look across the store and realize that I am the only one on the rear aisle. I only have two items left to pick up, and as I look at my watch I realize that I don't have the time to put off completing my task. If the man is going to be there, then, damn it, let him be, because I need to get in the checkout line by 11:30 p.m. It is already bad enough that I won't have the time to go through the bread like I want to, but getting to the checkout at the right time is really taking priority.

I gear back and start pushing my cart, slowly at first, and then faster, until I'm almost running with it across the store, straining to avoid glancing down the aisles. I reach the end of the store and turn my cart left onto the last aisle.

It's empty!

I quickly grab the second loaf of whole wheat bread

from the second shelf from the top, pushing the first one aside, before turning around to get the butter. When I turn around, I find myself staring face-to-face with the old man. His breath spills out from behind his wicked smile like garbage baked on a rock during the hottest day of summer. His skin is so dry that cracks run along his face into the depths of his matted beard. His eyes are a cloudy gray with a thick puss oozing out of the corners, and they are locked on me like some type of war missiles.

I quickly jump back, straining to pull the cart between us to serve as a barrier, but the man blocks me and pushes me into the bread. I fall back, shocked. As I try to catch myself, my hand hits a loaf of bread and loses grip, causing me to fall onto the floor. The man stands over me, and I find that I am too afraid to move. His bulk towers over me like a huge dark mountain, and before I realize it he is reaching into my shopping cart, removing things. When he takes my choice steak and slings it down the aisle onto the floor so hard that it snaps loose of its plastic and lands facedown on the floor, my chest tightens.

Next, he hurls the bananas over the aisle, onto the floor of the next aisle. I hear the thud of them hitting the tile. Now I can feel my breaths shortening.

All I can think is that I don't have enough time to replace the items before I run out of time.

The man takes my six-pack of beer out of the cart and tosses the cans on their sides, denting them. One can pops open and sprays the cookies next to the bread.

My cart is nearly empty, and as I try to stand up I find that I can't catch my breath at all. I reach behind myself to find a shelf for support, but the old man takes my wheat bread and begins pelting me with it. The bag of bread slaps across my face like a backhand. Again I fall back. As I try to stand, the man slaps me back down with a gnarled, bony hand that feels like a brick wrapped in crusted flesh. The pain bolts across my cheek, burning into the side of my face.

"Help!" I yell, not wanting to surrender to the madness of what is going on around me but having little choice in the matter. I can barely hear my own voice, but I don't have the air to yell out again. The old man looks down at me, and fear races over me when I realize that for the first time in seven years I won't make my schedule. My head swimming, I fall back, unconscious.

When I come to, I find a pimply-faced redheaded boy, who could be no more than twenty years old, kneeling down beside me. He's trying to assist me in sitting upright. The whole time I see his lips moving, but I can't make out what he's saying. The Olson's name tag on his shirt reads RUSTY. I look at him, straining my eyes against the fluorescent overhead lights of the aisle.

I watch his lips move, and I start to gradually make out what he is saying. "I'm sorry, mister," he repeats over and over.

My mind is muddled with thoughts of the old man and wondering what time it is. As I sit up, I frantically look around for the man. Rusty and I are the only ones on the aisle, though. I look around for my bread and the dented cans of beer, but they are no longer there.

"I'm so sorry," Rusty says again.

"Rusty? Rusty, look, what's going on here? A man just assaulted me with food from my cart."

Rusty stops for a moment and looks at me, his eyebrows raised in curiosity. He doesn't seem to understand what I'm talking about, so I repeat it.

"Rusty, an old man just assaulted me in this store. I need for you to notify the authorities right now!"

"Sir," Rusty says, "I don't know what you're talking about."

"What do you mean?" I rise to my feet and look for my cart. It is resting off to the side of the aisle with a small bag of tied-up bananas, a package of choice steak, a loaf of bread, and a six-pack of Budweiser.

"There's no one else who's been over here. I had just finished mopping the floor, and I forgot to put the sign down. I just started working here last week, and I can't take it if they fire me. I have a kid at home. Please, mister, if you're okay, let's just leave this between us."

I look at Rusty, and I can see in his eyes that he is genuinely scared. I touch my back and twist my waist to see if I'm all right. I don't feel any pain, but when I glance at my watch I see that it's now 11:40 p.m.

My heart is aching now. I reach for my cart. "You know what, Rusty? I just want to get my stuff and get out of here. No harm, no foul, right?"

"Y-yes, sir," he responds and stands back from me.

I grab the first package of butter I come upon and push my cart toward the checkout. My stomach is all out of sorts, and my head is starting to hurt like hell. There is no line on the only open checkout lane, and when the cashier recognizes me, she tries to weigh my bananas and ring me up as quickly as possible. It's too little, too late, though, and I'm already frustrated and upset, so I just reach in my pocket and pay her from the twenty I had folded three times and placed squarely across the bottom of my front right pocket.

My head feels like fireworks are going off inside my brain, and now I only want to go home and sleep off this night. I grab the paper bag, tucking it in my arms like a toddler, and I walk out of the store into the cool night. Each step I take is heavy and my vehicle seems so far away. The cars drifting randomly through the night don't even register to me.

I place the bag on the backseat of my Jeep, plopping myself down in the driver's seat. I feel as if all of the wind has been snuffed out of my sails. I can't explain why I feel so dejected. I just do. I feel dirty and worthless. I only want to get home now and be inside the safe confines of my own home. Everything just feels totally out of sync.

I crank up the vehicle and pull out of the parking lot. My eyes are heavy, and I find myself almost completely consumed in disappointment, so much so that it takes me a moment to recognize the stench rising from my backseat. Then it hits me! I know the smell, and I remember from where I know the old man!

I see myself, not yet ten years old, standing with my father in front of a fast-food restaurant. A ragged, homeless man approaches us, and the scent of garbage and cheap liquor is screaming from his pores. He asks my father for change, and my father hands him a few folded dollars. I remember asking my father, "Why did you give that nasty old man your money?" My father responded, "Sometimes people need a little help from time to time." As we walked away, I told my father that I would never allow myself to get to that point, where I was smelling rotten and walking up to strangers. My father then looked me dead in my eyes and told me, "Son, sometimes we can't always control our circumstances."

My father's words still ringing in my ears, I look in the rearview mirror and am now horrified to see the old man, sitting hunched over, quietly tossing my groceries out of the window into the dark street.

Dream Girl

Dameon Edwards

"Typical," Damon Mitchell muttered to himself, tossing the crinkled issue of last month's *Essence* back onto his cluttered desk.

Left in the office about a week ago by either one of his residents or resident assistants—he hadn't really cared to discover whom—Damon finally yielded to the glaring headline beside the pretty mahogany face beaming from the glossy cover: WHERE ARE THE GOOD BLACK MEN? it had brazenly asked.

Pushing his paperwork to the side, Damon had chanced the waters, peeking at the article. After several paragraphs, he had read enough to confirm his initial suspicions. It was yet another griping missive featuring so-called professional, got-it-together women bemoaning the dearth of "worthy" black men. Brothers who had jobs, were "spiritual," respected them, and weren't afraid of commitment, yadda, yadda, yadda . . .

Damon, himself a young black man with a college degree, a job, and a car, who hadn't been on a date for almost a year, knew such "heartfelt" testimonials were full of shit.

His last tepid romance had evaporated as quickly as morning dew. Cheryl, a paralegal he had met by chance at a bakery he used to frequent downtown, had first started in on him by telling him that he was moving too fast, pushing too hard.

At that time, Damon had been listening to the crap *Essence* and its ilk were selling, trying to be attentive, attempting to show her that he was the one man who was different, that he wasn't afraid of settling down.

But he had forced himself to accede to her wishes and had backed off. Restricting the previously daily phone calls, e-mails, and text messages first to every other day, and then to two-, three-, four-, and five-day stretches.

His contacts became less frequent, but no surprise in hindsight, so did hers. Until eventually she didn't call at all. The wound left by her abrupt dismissal still hadn't healed. Damon knew he could be pushy at times, even needy on occasion, but he couldn't have been all that bad.

He had always paid for their dates, always picked her up in his car. He had laughed at her jokes even when they weren't all that funny, tolerated her need to forage in every discount shop and boutique she discovered, and really tried to listen and empathize with her when she raged about her bosses at work. But it had all been to no avail.

At first, unwilling to accept the finality of their breakup, he had left message after message, via phone and computer, seeking answers from her. She had never responded.

Her coldness had hurt him, pissed him off even. He

had contemplated, on more than a few occasions, driving over to her apartment to demand an explanation, or at least to see if another man had taken his place.

But he had never done so. Not so much because he was afraid of what he might do, or whom he might find, at Cheryl's apartment. He was disgusted by the thought of what he *would* do. Which was nothing but cry and beg Cheryl for another chance, or even worse: ask her to be his friend.

The one thing he hated almost more than anything, being the neutered *friend*. Always reliable, infinitely understanding, and forever listening as women wringed out their frustrations about how bad their boyfriends were treating them, but never once letting the thought enter their minds that the friend they were leaning on might be the better choice for them. Instead they were more content to often use said shoulder like a tissue, discarding him as soon as he was no longer needed.

Damon had been down that road far more times than he could count. The very thought of contemplating such self-castration dissipated the nagging curiosity he had over the breakup. He had forced himself to let it go, or at least to continuously tell himself that he had moved on, which was good enough.

He just accepted the maxim that he would never understand women. He was almost thirty now and he felt as confused around them as he had since puberty.

But he had at least discovered one thing about females along his journey: For the most part, they were confused themselves, if not outright deceivers, then self-deluded about what they really wanted in a man.

In almost every magazine, book, TV talk show, or movie, black women complained about black men, declaring them dogs, cheaters, abusers, freeloaders, ad infinitum. But it was these same louts, the thugs, the bad boys, that these women were constantly spreading their legs for. It didn't make any sense. It wasn't logical. But it was real. Women were just creatures of drama, unable to leave a pot unstirred, he had bleakly realized.

Not at all like the women at the club. . . .

Damon smiled at the familiar hardening in his pants that occurred whenever the thought of Tamales slid into his mind. An hour out of town, Tamales was the best shake joint Damon had ever been to. Most of the women were fine, the drinks were cheap, and the music decent, though a little hard-core for his taste. Best of all, the dancers knew how to treat a brother. Like a real man, he thought: attentive, accommodating, willing to listen to *his* needs, concerns, and desires for a change.

So what if it was all an act that ended when the cash ran out? So-called real relationships were often fueled by the green, too. His own relationship train wrecks, along with the stories he had heard from his relatives and friends, attested to that.

Damon tapped the keyboard on his computer, deactivating the screen saver. Not a fan of watches, he checked the time in the right-side bottom of the screen: 5:45 p.m.

Only fifteen more minutes. *Time's stretching out forever today*, he sighed. But of course, Fridays were always like that. Fridays that fell on the first of the month, *payday*, were the worst.

Leaning back in his chair, he was content to let the dwindling minutes run out like sand grains in an hourglass. He closed his eyes, holding back a yawn as he imagined sitting in front of Tamales' main stage, with his favorite dancer, Hypnotize, opening her legs for him, pulling a hot-pink G-string to the side to show him a special treat. . . . Unbidden, his hand made its way to his crotch, massaging his expanding hardness.

"Mr. Mitchell," an amused voice softly trilled.

Damon almost fell out of his seat. Scrambling to recover, he began shifting books and papers around on his desk. Damn, he had forgotten to close his office door. Fridays were usually slow, with most of his residents either at the cafeteria or heading home at this time of day. He hadn't expected anyone to walk by his office, or stop by to see him. But of course, he hadn't expected to be fantasizing about the pussy he would hopefully be seeing shortly, either. *If Hypnotize accepted my apology, that is*, the sour thought cooled his anticipation.

"Girl, don't ever creep up on a man when he's sleeping," he huffed jokingly, trying to play off both his arousal and his trepidation.

Aria, one of the shapely cheerleaders residing on the second floor of Hayes Hall, merely smiled at him, her hazel eyes bright. "My light went out."

Not sure if she was giving him a pass or not, but grateful if she was, Damon slipped into his professional, dorm director mode. "Which light? Overhead? Closet? Desk?" She pointed at the ceiling.

"Overhead, huh?" he asked.

Aria nodded.

Normally, he would advise residents to write a service request and leave it in the tray on the counter outside his office for Housekeeping to attend to on Monday. *But what the hell?* Damon thought. By the time he finished installing her bulbs it would be past time to get off. Plus, he didn't mind spending a few minutes gazing at Aria's luscious form before the real fun began.

"I'll have to go to the housekeeper's closet to get you two new bulbs." He got the statement out before a yawn finally escaped from his lips. He shook his head, hoping he wasn't getting sleepy. He had been hitting the sack pretty early lately. He hadn't really known why, chalking it up to advancing age. It wasn't a real concern because he didn't have much to stay up for anyway. But this Friday night, payday, was a different animal. He was going to Tamales, if not by willpower, then girded by Red Bull. Jangling the large ring of keys in his pocket, he gestured gallantly with his free hand. "After you, Ms. Jenkins."

Damon didn't even hide his smile as Aria bounced out of his office, her apple ass straining against tight purple shorts. He was going to have a good time tonight whether Hypnotize could be mollified or not.

The third beer eased Damon's mind but not his disappointment. Slouching farther down in the wooden chair at the back of the room, he sighed at both the empty stage and its ancillary, the blinking string of Christmas lights adorning each only highlighting their barrenness. Beyond the main stage's single pole, he saw his reflection in the large mirrors covering the wall behind it.

Damon shifted his eyes away, not wanting to see himself. Afraid of what he would see glaring back at him: a chunky loser clutching a sweating bottle of beer, eagerly awaiting the arrival of women who would be in his company only if he paid them to be.

Damon instead turned his attention to the nearly deserted club. Two guys, with the worn-down, disinterested mien of locals, played pool at one of the three pool tables beside the bathroom and dancers' changing room.

At the bar, the club's burly owner, bartender, and bouncer, a walking slab named Vern, polished a beer mug absently, a similarly bored look mixed into his perpetual scowl.

The only dancer who even appeared to be in the vicinity of Tamales squatted on a stool by the bar, her porcine face stuck in the video poker machine on the bar top.

Damon had never seen how Peaches got any business. Her very noticeable gut hung down from her frame as if gravity was drawing it to the floor. He imagined that he could see her stretch marks and varicose veins even from where he was sitting. But of course, he had been here enough times to see her ply her raunchy wares for old men who didn't want to go home just yet to their wives, and young boys who couldn't distinguish between easy and stank.

Damon glanced at his watch. He hated wearing them, the bands always cutting into his wrist, but he really didn't like losing track of time, or too much of his money, in a place like this. He liked to maintain a modicum of common sense, of self-control, a feeling that he could leave any time he wanted to.

He had made the watch a part of his pre-Tamales ritual, which also included a shower, a fresh set of clothes, and even a few dabs of cologne.

It was approaching ten o'clock. He belched his displeasure. This had to be the slowest Friday night in the history of Tamales. Usually the girls would start filing in at nine on Fridays because of the good crowd and flowing money. Tamales usually fielded ten to fifteen honeys on Friday.

Of course, his girl, Hypnotize, would usually arrive about thirty minutes after the others, making a grand entrance, usually in something low cut, pumps accentuating the curves of her stallion legs. The night she had first come to his attention Hypnotize had been really bold, sashaying straight into Tamales wearing nothing but pasties and a thong.

She had playfully bumped her hip against his shoulder before ascending the steps and dispatching the pretender to her throne. The poseur, a lithe beige newbie calling herself Star, had cut her eyes at Hypnotize, rolling her neck to get Vern's attention. Damon had followed the rookie's eyes. Ensconced, as usual, behind the bar, the big man had merely shrugged.

Star had snatched up her bra and a few, but not all, of the dollars the patrons had thrown on the stage for her, and stomped off. The DJ had continued playing records, unperturbed by the spat. And Hypnotize had not disappointed.

Damon had never seen the rookie again. Surprisingly, he had felt a little sorry for the girl. Hypnotize had jacked her spot, and Vern should've intervened. A supervisor himself, he knew how unwise it was to play favorites or choose sides among subordinates, but then again, he really couldn't blame Big Vern.

Hypnotize was a star, in fact, the real star of Tamales. Five seven, butter pecan skin, and a voluptuous figure with tits and ass for days on end, she was the belle of the ball. Intricately woven, reddish-tinged microbraids wreathed her heart-shaped face, going all the way down to the small of her back. Despite her stunning physical dimensions, Damon had found her eyes, of all things, to be her best feature. Large, brown, warm, and soft, they reminded him of the thick chocolate chips in the cookies his mother would make when she felt in the mood for baking.

They weren't the hard, predatory orbs belying the practiced smiles on many of the other dancers, constantly scouring customers for the biggest paycheck. And blessedly, they weren't the dulled glaze of the girls willing to do anything for a hit.

No, Hypnotize was different. Actually demure, after a fashion. Nothing at all like her onstage persona, he would come to find out. Damon had almost spilled his beer when she had asked him to buy her a drink about a month after the Star incident.

He had promptly done so, and she sat down across from him, ample breasts spilling out of her powder-blue top. Hypnotize had sipped the Long Island iced tea quietly, her tongue flicking delicately over the straw every few seconds like a serpent seeking a vibration or scent.

Damon had known he was ready to be her prey from that moment on. But she hadn't asked him for a table, lap, or private dance like so many other girls did almost immediately when they approached him. She had asked him something much more shocking. Hypnotize had asked him his name.

"Da-Damon," he remembered stuttering, not sure if he should've supplied a fake name instead. He hadn't wanted anyone to even know he had set foot in Tamales, much less know he was a damn-near fixture. Damon had never liked people being in his business. Her eyes had sparkled at him, and she had rewarded his awkwardness with a flawless smile.

"So . . . what do you do, Damon?"

"Why do you want to know?" His response sounded too harsh and tinged with suspicion even to him. But he wasn't in the mood to be conned. He was a good customer and a great tipper. He had even been gentlemanly with all the girls who had performed for him in the VIP, always asking before he squeezed their nipples or smacked their asses.

A frown marred her delicate face. She picked up her drink. "I didn't mean to disturb you. Thanks for the drink." She then made to get up.

Damon gestured a bit dramatically for her to stay. Could she have really just wanted to know his name and what he did for a living? He hadn't met many women, and no exotic dancers, who had seemed all that interested in him unless something was in it for them. Could Hypnotize, the diva of club Tamales, actually be different? The thought fluttered on hopeful, beer-soaked wings through his mind, before he reluctantly dismissed it.

"I'm sorry," he said. "Please, don't go." He had never been good reading or using the signs, gestures, and phrases of seduction. He had always preferred things more straightforward. "Didn't mean to come off so gruff. I . . . I work at Dunlap College in West Point. I'm a dorm director."

"Really?" She leaned in closer. He would never forget the perfumed scent of her skin that night.

"Yeah." Damon smiled sheepishly, unable to resist being pulled into her orbit.

"So, what's it like?" She reached across the table, touching his arm with manicured nails. Her touch was as warm as her eyes. "Do you deal with guys or girls? Upperclassmen? Freshmen?"

"I run a coed building . . . upperclassmen."

"That must not be too bad. You must be glad you don't have to deal with any badass freshmen."

Damon found himself nodding at her declaration. He had been assigned to a freshmen hall his first year on the job. It had been one of the most wretched experiences of his career.

Seeming to peer into his mind, she nodded with a wistful twinkle in her eyes. "I know I raised enough hell when I was a freshman."

"Do you go to school around here?" He squeaked over the lump in his throat, his heart racing at the thought that Hypnotize was a Dunlap student. He had heard about several girls from the college who danced locally in West Point. That had been another reason he had decided to seek his pleasures far away from familiar eyes.

"No . . . well, not yet, at least. I had gone to school at Clark for a year before coming back home."

"Why did you move back?" he asked, genuinely curious.

Her face closed up at the question before she stared down at her drink.

"Didn't mean to pry," he said quickly.

"No, it's okay." She paused, looking at him again, really looking at him as if she were judging him. He fought his natural instinct to turn away from such scrutiny. To this day, he was glad that he had.

"I . . . dropped out after I got pregnant."

He couldn't help but gaze over her body, even looking under the table, the brazen, alcohol-fed reaction eliciting a self-conscious chuckle from her. "Damn, you came through all right." Even in the murky lighting of the club, her skin shone luminous and unmarked by the strains of childbirth.

"Thank you." Her smile was even more radiant.

"May I ask you a question?" He then leaned in closer to her.

"Yes, Damon?"

"Why . . ." His liquored suaveness had forsaken him, leaving him to stumble over his words. "Why are you talking to me?"

She laughed. His face had grown hot as the dam of past rejections had burst open. Sensing his distress, Hypnotize quickly said, her expression sympathetic, "I've seen you come in here a couple of times. And you seemed nice. Smart. You don't bullshit the girls or act like an asshole like some of the other customers do."

"Really?"

"Really."

"You've never danced for me, so how would you know how I act?"

"We girls talk," Hypnotize said conspiratorially, her gaze coasting over to the changing room. "In there."

"Really?"

"Really." A fit of giggles shattered her serious expression.

"Since you know my name . . . it's only right that I know yours." Damon rarely asked dancers for their real names. It hadn't really been all that important, and plus, too much reality shattered the illusion that he had paid to see.

"Marie. My name's Marie."

He stiffly shook her hand. "What about your baby? Boy or girl?"

"A boy. His name's Joshua." She made to reach for

the obligatory photos, before smacking her blemish-free forehead in mock consternation. "Sometimes I forget when I'm half naked."

"I wish we could all be so fortunate." He had been proud of his quip. From that moment on, Hypnotize had become his favorite dancer. Snicka, Blaze, and Honey Bunz had all been forgotten.

Damon glanced at his watch again: 10:45. Okay, it didn't appear that Marie was going to show, he realized. *Probably because she knew I was going to be here*, he surmised. He was a creature of habit, after all, and Marie knew him in a lot of ways better than his own family did.

The last time he had gone to Tamales, things had ended a little shaky between them, but he had hoped that she wasn't still mad at him. He had given her a whole month to hopefully let things settle down between them. After her set, he asked her to go to the VIP. After the second private dance, and in between records, she sat on his lap. Automatically, his arms coiled around her slender stomach. She leaned back into his embrace, resting her head on his shoulder. It was at that serene moment of blissful tranquility that his nature got the better of him.

I'd had too much to drink that night, said something I shouldn't, he tried to convince himself for the umpteenth time. He was surely not the first guy, and definitely not the first patron, to ask her for sex. Sitting up, Marie had just looked at him, with a lopsided smile that slowly dissipated before the light dimmed in her eyes.

"You're serious?" Her tone was incredulous.

"Well . . ." He shrugged. "I . . . mean . . . we're friends and all."

"So? What's that got to do with anything?"

"Nothing . . . I mean. It's just been a long time . . . since Cheryl. You know."

"And what's that got to do with me?"

"I . . . I've got money. I'll take care of you."

"What? I can't believe you just came at me like that."

"Like what?" Treacherous anger shredded his buzz. "I know what kind of shit goes on in places like this. I'll take care of you."

"Like hell." She grabbed his arms. He wouldn't let her go.

"Let's talk about this," he pleaded. "I didn't mean anything by it."

"I'm not a ho, Damon," she bleated, tears brimming in her eyes. She tried to break his grip.

Then what are you? He remembered the vicious thought sluicing through his mind. But gratefully, a modicum of sense had by then returned. "I'm sorry, Marie. I just . . ." The words had faded away with his resolve. He had let her go, and Marie had jetted out of the VIP.

Despite their friendship, Marie established boundaries early on. She gave him her e-mail address, and even accepted a gift or two, but not her cell number and no dates. As long as he'd had Cheryl, sex with Marie had been a fantasy often used to get him off after one of his Tamales excursions.

But after Cheryl, he had allowed the crushing loneliness and the burning horniness to get the best of him. After making an ass of himself at the club, he had sent several e-mails to Marie, trying to explain what he did and why he did it. He was a good guy, just out for a little fun. And though he might run out every now and then, he didn't mean anything by it. He was just a man, after all.

She hadn't replied to any of his electronic entreaties. He had hoped to see her tonight, and see if she was willing to let bygones be bygones. But if she wasn't, if she thought he was perverted or something, not only was their friendship over, but she would surely ruin his reputation for courtly behavior with the rest of the girls. If he couldn't smooth things out, he would have to find a new club.

Not only did she seem to be avoiding him, but she must've convinced the other dancers to join in a coven against him. Downing the remainder of his beer, he placed it beside the others before making his way to the exit.

Detouring at the bathroom, Damon dispensed most of the beer in the bathroom's urinal, afraid to even go into the bathroom stall, the stench from it permeating the walls. He zipped up and ran some cold water on his hands, a veteran enough to know that there was no soap in the soap dispenser hanging from the wall above the sink. He took a quick glance in the mirror, checking to see how red his eyes were.

Pleased with the results, he squared his shoulders, opened the bathroom door, fortifying himself to leave Tamales forever . . .

And then he saw *her.*

Standing calmly on the stage, decked in a sable sarong with matching bra, her svelte body radiated passion and poise.

"Fellas, Tamales is proud to bring to the stage, all

the way from the Islands . . ." The DJ's voice took on a faux Caribbean patois. ". . . Noir."

Damon absently closed the bathroom door without taking his eyes off her. *Noir*. The word rolled around in his mind, its shadowy and sensual connotations thrilling him.

Ghosting to the stage, feeling disconnected from his legs, or the rest of his body for that matter, Damon blinked in surprise when he actually found himself eyeing Noir's pierced navel.

He took a slow, loving appraisal of her as his gaze made its way to her face. Rich skin a shade beyond sepia, purple, or coal, as Stygian as the night itself, the woman's body seemed to have been carved by a sculptor more than formed in the womb of a living being. Lighter-skinned women, especially redbones like Cheryl or Marie, had always been Damon's preference, but none of them compared to obsidian Noir.

Continuing his inspection, he felt a primal energy coiled within the woman's taut muscles. Unlike supple, voluptuous Hypnotize, Noir was angular. Hard.

Both haughtiness and fierceness warred behind her dark eyes as she looked down at him, though her aristocratic features were impassive. Her regal face was crowned with a short, kinky natural. She reminded him of one of the ancient Egyptian or Abyssinian queens in the Art History textbook a resident had given him after she had been unable to sell it at the "Book Buy Back" last semester.

Strange that he was thinking of crazy shit like that now of all times, he thought, while the most enigmatic and fascinating woman he had ever seen stood before him. Even the DJ respected the sanctity of the moment, of Damon's discovery, because he had refrained from his cacophonic ministrations for a brief respite. An eye in the hurricane, Damon realized as soon as the music began and Noir quickly dispatched both bra and sarong, her onyx body twisting into a carnal dervish. It was the performance of a lifetime, for the both of them.

After the last dance hall number had ended for her unusual solitary set, Damon was waiting by the steps as Noir descended the stage, bra hanging from her neck as she wrapped the sarong around her dangerous hips. In heels, she met his gaze at eye level. A fine coating of perspiration made her dusky skin shine as if polished.

"That was awesome," Damon struggled to say, reaching into his pocket to hand her a ten-dollar bill. He had already left a great portion of his paycheck, in ones and fives, on the stage. Noir hadn't even acknowledged his generosity, and he was shocked that she didn't seem all that concerned about the green littering the stage even now.

Every dancer, Marie included, was zealous about getting each dollar she felt owed them. But it appeared that Noir was different. But if she wasn't in it for the money, then why was she here?

"How . . . how did you learn to dance like that?" Damon asked, trying to fill up the vacuum. Noir had been content to stand there, merely gazing at him, her expression giving away nothing as she fastened her bra. *Well, say something*, Damon demanded in his mind.

Changing tactics, determined to get some kind of response from this woman, unable to be ignored, he asked, "The tattoo, on your back, I was trying to make it out while you were dancing, but you were moving so, so . . ." Images of her sinuous form seducing the lucky dance pole flittered through his mind, momentarily robbing him of speech.

She smiled all of a sudden, quickly turning her back to him. Still, he was able to make out only a letter or two of the heavily Gothic script running along her upper back. Its dark ink blended almost too well into her skin.

"Succubus," she said, her words clipped, precise, her accent perhaps West Indian. "It comes from ancient legend. Succubae were female demons that seduced men while they slept."

He shook his head. Damon hadn't expected too many sisters, especially those that shed their clothes for a living, to know anything about medieval mythology. "I know what a succubus is."

"You think so?" Though her lips were pinched, her tone was now playful. "I don't think you do."

"Well, yeah, I read about it . . ." he began defensively, for some reason feeling a need to explain himself.

"Do you want a private dance?" she asked, cutting him off.

"Well . . . . uh, sure." *Don't you mean hell yes*? his inner voice chided. *Hop on that shit!*

She wrapped a hand in his. Her grip was cold and leathery, scaly almost. "Come with me. Something tells me you're no stranger to this place." She led him toward the VIP lounge.

"No, well, yes. I've been here a few times." Noir looked back at him, her gaze disapproving.

"Okay." He shrugged. "More than a few." She was a fantastic dancer and a lie detector all rolled into one.

Moving beyond the beaded veil entrance to the VIP,

the best-furnished room in Tamales, Noir led Damon
to the long black leather couch placed against the back
wall. First taking care of securing access to the room
by greasing Vern with the remainder of his cash, he
hoped this dance was worth it. He had known what to
expect with Hypnotize. It had been one of the things he
liked most about her. But Noir was a totally unknown
quantity.

For a few terrible seconds, he wondered if Marie
would find out. He had been so focused on the stage
that he wouldn't have noticed if an elephant had shambled in behind him. What if she had seen him, giving
all his money away to this new girl, treating Noir like
he had once done her? Would she be mad? Jealous? Or
would she feel anything at all?

Staring up as Noir leaned over him, her eyes glinting in the variegated light of the disco ball twirling
from the ceiling, he realized that he really didn't care
what Marie thought. If she wanted it to be business,
then he would keep it at that level.

And he was going to have his fun, whether she
showed up or not. When the music started, Noir tossed
her sarong to the floor before unhooking her satiny bra,
an ebon nipple grazing his lips. "Take it," she whispered. He complied, sucking the hard, salty aureole
into his mouth. Noir pounced on him, grinding her
pelvis slowly against his groin.

He moaned, breaking contact as he seized her firm
ass in both hands. She roughly grabbed his head.
"Continue," she rasped.

Following her directive, he was proud when her
moans quickly outpaced his own. Lips locked on her
nipple, his hands roved her slick back, even chancing a
few ventures beneath her black thong panties. He

paused; afraid she would stop him, by slapping his hand away, cursing him out, or even worse, calling for Vern. But she didn't.

Her tacit permission opened something deep within him. He began nibbling on her breast, as one of his fingers sought her asshole. He delicately spread her labia with his other hand. When he poked a thumb inside her, the depth of her heat and wetness stunned him. Damon hadn't thought he could ever get a woman so excited.

His thumb made circles around her clitoris, her body moving in sync with the questing digit. She groaned so loud that Damon thought Vern might hear them. He knew the big man didn't give a damn about what happened in the VIP so long as everybody kept things quiet.

But he wasn't about to tell her to be quiet. Her gasping was turning him on.

"Do you want more?" she managed between breaths as the song faded.

Gazing at the panting girl, with flagging disappointment, he said, "Honey, I would really like to, but I don't have any more money."

The look she gave him was sad, pitiful. But strangely, not detached or condescending, a reaction that similar admissions had engendered in other dancers.

"I don't care about that."

What? "What?"

She cupped his face in her hands; her touch was still reptilian, but no longer cold, as if the heat he had created between her thighs had suffused her whole body. "I don't care about money," she repeated.

"What's going on here?" He looked around, scared

that cops were going to storm in at any second, or maybe Vern or another dancer. *Was this some kind of joke?* Perhaps Marie had put her up to this, to teach him some kind of lesson. She might be waiting just beyond the beads at this moment, ready to spring in and prove him to be the lout she tagged him as.

"I *want* you. I *need* you."

"Is this a joke? Hypnotize put you up to this?"

"Marie," she whispered. Even in the poor light of the disco ball, Damon saw her dark features twist with displeasure. She leaned her torso away from his still hungering lips.

"You know Marie." Damon nodded, things becoming clearer. "She put you up to this, didn't she? Trying to teach me a lesson about not wanting a woman just for sex, right?"

"I *know* Marie," Noir said, her voice icy. "Is she what you want?"

"Just what the fuck is going on here?" Damon asked again, anger beginning to simmer. "Is this some kind of game?"

"Only if *you* want it to be," Noir said, her voice filled with accusation. "I'm here because I'm not into games, and I thought you were the same way, but if you want to keep on chasing after Marie, then go ahead."

"So you do know Marie."

"Didn't I just tell you that?"

"I'm sorry," Damon said, on reflex. Noir grabbed his head again, this time more gently, caressing his cheeks.

"I know her, and I know you. I've seen your longing. Tasted your dreams." Her voice trailed off as her eyes glazed over.

Great, the one woman I've had success with is crazy, Damon thought, already whirling contingency plans through his mind to toss this woman off his lap and tear out of the club if she got violent. "I don't understand."

She smiled. It was one of the most serene expressions he had ever seen. Her eyes twinkled as she leaned in close to whisper in his ear, "I'm not supposed to tell you, but this is a dream."

"Bullshit!"

She twisted his head roughly, her nails digging into his bald pate. Damon bit back a yelp.

"Don't do that again," she warned. "I'm serious. This is a dream. You are my charge. I have been with you for a long time . . . since you were eleven in fact." She paused, peering deeply into his eyes with wistful fondness. "I was there for your first wet dream. And every one since."

His erection a memory, Damon didn't even try to hide what he thought of this strange woman's revelation. "Noir, I've never seen you before in my life. This shit isn't funny."

"My name is Nahema. Please call me by my given name. It is only fitting, since I know so much about you, and you know almost nothing about me."

"Bitch, I don't know shit about you!" Damon's anger felt soothing. He needed it to get some control back over this spiraling situation.

"I know about Mrs. Harland, your sixth-grade teacher, Tomika Simmons, your first crush . . . Aria Jenkins, the little cheerleader you jerk off over during your lunch breaks, and so many others."

"How . . ." The rest of the question hung in his throat.

She smiled, nodding with approval. "They were me. Well, actually I assumed their forms." She tapped his right temple. "In your dreams. Your fantasies. I fulfilled your every desire, performed, suffered, and *enjoyed* your most deviant whims."

"How . . . what . . ."

"I've seen how these mortal females treat you. *They* don't understand you. *They'll* never accept you." Her voice was filled with an unfathomable sadness. "They don't appreciate your passion. I do."

"You . . . do?"

"I want to be here for you. Forever."

"Forever."

She smiled, nodding. "Yes. Forever."

"How . . ." Damon didn't know whether to laugh or cry. If this was a dream, it was the weirdest dream of his life.

"Right now, in the corporeal world, you are dozing on your couch, preparing to disgrace yourself by apologizing to Marie, a *mortal*, who has never known your heart like I have."

He took in his surroundings. The black leather couch, the murky carpet, the disco light, the music blaring through the VIP's thin walls and beaded entrance, and the salty tang of Noir/Nahema's breast on his lips . . . It all seemed so real to him.

Damon shook his head, trying to clear his mind. But how did she know those things about him, about the women he had secretly fantasized over since his first strand of pubic hair had sprouted?

"Fine, don't believe me," Noir/Nahema huffed, pouting as she lifted off his pelvis.

"Wait." He grabbed her arm. "Let's say this is a dream. How can you be with me? What do you want from me? How can you be here for me? Forever?"

She hopped back on him, pushing him into the plush

leather. He couldn't help but feel like he was drowning, being swallowed up by something far beyond anything he had ever known or believed possible as Noir unzipped his pants and pulled out his dick, stroking it back to aching readiness. Pushing aside her panties, she mounted him, her heat engulfing his manhood, spreading out from his shaft to envelop his entirety.

As she rode him, slowly at first, increasing in force and rhythm with music only she heard, Damon had never felt closer to a woman. In fact, he felt outside himself, his whole existence becoming a pulsing, throbbing sun, entwining with her fiery star, exploding in an orgasmic supernova that he feared might incinerate the club around them.

For dizzying, terrifying seconds afterward, Damon couldn't see, he couldn't breathe or feel anything around him; only the slackening pulse of his heartbeat told him he was still alive.

"That's what it can be like, Damon," Nahema whispered into his ear. His vision clearing, he saw her looking at him, her dark skin aglow and smile beatific. "Every night."

"My . . . God . . . what do I have to do?"

"I live in your dreams, sustaining myself on your essence . . . in small doses." She lowered her head, her voice tinny, penitent. "I've been imbibing more of your soul lately in order to puncture the walls of the dreamscape to be able to talk to you like this . . . that's why you've been so tired," Noir admitted, her haughtiness subdued. She looked at him again, her gaze searching for acceptance. Damon nodded impartially, forcing himself not to roll his eyes. "For me to be with you permanently, in your world, a bigger infusion will be required."

"Infusion . . . like blood or something?" Damon was still dazed from their frenzied lovemaking. He wasn't sure what Noir was talking about, but if it allowed him to continue fucking her, he was down with it.

Nahema pursed her full lips, her confidence now resurgent. "Not quite . . . I need a body, a vessel to live in. I need you to find a person for me, with a soul I can consume totally so I can be with you on your plane."

"You're serious?"

Noir merely looked at him. Damon felt his intestines twisting. A frost layered his skin. "My God, you are serious."

"The only question you really need to ask yourself is, are you?" Noir replied, her eyes eager as she took him in again. Damon readied himself for another session, but the dancer slithered off him. Her hungry gaze never left him as she walked backward out of the VIP, saying nothing else, the clinking of the beads the only sound in the club, in Damon's whole world.

Her voracious eyes lingered long minutes after he woke up, on his couch, a damp stain soiling the crotch of his jeans.

Taking in his surroundings, his heart stalling in his chest, Damon forced out a breath. "My God, that shit was real," he whispered. "*I* was dreaming. *She* was right."

His thoughts a muddle, Damon stumbled to his bedroom. He glanced at the glowing red digits on his alarm clock: 9:30 p.m.

He still had time to make it to Tamales, still time to find Marie and attempt another apology. Still time to hear her curse him out, or laugh at him, or even worse, ignore him, dismissing him for the scrub he feared he was.

"There's another way...." The words wafted through his ears, coiling around his mind, piercing his heart.

"There is another way," he muttered to himself. If Nahema was right, then there was a woman waiting for him, wanting him, who knew all of his faults and secrets, and still found him desirable.

Wake up. His sanity tried to push through the fog. *It was a dream. And since it was a dream, wouldn't it make sense that Nahema would know everything about you?*

"You're right," he mumbled, the haze dissipating with the thought. He chuckled. Damn, was he that hard up for a woman that he was actually considering a dream woman to be real? "I really am pathetic."

Hoping that he had at least laid out his Tamales wardrobe before he had fallen asleep, Damon yawned as he entered his bedroom. He smiled at the neatly folded blue shirt and olive khakis lying in the midst of rumpled sheets and torn pages from the latest *Black Tail* magazine.

The shiny pages, each featuring a different nude black stripper/ model in various forms of invitation, ringed his Tamales gear, almost like a shrine to his lust. Damon usually bought two copies of each issue, one to keep and the other to play with. He could be frenzied at times in his quest to get off, but he didn't remember tearing through the magazine after work. *But I don't recall laying out my clothes, either.* He shrugged. He was a little off tonight, but he would get back on track once he had a beer in his hand and an ass swinging in his face.

He untied his shoes, pulled off his shirt and socks, and tugged out of his jeans, leaving them all in a heap.

Damon also doffed his sticky underwear, holding them with a hooked finger as he put them in the hamper beside his closet. He knew he should take a shower, but he didn't feel like it. He was already behind, and he wanted to get to Tamales and see if he could make amends.

When he reached across the bed, his penis twitched as a glossy image caught his eye. He picked up the picture of the smiling, honey-colored model, her head cocked to the side as the camera captured her from the plump backside. "*Every night*," Nahema's voice purred, as the image on the page transformed into Noir right before his eyes, a current surging off the page, running down the length of his arm, and squeezing his dick in an electrifying spectral grip. His ejaculation strafed the picture.

"My God," he gasped, shivering, his skin both hot and cold. "I've never. I've never come like that before. What the fuck is going on?"

He closed his eyes, hoping that when he opened them, the honey-hued model would still be smiling at him through his oozing come. He felt a bowel movement bubbling when he opened his eyes to find Noir still on the page, now spread-eagled, a teasing finger over her glistening chocolate-pink clit. Damon balled up the page and threw it against the wall. It bounced off, falling behind his bed.

I need to lay off the caffeine, or something, Damon tried to joke, though he felt hollow inside, guilty even, as if he had somehow hurt Nahema. *The bitch is not real*, sanity railed. *Get it together!*

"Get it together," he whispered to himself, exhaling away the craziness in a big gust. His peace of mind lasted all of a few seconds.

"That . . . took a lot out of me . . . to do that," Noir's voice wheezed in his ear. *"Hurry, Damon . . . I need you."*

He shook his head in denial. "This shit can't be real."

"Hurry . . . please."

Damon then grabbed his head, painfully squeezing his meaty noggin. "Shut up," he warned with quiet vehemence. "Shut up." *Am I losing my mind? Oh God.*

"You're not losing your mind," Nahema breathlessly continued, softer currents now brushing against his naked skin, amazingly bringing his flaccid penis back to life. *"We don't have a lot of time. I can only remain on the corporeal plane for a few moments. If you don't want to be alone anymore you have to make a choice . . . now."*

It was madness, he knew, but what if it was real? What if it was his one shot at companionship? Something he had always longed for, but never knew how to make a reality.

And she was offering it to him, begging to be in his life.

If he had one chance, didn't he have to take it? But how?

"Hurry." Gossamer lips brushed against his left earlobe, serpentine words dripped venom into his heart, burning away his loneliness, dissolving his fear. Phantom fingers fondled him once more before fading into the ether, perhaps never to touch him again. *Unless I did something about it,* Damon sadly understood, a plan already forming.

He went to his closet and pulled out a metal case. A black .22 caliber pistol was nestled inside it. Damon hated guns, but he had felt a need to have one just in case something crazy popped off. His neighborhood wasn't exactly high society.

He took the gun out of the case, his hands trembling as he loaded it with bullets. Placing the loaded weapon on his bed, he quickly put on his Tamales gear, thankfully unspoiled by his wild orgasm.

Next, he rifled through the mirror cabinet hanging over his bathroom sink, tossing barely used medicine bottles until he found the sleeping pills he was looking for.

As he stepped out of his apartment, in a blue pressed shirt and crisp pair of olive slacks with noticeable bulges in both pockets, Damon Mitchell no longer felt alone.

My Sister's Keeper

Chesya Burke

Naomi walked through the park alone. The night around her seemed to make her dark skin invisible. The path narrowed, forked, and split off into two directions. The right was darker than the left.

She took the right.

She did not hesitate, as she knew exactly where she was headed. She had been there before. She'd left behind the streetlamps long ago; all signs of civilization had faded. Only the night lay ahead. The branches of the nearby trees shook and arched, as if they were arms warning her away.

She tripped over a tree stump that had split straight through the sidewalk, stood, dusted herself off, and walked on. To the right, just past the shadows, she heard rustling in the bushes. She walked toward it.

Suddenly, a loud scream broke the silence and she jumped despite herself. But she knew that voice. She rounded the bend, passed the large oak, and saw them.

Two forms lying naked under the blanket of night.

Another scream erupted and Naomi realized it was a shout of pleasure, not pain.

"Colleen!" Naomi called.

The man jumped, surprised by her presence. This park should have been deserted at this time of night. And except for the three of them, it just may have been. Only the drunks and junkies even dared to roam these woods after dark.

He sat up, looked at her, angry.

Naomi recognized him right away; he was one of the local dealers, Torch. He was known for burning the skin off junkies who owed him money, with the lighted tip of a cigarette. Loved the smell of burning flesh, they said.

She didn't care, she had come this far for her sister, and she wouldn't leave without her.

"Colleen," Naomi said, her words bouncing off the trees and back into her ears. "Get up from there."

The girl didn't answer.

"Get up, we're going home," Naomi repeated.

"I ain't goin' nowhere," her sister said. From beneath the large, dark man her body was almost invisible.

"Get up, damn it!"

"She ain't goin' nowhere, girl, till I get my money's worth," Torch said. "Now get."

He lay back down and resumed pumping into her sister.

Naomi walked over to them and pushed him off. "Keep your filthy hands off my sister."

"Your sister seems filthy enough on her own. You shoulda been here a minute ago when she was suckin' my dick." He laughed.

Colleen stood up without modesty; breasts and pubic hair shone in the moonlight.

"Get outta here, Nay," Colleen said.

"Yeah," Torch agreed. "Before we make this a three-some. You ever done it before, lil' girl?"

Colleen stepped between him and her sister. "She ain't no ho. I'll take care of you."

"Well, maybe things have changed." He caressed his genital area. "Come on, let me show you what a real man can do."

"No," Colleen said.

"Let's go." Naomi grabbed her arm.

"Oh no, you don't!" Torch rushed at Colleen and pushed her to the ground. She fell face-forward into the grass. He kicked her in the stomach; she gagged, caught her breath, and coughed. "You stupid trick bitch." He kicked her again.

He ran toward Naomi. His angry eyes and teeth pro-truding through a wicked smile were the only things she could see in the darkness. But those were enough. He was going to hurt her. Bad.

He stopped when he saw the silver pistol in her hands, aimed at his head.

"You don't know how to use that piece, lil' girl. Now put it down before I bash your head in with it." He took a step closer.

"Don't come no closer, man. I swear to God, I'll shoot you. I mean it."

"No, you won't." He laughed.

On the ground, Colleen sat up and looked at Naomi. "Where the hell did you get that thing, Nay?"

Naomi spoke, not taking her eyes off Torch, the bar-rel still aimed at his face.

"You think I learned nothin' from Mama, when she

used to come out at night lookin' for you? I know where she kept it."

"Put it away, you'll hurt someone." Colleen stood, holding her stomach, a slick of blood on her lips.

"Not if he just lets us walk away."

"Hell no!" Torch shook his head. "I paid her for it, now she's gotta deliver. She took my stuff. Tell her to put the gun down, Chocolate," he said to Colleen.

"I'll pay," Colleen said.

"No, you won't," Naomi said. "Give him the stuff back."

"I can't. It's . . . it's gone."

Naomi glanced at her older sister just long enough for her to see the anger in her eyes.

"You usin' again, Colleen? Who am I kiddin'? Of course you are." She tipped the gun on its side, still pointing the barrel toward Torch. She switched off the safety. "Now you can either let us go, or I can shoot you. Right there where you stand. You know they won't find the body for days, and then they'll just think another dealer did it. So what ya think? Say?"

He stood there for a moment as if contemplating his options, staring into Naomi's eyes. When she did not waver, he bent down and scooped up his clothes.

"This shit ain't over, bitch," he said, stepping into his shoes and glaring at Colleen. "I'll burn my money out of your ass, if I have to."

At eighteen years old, Naomi had already taken on the role of mother to her fifteen-year-old sister, Malaya. As well as to Colleen, who at twenty had been a prostituting drug addict even before their mother had died.

They had no father to speak of, so none of them did. No one else to count on, except each other. And most of the time, they couldn't count Colleen, so there was only the two of them.

Naomi had already gotten Malaya off to school and done the breakfast dishes before it was time to go to work at the phone company. She had gotten the job through a friend of her mother's and had worked there a little over six months. It paid most of the utilities; the others just got shut off.

On the way out the door, she ran into Lady Black. Everyone in the neighborhood called her that because she was more proper and pleasant than most in that part. And her easygoing way called for respect, despite the fact that she was still black, like the rest of them.

The old woman always told Malaya stories of how things had been in the neighborhood when she had been younger. Malaya loved the Lady, and Naomi imagined that the Lady felt the same for her sister. If she had to admit it, she would have said that the Lady scared her more than anything. It was her eyes.

"Well, there, how is the most important part of the Three Musketeers?" She always called Naomi that.

"Off to work. Someone has to pay the bills." She smiled.

"Too bad it's you, huh?" The old lady's eyes had a way of saying much more than her mouth, and Naomi found herself turning away. Those eyes said too much.

Naomi shrugged.

"Where would the miss be right now, if she had her choice?" Lady Black asked.

"Oh boy." Naomi closed her eyes, letting the thought take her where it would. She opened them, a sad look on her face. "Where else could I go? Colleen and Malaya need me."

The old woman stared at her in surprise, as if she had never heard such nonsense in her life. "Why, anywhere you want, girl. Anywhere in the world."

When she left the old woman, she saw the old man from upstairs. He wasn't really old like Lady Black. About thirty-five, she'd guessed. She had come to call him that because he had made it a habit to chase girls much younger than him. The younger the better. Naomi had even caught him flirting with Malaya. She hated him.

"I saw your sister, Chocolate, gettin' in some old man's car," he said. "You think she was gonna do him?"

Pervert, she thought. "Her name's Colleen."

"Well, they call her Chocolate on the streets."

"Not all of us hang out in the streets." She didn't even bother smiling; he knew she despised him.

"Well." He smiled, showing all of his toothless gums. "Some of us make it our job to *work* the streets."

"My sister's not a whore!"

"Maybe you should tell *her* that." He smiled at her one more time before he walked away.

God, I hate him. He had no right talking about her sister that way. She knew that Colleen had problems, but she thought maybe if she could get her help, things could go back to the way they were before Mama died. Maybe things would be all right.

Mama had been less than forty when she was diagnosed with cervical cancer. Naomi remembered thinking how brave her mother had been when she'd sat all of them down and told them. They had cried, but

Mama had said simply, "Don't cry for me, I'm going home." She was dead two months later. Colleen was strung out by then, and Malaya was still in high school. And Naomi was working her ass off to keep them all together. She had to make Mama proud. She just had to.

On the bus ride to work, Naomi pondered just dropping everything and leaving. She, Malaya, and Colleen could just make a new start somewhere else. A fresh start. It would probably do them all good. But Colleen would never go; she considered this her home.

Naomi supposed the girl was right; it was home to all of them.

Mama had lived and died here. Perhaps they all would as well.

Time went by slowly in the projects. Most of the time, it seemed to stop completely.

No money.

No job.

No hope for the future; no reason for time.

Naomi worked her job at the phone company. Colleen—aka Chocolate—worked her corner. But most importantly, her job was to find her next fix. Malaya had just turned sixteen and had a longing to go to college. Naomi actually thought she could make it on a scholarship with her 3.8 GPA.

She was proud. She wanted Malaya to have more than she had. She wanted her to become more than just a junky like Colleen. Or a phone rep, like her.

"You really think I can?" Malaya asked one night, sitting at the table finishing her homework.

"Of course you can," Naomi said. "I've told you that."

Malaya twirled around, hands held high in the air, almost lost in thought. "Maybe I'll be a doctor. Get an office on the South Side here. Help some of us without insurance and money. What ya think? I could, right?"

"Yeah." Naomi smiled.

"But . . ." She drifted off as if she heard a voice in the back of her head telling her not to say any more.

"But what?"

"Colleen said that ain't nobody in this family never been to college and neither would I."

"She said that?"

"Yeah." The girl paused and Naomi saw the hurt in her eyes. "You know she ain't been home in two days?"

Naomi nodded. "I know."

"You gonna go get her? Can I come too?"

"No. I'll do this alone." Naomi allowed a single tear to fall down her sullen face.

"Mama used to cry, too," Malaya whispered.

Naomi didn't hear.

She found Colleen in the park again. She wasn't surprised. The surprise was that she was alone.

"Let's go home, Co."

"Did you bring your gun this time, Officer?" Colleen asked.

"I never know what I'm gonna find you with. Mama told me that. She told me to take care of you. Who is it nowadays? Anyone who pays, right? You'll fuck anyone who pays."

"Right!" Colleen screamed. She wobbled forward, and fell to the ground.

Naomi could tell she was high. Crack. "So you can buy that shit. Why?"

"Because . . ." She stood and brushed an invisible stench from her knees, like a pro.

"Because what, Colleen?"

"It's Chocolate to you. To everyone! My name's Chocolate."

"Let's go home now." Naomi reached out to her sister.

Colleen slapped her hand away. "I am home. Don't you see?" She twirled in a circle, her arms outstretched. She fell again, stood up. "Home. This is Chocolate Park. My park. My home."

Looking at her sister, Naomi began to cry. She knew that Colleen had been doing drugs for a long time. She even knew about the prostitution, despite her desire to deny it happened. But she had never seen Colleen like this.

Maybe, she realized, she had never allowed herself to see it. She loved her sister, damn it.

Colleen had taken it hard when she found out that their mother had cancer. She felt responsible, as if she hadn't been there for their mother when Mama had needed her the most. And of course she hadn't been, because of the drugs. Then when she died, Colleen had been stuck with all the responsibilities of two younger sisters. Motherhood.

But hell, so had Naomi. The difference was that Naomi was good at it.

"Do you want to join me?" Chocolate said. Naomi did not see her as Colleen any longer; her sister had died. "I can help you. You know, show you the ropes.

Even help you find johns. What ya think?" She raised her hands high. "I'm my sister's keeper, right?"

Naomi wiped her eyes. "Malaya ran into Torch today. He said he wants his money or his stuff. He said he'd kill you to get it. He said he'd kill her, too. Do you care?"

Chocolate didn't answer.

The drugs wouldn't let her care.

The day Torch raped Malaya, she had been walking home from school and he'd grabbed her and pulled her into his car.

He drove her to his apartment, and one by one, he and his buddies had their way with her.

When he sent her to walk home, he told her, "Tell Chocolate, I want my money. Or next time I'll kill you, bitch." And then: "You even think about goin' to the cops and my boys will kill all three of you."

How do you choose one sister over the other?

Naomi got the call at work. Her sister was hurt. Malaya had gone to Lady Black's apartment; their phone had been long disconnected.

When Naomi walked in, she saw her. Malaya's eyes were swollen shut and had a deep cut on one lid. Torch had knocked out one of her teeth and it had lodged in her lip, so the girl could barely speak. The entire right side of her face was bruised and she had small circular burn marks on her face and body—from a cigarette. Torch's.

Naomi could tell that Malaya had been crying, but now she put on a brave, strong face for her.

Naomi couldn't do the same; she cried. "Oh, my God. What did he do to you?"

Malaya sat up on the couch. "He didn't do this." The pain from her embedded tooth was obvious.

"You mean, Torch didn't . . ."

"Oh yeah, he did it with his buddies." She covered her mouth as blood ran from her lips. "But Co, she let it happen. She's been hurting us for a long time. This is just another way."

How do you choose one sister over the other? Naomi looked at Lady Black, whose eyes once again told her everything she needed to know. Louder than words they shouted . . .

"Pack your stuff, we're leavin'. *Now*!"

Naomi found Colleen in Chocolate Park with her john. "Get up and leave. Now!" she told the man.

He looked at her strangely, but didn't argue. He stood up, zipped his pants, and ran off.

Chocolate just lay there, naked.

"Torch wants his money," Naomi said.

"I'll pay. I'll pay, okay?"

"When?"

"When I can."

"He raped Malaya. Him and his fucking friends. They raped her."

"What?" To Naomi's surprise, she looked concerned. "He what?"

"Beat her up too. Bad."

Chocolate covered her face. She cried; Naomi could see her tears glisten in the moonlight. But Naomi felt no remorse.

"How much stuff is worth him raping Malaya? Huh, Chocolate? How much?"

She sobbed. "I stole some of his stash. I was gonna pay it back, I swear."

"When?"

"When did I take it? A couple of weeks ago. I didn't even think he'd notice. I . . . I was gonna pay him back."

Naomi shook her head. "You fuckin' junky. What you gonna do about it?"

"Do? What can I do?"

"I don't know. Do something to keep him from hurting Malaya again."

"He'll kill me!" she cried.

"He raped your sister. Isn't that enough? And I know that's why you haven't been home, so he couldn't find you. You've been hiding out. But maybe if you go to him, tell him to leave Malaya alone . . ."

"I . . . I can't."

"He said he'd kill her next time. He said he'd *kill her*, Chocolate!"

"I can't."

Naomi shook her head. "I knew it. You're a coward. You won't even do it to help Malaya." She sighed. "I love you, Co." She held out her hand to the girl. "We're leaving tonight. I'm taking her and getting outta this stinkin' shit hole. Come with us, Co. Come with u—"

The shot came from behind Naomi. The echo bounced from tree to tree. Instinctively, Naomi ducked and fell to the ground.

When she looked up, the second shot pierced Chocolate's chest. The first had hit her in the stomach.

Naomi looked at the shooter.

It was Malaya.

The girl cried and dropped the gun. "We don't need her, Nay. Mama used to cry. Did you know that? I would hear her through the walls. She would cry. She'd cry for her—now she's made you cry, too. And me." She wiped her eyes. "But we don't have to cry for her anymore. We can forget her. She's with Mama now."

In the end, the choice was easy—choosing one sister over the other.

The hard part was burying Colleen in her Chocolate Park.

The Wasp

Robert Fleming

"Beware of the wasp's stinger . . . darn thing hurts."

—Willie Best (1934)

Before I got in here, my family had me locked up, in a psychiatric ward, for my safety. At least, that was what they said. Three times in Bellevue. How they caught me was when I went over to a girlfriend's apartment and she ratted on me, called my sister and told her that I was here. When I arrived there, I had no idea that she would snitch on me like that. I was telling her that I was sleeping in all-night theaters, in hallways, in the bus terminal, on subways, anywhere but home.

He was there, my husband. I was tired of being alone and hungry, but I was scared of him. He had beaten my ass so badly the last time that he put me in the hospital. I was tired of being his doormat. I told her that. I was afraid for my life. He told me he would kill me.

And he meant it. I got a protection order from the police, but it didn't do any good. My mother, before she died, told me that I should have left him a long time ago, but I was too afraid to do it. Also, he kept telling me that I wouldn't have made it without him. I was nothing without him. If I started a new life, he would find me and I would be sorry that I left him. He would make me pay.

"He's going to kill me," I told the cop when I was in the police station to get the protection order. "He means it. He was choking me under the water in the tub last night. I thought I was going to die. I don't want to die. I'm only twenty, I haven't lived yet."

"What were you arguing over?" the cop asked. "Some man you were flirting with? I know how you young girls are. You see something you want and you go after it."

I knew he was just saying that because he had an audience. The other guys chuckled. See, I knew men stick together. A lot of them think all women are sluts and whores. I'm not like that.

"Yeah, what were you arguing over?" another cop asked me.

"I don't want a baby and he does," I said. "I don't want to have a baby. I want to go back to school. I want to make something of myself. He's in a rush to have a kid and I don't want to do it."

"Why not?" the first cop asked me. "Every woman wants to be a mother."

"Well, I don't want to be a mother," I said. "My mother had nine."

"Different fathers?" the cop asked with a smirk. If it was a black woman, she had to have multiple fathers, not one, but several.

"By three fathers. But that is not it. I'm just not ready."

The cop laughed with the other men. He was white

and so was the other guy, but there were three black guys around the desk. It was a man thing. A woman should have babies and that was that. You were put here on earth to be a breeder. I knew that I was not put here to be a breeder. And I knew how hard my mother had it when all the men left. She was left to be a mother and father to these kids and it killed her.

"Is it about childbirth?" the first cop asked. He was trying to be nice, at least nicer than the other guys. "It hurts but then you forget it. The pain goes away. My wife had five kids. You know, we're Irish. We like big families."

"And you're Catholic," the other guy teased. "The pope doesn't like birth control."

"I'm not ready," I said. "I should have control over my body."

"Then you should not have gotten married," one of the black guys said.

"Are you a dyke?" another black cop said. "You like women?"

"Hell no," I replied coldly. "I just don't want kids." I thought about other young women who pushed their baby carriages, proud to be a mother, female superior, proud to be a breeder. They made you walk around them.

The first cop tried to lecture me about motherhood. "One day, you'll regret that you didn't have children. You'll be alone. Home, family, and the domestic life are all that matters, especially when you get old. You don't want to get old and miss out."

I heard about the biological clock, the fertile time running out and menopause setting in. Tick, tick, tick. I didn't think it was a disgrace. I tried to make them understand.

"Do you like cats?" the second cop teased. He was smirking and the guys laughed.

"I hate cats," I answered. I didn't get it.

"But if your husband wants children, you should give him children," the first cop said. "Being a mother is a part of marriage. Also, your parents would want to become grandparents. That's part of the cycle of life. Grandchildren continue the cycle of life, but you know that."

"My mother is dead," I said.

"I'm sorry," the first cop said. "You're not a feminist, are you?"

"No. I just don't want to have any kids."

The second cop laughed sullenly. "You want to be a whole woman, right?"

"What is a whole woman?" I asked, like he would know.

"Like biologically what you want to be, a woman and a mother," the cop said. "A whole woman. Normal. It isn't normal to be childless. It just isn't."

"It should be my choice, not his," I said firmly. "Can I get the protection order? If you don't give it to me, he says he will kill me."

The cops gave me the order, but with conditions. I knew what they meant. I had to submit to him. I moved out and tried to find a place to stay. The rents were outrageous. I spent a couple of nights with a coworker but I had to move. She tried to feel me up. I didn't even know she was lesbian. She had never tried anything before.

I rode the trains the following nights. I would wash up in the restrooms, change clothes from the two shopping bags I carried, and go to work. The coworker tried to whisper to me, telling that she wouldn't do that again if I came back. No way. I was scared being on the streets. But I had no choice.

One afternoon, I walked into my boss's office. He was a computer nerd who loved science. There were other nerds standing around, talking about some astronomers saying they had detected water at the most distant point from Earth in a galaxy two hundred million light years away.

I waved to the boss to get his attention. He waved me away. He was holding court and loving it. When I tried to approach him in the hall, he chided me for being brazen in barging into his office. I just wanted to ask for a raise. Maybe my timing was off. Maybe just a couple of dollars an hour would have made finding a room in an SRO hotel a bit easier. All because I didn't want to be a mother.

I really didn't know I was being abused. I thought it was love, love between men and women, the routine matters of the heart. My husband had hit me, repeatedly. I didn't like it, but I put up with it. I'd look in the mirror and my face would resemble a beaten boxer's face. Black eyes, bruised lips, twisted arms, aching limbs and ribs. True, he stomped and kicked me too. I believed he hated women. I knew he hated his mother but I think he hated females, women in general.

At parties, he'd loud-talk to his men friends with their girls: "See, she dances like a white girl. She dances like she fucks." He loved to shame me, embarrass me.

In bed, he laughed at me, said I had no rhythm.

My girlfriends said I should leave him, before he killed me. The papers were full of guys who wanted to control their women, gave them low self-esteem, and shot or stabbed them. I couldn't leave him. I tried, but I couldn't. So when I finally did, just ran away, I started to make up reasons why I should go back. I always returned.

That day about three years ago, when I got off work, Jack, my husband, was waiting for me. I was headed to the bus terminal to get to my locker so I could change clothes and wash up, but he dragged me to the car. He had a gun. I didn't argue with him.

"What is it you want from me?" he shouted. "You want a divorce?"

"No, I just want you to stop pressuring me about having a baby," I said, trembling. "I love you, Jack. I still love you. Give me time, please."

"We're married," Jack yelled. "I'm the man. I'm your husband."

"But you don't own me," I yelled in return. "I'm young. I want to live life. I want to go back to school and get a career. Is that so wrong?"

He poked me in the side with the gun. "Yes, it is if I say so."

"Why don't you want me to go back to school?" I tried to stay calm.

"Because I don't want them to be filling your head with all that nonsense," he said. "You don't need a career. I'm the man. I can provide for you and the kids. I can provide for this family. All you need to do is stay at home and take care of the kids."

"Suppose you leave me and the kids?" I asked, watching him start the car.

"I won't do that," he said, pulling out into traffic. "I love you. I just want you to do what I say. It's for the best. If your mother were around, she would agree. All she wanted to do was to have you happy. I'm a good husband."

"I want to do the school thing while I'm young," I said. "I can make you proud of me. You'll see. Then we can earn money, then we can have our babies and a good home. I want a house in a good neighborhood. I'm tired of being poor."

We pulled up to a light. A cop car eased alongside us. My husband tucked the gun between his legs. He shot a bitter glance at me, *keep cool*, and leaned forward to talk to the police officer in the next car.

"Do you know your turn signal on the rear left light is out?" the police officer was asking my husband.

"No, I didn't, sir," Jack replied. "I'll get that fixed as soon as possible."

"You better," the cop said. "I'll let you off with a warning."

"Thank you, Officer," my husband said, smiling.

The patrol car sped away. My husband didn't speak to me until we got home. He didn't ask me where I'd been. He acted like I had been at the job after a long day, but he didn't try to figure out what I'd been doing. My mother warned me about him. She said he was a strange man.

My husband marched me down to a gynecologist, or "pussy doctor" as my mother used to call them, so he could get me checked out. To see if everything was in working order. Jack was religious about doing the speculum bit, every six months, no abnormal Pap smear for me. He found a woman doctor, who was a friend of his mother. Sometimes, he would sit in there as she asked me questions. I hated it, no privacy.

"Are you having any irregularities in your menstrual cycle?" Dr. Reina Amado asked me. "Bleeding heavier or lighter?"

"No." I loathed him sitting there.

"Do you examine your breasts for lumps?"

"Yes." I glanced at him, this two-hundred-and-thirty-pound muscle boy, weight-lifting fool, watching me for any blemishes or flaws.

"Do you inspect your vulva for lesions, warts, or abnormal moles?"

"Yes."

"Do you examine your vaginal walls?" the doctor asked. "Is your discharge normal? Or is it indicative of a yeast infection?"

"Everything is normal down there," I replied.

"Take your clothes off and slip into the gown," she said and chatted to my husband while I walked beyond the screen. I returned and lay on the examining table.

I saw her wink at my husband. Maybe they were lovers. She wasn't that old. She put on gloves, rubber ones, and took out the speculum. Cold metal.

"Watch again and let me show you how it is done," Dr. Amado said, putting her hands on my body. "With one hand on your belly and two fingers inside your vagina, feel your uterus, fallopian tubes, and ovaries. Are your hands washed?"

"Yes." I hated my husband to see this. It was like watching me play with myself. I did as I was told, reluctantly.

"Now, with one finger in your vagina and another in your rectum, feel the area behind your uterus," the doctor said. "Good, that's it. Explore. Feel anything out of the ordinary?"

"No." I was ashamed. Totally humiliated.

"You might have a yeast infection, very slight," Dr. Amado said, holding up a glove to see a thick, curdlike discharge. "I'm going to prescribe some Monistat. Do you get these often?"

"No, it's my first time."

"Is it VD?" my husband asked the doctor. "Has she been fooling around?"

"No, it's normal," the doctor answered. "Some women just get them. It will clear up. Also, drink cranberry juice, lots of fluids. Okay, Maya?"

"Yes, all right." I knew Jack would be interrogating me all night, to find out if there was another guy, if I was fooling around.

Later, Jack was jovial in the car, but upset at my angry face. I was pouting. He said he'd slap me silly if I didn't lighten up. After all, he was my husband and not a stranger. I flinched when he raised his hand to slap me, but he stopped. He hugged me instead, cooing that he loved me, that he'd love me forever. He was the master of mixed signals.

In the beginning, Jack was the kindest man I knew. My family loved him. When he was just a boyfriend, he used to pick up groceries for my household, take my mother to the Laundromat, drive us to church, even ride with my mother to the doctor's office. He was so patient, waiting around when she went to the drugstore to get her medication. My mother had nine kids, but she was a lush, so the city took most of her young kids away. She couldn't take care of them.

And then she got liver cancer. The doctor told her that she would get sick if she didn't stop drinking. She loved bourbon, straight up. She drank like a fish. She didn't start drinking until the last of her husbands left her, and then she couldn't stop.

Yet my mother warned me about Jack; she could see through him. "Jack tries to act like butter wouldn't melt in his mouth, but I get a bad feeling about him," she said just before she got sick. "He reminds me of Felix, my second husband. Something doesn't feel right about him. Don't marry him. Please don't, Maya."

I was stubborn. I wanted Jack.

When we got married, I wanted to stay with my mother because she was not well. He didn't want to live with her. We got a place in Brooklyn in Brownsville, a dump, where we gave parties, drinking and drugging. I got tired of that. He didn't want to leave the house. We got into a fight because I went to work as a secretary. I was always good in typing and stuff. When we went out, he would always put me down, talking about my fat ass.

"Man, she definitely got a lot of junk in the trunk," Jack said, teasing me before the guys. "She got a J-Lo ass and she can fuck. I got to give it to her, she can tire a nigger out, but that's about all. She can't cook or do anything around the house."

He told me he was screwing a coworker, bragged about it. One night, one of his crew told him about himself, said he should respect me. "You shouldn't talk about how your lover swallows come all night," he said to Jack, who wanted to punch this guy out.

And jealous, oh man. Jack started to check the car's gas gauge to see if I was going where I should go. He monitored the phone bill to see if I was making any calls to guys, itemizing it. He was slowly isolating me and I wasn't having it. I told my mother about it and she said I should get out of there. He wants to control you, she said.

My sister Inez said I changed. I got really quiet, shy, and meek. I never went anywhere except when Jack took me. I never went to family events, except for my mother's funeral and Christopher's baptism. He would snap his fingers like he would do for a dog and I would sit on his lap or in a chair near him. He would smack me in public or punch me and I never thought about calling the police. I was scared to go against him.

"You don't know what he would do to me," I told my sister. "He's crazy."

One Easter, he beat me so bad that I had to go to the hospital. He broke my jaw and busted a few of my ribs. The doctor who saw me never asked me about abuse, so I didn't volunteer anything about my husband doing this to me. He never brought up domestic violence, so I didn't either.

I went that spring after the hospital visit to a place where women went for counseling. A woman who knew my symptoms understood everything about me. We talked and cried together, but I would not leave him.

I took a long lunch with some coworkers, a few laughs and drinks, and Jack was waiting for me when we left the restaurant. He didn't say anything when he called that afternoon. But when he picked me up, he was all smiles until he pointed the gun at my heart and said I was a bitch.

"Who did you fuck?" he said.

"I don't know what you mean, baby," I said.

"I saw you with that man," Jack said. "I saw you with him."

"That was my boss and there were four other people there too," I quickly explained. "We were talking at lunch. We were celebrating a deal that came through."

"Are you fucking the bald white guy?" Jack asked. "Is that the man?"

"He's my boss, damn it," I answered and he slapped me across my face with the gun, hard enough to bust my lip and bloody my nose. I saw stars for a time.

He didn't say anything until we got home. Then he started yelling and screaming about how I was going to have his baby, it was time for him to claim what was mine; then a baby would announce what was his. He blackened my eyes and I had to take off the next day.

"You oughta thank me for killing your black whore ass," Jack said, holding the gun in my mouth. "You know that. You cunt bitch! You will have my baby or I will kill you. That is final!"

I left him after that, a second time. I switched jobs. I cut off all ties with my family, my sisters, my brothers, my aunts, everyone. I got a new place. I got a new man.

I forgot all about Jack. I turned twenty-one.

Then one day, I got off at my subway stop, on the number two train, and there he was. He was driving a red Honda, was wearing a suit, and leaning against the car.

"Did you really think you could leave me that easy, bitch?" He held the gun at his side.

I saw it. He knew where I lived. I lived only two blocks from the train stop. I was screwed. I silently prayed and continued walking.

A day later, I got another order of protection, one of fifty thousand the city courts grant a year. The judge said it would be the only thing I would need to start a new life. The maximum time for the order was a year. I figured I could use that time to put my life together. The catch was that I, as a battered woman, had to accompany the police officer when he served the order. Since Jack had moved, we had no choice but to serve it to him on his job.

The officer handed it to Jack, who was a salesman at a department store. He sold electronics, such as TVs and stuff. I didn't want to go but the cop said I would be safe.

A crowd of coworkers gathered around Jack as he was handed the order. The cop said the words and warned Jack not to come near me. A boss was standing near Jack.

"You got me fired, you bitch!" Jack shouted. "You got me fired."

I knew that was not the last I would hear from Jack. I just knew it.

Three weeks passed. Daniel was my new man. Tall, thin, quiet, and almost serene. He looked like a basketball player, but he didn't play sports. He was a runner and ran in the marathons, the New York variety and the Boston one. He dressed very well, casual and classy. Always Bill Blass. I loved to drive his car, a vintage Thunderbird Sportster.

Now I was in his arms and nude, like that first time, for he held my heart within his cupped hands, a love I'd never known with any other man. His kisses were soft and heated. I could dream with him of a future and possibilities, unlike Jack where there was only darkness and hopelessness. I felt his dick inside me, the fire of it, the surging power of the hardened flesh. He took his time to drink in my scent and my sensitive nub, causing me to buck underneath him, easing him farther inside until he flowed so sweetly and tenderly. Skin on skin, sweat, touching and writhing.

Funny thing was that Daniel never liked to lie around with me. He kissed me on the lips and ran off to the shower.

I lay in the soiled covers, smelling the aroma of freshly made love, and wondered why it was taking so long for Daniel to shower. I listened. No water, no splashing. The door was ajar. I tiptoed to the closet, grabbed my robe, reached for the gun in the top drawer. It was loaded. I opened the door and eased down the hallway until I pushed the bathroom door open.

"Oh, shit," I gasped. Daniel was sprawled on the tile floor, his hands up to his throat, a gaping hole in his neck. Blood poured from the wound with every beat of his heart. He tried to speak, tried to warn me, motioned with his limp arm toward something.

I turned and faced Jack, his ugly face wearing a distorted smile worthy of his deed.

"If I can't have you, nobody will," he said, matter-of-fact. His gun was held down at his side. "I told you that I will kill you and anybody else that got in the way of our happiness. You will have my baby."

I shot Jack. He fell against the wall with the first shot, then pitched forward. I shot him again, this time in the chest. He slumped over with his gun hand trying to lift up, and I kicked the gun out of his grasp and shot him one last time. The bullet went through his forehead.

I dialed 911 and asked for help. They put me on hold. Daniel was still alive, but barely. His eyes were glassy and his hands were twitching. He was losing a lot of blood. He was going to die.

I went crazy that summer. They locked me up. I don't know how long. I was crazy as a motherfucker. Totally insane. I did shit I wasn't supposed to do. Early on in my imprisonment, I stuck my hand through a pane of glass. My mouthpiece tried to get me put in a minimum-security prison, but they decided on a place for the criminally insane. One of the guards there tried to dry-hump me, thrusting himself on my leg and ass, like a dog in heat. I felt his dick. It was soft and limp against my butt.

This blondie made him leave me alone. This other son of a bitch with him followed me all day. I kicked him in the balls and he yelped like a scalded cat. Every time I tried to get some shut-eye, somebody fucked with me.

These folks were real nuts. One girl swallowed crushed glass. Another chick jammed something jagged up in her pussy and bled to death. I would catch the inmates having sex all the time with each other, or with the guards.

When I told my sister Inez what was happening, she said nobody liked a tattletale. My other sister, Barbara, brought a couple of her church sisters to pray over me, made me hold a cross and read from the Old Testament.

"A woman is born of sin and trouble," Barbara said, pointing to my heart. "The Bible says that. Read the Old Testament. Remember Eve led Adam to sin. She ruined him. She turned him from God and all of His glory."

"What are you saying, sis?" I asked.

"You killed him, a man," Barbara replied. "God will never forgive you. Killing is a cardinal sin. Didn't matter what he was doing to you. You should have left him. You don't kill him, for heaven's sake. Now look at you, locked up in here like some animal."

I remembered how Barbara was working as a clerk on a temp job about two years ago, just barely making ends meet, and her boss, a cracker, offered to give her a raise if she would let him feel her ass. If he could see her bare buttocks. And she let him. A woman is a sinner, yeah, right. Damn hypocrite!

A year into my sentence, I was put in a straitjacket following a stunt I did. I tried to cut an assistant's throat with a jagged can top. They put me in a harness so I couldn't do any more mischief. That was when I made friends. Selma and Jan, both nutcases of the first order. Jan would tell the most outrageous lies imaginable. We would all listen to her and howl with laughter.

"When I was an actress, another actor brought in a soiled Kotex in a mayonnaise jar, saying it was used by Barbara Stanwyck," Jan laughed, cracking herself up. "Do you believe that?"

"No." Every woman patient on the ward screamed in glee.

"My father got drunk one night and called the FBI, saying he shot J.F.K.," Jan continued. "My mother thought he was crazy. She left him after that with a deacon from church. The old man went queer and ended up with a sex change in Soho as man and wife. My brother said the last he saw of him was when he spotted him with a bunch of skinheads in the Village, wearing a red Mohawk."

Selma always laughed at her lies. She was a stout girl, had her tits bandaged up. I caught her leaning over, sniffing Jan in her crotch with a broad smile on her face. "You don't use it much," she said, sticking out her tongue coyly.

I was tied up for several hours of the day, my "agitation" hours as the hired help called them, and Selma and Jan took turns letting me smoke. They fed me cigarettes while they railed against men and their superior, arrogant sex. Selma said she was married once, had one girl, who was assaulted by her minister. The girl never recovered, lost her head, was doped up on meds and had a seizure and walked out in front of a bus downtown.

"I understand why you don't want to be a breeder," Selma said, her lips in a snarl. "To be honest, I wish I had never brought a child into this world. They hate children. They hate babies. Men love sex, that's all. If we didn't have pussies, they wouldn't want to have anything to do with us. Think about it."

I wished I had kept my mouth shut. Jan had the bright idea of collecting all of the knockout meds from her pals on the locked wards. When they had a cupful of them, they fed them to me until I lost consciousness and fell back on the bed. Millie told me all about it later; how Jan held the flashlight so the girls could see, and how Keisha, another inmate, tied my arms down, and how Selma went to work with a needle and thread. Something about an African ritual or rite, closing the window of the body to the soul, Selma said to the girls.

When I awoke afterward, the pain was horrific. I

howled in agony. The nurses and orderlies rushed into the room, saw the bright pool of blood soaked into the covers, and pulled them back. I was writhing back and forth, out of my head with physical torment; it felt like a hot butter knife had been put between my bare thighs. One of the orderlies fainted and two nurses carried him out.

"Oh my God, how could anyone do this!" the head nurse yelled, pointing at my neatly shaved, stitched-up sex. "It's not funny. This is not funny at all."

Nobody was laughing, except me. The pain made me delirious, hysterical. Stitched up like a gaping wound. Neuter. A zero woman reborn.

Hell Is for Children

Rickey Windell George

Tears ran from Gail's eyes—wide in the dark. Rolled from the left, over the bridge of her nose, and into the salty pool that was forming in the right.

Rap music oozed through the wall at the back of her head, muffled but thumping, making her brain ache. This was not the sound, however, that was eating away at her insides, at her heart and soul. Somewhere near, in her own apartment, a sound like the howling of a wild dog swelled.

"It ain't right," she said, strands of saliva and tear water connecting her lips. "It just ain't right."

There was movement then in the bed beside her, a body turning, a man's shoulder coming into view beyond the slope of her silhouette. Then a three-inch Afro and a wrinkled brow, and at last a drowsy pair of arterial eyes emerged as he hoisted himself onto one elbow to look down on Gail's dark contours.

"Haven't you heard?" he said. "Hell is for children."

A fresh tributary of salt water broke across Gail's

face, dropped off her cheek, and stained the pillow. How many times had she asked the question of a few moments past? How many times had she gotten one stupid answer or another?

Somewhere in the bowels of the apartment, a cry broke through the hazy dark, clearly human this time, clearly the sound of pain.

"He's hurting," Gail said.

"Sheets never hurt nobody. Besides, ain't got no choice. You want him bangin' around, bouncin' off these walls all night?"

"How'd you like it?" she protested, anger burning like fire in her stare. "You want to be all tied down?" Gail was up then, back like a board, body thin as a rail, naked and black—midnight ebony.

A strong arm was slipping around her then, the long skinny fingers wriggling eagerly—*like the legs of a cockroach*, she thought, as the digits brushed her visible rib cage en route toward a breast. God in heaven, were those her ribs showing? Was she trying to starve herself?

"Get your hands off me, Karl." Gail snatched away, snatched up her robe from the floor on her side of the bed, and began on with it. She was as disgusted with herself as she was with him.

"Always the same bullshit," he said and flounced back down in the mess of sweated bed linens. Then breathing out through his mouth and wiping perspiration from his brow, he said: "Did it get hotter in here?"

Gail was on her feet now, tying the sash, eyeing Karl as she did. The radio man had said they'd broken a Louisiana state record the day gone by, he'd said it was hot enough to fry bacon on the sidewalk and that the thermostat wasn't apt to dip below ninety-eight even after sundown. Sweating atop the sheets and washed in the flimsy light flung in through the safety bars at the window, Karl's caramel-colored skin was lit in the shadowy shades of blue projected off the neon sign across the street. Even his high-yellow hard-on was cyan tonight. Once upon a time on a hot summer's evening like this, he'd stolen Gail's heart, and Lord knows her better judgment. Once upon a time, those drowsy eyes and that narrow ass of his were all she could think of. He was not especially handsome, but he'd seemed so to her. Now all Gail could think was what kind of no-account bastard he was, hot for fucking even with his son tied to the bed up the hall, moaning, sealed up behind a dead-bolted door like the hunchback chained in the bell tower.

Karl's lips were moving but the words were lost to her.

There was a moment of blurred unreality then. There was a trickle between Gail's legs that her fingers chased after. Her fingers coming back red, she determined that it must have been that time of the month, but could not even consider the whereabouts of a pad before another desperate moan was emitted somewhere in the dark beyond her room.

"—I get sick of this shit," was the tail end of whatever Karl was saying.

"Sick of what? You don't do a damn thing. You've never done a damn thing. All you're good for is tying him down and locking him up."

"He's got to be tied down, you know that."

"You should help me."

"Help you what?"

"Help me with Martin, goddamn it! He's your son, too."

Karl's eyes shifted, the whites bloodshot, the lids heavy. "I'm tired."

"And I'm not?"

Karl adjusted then, turned his back and narrow ass to her. "It's cause of you we keep going in these circles."

Another moment of unreality then: the room turning slowly, the little boom box on the dresser top, so easy to grasp and to pitch at a motherfucker's head. "I should give him away, right? Dial a number and make him go away?"

In the moment of silence that followed, the dark stream running down Gail's right leg arrived at her ankle. Then at last Karl's answer rang out. "We shoulda put him down the incinerator the day he was born."

Gail's breathing seemed it would stop that instant. It felt as though this man—this lanky son of a bitch in her bed—with the healed knife wound on his belly and the scar from that bullet on his chest, had stomped her in the heart.

He really didn't give a damn.

He didn't care if the boy lived or died so long as he was gone away somewhere, *in a place* was how the whites liked to say it. There wasn't a day that Gail didn't imagine the possibility, though she wished she could say there was. Her life was an unrelenting trial and it was because of Martin. If she were to put him "in a place," then everything would be so much easier. Each time she more than grazed the thought, however, she was reminded of the place where she'd spent her growing years: Sister Mary Hellena's home for orphaned girls, also known as hell on earth.

That was all right, though, wasn't it? Hell was for children, to hear Karl tell it.

* * *

Gail didn't remember leaving the bedroom but found herself in the darkened main hall moving toward the call of her child—now a mix of frantic shrieks and convulsive sobs. She could hear his bed jumping, banging, and creaking as he thrashed upon it. Martin's door was at the end, the last one on the left, and it seemed the walk—the dread—would never end.

The noise was earsplitting up close and the scent—God, yes, there was an almost unbearable stink—was heavy in the air as the room grew near.

"Defecation," the social worker liked to say.

"Shit!" Gail had corrected just days earlier. "Don't dress it up! He shits on the goddamned floor and then he plays in it!" Gail's arms outstretched almost like Christ on the cross, and turning in the middle of the room, she said: "He wipes down the walls with it. Sweet baby Jesus in heaven, I've seen him eating it."

The social worker was a fat white woman with a man's bowl haircut. She looked quite literally like someone had put a large soup bowl upside down over her head and simply shaved whatever hair there was that spilled out around the rim. Her eyes held all the compassion of ice cubes and her personality was none the warmer. "So toileting is still a problem?"

A problem? Gail thought, giggling at the stupidity of the question inside her head. Martin was fourteen and the size of a man, and he could not tell a toilet from a water fountain, or his ass from a stump in the ground.

"A problem?" Gail answered the question with the restatement of those two ridiculous words, and without realizing it she'd begun to turn again in the middle of her living room, like a child's spinning top slowly running out of steam. In snatches she glimpsed the kitchen through the entry: orange painted walls, white linoleum floor, a cutting board on the counter, a meat cleaver on the board—glinting silver light.

In turns the social worker sensed the change, saw the bulging capillaries in the other woman's eyes, felt the heat coming off her body. Gail was a woman on the edge.

Typically Martin spent his days at school, in the special class that he was taken to by way of the special blue bus. It was summertime, though, and school was over, and those few precious hours of reprieve were just a memory. It was the sound his body made hitting his bolted bedroom door that had pulled Gail's thoughts back from the cleaver. She liked to imagine that her son was trying to break the dead bolt, liked to give him credit, that at least his actions were efforts at escape. But he slammed the walls and the window boards and the floor equally as often as the door. Perhaps he just liked the sting of the impact?

"You're a stupid bitch," Gail said to the social worker. "Yeah, I got a problem. I have to lock my son in his fucking room all day. I have to board his window so he don't jump out. I need help!" Her hands went up to her head, gripping the thick puff of her hair, pulling—the pain had felt good, made her feel real. "Why won't somebody help me?"

"No one will come out here, Gail. Not to this neighborhood and not to deal with Martin. It's an awful thing to say, but you should really start considering the inevitable. Martin is getting big and these outbursts much more dramatic and frequent."

"I ask you to get someone out here to help me and all you can talk about is how I should give him away."

"It's my recommendation that we seek institutional-ization."

"You want to take my baby away from me?"

"Gail, I don't place this kind of suggestion lightly. Yours is an extraordinary case—"

Martin's door thumped and rattled with his weight again.

Gail's eyes locked on the fat woman, shimmering liquid hatred. "Get the fuck out of my house."

Now, in that long hallway for the some-odd thou-sandth time, Gail wondered if it wasn't time to dial the number. The fat lady had left in a rush, but not before leaving a card—a magic number that could make Mar-tin go away. Gail reached the knob and the mechanism of the dead bolt and she wondered if she could do it again. If there was help, if she was not so alone, per-haps she could go on.

The one Therapeutic Support Specialist brave enough to come to Kindred Green—Mr. Lucas—had not re-turned after the day Martin smeared ejaculate in his face. He'd been a godsend for the few days it lasted, helping with feeding and bathing, but when the boy had brought his dripping hands out of his oversized di-aper and slammed the slimy palms in Mr. Lucas's face, the heyday ended. The boy must have tackled him, taken him down. Martin had been cleaning his hands with the man's face—in his beard, across his nose, wriggling his gummy fingers in the man's gaping mouth— and giggling insanely when his mother, hearing Mr. Lucas's stifled screams, came and wrestled Martin loose.

Everything ended in screams where Martin was concerned—his or someone else's.

Martin was screaming as the rod of the dead bolt retracted from the jamb.

"I'm leaving!" Karl was in the backdrop, in the hallway now, but not on his way to lend a hand. He'd gotten into his jeans and was headed for the front door. Even now, Martin—all one hundred and sixty pounds of him—was wailing just on the other side of his bedroom door.

"Please," Gail appealed to Karl. "Don't leave me by myself again. Just help me settle him down."

The front door was already ajar in the man's grasp. The hallway's lone bulb played a game of tricky lighting in the murk, made sweaty highlights on the tops of the man's shoulders, made the rivers of moisture on his chest seem dark as oil.

"Please stay."

"What for?" Karl asked. "We both know how this goes. Sleepless night, wailing mongol—"

"Don't you dare call him that! He ain't no mongoloid. He's our son."

"Whatever," Karl said. "We know how this plays out, how it always plays out."

"If you help me it might be different."

Karl looked back. Was the expression smug or sad? Gail couldn't tell. Whichever it was, the front door closed just the same and then, utterly alone, she was pushing her way into Martin's room. Though she couldn't see their swarming little bodies she could hear the hum of flies swimming in the pitch-black. She fished for the light switch, found it, and gasped at what she saw.

Martin was there on his bed, one hand free of the

sheet ropes where the bedpost had broken. He was completely naked where he'd torn his pajamas and the giant diaper off with his free hand. Writhing awkwardly, straining against the remaining restraints, he was masturbating so fiercely that his penis appeared bruised and raw.

Gail thought about the sheets, how he must have fought to get that hand free. It was so very wrong to tie him down, but at the same time bizarre compulsions ruled his sad life, and it was impossible to predict what he would do. It was impossible to keep him safe at night without restraint. The boards at his window, which allowed only a peek of light in the day, seemed equally cruel, but what was she to do? He'd put his fists through the glass once already.

Was it time to dial the magic number? Gail's vision blurred and she saw the monstrous nuns of her childhood, vaguely recalled the things that one of them had done to her with kitchen utensils—spoons, forks, in one case the handle of a rolling pin.

When Gail's eyes refocused she saw that she'd been right about the flies. Dozens were milling about, laying their eggs in the shit-smeared sheets. Only now did she see the filth that covered the boy and the linens, even his pumping hand. Then she spotted the roaches, silent and stealthy by comparison to the flies, and far more numerous. There were at least two hundred of them, up from the cracks and dark spaces, feeding on the boy's feces and spilt semen, and drinking the sweat off his lopsided body. They scattered in the light now, at least a dozen of them scurrying by and over Gail's bare feet, the little antennae probing, tickling. She did not jump or even stir.

Martin reared his body up toward the door and

moaned. It was nothing intelligible, just a guttural sound, but to Gail it said Mommy.

Down syndrome coupled with mental retardation and a severe sensory disorder had made her fine boy into this puffy-eyed monster, and not a day went by that she didn't wish she could take the affliction away even if it meant carrying the burden herself, or that he could simply have been born ordinary, or if none of those options, then not born at all. She hated herself for some of the things she thought, but how could she help but to think them?

How much more could she take?

Just then, Martin raked his man-sized hand across the wall at the head of the bed and left a series of brown streaks that a fresh set of flies swarmed toward.

In the corner, the movement of other flies captured her stare. Her bucket was there at the center of the flurry, the washrag slung over the lip of the pail, soiled already from the last change. Gail's eyes glazed over before spilling salt sorrow, and then she shut the door. She thought of the place she'd grown up, of the nightmares she'd endured. She thought then of the room in which Martin lived, of the bed he was tied into at night, of the window that offered no light and the stench and the shit and the roaches and the flies.

Hell *was* for children.

Gail went to the card that was taped to the refrigerator, and next to the phone hung from the kitchen's west wall. Spanish music invaded this room, seeped through the cinder block.

"I can't take this anymore," she said as a female voice filled the line. "I've tried and tried to be a good mother, but I can't do no more. I'm all used up. All used."

When Gail was done on the phone she went to the hall closet and then out the front door.

She knew where to find Karl. He never went far, just far enough not to have to hear the mongoloid's crying. This was usually no farther than the lobby or the back steps where it was easy to score cheap weed. Gail found him in a corner, on the floor smoking some herb. He'd already been to the back steps and come out to the lobby proper to relax and enjoy his smoke.

"I did it," she said, eyes red and runny, nose running as well.

Karl looked up from where he was perched on the linoleum, his back to the wall of silver mailboxes.

"I called about Martin," she said. "They'll be here to get him in under an hour."

A grin broke across Karl's face as he made a move to come to his feet. Perhaps he was going to strut over and hug her, maybe he was going to cheer. Whatever the case, Gail's robe came open; her nude skeletal body was glimpsed only in the snatches between flowing fabric as the hunting rifle came up and out of the shadows there. Karl's smile slipped, the thinly rolled cigarette dropped from his lips, and before he could scream or even speak his terror the trigger was pulled. The lobby shook with the sound of thunder as the gun blast hit him squarely in the chest, aimed at blowing his lungs out his back it would seem. Rivers of blood from places so deep that they were black washed down his chest, and at the same time the silver mailboxes at his back were spatter-painted red. All this happened before his husk had even slumped to the tiles, and Gail was back on the elevator well before the dark puddle had spread from his cooling corpse.

Gail went then to her son, to his nonsensical wailing, that to her sounded so much like "Mommy, help me." With the smoking gun in the lock of her arm she ripped down the boards at his window. Using her fingers and teeth she undid the sheets that bound him to the bed. And there, in the mess of his excrement and other excretions, she held him and kissed his brow, and when he was calm and quiet she put the gun up under his chin and settled him down once and for all.

The last bullet Gail kept for herself.

Returning to her bed, she let the robe drop into a pile at her feet as she sat wide legged on the edge. Turning the gun upside down so the trigger was facing up, and hunching over a bit, she pressed the still steaming barrel to her vaginal lips and pulled the trigger. It was something she should have done long before she'd ever let Karl inside her, something that would have prevented there ever being a Martin.

As the thunder rumbled a final time, the bullet ripped through Gail's body, first mangling her uterus and then lodging deep inside her, rupturing organs along the way. She was dead even before her body pitched, before her head fell upon her pillow. A tear rolled from her left eye, over the bridge of her nose, and into the salty pool that was forming in the right.

Rap music oozed through the wall at the back of her head, muffled but thumping, making her brain ache. This was not the sound, however, that was eating away at her insides, at her heart and her soul. Somewhere near, in her own apartment, a sound like the howling of a wild dog swelled.

"It ain't right," she said, strands of saliva and tear water connecting her lips. "It just ain't right."

There was movement then in the bed beside her, a body turning, a man's shoulder coming into view beyond the slope of her silhouette. Then a three-inch Afro and a wrinkled brow and at last a drowsy pair of arterial eyes emerged as he hoisted himself onto one elbow to look down on Gail's dark contours.

"Haven't you heard?" he said. "Hell is for children."

A fresh tributary of salt water broke across Gail's face, dropped off her cheek, and stained the pillow. How many times had she asked that question? How many times had she gotten that stupid answer?

Hell was for children, and for mothers and fathers, too.

Somewhere in the bowels of the apartment, a cry broke through the hazy dark, clearly human, clearly the sound of never-ending pain.

Flight

Lawana James-Holland

Illinois, 1669

Jean's eyes flew open as he sat up abruptly, his breath coming in quick, heavy bursts. His entire body was covered in sweat. He lay under an animal hide, naked except for a breechcloth. Shapes loomed near him in the darkness, flitting in and out of view.

"Good, good. Your fever has broken," a soothing voice said with relief. Jean's eyes adjusted to the dimness, and he saw a smile on the face of his Inoca wife, Kilswa. She cradled his head in her lap. Her knee-length, red deerskin skirt was soft against his skin. He managed a weak smile and reached up to touch her smooth ochered face, her cheeks marked with tattoos. Trailing his fingers along her side, he began to trace the lines of the geometric tattoos on her arm.

"How long have I been asleep?" he asked.

"A long time. We were all very worried and thought for a moment that you would not make it. I asked a healer to come and treat you. You were calling out in your sleep."

"My love, I had a dream that I was a hawk being chased by a winged creature with skin tougher than animal hide. It was so fearsome, but it was not able to catch me."

Kilswa's eyes widened. She gently laid his head down and got up.

"Wait. I will be right back!" Her long braid bounced along her back as she rushed away.

Jean looked at the small, reed mat dwelling they had put him in since his illness began. He missed the comfort of the longhouse they shared with another family. He smiled at the talisman that the healer had hung above him. Protection? Better health? Jean didn't know which one it was for, but he was glad for the extra help. A clay pot filled with water sat nearby, and Kilswa had been busy making clothing. The unfinished garment lay neatly folded, and he realized that it was for him.

How long had it been since he had come to live with the Inoca? Four years now? Five? The Inocas of this area had taken him in as one of their own, and he thrived in the freedom—freedom being something he had not known in a very, very long time.

Jean closed his eyes. In his mind, he could still hear them screaming. . . .

When his master had proposed leaving Martinique, Jean had no choice except to go with him to New France. What else could he do? Father Cormier and the Jesuits were determined. Jean saw it as the possibility for an adventure. How had their missionary expedition gone so horribly wrong?

It was with great nervousness that his party of ten had started passing through the lands of the Seneca—the westernmost nation of the great Iroquois Confederacy. They came across a band of warriors en route to the lands of their enemies on their border. The warriors' heads were shaved bald, with dark locks of hair hanging down their backs and bristling porcupine hair roaches with a feather that mimicked their motions. Jean noticed that every warrior, with his black-painted face, could not take his eyes off him.

In his travels with the missionaries, Jean had been in contact with the native people of these lands whose laws, beliefs, and understanding he knew the French did not comprehend. As they traveled through the wilderness, Jean recognized it as a chance to try to learn their languages and more about the communities they encountered—something that did not interest the others. He had flinched when the Frenchmen called them "savages." Wasn't that what they had called his own people whom they had taken him from as well?

There was so much he didn't know about those whom they encountered, but what Jean *definitely* knew was that the Iroquois were the ones they wished to peacefully deal with, most of all.

The Senecas had been surprised to come upon them, but after much examination of Jean, they were willing to let the party go on their way and offered to share food with them, first. Jean shared some beads with them in exchange. Father Cormier and the others thought stopping would be fine, as they needed a rest anyway. As night fell, Jean walked with Father Cormier to where one of the warriors lay on the ground, sick and in pain. One of his colleagues was with him, squatting beside him.

"I do not believe he is going to make it," Father Cormier said, shaking his head as he looked at the ill man. "This is an opportunity for God's work. We must do whatever we can do to convert these savages."

"Father, I do not believe that is a good idea. I believe we should go on and let them be," Jean said. The other warriors nearby watched him intently.

"Just who do you think you are to question me? You are but a slave!" the priest said, sniffing at him dismissively. Jean's lip curled and he threw his hands up in disgust. He was sure the warriors didn't miss that either.

Father Cormier stepped over to the sick man and made the sign of the cross over his body. The warrior beside him sprang up, shouting, and the others who saw him instantly became angered as well. Jean's eyes widened, surprised by the sudden reaction. He understood only one word of their language: *Curse*.

Oh no. They think that the Father has hexed him.

Before any of them could react, there was a loud *crack* as Father Cormier was struck with an ax, a look of surprise on his face as it split open. The blood spurted out onto Jean. He jumped back and watched the priest's body fall onto the ground before him. The rest of the warriors went into a frenzy, pulling out their knives, ball-headed clubs, and axes. Screams pierced the air as some of the other Frenchmen met the same fate. Jean could only watch as the men in his party were bludgeoned with the heavy clubs, their skulls crunching and splattering brain matter.

One of the men ran to Jean, face covered in blood, holding his stomach.

"Jean . . . Jean, help me." It was the man whom Jean recognized as their interpreter. Jean looked on in horror as the man removed his hand from his stomach and his intestines rolled out of the wound.

They had unwittingly become part of something bigger than their mission. They were caught up in the middle of a war in which being French meant you were in league with their enemies—especially the Inoca.

Easily outnumbered, they were rounded up. Jean listened to the pleading and shrieks of the French missionary party as they were tortured and put to death one by one—Jean's former master included. Despite his terror, Jean somehow felt liberated by that action.

He watched as the warriors severed or burned the men's fingers and bodies, taunting them as the Frenchmen screamed. The warriors seemed to take particular pleasure in stabbing a smoldering stick into the eyes of a very large trapper named Jacques, and were disappointed when he finally cried out. Jean was sickened when they cut open the man's chest. The same warrior who had killed Father Cormier reached into Jacques, and with one motion, snatched out his heart and bit into it with a relish. The others began to chant and sing.

When they got to Jean, they tried to burn him on the hands and feet. The pain was searing, but at least he was still alive. If this was the way they did things, then he would die with pride. He was resolute, looking the warriors in the eyes as they taunted him, shouting and trying to get a rise out of him. They wanted to see him flinch, and he refused to give them that satisfaction. Years of dealing with ignorant white Frenchmen had taught him how to repress the desire to fight back, no matter how much he was seething inside. Something in him knew that this was not the time to repress how he felt. He stared down the warriors with contempt, as if daring them back.

This was his life. He was a man, and a man would not die crying out with pitiful wails as his master had. He saw something change in the way his captors viewed him from that moment on. What was it? *Admiration*?

They tossed him to the side near their camp, and he realized that only he had been spared from the execution that had followed for everyone else. Jean was certain that it hadn't been just his defiance, but also his chocolate-colored skin that had saved him.

Everywhere his party had traveled, he had been a star attraction. The men were certain that he must be brave, the women certain that he was handsome. Everyone wanted to touch his skin, certain that if they rubbed hard enough it would come off like the paint they wore.

Although he had been spared, Jean was uncertain of how long that status would last. As soon as night arrived, he escaped. He regretted his heavy footfalls, certain that he must sound like a loud, large animal barreling its way through the forest. Each step on his injured feet felt like the fire that burned him, but he knew he had to keep going. Calls rang out to the others in alarm, which only urged him more. He ran through the woods with no idea of where he was going, the branches and thorns tearing at his skin. *Will I be fast enough*? he thought as he ran blindly in the dark. Soon, he heard the roar of rapids in the distance. As the warriors closed in on him, he continued toward the sound of water.

Mon Dieu, he thought, reaching the dark roiling water. *What other choice do I have?*

The warriors cried out when they reached him, stretching out their hands to grab him and pull him back. He saw their mouths open in horror as he leapt into the water instead.

The coldness almost knocked him out. Jean could

not see anything as he was buffeted about against the rocks, their sharp edges tearing his skin. The waves rolled over him, and he struggled to stay afloat.

The swift water swept his exhausted body along, and he soon lost track of time. At dawn, as the sun rose, he was spurred to action and used the last of his strength to grope at anything he could possibly cling to. He barely grabbed on to a large branch that had fallen, and tried to pull himself up and out of the water before he collapsed.

With the daytime came feminine voices. He could hear the women speaking to one another, one more forcefully than the rest. He heard footsteps coming closer to where he lay on the shore.

I do not care. Let what happens to me happen. I am so very tired.

The dominant voice issued an order to the others—who he could hear were now running away.

Jean couldn't help but think that her voice was sweet even as she poked him with a stick. He understood nothing she was saying, but he could tell she was trying to calm him. She poked him again and he coughed, his eyes opening.

She laughed, and the first thing he saw was her beautiful smile.

Years later, that woman who had discovered him was now his wife. Kilswa had returned to him—this time with the chief, a few of the other elders, and Keemoraniah, the head of the warriors.

"Chief Wataga," Jean said, trying to sit up to acknowledge the older man properly. He stood before Jean dressed as if for a special occasion in a breechcloth and leggings decorated with red, triangular stone pendants. He also wore long necklaces of white shell beads and ones of woven bison hair decorated with feathers. His headdress was a garlanded crown of multicolored feathers. As he smiled at Jean, the worn lines in his face relaxed.

"No, no, do not get up. You need your rest. I wanted to hear more about this dream Kilswa told me about."

Jean repeated it to him and the other men looked grim.

"What is wrong?" Jean asked.

"That beast you dream of is a thing of flesh. It is very real. I encountered one the first time as a young warrior, and we were successful in our mission to eliminate it. We did not realize that there was another one as well until recently. They have probably been spawning all along. This is a menace that has been threatening us for eons."

"So you are saying that this monster is *real*?"

"It is the *piasa* and it is a murderous thing. This storm bird is not something to be respected as it has terrorized us for long enough. It feasts upon whoever is unlucky to come across it and I am certain that its lair is filled with the bones of too many of my people. Something must be done about it."

Kilswa was now kneeling beside him. Jean reached for her hand.

"There is more," Chief Wataga said. "It has to do with the hawk that you saw in your dream. This fever allowed you to envision your manitou—your protector spirit. We Inoca believe that Kitchesmanetoa the Creator watches over us all, but we all have manitous that are our own. They help to guide us and give us the strength that we need in our lives. As a hawk is a sign of a warrior, I want to select you as the final one who is to accompany me on a mission."

"What mission is that?" Even in the heat, Jean felt a chill as he asked.

"As one of the warriors who is to travel with me to end this. We are going to kill the *piasa*."

All were quiet as they made their way toward the high bluffs overlooking the river. Jean looked at the warriors silently walking with him, their nervousness palpable. Even in the midst of knowing that they were all walking toward a destiny for good or bad, he took comfort in the peacefulness of the woods surrounding them.

Chief Wataga walked with him at the rear of the group. He laid a hand upon his shoulder. Jean noticed the way the warriors flanking them gripped their weapons. These men were fearful just as he was, yet he knew they were not going down without a fight. Their bows and arrows were slung across their shoulders. Their hair hung long, dark, and shiny on the sides of their heads, the tops cut short and bristling. All of them were tattooed with triangles and lines and interlocking crosses—markings that never ceased to interest him, as they all were marked in much the same way.

"If you are to join us as a warrior, you must look like one as well," they had told him as they painted him with ocher that morning.

Jean had learned that the woods are never as silent as you thought they would be. Sometimes the wind could be as loud as the movement of animals or even louder than one's own thoughts. There was so much he had learned after being taken in, and most of all it was about being your own person. Almost all of his life he had been a slave, and for the first time since he was a child he was truly free and part of a people who were free as well. What had the Jesuits been thinking?

The woods started to become sparse as they came closer to the rocky bluffs. He was unprepared for the sight of the cliffs and the view overlooking the river.

What beauty there is in this place of ugly death, Jean thought grimly.

Keemoraniah slowed his pace. The woods began to open into a clearing, and he motioned for the other warriors to get into position. He then nodded at Jean and Chief Wataga to follow him.

What are we doing? Jean wondered as they took a central position. *We are too exposed.*

It was then that the chief looked at him, as if reading his mind. For a moment, Jean panicked with the realization: *He is drawing out the creature. And we are the bait. The Inoca saved my life and I am now expected to participate in saving theirs.*

They heard it before they saw it. A loud screech resounded through the quiet.

So quickly?

The warriors were all in position, crouched in the underbrush. The chief stood tall and unflinching as the *piasa* approached.

Jean's mouth dropped as it rose before them.

No, he thought. *It cannot be. The beast from my dreams. The chief was right. This is no monster at all, but definitely an evil creature of flesh.*

He could not take his eyes away from it. The monster was the length of at least four men, with rough, leathery greenish brown skin and gigantic wings like sails. Its eyes were focused on them as it opened its long beak—showing its rows of sharp, fanged teeth.

Its claws had long talons and one of the warriors cried out upon seeing it, gaining the beast's attention. The *piasa*'s wings started to beat the air, holding it in place as it contemplated attack. Jean was entranced. The beast was both magnificent and horrible.

One of the warriors stirred in the underbrush, and the *piasa* swooped toward him with its mouth open, faster than what Jean thought such a large beast could manage. The warrior tried to duck, but misjudged. The *piasa* ripped off his head with a single bite. Blood spurted from the severed neck.

The warriors regrouped and tried to stay as still as possible. *What are they waiting for?* Jean thought.

It was then that Chief Wataga did what Jean feared most: He called it to *them* instead.

The *piasa* rose high, and then suddenly swooped down upon the two of them. They rolled out of the way, avoiding the beast's deadly teeth. The warriors' arrows whizzed through the air, but bounced harmlessly off the creature's tough hide.

"Underneath!" Chief Wataga cried out. "I saw its vulnerability as I rolled. There are soft parts underneath!"

Another warrior stood up from his hiding place, trying to get a better angle on the creature, but it was too fast for him: It flew down upon him and tore his body into two pieces—one piece in each claw, his shriek echoing through the air.

Jean recovered and watched the creature rise again, poised to strike. With trembling hands, he raised his bow and fitted an arrow. He let the arrow fly, and it struck the *piasa*, startling the creature, but not wounding it. The *piasa* dropped the dead warrior's body parts over the edge of the bluff, and as it started to come down upon them again, the chief stood instead of rolling. The *piasa* pierced him with one of its claws, trying to sweep him up and take him away.

"No!" Jean yelled. He fitted another arrow and let it fly—taking care to avoid the chief. The arrow hit a tender spot under the monster's wing. The monster recoiled, but held fast to the chief. Jean leaped, tried to grab on to Chief Wataga's body and hold him down. They were trapped underneath as the creature thrashed about, alternately trying to claw at them and tear at them with its teeth. As Jean and the chief tried to dodge the creature's attacks, Jean's skin was becoming damp with not only the chief's blood, but his own. It did not matter. He was not going to let him go—this man who had spared him.

A life for a life.

Jean had never been so terrified in his entire life. Not during the boat ride that brought him to Martinique from his village—when those around him died left and right as the dysentery dripped and pooled around him. Not when the others were killed in his missionary party or even when he escaped the Seneca by leaping into the dangerous rapids. This was a fear that no one could even dare imagine.

This was also a fear that Jean refused to let take him—or his leader—and as he looked over, he realized the chief had not flinched once.

Jean struck at the *piasa*'s reptilian claws with his short dagger. Chief Wataga started to sing, and Jean knew it was the song of preparing for death. They locked eyes, and the chief never stopped singing, his voice becoming ever louder, stronger, and clearer.

The other warriors fired arrow after arrow, in a barrage. Chief Wataga staunchly continued singing as Jean tried to strike the creature again and again, while trying to avoid the powerful wings and the sharp beak.

Arrow after arrow struck the *piasa*, yet it kept its hold on Chief Wataga and started to pull him—and Jean—closer and closer to the edge of the bluffs.

Jean cried out as they reached the edge, but refused to let Chief Wataga go. He was close enough now that he could look over and see the water, fifty feet below. This was one fall into the water that he knew he would not survive.

Creator, protect us, he prayed. All around him was the whizzing of arrows as the skilled warriors plunged one after another deep into the monster's underbelly. The *piasa* lifted its wings again. Keemoraniah stepped clearly into view, pulled his arrow as far back as he possibly could—and released it, striking a vulnerable section of the *piasa*'s underside.

The *piasa* screeched, and finally released Chief Wataga. The chief collapsed on the ground, rolling onto Jean.

With one last, piercing shriek, the *piasa* dropped into the water below.

Jean started to drag Chief Wataga toward the edge of the woods. The other warriors stood guard at the bluff's edge, in case the beast returned.

"Sit me upright for when they come to me," Chief Wataga said. Jean did as he was told.

"I have only one question for you," Jean asked. "And that is, why?"

Chief Wataga slowly opened his eyes.

"If anyone should know, it would be you," he said softly. "I just wanted you to see it for yourself. This new life you've been given didn't start when we found you, or when we adopted you as one of our own. This new life of yours has always been more than just yours. I hope you understand that better now."

He closed his eyes again. Jean felt Chief Wataga slipping away as the rest of the warriors surrounded them.

The death song began anew.

A life for a life.

Hadley Shimmerhorn:
American Icon

Michael Boatman

Nobody inside Deke's Valhalla Stop-n-Drop felt much like eating. They were watching the walking dead people on the flat-screen television over the counter.

Hadley Shimmerhorn, nineteen years old and pretty as a dream, was staring at the Dukes of Hazard clock over the door, and quietly mouthing the words to "Ain't No Mountain High Enough." She favored "Mountain" as an audition piece because it demonstrated both her vocal range *and* her flair for drama.

Only twenty-five hours to go, she thought. Twenty-five hours until the producers of "America's Favorite Reality Show" would learn that Hadley Shimmerhorn had what it took to become the next American Icon.

The sound of snapping bones snatched Hadley back into three-dimensional reality. She glanced up at the television, and for the first time in her nineteen years, horror silenced the angry blackbird in her head.

On-screen, a dead man was eating Katie Cleric.

Cleric was the perky hostess of *Rise n' Shine*, Hadley's favorite morning show. As the dead man rifled through Cleric's entrails, the camera zoomed in on the expression of startled wonder that had flash-frozen itself onto her face. Hadley could see flecks of blood between Cleric's perfect white teeth.

Cleric's cohost, a lovable black weatherman type, uttered a gobbling croak, stumbled, and crashed through the wall-sized window behind the stage. Two dozen deceased midwesterners swarmed through the broken window, fell upon the lovable black weatherman, and tore him limb from limb.

Holy crap, Hadley thought. *It's really happening.*

Then the screen went black.

Emmet Pearson, the one-legged mailman, spoke first: "What the fuck was that?"

Clovis Holyfield, the only female driver for National Cargo, grunted through a mouthful of tuna on rye. "They were rabid."

"Bullshit," Emmet snapped. "They was terrorists."

Clovis shook her head. "Those motherfuckers were crazier than a shit house full of red monkeys."

Joe Swanson, owner of Swanson Quality Used Cars and Trucks, reached over the counter and pinched Ruby Ling, the only waitress who'd bothered to show up for work.

"Hey, Pocahontas, any sign of my goddamn pancakes?"

Ruby Ling's jaw dropped, and then she burst into tears.

"Why you always gotta be such a dick, Swanson?" Clovis said.

"Wonderful," Swanson grumbled. "Black Butch speaks."

Swanson's dealership sat on the other side of Route 45, directly across from the Stop-n-Drop. Every morning at seven-thirty sharp he dodged rush-hour traffic to come over and hassle the waitresses.

"That asshole would crawl through hell wearin' gasoline panties for cheap hash browns," Deke always said.

Friedrich Jackson raised his hand. "What's happening on the other channels?"

Friedrich was Hadley's favorite busboy. Hadley was pretty sure that Friedrich liked her back, even though he was black and she was biracial: half black and half white.

Emmet fidgeted on his wooden leg. "Try CNN, damn it."

Nestor Mendoza, the grill man and most senior employee at the Stop-n-Drop, turned up the volume as Hadley eased around the cash register and stood behind Friedrich.

"—in downtown Chicago. I'm standing on the roof of the Burger World across the street from the *Rise n' Shine* television studios, where this tragedy seems to have begun. We don't have much information, but this much is known. Katie Cleric and Ben Stoker, two of America's most popular on-camera personalities, are dead—devoured, apparently, on national television."

"Oh, fer Christ's sake," Swanson grumbled.

"Saudi operatives," Emmet said. "Goddamn A-rabs are takin' terror to the next level."

Clovis made barking noises.

"Quiet, please," Mendoza said.

Hadley leaned forward and placed her hands lightly

on Friedrich's shoulders. She felt him shiver at the contact.

"—where hundreds of these terrorists have descended on Michigan Avenue, attacking innocent shoppers, pulling people out of cars—Donnie, get a shot of the street."

The camera operator panned down to Michigan Avenue.

"Holyyy shit," Friedrich said. He flinched. "Sorry."

Hadley smiled. "No problem."

Chicago's premier shopping drag was choked with screaming tourists. They were being run down and slaughtered by people like the one that ate Katie Cleric.

Some of the attackers moved with a stiff, jerky gait; they reminded Hadley of the time she'd gone to visit her grandpa Roosevelt after his seventh stroke. She'd found him doing the Lindy Hop with twelve other stroke victims as part of a rehabilitation program called "Swing Dancing for the Senior Spastic."

A lot of the people on Michigan Avenue moved like Grandpa's friends at the convalescent home. Many of them had been mutilated. Hadley saw one man with half a face fighting to drag a little old lady through a locked revolving door. When he couldn't get her through the door, the half-faced man sat on the old lady's chest and banged her head against the sidewalk until she stopped kicking.

But some of the attackers acted like normal people. The camera tracked one woman, a redhead wearing a black blazer, skirt, and white sneakers. A smallish man wearing a pink suit ran toward the redhead, with five stroke victims in hot pursuit. As Pink Suit passed the redhead, she stuck out her right foot and tripped him.

The five strokers fell upon the pink-suited man. But as the redhead approached, the attackers pulled back. One of them was chewing the pink-suited man's toupee.

The redhead dragged Pink Suit into an abandoned taxi and slammed the door. The taxi began to rock violently on its wheels. One of Pink Suit's hands clutched the steering wheel and jerked it, hard, to the right. A second later, a jet of blood splattered the front windshield.

The seven people in the Stop-n-Drop stared at the screen. Then Ruby Ling vomited all over the Dirty Harry jukebox. Mendoza thumbed the channel scan button on the remote.

"—movable slaughterhouse—"

Click.

"—people being devoured in broad daylight—"

Click.

"—shit, shit, shitting shit!"

Click.

"—walking corpses, although at this time that has not been confirmed."

"Freeze it," Hadley snapped.

"What's happening?" Friedrich whispered.

Hadley stared at the television, her heart thumping a heavy backbeat through her veins.

Because she knew what was happening.

Just like she knew what was going to happen next.

Mendoza increased the volume.

"If you're just joining us—Terror in the streets. America is under attack by what can only be described as a ravaging army of cannibal terrorists."

"Saint Theresa," Emmet whispered.

"—reports are flooding in claiming that these canni-bals are the recently dead, returned to life. But those reports are being dismissed by authorities."

"*Rabies*," Clovis snorted.

"Quiet, Butch," Emmet snapped.

"—earlier today, the president was airlifted to an undisclosed location following an attack at a corporate fund-raiser in Houston. He was unavailable for com-ment. I repeat, this nation is under attack by an army—"

As the people in the Stop-n-Drop began to shout, Hadley walked over to the big picture window that faced the empty highway and looked out over the flat suburban landscape.

To the north, Chicago beckoned like a waiting wan-ton, her famous skyline visible even from Valhalla, thirty-five miles to the south. Hadley's eyes wandered over the landscaped greenery that extended into the horizon on every side: a verdant circle punctuated by little dots of white and gray, like the stone teeth of a gargoyle. She shuddered as the cold hand of irony made a fist around her heart.

I always knew this would happen.

Music burning in her head, Hadley spoke quietly. "Everybody shut the fuck up."

Five pairs of eyes swiveled toward her.

"Friedrich," she said. "You and Oscar go get some boards, hammers, and nails, we've gotta cover the win-dows. Clovis, I'm gonna need the sat-telephone out of your rig."

"What the hell for?" Clovis said.

Hadley kept her voice level. *They don't know.*

"The landlines are probably jammed already," she said. "Without a way to communicate, we're ass-slammed."

Ruby Ling wiped her chin and belched softly. Friedrich ogled Hadley as if she'd just sprouted wings.

"What's the Tragic Mulatto goin' on about?" Swanson said.

"Mr. Swanson, you'd better go get your people and bring them over here," Hadley said. "There's way too many windows in your store. Your employees are sitting ducks."

"Now, wait one goddamn minute," Swanson said. "What makes you think the police can't handle this thing? They've probably got it under control already."

"Gee, you think?" Hadley snapped.

"Yes, I think," Swanson shot back. "Hell, this whole thing is probably some kind of publicity stunt. They said it started in a TV studio, for Christ's sake. There's no reason for us to fly off the handle here."

The scream from the kitchen stopped the argument.

"What the hell—" Mendoza said. "Eduardo?"

Mendoza went into the kitchen. "Eduardo, *que paso?*"

Hadley and the others went through the double doors.

The back door to the restaurant was wide open.

"Eduardo?" Mendoza said.

Eduardo screamed again: *"Dios mio, ayuda me!"*

"Parking lot," Emmet hissed.

Outside, Eduardo Corona, one of the busboys, was fighting with two dead men. One of the strokers, a black man with his hair in cornrows and a butcher knife stuck in his throat, grabbed Eduardo from behind. The other corpse, a bone-thin white man with a purple Mohawk, grabbed Eduardo's right hand and crammed it into his mouth. Eduardo shrieked. Then the black stroker bit him on the back of the neck.

Eduardo's sneakers drummed on the cement like a man dancing on an electrified cattle grate, and his fingers came away in Mohawk's mouth.

Ruby Ling screamed, "They're killing him!"

But they were too late. As they watched, Mohawk darted in and bit off Eduardo's nose. A second later, Butcher-knife tore the busboy's throat out. Mendoza cursed and ran back into the Stop-n-Drop.

"My God," Clovis said. "Look."

Across the parking lot, a man was staring into the morning sun.

"Hey," Swanson said. "Hey, that's Pete Garrison!"

The sun gazer's head turned toward them.

"Jesus Lord in heaven," Emmet said.

The sun gazer held out his arms and staggered toward the four humans.

"It's ol' Pete Garrison," Swanson drawled. "He owns the Dippin' Donuts over at the mall."

Hadley stared. Garrison's eyes gleamed with a thick, white glaze. His hair stuck up in wet, brown cowlicks all over his head. His lower jaw worked soundlessly, as if he were trying to chew something too big for his mouth. A tatty green bathrobe hung off Garrison's shoulders. It flapped open on the right side, revealing a sagging belly and a nest of gray pubic hair. The left side was plastered to his body by a swath of dried blood that extended from his upper torso to his outer thigh.

"Hey, Pete," Swanson said. "Time to make the donuts?"

Swanson laughed. Garrison lurched.

"Pete, it's me, Joe Swanson."

"He's dead," Hadley said.

"That man is not dead," Swanson snarled. "He's president of the PTA, for Christ's sake."

Over by the Dumpster, Eduardo's prayers had faded to a litany of startled gasps, snatched between the strokers' bites.

"I don't know, Joe," Emmet said. "He looks dead to me."

"Next person uses the D word is gonna get knocked on his keester," Swanson said. "In case you geniuses hadn't noticed, he can't be dead . . . *because he's walking around.*"

"He's walking around butt naked," Emmet mumbled.

Swanson scowled and turned as Garrison reached him.

"Listen, Pete," he began. "Tell these idiots you're as right as rain."

Garrison grabbed Swanson, pulled him close, and bit a hunk out of his right cheek.

"Jesus God!" Swanson cried. He fell to his knees, his face spouting red.

Mohawk spat out Eduardo's knucklebones and stood. At the same time, Mendoza flew out of the back door wearing his motorcycle jacket, clutching a meat cleaver in one hand and Deke's Mac-10 semiautomatic in the other.

As Garrison bent over to paw at Swanson, Mendoza reversed his grip on the assault rifle, swung it once around his head, and caught Garrison across the bridge of his nose.

Crrrraack.

Momentum lifted Garrison off his feet. He hit the cement and lay still.

Mendoza spun as Mohawk and Butcher-knife reached for him, swung the meat cleaver, and buried it in Butcher-knife's chest. The black corpse staggered backward five steps and sat down on its rump. Meanwhile, Mohawk grabbed Mendoza by the hair net.

"Help me, you assholes!" Mendoza snarled.

He leaned forward and flipped Mohawk over his shoulder. The stroker hit the asphalt, twisted, grabbed Mendoza by the collar, and dragged him down on top of him.

Mendoza dropped the shotgun.

Hadley moved without thinking.

She ran for the cleaver.

As the black corpse stood, Hadley grasped the handle of the meat cleaver and pulled. At the same time, she kicked out with her right foot and shoved Butcher-knife backward.

The stroker stumbled and tripped over its own feet.

Mohawk was busy trying to bite Mendoza's arm, but having difficulty chewing through the thick leather of his motorcycle jacket. Hadley swung the meat cleaver over her head and split Mohawk's skull clean down the middle. The meat cleaver sank in up to the hilt. The skinny corpse shuddered and fell.

Hadley was vaguely aware that Ruby Ling was screaming her name, but the music pounding through her veins muffled any other sound.

Ain't no mountain high enough, she thought.

A million miles away, something exploded. Ruby Ling screamed again. Then Hadley was grabbed from behind. She whirled and looked into the face of Pete Garrison.

As Garrison clutched at her, the left side of his bathrobe fell away. Hadley stared at the foot-long trench of gnawed meat that gaped up at her from Garrison's torso. His penis had been chewed to a raw nub of veins and skin.

Garrison opened his mouth.

"Eat this, shit bag."

A second later, there was another explosion and Garrison's face blew off. It flew over Hadley's right shoulder, sailed across the parking lot like one of those floppy Frisbees you could get for your Golden retriever, and stuck to the front window of the Payless Shoe Store.

Garrison dropped.

Clovis was standing there, her brown hands clutching the dual pistol grips of the smoking shotgun. She spat on the asphalt. Then she kicked Garrison in the nuts. "I'm a Krispy Kreme girl m'self."

"I love two things in this world," Hadley said, later.

"One of them is singing American R-and-B classics, preferably from the Motown catalogue, circa 1964 to 1979."

Hadley spoke slowly. She wanted to make sure they all understood what she was going to tell them next.

"The other thing I love—is zombie movies."

"Zombies?" Emmet said.

Hadley nodded. "Romero was the first, the prophet of the postmodern Living Dead genre. But there've been many others. I've seen them all. Trust me, people, we have a very bad situation on our hands."

They'd nailed up everything they could find over the front and side windows: three doors, two of the old wooden tables left over from before the last renovation, and the polished wood sides of the jukebox.

Mendoza was busily breaking down some wooden milk crates he'd scrounged out of the Dumpster where they'd stashed Eduardo's body.

"It's not going to be enough," Hadley said.

Mendoza looked at the front windows and nodded. "I'm gonna find some more wood."

Swanson sat alone in one of the booths with his face to the wall, a cold compress pressed to his torn right cheek. Seeing Pete Garrison shot had taken something out of the normally rambunctious used car salesman.

But Hadley was worried about that bite.

She'd seen enough to know what happened to the victims of a zombie bite. So far, the phenomenon had behaved exactly as Romero had predicted, save for one critical point: Garrison was the only corpse from the parking lot attack who'd shuffled along in classic movie zombie fashion. Hadley was pretty sure she could outrun any stroker that moved like the ones from the Romero films.

But the black corpse with the butcher knife neckware had displayed only slightly less coordination than a normal human. And Hadley remembered the eerie speed with which the skinny corpse had attacked Mendoza.

It was so fast, she thought. *Faster than Mendoza.*

She'd heard the busboys telling stories about Mendoza's boxing days back in Mexico. He'd even fought professionally before his right lung collapsed during an exhibition bout.

What if all the others are like them? Hadley thought.

"We've got to get out of here," she said.

"Bullshit," Emmet drawled. "I got one good leg, girl. You expect me to run all over creation from those freaks?"

"He's right," Swanson said. He stood and stepped out of the booth. "Why not wait here until the police show up?"

"Phone lines are *down*, man," Clovis said. "My sat-phone's clogged with so much traffic I can't copy what anybody's sayin'."

"Riiight," Swanson said. "Bet you'd like to keep us locked up in here, right, Butch? That way, you can paw all over the Tragic Mulatto whenever you want."

"What the hell are you babblin' about?" Clovis said.

Swanson stalked around the counter toward Clovis.

"Oh, I've *seen* you," he said. "Checking her out when you think no one's looking. You're hot for her box. Aren't ya?"

Hadley sensed something ugly crackling through the air. A crazy fire was burning in Swanson's eyes. His face bristled with reddish purple splotches and his eyes bulged from their sockets like soft-boiled eggs being squeezed out of a hen's backside. Hadley gripped the cleaver even tighter.

"Hey—" she began.

"Swanson," Clovis interrupted. "That freak must have bitten you up your ass, 'cause that's obviously where you keep your brains."

Swanson's eyes bulged even more. A thick purple vein popped out in his right temple as he spoke through clenched teeth. "You dirty—black—*dyke*."

Clovis stood up.

"Bring it on, Condoleeza," Swanson crowed. "I'll show you what a real man's good for!"

"Listen," Friedrich cried, pointing at the television. "Everybody, listen!"

"—confirmed reports that the bodies of the recently dead are returning to life only to attack the living. This phenomenon is being reported in cities all over the world, and where the dead walk, murder and cannibalism soon follow. CBN News is warning everyone able to hear this broadcast—*stay inside*."

"Ahhh," Swanson said.

"—secure all doors and windows, find a safe place to hide with your loved ones. *Do not answer the door for any reason*. Some of the recently dead are masquerading as policemen, door-to-door salesmen, even Jehovah's Witnesses. *Some of these assassins are even able to pass as ordinary human beings*. They are extremely dangerous. We have some disturbing footage to show you now. Parents, we warn you. If children are present these images may prove distasteful."

"See?" Swanson said. "We're s'posed to stay where we are."

"I have to agree, Had," Friedrich said. "I think we're—"

Hadley reached up and turned off the television.

"Hey!" Emmet squawked.

"Has everyone forgotten where we are?" Hadley said. "We're right in the middle of *Valhalla, Illinois*."

"So?" Swanson said.

Hadley bit back the urge to stab him in the neck.

"Mr. Swanson, there are seventeen cemeteries within a two-mile radius of where we're standing."

Emmet stood up as if someone had just goosed him with a cattle prod.

" 'Where the Midwest Comes to Say Good-bye'," he murmured.

"Everyone in Valhalla either works at a cemetery or knows someone who does," Hadley said. "Route 45 runs past six funeral parlors, three hospitals, five retirement communities, and *nine different cemeteries*."

"Industry town," Emmet moaned. "Two thousand families clustered around seventeen boneyards—"

"I see your point," Friedrich said.

Just then, the front window exploded and Deke Simmons staggered into the Stop-n-Drop.

Back when he was "Deacon Simmons," beloved linebacker for the Chicago Bears, Deke had always called himself "one big black son of a bitch," but he also had a heart of gold.

Six weeks earlier, Hadley had wandered into the Stop-n-Drop, needing to make a demo for *American Icon* but hard-up for extra cash. Deke had recognized her: a week earlier she'd sung the National Anthem at Deke Jr.'s Little League baseball game.

"Talent like yours might brighten up this dump, Songbird," Deke had said. And he offered her the cashier's job on the spot.

Someone had smashed Deke's face back into the cavity once occupied by his skull. Now he looked like an ebony Cabbage Patch Doll, his head shaking back and forth, one eye bulging, like a man trying to pass the world's biggest kidney stone.

Deke turned as Mandy McCafferty shuffled in through the broken window. Mandy usually waited tables on the early shift. Now a big black frying pan dangled loosely in her right hand. Hadley saw several glittering yellow objects clinging to the gore clotted along the edge of the pan.

Those are Deke's gold teeth, Hadley thought.

She'd heard the gossip about Deke and Mandy, had caught them loitering around Deke's Winnebago, parked out back, more than once.

Someone had torn big hunks out of Mandy's throat and the sides of her neck. The top half of her yellow "I Tumble For Timberlake" T-shirt was stiff with blood.

From the waist down, Mandy was naked.

Emmet turned and clunked toward the front door. Mandy spun and hurled the frying pan across the counter. The flying skillet struck the back of Emmet's skull and sent him sprawling. Mandy whined and lurched toward Emmet's body.

Deke headed straight for Hadley.

"Deke?" Hadley said. "Deke?"

Mendoza jumped on Deke's back.

Deke spun, his coal-black arms beating at Mendoza's face. Mendoza snarled and jammed a screwdriver into Deke's ear. Deke howled, lifted the fry cook over his head, and hurled him at the side window. Mendoza crashed through the glass. He struck the ground with a loud crack, and lay, unmoving, on the sidewalk.

Deke turned, Mendoza's screwdriver dangling from his right ear. Its yellow handle flopped against his cheek.

"Holy jumping shit," Friedrich said.

Deke swiped at the screwdriver and howled like a dying rottweiler forced to listen to Britney Spears's cover of "Doctor Feelgood."

Over in the corner, Swanson and Ruby Ling were making out against the jukebox. At least, it *looked like* they were making out. Swanson's face was buried in the crook between Ruby Ling's neck and shoulder, while Ruby Ling's hands were entwined in Swanson's hair. Then Swanson pulled away, blood streaming down his chin, and Ruby Ling fell, spurting red violets across the floor.

"Son of a bitch went over and never told anybody!" Hadley screamed.

"Finger—lickin'—*goooood,*" Swanson groaned.

Clovis shot Mandy in the face, blasted her back through the broken window. Then Swanson tackled Friedrich.

"Help me!" Friedrich screamed.

Deke lunged at Hadley, forced her to retreat. Hadley aimed a halfhearted swipe at the ex–NFL star's hand and dodged around him.

Swanson was dragging the struggling Friedrich toward the restroom. Hadley ran toward them, knowing she was too late: Swanson was one of them.

One of the quick ones.

"Clovis!" she screamed.

Clovis was behind the counter rifling through the drawers and shelves. "Where the hell did Deke keep the goddamned ammo?"

Swanson punched his hand through Friedrich's chest, ripped out something red, and stuffed it into his mouth.

Hadley swung the meat cleaver up, intending to sever Swanson's head from his shoulders. But Swanson whirled and backhanded her across the face. Hadley flew across a nearby table, bounced off the vinyl seat of a nearby booth, and slid out of sight. The meat cleaver landed a few feet away.

Two more zombies staggered in through the front window. At the same time, the kitchen door banged open and Eduardo stumbled, noseless and extinct, into the truck stop.

Clovis jumped onto the counter. Eduardo climbed up after her.

"Shit," Clovis hissed.

At the last moment, she spun, ran toward the edge of the counter, and leapt into space, then reached out and grasped the blade of the big overhead ceiling fan. Eduardo grabbed Clovis's leg and bit down on one of her engineer's boots. Clovis kicked him in the face with the other foot and freed herself, using the momentum to swing up and hook her legs over the fan blades.

Clovis hugged the ceiling fan, spinning lazy circles above outstretched zombie hands. Eduardo fell off the end of the counter and hit the floor. Hadley heard bones snap.

"We gotta get to my truck!" Clovis screamed.

Swanson finished whatever he'd snatched out of Friedrich's chest. He turned and glared at Hadley.

"Low—low—prices," he moaned.

"Oh, crap," Hadley yelped.

Swanson got to his feet.

"Move your ass, girl!" Clovis said.

But Hadley was wedged between the booth and the table post. Her right leg was bent backward at an awkward angle, her foot pinned beneath her in a kind of hurdler's stretch. "I'm stuck!"

Having decided to abandon his pursuit of the spinning Clovis, Eduardo dragged himself toward Hadley, his broken leg trailing dejectedly behind him.

Hadley's every move wedged her more tightly between the seat and the post. The other zombies, sensing easier prey, shuffled toward her. Swanson grabbed Hadley's right foot and pulled. Hadley cried out as her legs were pulled apart.

Then Swanson was grabbed from behind and hauled to his feet. Hadley was pulled forward even more, her foot gripped in Swanson's fist, until her back leg straightened out and she slid out from beneath the table.

Deke had Swanson in a choke hold. The salesman fought with a maniac's intensity, biting Deke's forearm, dragging long red runnels into the skin of Deke's neck and face with his fingernails. Deke grabbed Swanson by the scruff of the neck, reared back, and slammed his face into the table—

Bam, bam, bam, bam, bam!

—until Swanson stopped fighting.

Over near the jukebox, Ruby Ling sat up and giggled.

Hadley stood.

Deke turned and glared at the other zombies. They stopped and regarded him with the air of conscientious objectors. In a flash, Hadley understood: Somehow, Deke had become one of the quick ones.

Hadley edged forward, her fingers reaching for the screwdriver sticking out of Deke's ear. Deke backed away.

"Nnooo," he moaned. "Helllpsssss meee."

Hadley nodded, gratitude filling her eyes.

Clovis climbed down off the ceiling fan.

"Songbird," she said. "I hear more of 'em comin'!"

"Moooorrree," Deke hissed. "Lotsss—more."

"We have to go, Deke," Hadley said.

Deke nodded slowly. Then he opened his mouth. Hadley tensed, ready to bolt.

"Siinnng."

Over by the front door, Emmet got to his feet, the back of his head leaking, and turned toward Clovis. Deke lifted a hand. Emmet whined, and stood still.

"Sinng," Deke said.

Hadley nodded. At first her voice was barely audible over the moaning of the walking corpses. But slowly, the song gathered strength. Hadley sensed that hers was the last song these dead would ever hear, and the knowledge lent her a kind of strength she'd never consciously possessed.

More and more strokers were stumbling into the truck stop. Hadley lifted her voice and sent the song out over the heads of her audience until it echoed up and down Route 45.

When she was done, Deke nodded. "Sonnngbirrrrd."

There were nearly fifty dead people milling behind him.

"*Hadley,*" Clovis said.

Deke faced the strokers who blocked the front window. The corpses shuffled and parted. Hadley and Clovis walked quickly through a gantlet of the whining dead.

Hadley climbed up into the cab of Clovis's eighteen-wheeler. Behind her, Deke stood in the window shaking his head like a man trying to dislodge a trapped mosquito. The yellow screwdriver bounced against his shoulder.

In the northern distance, black towers of smoke rose into the afternoon sky: Chicago was burning.

"Three million dreams," Hadley whispered.

"What?" Clovis said.

"Nothing," Hadley replied. "Better head south."

Clovis nodded. "Long as you keep singin'."

They thundered out onto the highway.

As they passed, the dead paused. But a terrible hunger tugged most of them toward the burning in the north, and they walked on.

But some of them cocked their heads to mark the passing of a newborn star.

Nurse's Requiem

Maurice Broaddus

"Is not wisdom found among the aged? Does not long life bring understanding?"

—Job 12:12

Daniel nearly vomited the first time he rolled the old lady from her sloshy pool of excrement. His arm buckled, almost dropping her, but Jake supported her with his free arm. With a few tugs on the incontinence pad, Jake pulled the stained one free while rolling a fresh pad under her. Daniel became all too aware of the odor that assaulted his nostrils. Feces still covered her matted, gray pubic hair. He tried to be gentle when he wiped her clean, but she still groaned at his efforts.

"Can you hand me a new gown?" Jake asked.

"This has seen better days," Daniel said with a gallows chuckle, holding the soiled gown as if it threatened to rear up and bite him. His friends often wondered what made him choose to work in a retirement home, the Devil's playground. He grew up in a close-knit Bible-believing church that bordered on religious fundamentalism. So when the demons revealed them-

selves in order to openly live among mankind, he recognized it as a change in Satan's tactics and rejoiced.

The end days were upon them.

In the meantime, he had to be about the Lord's work.
Daniel always had a heart for the elderly; recalling his
lessons that whoever mistreats the least of these, wid-
ows and orphans, mistreats Him. However, the Regional Healthcare Center, home of the damned, was a
repository of the best forgotten. Daniel had three nights
of orientation for being a certified nurse's aide, which
meant that he had to be paired with someone. Tonight,
he toured with Jake. Jake was "high yella," Daniel's
mother would've said. He had a large forehead, exag-
gerated by his receding hairline, quite visible despite
his shaved head. And he had a slim, though muscular,
build.

"Thank God you a dude," Jake said.

"I'm pretty grateful." Daniel didn't want to jump to
any conclusions. All of those Hollywood types and
rappers thanked God. God didn't seem to really matter
to them; like *God bless you*, it was something to say.

"Nah, I mean it. The rest of the staff is women."

"Kind of what I expected, you know, being a nurse's
aide and all. Is that so bad?"

"You ever listen to a roomful of women cackle?
Plus, I'm still with my baby's mama, so it's not like I'm
looking."

They peeked in the next room. A rather obese man
breathed with a wheezing snore. A teddy bear rested
next to him.

"That's Mr. Reams. If he's asleep, let him sleep,"
Jake said.

"But shouldn't we check to see if he's wet?" Daniel
asked.

"How long have you been an aide?"

"Tonight is my first night of clinicals. After ten days, I can take my CNA test."

"Yeah, you sound like you just got out of those state board classes." Jake sighed. "He got a catheter due to his . . . condition. No legs and shit. So if Mr. Reams is asleep, let him sleep. Same with his roommate, Mr. Black. Let them sleep, or they stay up all night bugging the shit out of you."

Daniel followed him back to the lounge area and plopped down next to Jake, not noticing the man on the other side.

Jake leaned forward to say, "Hey, Mr. Black."

"Hurm," a razor-sharp, yet gravel-filled sound replied. "You gotta cigarette?"

"It's too early for cigarettes, Mr. Black."

"Baby, you gotta cigarette?" Mr. Black said to Sh'ron, another CNA, who sat across from them, wrapped in a blanket.

"Baby, you gotta cigarette?" Jake mimicked, silencing him. Daniel felt a pair of eyes on his back. Mr. Black. He kept studying him when he thought Daniel wasn't looking. Whenever Daniel turned back to him, Mr. Black looked away. Not that Daniel stared at him too long; there was an ugliness to his yellowed, bloodshot eyes and wrinkled, flabby jowls, like a fat man who had lost his fat and was left with extra skin.

"No one told me we had such a good-looking man up in here." Sh'ron's voice had an annoying nasal rasp; a beautiful picture spoiled by talking. Her deer-brown eyes studied him like he was the last rib at a barbecue. A mole accented her left cheek in an intriguing way; bright red lipstick anointed her full sensual lips.

"Thanks," Daniel said.

"You in church?"

"Yeah."

"I could tell. I bet you in pretty deep, huh? Guess you off-limits."

He smiled, both embarrassed and flattered. Mr. Black shifted noisily.

"C'mon, man, let's go get a Coke or something. Anyone else need anything?" Jake stood. Muffled half grunts and shrugged shoulders were their only response. In the silence that accompanied the slow elevator ride, Daniel noticed the tattoo on Jake's forearm: a heart, with wings on either side of it, with a pair of horns on top and a tail extending from its tip. Twin pitchforks crossed in the background. Three letters inscribed the heart: *B G D*.

"Black Gangsta Disciples," Jake said.

"Huh?" Daniel felt stupid, as if caught peeping in his sister's window.

"Yeah. Black Gangsta Disciples. I used to run wild in the streets. You know how we do, deal a little. But I'm through now, walking a different path."

The elevator spat them out at the lobby entrance. A statue of Mary greeted them. Her fingertips were broken and cracked, another neglected mother. Bits of wire peeked through her worn hands. Her hollow and dead eyes held Daniel's gaze for a moment. He could see how a fallen Mary might amuse the guests. A nurse cleared her throat, looming over them with a toxic glare of instant dislike, like a cat tossed amid a pack of hyenas.

"I see that no one's told you the rules." She pointed to the silver cross dangling from Daniel's neck. "Those may agitate the residents."

"That kind of goes against my First Amendment rights."

Jake rolled his eyes.

"That's why we usually don't take your kind," the nurse said.

"What kind is that?" Daniel asked.

"You have the stench of a Jesus freak about you."

"Don't mind her, she's all right," Jake said once they were out of earshot. "She's a little uptight, but a good nurse."

Daniel didn't pay her any mind. She was the least of his concerns. Here, surrounded by the sick and the possessed, he would be tested. It was one thing to have faith in the unseen spiritual; it was quite another thing to know, to confront the reality of belief. The opposite of faith was certainty.

"How do you like it so far?" Jake warmed up a burrito.

"It's different. A lot of people to remember."

"Don't worry about it. This place works short every shift. Never enough people because they don't wanna pay shit. State would shut this place down in a second if they knew how this place was run." The microwave's ding interrupted his thought. "Gotta have a balanced meal."

"This is all the balanced meal I can keep down." Daniel raised his Coke can.

"Daddy, Daddy! No, Daddy, please, don't make me," Ms. Mayfield, a wisp of a woman, cried out. Coarse black hairs sprouted from her chin. She reminded Daniel of his mother, in a way, what his mother might become. His mother, too, had been diagnosed with Alzheimer's. At some point she'd stop being that little girl who trusted Jesus. She'd have lost her mind, no longer there in any real way, simply a body.

Ripe for *them*.

Daniel lived with the constant fear. The possibility that he would grow old and forget who he was and what he believed. He knew the Devil was real. Daniel always thought it curious that Jesus was always casting out demons, and yet these days doctors were quick to diagnose people as mentally ill. Then demons appeared in their midst, telling them what their doctors were too smart to see. Only the sadness of the situation kept Daniel from making any "I told you so" pronouncements.

Ms. Mayfield winced in pain, then touched her forehead. A calmness overtook her face. She reached for him with one of her wrinkled, skeletal hands, startling him with both her suddenness and her strength. She pulled him close. Images of her withered desires sent him reeling back. However, she chanted something in what sounded like a mix of Latin, a north European dialect, and gibberish. Yet her tones were cautious, almost concerned. Her eyes virtually shone with clarity. As quickly as it started, her "lucid" outburst ended and she fell back, exhausted.

The odor was utterly appalling, so he removed her sweat-and-urine-soaked gown. Her age-laden breasts fell flat against her chest. He found himself unable to look away, at once revolted and drawn to the sight of her full, wrinkled nakedness. Daniel mulled over her wardrobe selection, settling on a pink, flowery housedress suitable for milling about with the other residents.

She curled into the fetal position, almost pleading to be let back into some unseen womb, murmuring to herself. On her nightstand was a photo album. Curiosity got the better of him and he flipped it open. Pictures of crows from magazines had been placed like scrapbook photos.

"We're all crows. My children and I. All crows," she said with a burst.

He pushed her wheelchair to join the elderly gathering in the television cul-de-sac, like the set of a geriatric sequel to a zombie movie.

"You come in tomorrow?" Jake asked.

"They have me scheduled to work Monday through Friday this week and next week. They want my clinicals to be over with quick so they can transfer me to Southside."

"Yeah, but you coming back?"

A nostalgic wave of melancholy washed over him, unbidden, with memories of Aaron. The two of them grew up in the church together, best friends since they graduated into the church youth group. Daniel's friendship with Aaron revolved around the two of them being bad influences on each other. Aaron, ever the pastor's kid, enjoyed slumming with Daniel, mostly because hanging with him annoyed his parents. For his part, Daniel enjoyed the cool status reflected onto him by Aaron's presence. Aaron was the envy of all the kids: the pastor's son, tall and athletic, blond curly locks, handsome with a clever wit about him. Daniel's parents insisted that he go to church even if they didn't. He had been unnoticed by the other kids and knew only the distracted attentions of his Sunday school teachers. Somehow it came up that his father drank and smoked, two of the bigger sins in their little corner of church, and Daniel noted the sudden interest stirred in others about him. On occasion, he raided his father's cache of alcohol, and he and Aaron whiled away long evenings talking about girls and life. That was about as wild as they ever got, but in their circles it was wild enough.

Life had a way of falling into place for Aaron. He married his high school sweetheart right after graduation and had a beautiful son. Then one day, they were about to go to "Friends and Family" day at the church. They were in a hurry as they usually were (it wouldn't look good for the pastor's son not to be there early). He was going to pull the minivan around front to meet her. She'd left the baby unattended for only a minute, not realizing it lay in Aaron's blind spot.

He never saw the baby carrier.

The accident shattered them. Oh, the couple said all the right things about God's will, about all things working for good. They were allowed to grieve, but even Daniel felt the pressure for them to put it behind them, to move on, to never question or doubt. It was as if everyone was afraid that real grief—real faith-shattering tragedy—might expose the house of dogmatic cards that they called faith for what it was: a series of failed homilies that they depended on to guide them, rules without love or anything real to offer.

Watching everyone walk around with plastic, "everything's for God's glory" smiles left Aaron stumbling after his faith. He confessed to Daniel (begging him for faith, it seemed, looking to him to restore the shattered remnants of belief), asking what he'd do when he woke up screaming in the night from the silence of his unanswered prayers.

That was the night before Aaron shot himself.

"Lord, I believe. Help me with my unbelief," Daniel whispered. A call button from one of the empty rooms was jammed—and with maintenance not due in until morning, the signaling bleat snapped him from his revelry. The incessant drone stabbed Daniel through the front of his skull, fraying his nerves. He filled out ADLs, Activities of Daily Living, which on the third shift meant logging what time he turned each resident. The splatter of dribbling water drew his attention. At first, he wondered who'd left the sink running, until he noted how close the sink sounded and that the water smelled like piss. Mr. Reams, with his subdued wheeze, slept through his bladder release. Daniel hadn't realized how young Mr. Reams was, at least compared to the others. Daniel found out Mr. Reams had lost his legs in Vietnam. He came home from the war and got into a fight with someone who shot him point-blank with a shotgun. The wound left his side horribly scarred and him barely able to see; he had to force his eyelids apart to detect any image. Still asleep, he cuddled his bear tighter.

"Him and that damn bear," Sh'ron said.

"You ever hear him when you put him to bed?" Jake said to Daniel, who shook his head. "'Cover the bear. It's the type of woman I like. Don't want shit, don't ask for shit.'"

Daniel grew a little uncomfortable with the conversation since he feared where it might lead. Spying Mr. Black creeping out of Ms. Mayfield's room provided the perfect reason to excuse himself from the conversation. Mr. Black liked to pretend he was a CNA, except that he deposited an article of clothing at each stop. He was down to a T-shirt and his boxers.

"Why don't you go watch TV, Mr. Black?" Daniel asked.

"Hurm. I wouldn't enjoy that."

"Sometimes I wonder if you are doing this on purpose."

"No, I'm not doing this on purpose." He took off his boxers.

"Come on, Mr. Black. I don't have time for this."

"Why are you here, then, surrounded by old folks?" Mr. Black asked with a rising sharpness to his voice.

"Morbid curiosity." The words spat out more sharply than Daniel intended.

"Tell yourself that if you want." Mr. Black's eyes alit with dark perspicuity. "You live in a world of the weak and the wounded. Being here lets you feel superior to your fellow believers."

It dawned on Daniel how difficult it was to tell the demon-possessed from the mentally addled. He thought he had Mr. Black—still standing naked from the waist down, a collection of wrinkled flesh—pegged as merely senile.

"I'm not afraid of you. My soul is safe," Daniel said, comfortable in such tiny leaps of faith.

"Your soul? Hurm. Your soul is barely worth a dollar to me. What am I going to do with it? I can't compete with the magic of being saved. Take comfort in your manipulator, accepting Jesus every time you doubt or feel doomed, while finding yourself alone after every prayer. I prefer the certainty of clean sheets and three meals."

With that, Mr. Black shambled down the hall.

* * *

"Who's there?" Mr. Reams growled. He sat up, his stubby fingers on either side of his eye, stretching it open. It darted about like a scavenging rat, bloodshot with a cloud pooling over it.

"It's me, Mr. Reams," Sh'ron said.

"Who's that with you?"

"He's only been here a few days. Can we do anything for you?"

"Just empty my urinal," he snarled. It came out *"Emy mah urnal."*

Mr. Reams rolled away from them. Huge swatches of bandages covered his backside, shielding the pink raw flesh, a succulent sponge oozing blood from its center. Decubitus ulcers were fairly common; though caught early, the bedsore had fingernail marks around the wound.

As they walked back to the lounge, Daniel could feel the mental pull of the place weighting him down. He hoped to lose himself in some reading. Forget the despair, the subtle groaning of the soul, the environment that gnawed with teeth of confusion, apathy, doubt, futility . . . the gamut of nightmares that were his activities of daily living. He recognized the handiwork of the Devil when he saw it. He knew Satan's many voices when they spoke: Mr. Black, his mother, his own. The voices that spoke of the cracked and fragile thing that he called faith as being little more than a trick of the weak mind. Though raised in the church, Daniel had never quite made the faith his own. It was more like other people's expectations of it in him. Still, it was easy to put on the show; the show was reflex ingrained in him, and that was all anyone looked for. If you parroted the right answers, you were in. And you learned not to ask the tough questions, or your soul was in danger of damnation. Questions like why a good God would allow any of His people to be flesh puppets for the fallen. This place, Daniel believed, was a test. Once and for all his doubts would be put to rest; unquenchable fires purifying the quality of his faith.

His doubts scared him the most, plaguing him most whenever he thought of Aaron.

"How's Aaron?"

"What'd you say?" Jarred from his thoughts, Daniel felt like a man in the throes of a nightmare startled to full wakefulness. It took a moment for his eyes to focus, for him to recognize Jake.

"I asked, 'What're you reading?'" Jake stared at him with mild concern. "Your test is coming up soon."

"A book on unseen spirits. You know, angels and demons, that sort of thing."

"Why?"

"Jesus was always running around dealing with demons."

"And look where it got him." Jake's fingers danced with antsy frustration along the end table's edge.

"We only fear the spirit world because we don't understand how it works. That's why I've been studying. Haven't you ever wondered how demon possession works?"

"Sometimes, I guess."

"All right, check this out. Say you're driving in your car minding your own business. Pretend that your car is your body and you, the driver, are the soul. Possession is like being carjacked." Daniel paused to let the lesson sink in. The weight of his book shifted from hand to sweaty hand.

"Carjacked. I like that."

A balding woman wheeled herself down the hall, inching along by her foot pulling her, an eerie, determined intelligence in her eyes. She slumped forward in her wheelchair. Concerned, Daniel rushed to kneel alongside her. She bolted upright in her chair, glared through him, and let loose a barrage of expletives and ravings that caught him so off guard that he fell over.

"I don't think I'll ever get used to them. They're so . . ."

"Real?" Jake offered.

"You know, my girlfriend used to have to drive by a cemetery on the way home from school. Then one day, the city put up a stop sign right in front of the cemetery. A friend told her that one time, when he stopped at the stop sign, he looked into the cemetery and saw a ghost coming toward him. My girlfriend laughed this off, so I asked her, 'Do you believe in ghosts?' She said, 'No,' so I asked, 'Have you ever looked into the cemetery since then?' She said, 'No, if I looked, I may see a ghost, and then I'd have to believe in them.' "

"I still don't get what would make demons possess a bunch of old folk." Jake laid down the remote, only to pick up a cigarette. The smoke curled up around him. A defiant gleam in Jake's eyes seemed to dare Daniel to come up with something even close to rational.

"It's the deal we made. It wasn't easy coming to a detente that would allow us to . . . accommodate demons. They need a home in a host body to give them rest and allow them to express themselves in the physical world. Remember, they're spirits. Wandering about is like hanging out in a desert. I remember a story in the Bible about a demon called Legion."

"'For we are many.'" Jake tamped his cigarette into a cracked, black ashtray. Something about his casual sureness gave Daniel pause.

"Right. He and Jesus crossed paths and Legion asked if Jesus was there to torment him . . . them before the appointed time. Jesus said no, but he was going to cast them out from the man the demon had possessed. Legion begged to be put into a herd of pigs, so he was. The same principle's at work here. To be frank, senile people have little left of their minds to offer much resistance. For all we know, they may suffer from a preexisting mental or spiritual problem that the demons merely took advantage of."

"That's where I have a problem. You can't tell me that all of these crazy old people are demon possessed. Some of them are just sick or old. Look here."

He grabbed a few of the patients' charts from the nurse's station. Some patients were brought in for Alzheimer's, some had become noncommunicative, some physically abusive. Senile dementia, hallucinations, simple schizophrenia, history of seizures—theirs were a veritable laundry list of sundry ailments.

"Not every case is possession, but it's possible that some of the diagnoses of mental disorder could be," Daniel said.

"So what would you do?"

"That's easy. The Bible kept it simple. All we'd have to do to exorcize the demon is—"

"We? Oh no, my brotha, you been misinformed. *We* ain't doing shit. Ain't no way I'm about to go up against no pea-soup-spitting, head-spinning motha-fucka."

It amused Daniel to see Jake slip from his professional persona when he got worked up. Somehow it reassured him, like they were connecting on a personal level. Daniel pressed on. "C'mon, Jake, we have to do something."

"There's that 'we' again. Call me funny, but if a bunch of demons ain't bothering me, there ain't no need for me to be bothering them. If all I have to do is wipe they ass and get them a drink every now and then, I'm Mr. Status Quo."

"It's kind of our responsibility . . . as nurses' aides. You see, once the demons have found a home, they act like anyone else and hang on for dear life. Unfortunately, they also torment their victims and try to kill them."

"That sound you hear is my bullshit detector going off. Is this why you wanted to work here?"

"What would it take for me to talk you into this?"

"You don't have enough words. Shit, English don't have enough words."

"Even if you saw . . ."

"Even if I saw what?"

(*"How's Aaron?"*) The floor alarm cut off whatever reply he might have had. Only a resident wandering through a restricted exit could have triggered it. Ms. Mayfield stood before them, more horrible given the humor of her filthy appearance. She had covered her gown in her most recent bowel disgorgement, but she paraded about like she was the height of fashion. Having bathed in a bed of her own ordure, she was a sour bouquet of sweat and excrement.

"Where you going, Ms. Mayfield?" Daniel asked.

"I wanted to be where everything was happening."

"You know I'd come get you if anything happened."

"By the time you get me, everything will be over last year. It's cold in here."

"Go lie down, then, sweetie," Daniel said.

"I can't. It's thundering something fierce."

"When it thunders, the angels are rolling out the rain barrels, and when it rains, one of them done dropped a barrel or two and bust it."

"What do devils do?" she asked.

Daniel chuckled.

"You're different from the others here. What do you do when God's promises fail you?"

"They won't," Daniel said. "I know . . ."

"You *know* very little. We know. Black was right about you, you wear your story like a poorly chosen hairstyle. You grew up in church parroting your parents' faith. You'd done it for so long, dressed it up in clothes of youth group and mission trips that everyone thought it was the genuine thing. Even you. Except on those dark nights when you fear that you have nothing to call your own. Thus, no matter how often you fall on your knees, you lie in bed terrified that you'll be left behind. Don't tell me what you know. I've been *there*. Sang with the hosts. Seen Him. There's no room for faith here."

No one understood. He barely understood. These creatures were an offense before God. The idea of Jesus' miracles terrified him. They weren't miraculous, they were unnatural. He'd grown up sympathizing with Doubting Thomas. When Jesus returned from the dead (returned from the dead!), even then some didn't recognize him; as if their minds refused to accept it. The horror, the abomination. Thomas said he wouldn't believe until he saw the Christ's wounds for himself. So he stood there, tracing the open gash along Jesus' side, his fingers feeling the torn flesh, still struggling to believe.

Like Thomas, Daniel feared that even had he put his fingers through the pierced flesh of Jesus' hands, he still wouldn't believe. Better to submit to the authority of his church elders, those who better understood such things, and trust in them. It was somehow easier to trust in principles, their clear (and safe) black-and-white tones. The demons, their presence, their reality threatened to unravel it all, to color his world in faded-blood shades of sepia.

The windows of the sullen yet formidable building stared at him with a stern blankness. Daniel listened to Mahalia Jackson finish her dirgelike rendition of "In the Upper Room," keenly aware that his shift had started ten minutes ago. He'd been working at the Regional Healthcare Facility for under a month.

A chill wind rocked the car.

(*"How's Aaron?"*)

With Mahalia's last note, Daniel walked duty-bound to the front door, scourged by the biting fall wind. The mournful quality of the dingy, amber-colored walls increased his anxiety. Holiday decorations, reminiscent of the ones his fifth-grade teacher used to do, hung in feigned cheerfulness.

The first-floor nurse's station stood abandoned.

The elevator door waited, its doors agape with expectation. The car rose with a tenuous tremble, as if old, insecure muscles strained to pull it up. He stood near the back, part of him bracing for the impact sure to come when the cables snapped. The elevator stopped a foot shy of the third floor out of spite. The stale, fetid air of looming death greeted him.

He felt a singular sense of disquiet. Two aides had already quit that day, one leaving a note that read "I will never be back again in life." The smell wafting about the halls was particularly stomach-turning, probably due to the addition of his own anxious sweat. He focused on his enemy to keep his nausea from overflowing. Jake whispered into the phone at the nurse's station; the frustrated look on his face screamed that his baby's mother must've been needling him about his responsibilities. A horrible howl came from the room Sh'ron exited from.

"Mr. Black was going through some of the barrels looking for a shirt," Sh'ron started. Neither he nor Jake even glanced up, but she continued anyway. "I'm thinking about tying him down, before he goes through everything and makes a mess."

Daniel wished that the state would do an inspection tonight: Regional would be shut down for sure. He realized that only he, Jake, and Sh'ron were on as aides. That would be great except that they were it for all three floors. The lone nurse in the building spent her evening running back and forth among the floors. Her standing orders were that if the residents gave them any problems, tie them in restraints. State regs be damned, Daniel guessed, when they worked this short.

Sh'ron had a broader definition of residents giving her problems: All the residents in her hall were tied down. They would probably stay that way, unturned and unchecked, until it was time to wake and dress them. Daniel wasn't up for idle chatter tonight, though.

Behind the nurse's station, his right knee danced up and down with its own nervous energy.

"Is it me, or do the residents seem extra agitated?" Jake asked.

"It's him." Sh'ron thumbed toward Daniel.

Daniel's doubts picked at him like an unhealed scab, needling him with the Devil's voice. How long could he tread water believing, not believing, as he did? He wanted to surrender to the doubt, let the insecurities rush over him like a quick slice across his wrist and give in to the gentle caress of the abyss. He needed the church, the danger of community, to feel real. Yet he knew he was cut off. Something within no longer worked, connected, leaving nothing in him for belief to latch on to. No love to fill those empty spaces, those cancers of his faith.

"I'm going to go pray over Ms. Mayfield," Daniel said.

"No, Daniel, wait." Jake grabbed his arm.

"Look, all I'm going to do is pray for the demons to leave in the name of Jesus Christ. If it works, fine. If not, all I've done is pray."

He would have his answer: Would God's might truly protect him?

Daniel crept into her room. The last sharp stabs of light from the hallway faded with the door closing behind him. The parking lot lights spilled through the curtains. Daniel noticed a few facedown picture frames along her dresser. He flipped them over to see that every picture of Ms. Mayfield, even photos that caught only a thatch of hair or a passing elbow, had been circled. Probably done during her last lucid moment to remind herself that she wasn't forgotten.

"Who's there?" she stirred.

"It's me, Ms. Mayfield."

"I keep hearing voices in my head."

"Have you ever prayed against the voices?" he asked. She flinched as if in pain. "I mean, have you ever thought about talking to Jesus about your . . . problems?" She continued to grow uncomfortable, writhing slightly, and quietly wincing.

"I don't want to pray. I don't like it," she muttered.

"That's okay, you don't have to."

He laid his hands on her and prayed. Trying to sound stern, yet compassionate, he exhorted the demons to leave in the name of Christ. Her hands fell to her chest, her head rolled to the side, and she fell into a deep sleep. He peered at her face: peaceful and melancholy.

"It's all futile, you know," Mr. Black said from behind him. "You feel it? The wisps of that fragile thing you call faith escaping through your fingers. You don't know what to do with your terror, shame, and grief."

"What do you want from me?" Those bloodshot yellow eyes, those veiny egg yolks, followed his movements.

"Hurm. It's what you don't want. You don't want to have to think, to struggle with reality. You don't want God, not really. You want something that will make you feel good, something bigger than you to lose yourself in. Something safe. God is none of those things."

"I'm doing His work. There's Ms. Mayfield. Her soul's safe now. She won't be joining you in hell."

Ms. Mayfield's eyes sprang open. She spoke through a contemptuous grin of utter, hostile malevolence. "Let that belief comfort you at night, but know this—hell is empty. We have no more a wish to be there than you. We just want to live in peace. To *feel*."

Daniel backed away from her. He felt movement behind him, a shifting among the shadows. Mr. Black opened the window. His flabby jowls made him look all the more like the Devourer. He gestured for Daniel to join him. "Tempting, isn't it? To jump in, unthinking, and embrace the decrepit whore you call faith. Pimped out to a God that doesn't listen to you. The irony is, if you find proof, you no longer have faith. Then what do you have?"

Daniel wanted to escape, be free of the constant harangue. He leaned forward, peering out the window. The sidewalks loomed far below him. He wanted to let go. Nothing made sense to him anymore. Nothing about the world that he lived in felt right. The way he lived, the way he moved, down to the core of his being—God seemed so far from him. The tattered edges of his faith clung to life like a man residing under hospice care. The weight of Mr. Black's glare pressed in on him long before Mr. Black spoke again.

"It's the ultimate test. The final answer to all of your questions."

Daniel mouthed the words to the Lord's Prayer, and it lodged like a cold stone in the pit of his stomach. His mind tried to latch on to something to anchor him. Reading the Bible first thing in the morning used to bring him such simple comfort. Now it was like reading the love letters of an ex-girlfriend. The prayer died on his lips. He doubted it would be answered anyway. For that matter, he doubted if he would be heard. He doubted if there was ever a hearer in the first place.

Daniel keeled forward through the window.

He didn't make a sound as the pavement rushed to greet him.

"What the hell's going on in here?" Jake rushed in. He joined Mr. Black at the window.

"Hurm. Seems someone's been asking the wrong questions," Mr. Black said, "had himself a bit of a fall."

Jake stared down at Daniel's broken body. "May you be in heaven a half hour before the Devil knows you're dead."

Mr. Black handed Jake a dollar.

"Oops, too late."

Wet Pain

Terence Taylor

I once saw a sign on a pillar in a New York City subway station, WET PAIN, written in bright red block letters on glossy white card stock. Back then I thought it was a joke or mistake, meant to read WET PAINT, but maybe I was wrong; maybe it was a warning of a different kind and I just missed the point because I didn't know enough to understand what I was reading.

That's how I feel about what happened to my good buddy, Dean, that I saw the danger signs all along but never realized what they meant, what they really warned me about. Not until he opened my eyes and I saw a side of the world I never wanted to see.

It all started when Dean moved back to New Orleans.

We met almost five years ago, on a job.

Dean was master electrician and I was tech director for a live multimedia press conference announcing the

UPN Network's new fall season. The client reps for the ad agency handling it were assholes, cut corners in all the wrong places, so we had to cover each other to survive. We worked together on floor plans for his lighting and my video equipment to do what they wanted with what they gave us, and made it through a two-week job from hell without killing each other or anyone else.

We stayed in touch. No one expected a white reformed redneck from New Orleans and a black gay geek from Park Slope like me to become best friends, least of all us, but we did. We were opposites in taste, education, upbringing, everything but how we saw the world and thought it should work; Dean called us "twin brothers of different mothers. . . ."

I made regular treks out to New Jersey for dinner with the family, but didn't know his wife, Lynn, was a black girl from the Bronx until my first visit almost a year after meeting Dean. I must have looked surprised when a stylish black woman opened the door instead of the suburban southern belle I'd expected. A short Afro crowned a dark pretty face, big gold hoops hung on either side of her broad smile. She feigned shock when she saw me, raised her eyebrows, and widened her eyes as she turned back to yell at her husband.

"Omigod, Dean! You didn't tell me he was a *Negro!*"

I loved her immediately.

After dinner we discussed Dean's colorblindness over beers on the back porch while their three-year-old, Milton, an only child then, ran around the yard in circles. Dean was built like a truck, six feet tall capped with a military-style crew cut. Lynn was small, compact; she nestled under Dean's free arm on the couch while we sipped beer and the two of us talked about her husband like he wasn't there.

"Dean says since he doesn't care about race he sees no reason to bring it up. I think it's passive-aggressive. You just know he only married me to see if it would kill his cracker family. . . ."

"Worth it, even if I am stuck with her," Dean said with a grin. She smacked him lightly. He winked at me, took a deep swig of beer.

"Anyway. I say ignoring color implies something's wrong, when difference should be recognized and celebrated," finished Lynn.

"Just sounds like a cheap way for them to get off the hook to me," I said. "'Black people? What black people? Everybody looks the same to me!'"

"Yeah, I get it." Lynn slapped Dean on the thigh with a grin. "No black people, no reparations! 'Slavery? What slavery? We don't owe you *shit!*'" We laughed like coconspirators, while Dean waggled his empty bottle until Lynn passed him another beer.

"Y'all need to keep me on your side," he said as he twisted off the cap. "We remember not the words of our enemies, but the silence of our friends. . . ."

"Smart-ass," said Lynn. "He quotes King, but doesn't fool me. Shakespeare said even the Devil can cite Scripture for his purpose."

"Never marry a teacher," laughed Dean. Lynn kissed him hard, and he kissed her back; they kissed a lot, had an easy affection for each other I envied.

Between jobs I'd hang with Dean at his place or mine, kick back, knock down tequilas, and take apart the world. Most of the time we talked by telephone. I had a headset that let me chat with both hands free while I drew floor plans at home on my Mac. He'd call on his Bluetooth earpiece from location while his crew set up lights and we'd burn up free long-distance by the hour while we both worked.

Lately more conversations were in person, less about Dean's dreams than nightmares about the war and a looming recession. A downturn in New York's economy after the Twin Tower bombings cut back on jobs for both of us; a few years of the Iraq war hadn't made things any better. I was single with low expenses in a rent-controlled Brooklyn apartment, but Dean had a family to support in Jersey, a wife and two kids.

Debts grew and no work was in sight; his wife's teaching salary wasn't enough to pay the bills. They'd already gone through their savings and started cashing out their IRAs, no matter how much they lost in early withdrawal.

"Freelance sucks, bruh. You know what they say," he said with a sigh. "Sometimes ya gotta chew off a leg to set yourself free."

Then his mother died.

I heard the phone ring as I walked upstairs with my grocery bags, but couldn't get inside my third-floor apartment in time to answer before it went to voice mail. There was a short message when I checked, no name, but I knew it was Dean.

"Greg, give me a call on cell, will ya? No big, bruh. Just need an ear, okay?"

He was down in New Orleans with the movers, getting furniture and boxes unloaded and into his mother's house before the wife and kids arrived from New Jersey to help unpack. I called him back on my headset phone while I put away groceries.

"Dean! How's life in the Big Easy?"

"Nothin' easy 'bout it, bruh." He paused. I heard a ring top pop, followed by what sounded like a long swallow from a tall cold beer. "Got everything in, so I'm takin' time off with my ol' pal Sam Six-pack. Don't think he's long for this world."

"How's the place look?"

"Like hell, but always did. Still can't believe what this dump is worth. Glad now I didn't burn it down as a kid. Lord knows I tried."

He grew up in New Orleans, a short walk from the main tourist drag of the French Quarter. Dean and his generation moved out first chance they got, but his widowed mother stayed in the family house until the end, in a quiet neighborhood called Marigny.

"Named after Bernard Marigny. His only piece of history's bringing craps to America in the 1800s and sellin' off the land we live on to pay his debts."

"From losing at craps?" I asked.

"My roots have cursed me, bruh. It's why my fortunes rise and fall." Dean had been out of work for over a year, had a family to support. "You know what houses in the French Quarter sellin' for now? Shit. Had no choice but to move back, and cash out Ma's place to stake a new start."

The move to New Orleans was only temporary. Lynn made that clear. Even in the early twenty-first century she didn't look forward to being the black half of an interracial couple in what she still considered the Deep South, no matter how "New" everyone said it was.

I finished unpacking groceries and started making lunch, commiserated with Dean about the twin nightmares of a major move and low cash flow. He sounded more down than usual; I wrote it off to the stress of moving. It was only later I'd look back and see it as the start of something more. By the time I made a sandwich and heated a bowl of soup, he'd finished three beers and was opening his fourth. I signed off to eat, but couldn't get the last thing he said out of my head.

"They say you can't go home again, bruh, but they're wrong. It's not that you can't, only that you shouldn't. Sometimes leaving home's the best thing to do, and you should stay away like you had sense."

"Too many memories?"

"Too many ghosts."

I laughed as I sat at the table to eat. "Don't tell me you believe in ghosts."

"Don't matter, bruh," he said. "They just have to believe in you." That was the phrase that struck me.

They just have to believe in you.

Dean called back a few days later.

His mother had lived on the ground floor of her worn yellow clapboard corner house and kept everything else stored in the small narrow rooms upstairs, packed so full over the years Dean could barely get in to clean. He'd dug in, found things he'd forgotten and others he never knew about. Old family photos, even a few original daguerreotypes, trunks of antique clothes, books, family papers. Some he packed in garbage bags to throw out, some he put aside to be appraised.

"Might be sumpin' worth a few bucks. Maybe I'll give it all to some local museum. The Dean Duvall Collection."

"Yeah, they could name a wing after you."

"Be some 'preciation, bruh. More'n I get round here."

Dean's speech was slurred, his accent the bad cliché movie redneck he always affected when drunk. It sounded like he'd been sitting with Sam Six-pack again, plus a few of his pals. I looked at the clock. It seemed a little early even for Dean to be in the tank.

"What do you mean?"

"Damn wife, f'true. Don't matter what you do, never enough."

"It's just the move. She'll settle down once you get the place cleared out."

"That's what they say."

I tried to lighten the mood. "Hey, how's the famous food down there? You have a chance to go out and check some of your old haunts?"

"Only haunts I seen been up here, bruh. No time or money for fun. Wife makes sure of that."

"You're upstairs now?" For some reason the news startled me, sent a shudder through my body, like some childhood fear was triggered by the thought of him crouched in a long low dust-filled upper room while we talked, sunlight streaming through small windows to cast long shadows while he labored late into the afternoon, alone with me and the ghosts.

"Where else I gon' be, bruh? Takin' care of business while we talk. All I do's take care of business. . . ."

We talked a while longer, but conversation never strayed far from complaints about his wife and kids weighing him down, giving him a hard time. I wanted to be supportive but felt drowned in his self-pity. When it was clear I couldn't pull him out of it I had to escape before I sank, told him I needed to get to a store before it closed, the best excuse I could think of to get off the phone.

"No problem, bruh. Catch ya later. Oh, and keep an eye out. Got a little surprise headed your way. . . ."

He wouldn't say what it was, no matter how hard I pressed. The way he'd been talking I wasn't sure what to expect. I hung up and poured a drink, stared at my computer screen instead of working or going out, and wondered what was happening to the man I'd known in New York.

A few days later my present arrived.

The bell rang and the mailman called me downstairs to sign for an oversized delivery sent Priority Mail. It was a long flat package wrapped in taped-together brown paper bags, thickly padded inside with cardboard for protection, DO NOT BEND! and FRAGILE! PLEASE DO NOT FOLD! scrawled all over it in Dean's blocky print. I carried my gift upstairs and opened it on the dining table where I had room to lay it out flat.

I unwrapped it and carefully removed the packing.

Inside was an old panoramic photograph over three feet long, brittle, cracked, the black-and-white image gently faded to sepia browns on thick, yellowed paper. It was a huge crowd at the base of the Washington Monument, ghostly pale women and children in the foreground, scattered in a semicircle around the edges of an open clearing.

Outnumbering them many times was a multitude of men that extended back to the horizon as far as the eye could see, dressed in dark street clothes or light robes, with and without hoods, many with left arms outstretched in a salute to the monument, to their fellow Ku Klux Klansmen, to their families, their country, and their God.

In the middle of the photo, Klansmen and their women stood around the edges of a massive American flag, long enough to take twenty to hold aloft at chest level, displayed proudly as if at a patriotic event, and on that day it was. I felt a chill despite Brooklyn's late summer heat.

The casual audacity of it scared me the most, the easy social exchanges among people in the crowd, that the photographer had snapped the picture and labeled it in precise handwritten text at the bottom, as if it were a quaint scene of any other approved public assembly:

Gathering of the Klans
Virginia Klans arrive at Sylvan Theatre
*Potomac Park * Washington, D.C. * August 8, 1925*

I went to my computer, did a quick Google, and confirmed that there had been a big meeting in Washington that year and read some history of the first Klan, founded in 1865 by Masons. They donned masks to inspire terror in their enemies; the white robes and masks were either to imitate the Knights Templar who fought in the Crusades or to pose as avenging spirits of Confederate dead come back as ghouls.

One site said by 1925, the Klan numbered four million, its members unlikely to be convicted by local southern juries even if arrested. I stopped reading and called Dean on the phone. He picked up after one ring, knew it was me without asking.

"Bruh! Guess you got my little package."

"Pretty big package for a white man," I joked.

"Yeah, well, saw it and thought of you." He laughed, long and loud.

"Not sure how to take that, but thanks. I'm touched. It's probably a collectible."

"Don't say I never give yuh nothin'."

"Did Lynn see it?" She'd marched in demonstrations against Bush and the Iraq war, organized petitions for feminist and civil rights issues; I could only imagine what she had to say when he brought it downstairs.

Dean laughed. "Yeah, took one look and said if I wanted to live with it, I could move my picture and skinny white ass into the garage."

"No surprise there."

"Guess not. Nearly told the bitch where she could put it, but like they say, you gotta pick your battles."

I paused. Despite their differences, Dean and Lynn were one of the most functional couples I knew. "Since when are you two fighting?"

"Ain't no fight, bruh. Just me layin' down law on who's boss around here. You know what they say, give 'em an inch and they'll take your balls!" He guffawed.

I tried to laugh it off, but was disturbed by the force of his cracks about Lynn. Dean had made the usual guy jokes about his wife in the past, but never anything this hostile. I asked to speak to her later and he either didn't hear or ignored me.

"Me, bruh, I think it's a piece of history. Real Americana."

"I'm with you. What's the story? You related to any of these guys?"

"Hell, probably all of 'em. You know how inbred those old bastards were." He laughed and coughed.

"Did you know you had Klan fans in the family?"

"Bruh, I'm learning more than I need to know. You'd never believe the shit I found. Scrapbooks of lynch photos, newspaper and magazine clippings, pages of

hangings and burnings, fuckin' museum of the misbe-
gotten. My roots. 'Fraid some's worth somethin', or I'd
burn it all." He started to drift. "Need cash now. Never
get this place cleared in time. . . ." When I asked to talk
to Lynn again, Dean made an excuse and rambled on
until he ran down like a spent windup toy. While I considered ways to get past him to talk to her, I got off the
phone and rewrapped the photograph.

I took it to a local frame shop in Park Slope. The
teenaged white clerk behind the counter did a double
take when he realized what it was, smiled slyly while
he took my order as if in on some secret joke between
us. His manager came in from lunch as we finished up,
a professional-looking young woman, styled with current fashion magazine cover perfection. She glanced at
the photo with a polite smile of feigned interest that
dropped as soon she read the caption.

"Is this for a museum or gallery?" she asked, pushing back frosted blond hair for a better look.

"It was a gift. A friend found it in his mother's house
in New Orleans."

She arched her eyebrows, as if wondering what kind
of friend he really was. "Well. I wouldn't want to live
with it."

"Sometimes it's good to remember it wasn't so long
ago."

"I suppose. . . ." She looked unconvinced. "I know
my grandparents don't keep postcards of Auschwitz."

"They were there. The rest of us need reminders."

"I suppose," she repeated, smiled professionally but
failed to conceal a scowl as she turned to walk away. I
pictured her coming back that night, turning off the
alarm, unlocking the door, and tearing the picture to
pieces with her well-manicured nails, savaging it with

the sharp stiletto heels of her designer shoes, then dismissed the image. This was the civilized Slope where we publicly aired our differences in the light of day, not Dean's inscrutable South that sent me souvenirs of a time when they were settled under cover of darkness.

I got busy on location for a job and lost touch with Dean. After a few more calls like the last one I was glad for the break. We traded messages on voice mail, but by the time my job was over, I was too tired to deal with one of his repetitive rants, so I put off calling back until I'd regained my strength. Hopefully by then things would have improved.

The phone rang one night after I fell asleep on the couch watching TV. It woke me enough to fumble for the phone without thinking to check caller ID, and I caught it just before it went to voice mail.

"Yah?" I said.

"'Bout time! Who do I kill to hear back from you, bruh?"

"Dean." I stretched, carried the phone to the kitchen to get coffee and a drink. A double. "Sorry, I got tied up on a gig. Had to spend more time on-site than I thought. You always say beggars can't be choosy."

"I ain't mad at you. Do what you gotta, I'll do the same."

He was so drunk I could barely understand him. It was exactly the call I'd been trying to avoid. "How's Lynn?"

He snorted, blew his nose, and laughed. "You know what they say, the darker the berry, the sweeter the juice . . . Bitch is fine, boy, why, you want some of that?"

"Boy? Excuse me?" My voice went up like a Richard Pryor routine. "Don't call me boy, asshole. And stop calling Lynn a bitch. I don't like it and I doubt she does." I'd had arguments with Dean over politics and art, but never really been mad at him until now.

His voice came back low and deep, dead serious. "I'll call you whatever I want to, boy. You ain't got no right ta tell me what to do, no more'n that black bitch downstairs."

There was a moment when I was going to respond with an easy retort, tell his cracker ass what I thought as usual, but there was something in his voice that stopped me. When he said those words it hadn't been the slurred accents of the drunk who called me. It was the voice of authority, clear and decisive, stating a truth. I wouldn't be challenging Dean, but everything he thought and believed in. I wasn't sure enough of what that was anymore to start a fight. Not without knowing what I was up against.

"We'll talk later. When you sober up," I said.

"Ain't drunk, boy. I'm high on life." He laughed like that was some kind of joke. "Yeah, that's it. High on . . ." He started to cough again, from a chest thick with phlegm.

"Enough with this boy shit, okay?"

Dean wheezed as he chuckled into the phone. "High on lives, boy. We high on lives. . . ."

I disconnected and turned up the TV to drown my thoughts.

I'd never been called boy by anyone before, and to have a good friend be first made it all the worse. I felt trapped in the apartment, the scene of the crime, and needed to get out, so I called a nearby friend and asked him to meet me at Excelsior, a local gay bar only a few blocks from us.

Winston was tall, dark, and dressed to kill as always, already posed cocktail in hand at the long curved wooden bar when I arrived. He'd just had his shoulder-length dreadlocks done, still moist and glistening with fresh oils, and toyed with them while we talked.

It was a quiet night at the bar, still early, and the jukebox played soft music instead of blasting dance hits. Excelsior was like any neighborhood bar, only gay, one of the few bars I'd ever felt comfortable hanging in. I'd met Winston there when he'd introduced himself to one of my friends who appealed to him. They lasted one night, but Winston and I ended up friends for years.

"What can I say, honey?" he said after I told him about my grim conversations with Dean, raved and ranted the rage out of my system. "I'm from Louisiana. White folk down there can be that way. Friends for years until you hit a rough patch that shows you who they really are. He's just getting back to his racist roots."

"I can't believe that."

"I tell you true. It's pack nature. When the choice is between you and their own . . ." He waved a hand to finish the rest of the thought while he downed the last of his drink.

I told him he was crazy. I told him he was wrong. I told myself to stay calm and give Dean time to redeem himself.

"Sometimes friends need a vacation from each other, boo. Let it go," Winston said as I finished my beer. "Forget it and him."

We walked out the door and hugged as we said good-bye. There was a crash of breaking glass against the sidewalk behind us as we heard voices yell, "Faggots!" from the street, then the roar of an engine.

People ran out of the bar before Winston and I understood what had happened and described it to us. A car full of teenagers was passing when one of the kids threw a bottle while the others jeered and cheered him on; then they took off through a red light. Regulars made sure broken glass hadn't hit us while the owner, ordinarily a quiet gentle man, ran out with a cell phone in his hand, snapped out orders to his burly partner behind him.

"I'm on hold with the local precinct. Did anyone get a plate number?" Someone waved, and he went to talk to her while I checked out Winston. He was furious.

"Goddamn them! How dare they! Goddamn motherfuckers!" He stamped back and forth in front of the bar, cursed while people tried to console him, or encouraged him to let it out. The owner came back over to me.

"Lord, Greg, I am so sorry. The cops are on their way. I don't know what to say. We've been open for years and that's never happened. Never. Come in if you need a drink while you wait. On the house." Winston headed back inside before I could answer for either of us. He turned at the door and gestured to the street, in the direction the car had sped off.

"Pack nature," he said, and disappeared inside.

Over the next week I noticed a rise in news stories about hate crimes: synagogues and cars vandalized with swastikas, fires in Baptist churches, Hassidic Jews attacked by Latin teens, black men beaten with bats by

a white gang in Howard Beach, a turbaned Sikh assaulted for the Twin Towers. I was extra watchful on
the subway after a news story about an outpatient off
his meds who'd pushed a girl onto the tracks, stopped
wearing my MP3 player so I could keep my ears open
for suspicious sounds behind me on the street. I couldn't
tell if the surge was real or if what happened outside
the bar made me pay more attention to stories that were
always there. It was as if whatever shadow Dean was
living under had made its way up here to look for me.

I picked up a voice-mail message that my picture
was ready, and stopped on my way back from the city
to pick it up. When I got it home I saw they'd done a
great job, despite the manager's reservations. The mat
was a narrow strip of ivory with a thin bloodred border
on the inside. The frame was rounded, high-gloss
bloodred to match the border. The best place to put it
seemed to be over my desk, so the long-dead Klansmen could watch over me while I worked at my computer.

When I was done hanging it I sat in my chair with a
shot of tequila to take a look. Smoldering eyes stared
down in disapproval, an allied assembly of racists who
would gladly have lynched me for being the free nigger
cocksucker I was. I was everything they'd tried to prevent; I thought trapped in framed glass their world was
harmless, frozen in the past, too far away to hurt me,
but Dean had proved me wrong.

I stared up at the panorama, examined faces and details while I tried to forget my last conversation with
him, tried to let the anger die down, but drink only fueled my fury. The rest of the night was spent brooding,
as I gulped tequila and smoked weed, tried not to call

Dean and start a new fight, used all my years in therapy to try to understand what made him change. I'd picked a bad combination; the tequila broke down my defenses, left me open to paranoid fantasies inspired by the weed. They came all too easily and all made sense when I was stoned.

There were only two explanations, internal or external.

If the answer was internal, Dean was having a mental breakdown. The expenses and pressure of the move had been too much, even for him. He was striking out at the only ones in reach, his family and me. If it was external . . .

All I needed to spur my stoned fantasy was the photograph in front of me. The crowd of Klansmen swarmed in a ring like white blood cells gathered to engulf invaders, a mass of individuals united to think and act as one killing organism. What if evil wasn't born of any single thought but was the product of a group mind, spread through the body of society like a virus that ate into healthy heads and converted them, made them its own?

What if there was an evil infecting America, demons, haunts, call them hungry ghosts? Something that followed us from the old world and made its home in the heartland where it grew and nourished itself on lynchings, serial killings, race riots, and state executions. It could have started in Spain during the Crusades, accidentally unleashed by the same Knights Templar that inspired early Klan leaders, Crusaders foolish enough to test powers they didn't understand and couldn't control.

Maybe alchemy or incantations woke an ancient

hunger that followed them to inspire the tortures of the Inquisition, the violence of the French Revolution, sent somber pilgrims across the sea to murder natives for their land, advised judges to hold witch-hunts in Salem, donned hoods of the Ku Klux Klan to spread terror through the South, ordered officials to inter Japanese Americans and drop the atomic bomb, while its fore-bears in Europe bred the Holocaust, traveled with soldiers to My Lai and Abu Ghraib, pushed misfortune into disaster, whenever, wherever it could to make things worse, fed our fear of each other to nourish itself. I didn't know what it was, what form it took; maybe it was hidden in all our hearts, passed down from generation to generation like a congenital disease.

So here was Dean, freshly infected by the Old South he'd fled. Whatever it was had slept buried in boxes of his family's racist memorabilia, waited for the right host, and woke when it found Dean in its reach, weak, afraid, and alone, sank in its fangs, fed on his soul, and regurgitated what was left back into his brain like poison.

That was the hate I heard, not Dean's, but the raw fury of the hungry ghosts of America, speaking through Dean's mouth like ventriloquists through a dummy.

I fell asleep on the couch in front of the photo, sure I had it all figured out, and was going to let Dean know first thing in the morning.

I woke with my worst hangover since high school.

There'd been some major epiphany the night before, but the details escaped me, scraped away with the rest of my memories of the night by pain. I cleaned up as well as I could, put dishes and glasses in the sink before I made coffee. There were scribbles on a pad on the desk, a map or diagram like a family tree with roots in Jerusalem ending in New Orleans, branches through Europe and North America, "Knights Templar" and "Ku Klux Klan" scrawled at either end. I remembered something about evil as organic or viral, that the photo had seemed significant; all that really remained was a churning in my stomach, a sense of foreboding, that there was something very wrong with Dean and not just a drinking problem.

I decided to call Lynn later and ask her how she felt. It was possible I was only overreacting to Dean blowing off more steam than usual. It was a tense time for them; I had to remember that when I brought up the subject with her.

In the living room I turned on the TV. After 9/11 the biggest change in my life was that I turned on local news as soon as I woke up, to see what had happened overnight. It looked like a quiet morning until they got to the weather.

While I sipped coffee and washed down a handful of aspirins for my head, the forecast went from New York's heat wave to a hurricane off the coast of Florida called Katrina. I didn't pay attention at first, but when they started talking evacuation and New Orleans I turned it up, heard enough to make me swallow my pride and call Dean.

The phone rang for a while. No machine or voice mail picked up. I imagined the sound ringing through the worn yellow house, echoing off bare cracked walls. I got ready to hang up. Maybe they'd left already. The ringing stopped. There was silence, then Dean's voice, rough, as if he'd been sleeping. Or drinking.

"Yeah?"

"It's me. I've been hearing bad weather reports. . . ."

"Bruh, wassup?" He dropped the phone. I heard it rustle as he picked it up and put it back in his ear. "I'm busy here."

"Yeah, look, there's a class-four hurricane coming in, they're talking about evacuating New Orleans."

"S'what damn bitch downstairs says. Not leavin' my home, boy. Don't need damn niggers tellin' me what to do. Niggers and illegals why I ain't got no work, why decent God-fearin' white men can't find jobs no more. . . ." His breathing was heavy, labored. I knew Dean had a temper; I'd seen him reduce teamsters to near tears, but he'd never lashed out at me.

"Slow down. Stop." I held it together, kept myself from launching into a speech. "This isn't like you."

"Maybe you don't know me good as you thought."

"No. I know you. Something's wrong. It's like something down there . . ."

Dean laughed it off. "What, boy? Go ahead and say it."

I couldn't.

A flash went off in my head and I saw the photograph.

I remembered everything I'd thought sitting in front of it the night before, as insane as it all seemed now. The infectious pack nature of ancient evil accidentally unleashed by the Knights Templar and carried to the new world like a plague. Dean taunted me as if he knew exactly what was in my head, dared me to say the words and hear how ridiculous they sounded out loud.

"Say what's on your mind, boy."

It was as impossible for me to believe Dean was possessed by evil spirits that fed on racism and fear, as

it was to believe he'd always been like this, that his
easy smile and our long hours of conversation had
been a mask, a pretense. That was more terrifying than
believing in monsters.

"What is it, boy? You think I been bit by a hungry
ghost? Superstitious enough to believe in nigger crap
like that?" He started humming, some old rock relic I
couldn't quite make out. I heard things move in the
background, like he was pushing boxes around, or digging through them like he'd lost something.

"You have to get out of there. Forget this fight. Go
downstairs, pack some bags, lock up, and get the family out of town for a few days. Just go to the airport, I'll
charge tickets, you can fly up here. . . ."

"Can't leave. Got work to do, boy. Maybe your kind
don't get that, but down here we take care of business."

"Let me talk to Lynn."

I heard a dial tone and got a busy signal every time I
called back. After a few tries I got the message and left
for a drink to slow the creeping dread in my gut.

Excelsior was having another quiet night.

There were still enough people for me to blend in
and be alone in the crowd. I ordered a beer and before
I'd half finished it saw a blond white guy in his late
twenties notice me from the end of the bar. I wasn't in
the mood for company, but before I could break eye
contact he smiled and wandered my way. He wasn't my
usual type, small, wiry, and a little too friendly, like a
terrier, but cute.

"Hey," he said when he reached my side, and sig-
naled the bartender as if he was just there to order.

I nodded.

"I don't usually see many black guys here. Too bad."

"Yeah, well, at these prices, you won't see many more."

He pulled out a twenty and slapped it down on the bar. "Next one's on me, then. Gotta keep you coming back."

"I'm kidding," I said. "It's an old joke, about a bartender and a horse." I let him buy my next beer, anyway.

"Yeah? Comparing yourself to a horse?" He swayed a little, rested his hand on my thigh as his smile broadened. I could tell he was more than a few beers ahead of me. "What's funny about that?"

"What? No . . ." I laughed and started to explain, realized we were past any pretense of intelligent conversation. He leaned closer and I let him kiss me as his fingers explored the front of my pants, found what he was looking for, and squeezed. His mouth tasted of beer and cigarettes, but his tongue was warm and wet in my mouth, and his hand was doing a good job of convincing me to let him go further.

I didn't bring guys home from bars often. The few nights I did were like this one, when all I needed was someone warm beside me to pull my mind from whatever bothered me back to my body and its needs. We left our beers unfinished and walked the few blocks to my place.

Outside, back in the real world, we looked like a couple of straight buddies barhopping down Fifth Avenue, while he whispered dirty comments under his breath about what he'd do to me once I got him home.

We raced up the stairs and into my hot apartment, tumbled onto my bed, moist shadows in the dark, undressed each other, and twisted on the sheets like snakes tying each other into knots until I heard the words hiss out of his wet lips . . .

"Yeah, that's it. That's my sweet nigger."

I shoved him away, rolled out of bed, and turned on the light, stared at him like I'd just walked in on a naked stranger.

"Okay," I said. "I don't need that right now."

"What's wrong?" He looked sincerely baffled as he stood, his pale boner poked up like a raised eyebrow. "Shit, what I said? Everybody says it. No big deal anymore, right? Hip-hop made it okay, they say it on MTV and BET all the time, know what I mean, mah niggah?" He said the last with a broad urban accent, laughed as if it was funny, then saw I hadn't joined him.

"Do you know how many black parents and grandparents died to keep me from being called that? I don't care how you spell it. You gots to go. Now. Get the fuck out of my house, faggot." I shook my head, pulled on my pants.

"Damn, bro," he started, but stopped when he caught the new look I gave him and put on his clothes.

"Yeah. Not so funny now, is it, queer? Didn't we make those words okay, too?"

I walked him out, silent, as furious at myself as with him for playing his hot black stud long enough for him to think he could say those words and have them excite me. After he left, I double-locked the door behind him, as if that could keep out what I was trying to escape.

Whatever it was.

The storm was coming.

They were past warning; it was on its way, tore along the Florida coast. I flipped channels to follow the coverage, stayed whenever I saw long lines of cars leaving New Orleans, the mayor and the governor of Louisiana urging citizens to abandon their homes and get to safety.

The hurricane was hyped so hard by the media it was hard to believe they were serious, that it could really be that bad. What they predicted sounded epic, the kind of biblical disaster we were used to seeing in other countries on TV. The idea that New Orleans could be washed out of existence seemed insane despite digital simulations that showed us how and why; how could anyone in power leave levees that unprotected in a city built below sea level? I stopped only to make dinner, watched coverage until I fell asleep on the couch as the sun went down.

The phone rang. I woke in the dark.

"Hey, boy."

It was Dean. A bad connection or my imagination made his voice sound distorted, off-pitch; it slid in and out of range like a digital movie effect.

"Can you hear it, boy?"

I reached over and turned on the light next to the couch. The room looked the same as always, possessions intact, the clutter I never keep cleared for long still strewn, but it all felt alien, like I woke up in free fall, my apartment inexplicably in outer space. There was an air of exploration, like I was in a new world where anything could happen, finding my footing for the first time.

"It'll be here soon."

"What's that? The storm?"

He laughed, the same choked chortle I'd heard before, like he was dying of consumption. "Ain't no storm. It's the dark that's comin'. Not dark like you, nigger, but real dark, deep dark, deeper than night, blacker than black, so deep nothing gets out. It's calling me, boy, like God called to Abraham. It's awake and hungry and ain't going back to sleep until it's been fed."

I froze; his words echoed the fantasy that haunted me since the night I'd fallen asleep in front of the panorama. I'd never admitted it to him, never spoken the words aloud. There was no way for him to know. "What are you talking about, buddy? Doesn't sound like you."

"You sure right there, boy."

"What's that supposed to mean?"

"You're so bright. What do you think?"

I looked up at the sepia-toned Klansmen over my desk. Some looked directly into the camera like they could see me, made me half afraid Dean could see what they saw, that they were all connected across time and space. "Cut it out."

"Why? Not so sure there's not somethin' out there can push people past the limit? Put icin' on the cake, turn a simple muggin' into vicious murder, date rape into a weeklong torture session? Not so sure you're always in control?" His voice was soft, seductive, an old-time movie country lawyer selling his case to the jury, Daniel Webster defending the Devil.

"You're talking crazy." I was frozen, unable, unwilling to believe what I feared the most.

"You want to hear crazy? Listen to this, nigger." He was on his feet, walked downstairs to the tiled kitchen wearing the headset phone.

"Hey," I started, but he cut me off.

"What?" Dean laughed and coughed at the same time; one rolled into the other, almost a death rattle, dry but filled with mucus. "You ain't a nigger? Any more'n that nigger bitch asleep in the bedroom?"

"Stop it."

"Stop what, cocksucker? I'm just getting started."

He laughed again and I knew this wasn't some kind of game or sick practical joke. Money stress, the move, something had pushed him too far to come back, over some edge I hadn't seen coming—that or something else. I heard kitchen drawers open and close, silverware rattle.

A butcher knife clanged as it hit a cutting board.

I recognized the sound because I knew the knife, had used it to help make dinner in their Jersey home, sharpened it myself the last time I was there and chastised Dean for not keeping a better edge on the blade. I wondered if he'd taken my advice, wondered how sharp the knife was now as I listened to his footsteps leave the tiled kitchen and walk into silence on the carpeted hall.

"Hey, what's up?" I asked, tried to sound casual.

"Just cleaning house, boy. Got work to do. Some folks don't seem to know their place. But I'll be taking care of business every day, and every way. . . ."

He started singing the old Bachman Turner Overdrive song aloud. I recognized it when I heard the lyrics; it was what he'd been humming for weeks upstairs while he talked to me on the phone. The way he chanted the words broke the spell that held me frozen. The only place he could be going was to the bedroom.

With a butcher knife.

I stood up with no idea where to go. To the police? The airport? Even the fastest flight would get me there hours too late. I couldn't hang up as long as I could use the phone to hear what Dean was doing, and I couldn't call his local precinct on my cell without him hearing me.

I started to panic, then stopped. There was still one thing I could do. I went to my computer and searched for the police station nearest the house in Marigny, found the precinct closest to them and an e-mail address, sent a short but explicit note that explained what was happening, where, and that I was on the phone with him now. Then I sent it again a hundred times.

"Dean? What's going on, there, buddy?"

"Gonna put her down, bruh, put the black bitch down like a rabid dog, and take care of her little black bastards. Then we're comin' fer you, boy, every last one of you, until every nigger knows their place."

He kept humming the song, moving to the back of the house a step at a time with a little laugh every now and then. To be sure the police got my message I found their fax number and computer-faxed fifty copies of the note in large type so someone would be sure to notice it pouring out of the machine. For once I was glad to be a geek.

"Listen to me, Dean—"

"Shhh . . . Bitch is still asleep."

In my earpiece I heard the bedroom door creak open, Lynn's sleepy voice in the background, too slurred to make out what she said.

"Hey, baby," whispered Dean. I heard Lynn gasp and try to scream; instead there was the sound of struggle, a punch, and I heard the breath go out of her with a dull thump. I remembered how much bigger Dean was, imagined him throwing Lynn to the bed like a rag doll.

"Damn it! What the fuck are you doing?" I shouted into the phone, helpless to stop him any other way.

"Quiet, boy, got my hands full right now." His voice was strained, breathless. Lynn screamed for the children to run, until he gagged her. I heard sheets rip; Dean's breath came in short bursts as they struggled.

"Jesus Christ!"

"Don't you take the name of our Lord in vain, mother-fucker," he snarled. "God don't care what happens to this nigger bitch any more'n he cares about your black ass."

I listened to him hum that damned song as he went about his work. "Still there? What do you think, bruh? Is Dean at work here? Or somethin' else?"

He headed down the hall to the kids' room. I heard them weep as he entered, pictured Dean shoving seven-year-old Milton back down the hall to the master bedroom by the neck, two-year-old Shana tucked under his other arm like a football. Dean wouldn't need the knife to handle the kids. I heard him throw them to the floor, slap them to shut them up while he bound them.

A new e-mail came in from the police that my messages had been received. "Is this for real? We're in the middle of a citywide evacuation. . . ."

I typed a fast reply, "I swear to God, I have him on the phone now trying to slow him down, you have my permission to tap into my line if you have to verify," and hit Send, waiting until they confirmed to relax. I just had to keep him talking until they got there. I tried to keep the excitement out of my voice.

"Dean? You still there?"

"Yeah, boy."

The children's panicked howls had subsided to sobs; all I could hear from Lynn were moans and muffled cries through her gag as Dean snickered.

"They say beauty's skin deep, don't they, bruh? That true, nigger? Let's take a look."

There was a wet rip and new shrieks from Lynn; then she must have passed out from the pain; when I didn't hear her anymore I couldn't hold back tears. I felt helpless, even knowing help was on the way. The only question was if it would be in time.

"In the name of God," I said. "If there's anything of you left in there, stop this before it's too late."

"You started this, boy. You needed proof. Satisfied? Believe in us now, nigger?"

I must have screamed, and it all poured out, the rage, the fear and pain, and I denied him at the top of my lungs; I didn't believe, it wasn't anything but Dean at work and he was going to burn in hell if there was one, and if there wasn't I would build one to hold him . . . I don't know what else I said; it was drowned out by the sound of sirens in the background as the police finally came, close enough that he knew he could either finish his task or flee. I prayed Dean was still sane enough to run.

He hissed into the phone, "You did this, boy. Don't know how, but it was you, you nigger bastard. We comin' fer you, boy. Comin' fer you . . ."

And the line went dead.

Someone from the precinct had the mercy to call an hour later to let me know Lynn and the kids were safe, the longest hour of my life. They found Lynn tied spread-eagle, tortured, bleeding, the kids hog-tied on the floor, forced to face the bed. They couldn't find Dean. He got away before they could get inside.

I lost contact with Lynn and the kids until friends told me they'd been safely evacuated after the rescue to her mother's house in the Bronx.

"The kids are fine as they can be," she said. "The house sounds like it's in one piece. Our street wasn't hit bad, no flooding, just lost a few windows and shingles. Neighbors next door rode out the storm, they're keeping me posted when they can." There was a brief almost unnoticeable pause. "Still no word about Dean," she added, as if he'd wandered off at the mall.

"How are you?"

"Oh, well. Everything works. Thank you for that. If he'd had more time . . ." She sighed, tried to laugh it off. "I won't be wearing shorts or sleeveless tops for a while, but didn't much anyway."

I never asked what Dean did to her in the bedroom that night, what the children were forced to watch. All I knew was what I heard; that was bad enough. I was afraid to know any more. Facing what Dean was capable of meant either admitting I hadn't known him at all, or that something else wore my friend like a Halloween costume and tried to destroy everything he loved.

I watched CNN news coverage of the hurricane aftermath with the same mute disbelief I felt witnessing the fall of the Twin Towers. It was hard to believe it was real, happening to us as we'd seen it happen to so many others in the last few years of earthquakes and tsunamis.

As days went by I couldn't tell if the crisis was under control as the government claimed or if the city had descended into the surreal hell described on the news. Official reports tried to play down the crime, TV showed waterlogged devastation and hinted at unspeakable acts committed in the stadium, while online blogs painted a worse picture of the troops' behavior. Poor black residents were made to look like animals, patrolling soldiers portrayed as storm troopers; if Dean was host to something that fed on fear, it was feasting now.

I went to a party planned before the hurricane that became a benefit for Katrina victims. I'd planned to skip it, but Winston talked me into it.

"It's a healing thing, baby. Not just for you, but all of us, so you're going. Meet you at your place at seven."

It was at a loft in DUMBO, high under the Brooklyn Bridge, with a view of Manhattan outside factory-sized windows. I saw faces I hadn't seen in ages, heard stories about friends and family in affected areas who were struggling to recover or helping others. The events of the last week started to blur with more drinks, passed joints, and mellow music, lulled by human voices exchanging soft consolation.

My cell phone rang, and I opened it. The signal was weak, so I stepped out onto the fire escape to get better reception. The number was blocked; the screen said Unknown Caller. I slipped the earpiece on and pushed the Talk button.

"Yeah?"

"Hey, bruh."

"Dean." It wasn't a question. I had no doubt it was Dean's voice, weak as the signal was, even if I knew it couldn't be him.

"Oh, my nigger," the thing that spoke like Dean breathed into my ear, from a place no calls could come from, would not come for days. "Oh, nigger, the things we have seen. You would tear your eyes from their sockets to forget them." Then it laughed, a thick sound still filled with phlegm. "But not us, bruh. Not us. We like to watch."

I shivered even though the air outside was warm as I listened to the impossible voice, looked back through the window to watch the party still going on; music played, couples swayed on the dance floor, a distant world flickering light-years away, one I could see but never reach again in my lifetime.

"Where are you?"

"Like to know that, wouldn't you, nigger? Like to know we're not waitin' downstairs for you, in your closet or under your bed. Never know for sure, will yuh, bruh?"

I didn't want to hear the answer but had to ask. "Who are you?"

"Call us Legion, for we are many."

"You lie," I said. "There are no demons. Just excuses."

"Come on, boy," it said. "All people really want is a way to blame bad on someone else, God or the Devil. An easy explanation for why y'all take an eye for an eye instead of turnin' the other cheek, why niggers get dragged to death behind trucks and fags tied up to freeze to death, even now. . . .

"So it ain't your fault. It's ours. Don't say we never give yuh nothin'." I could hear the sounds of female shrieks and deep male laughter in the background. It chuckled again, just like Dean. "Gotta run. Got a date with an angel."

The screams grew louder as the phone approached them and disconnected, after one last laugh from my dead good buddy.

* * *

They found me asleep on the fire escape, phone still in my ear, said I told them I dreamed I was on the phone with a long-lost friend, and then was in New Orleans looking for him.

I said I stood on dry land under a full moon at night, looked east at a flooded road ahead, water as far as the eye could see. The flood whispered to me like sirens of old; I felt a pull, looked down, and saw water rise over my feet and up my shins before I could back out.

Hushed voices rose with the waters as they covered my waist, my shoulders and head. Fully submerged I could hear them clearly as I watched my last breath bubble up out of my mouth to the surface, now yards away. My ears filled with an infernal chorus of "Dixie" as I struggled to ascend. . . .

I looked down and saw the singers drift up from the depths in tattered Confederate gray, white hooded robes, sheriff uniforms, army fatigues, anonymous black suits, faceless men bound only by hate and fear. They sang as one, swung swords, sticks, billy clubs, pistols, rifles from muskets to AK-47s in rhythm to the steady beat of an unseen drum, like the inhuman sound of a giant heart.

Dean rose to the head of the hellish choir, a noose in one hand; his other gripped my ankle and pulled me back down as I fought my way up toward the light. . . .

They found Dean a few weeks later—what was left—wedged between a Dumpster and the side of a truck someone had loaded with the last of their worldly goods or loot, too late to get out of town. Dean's death went unnoticed in the torrent of news from Katrina, the far greater losses and atrocities; it was a small story worthy of note to only a few, but it was our story and we took it hard.

Life quieted down after that; Dean's recovery led to our own.

I went to New Orleans a few months after the waters receded to help Lynn sell the house. The city was like an invalid who'd nearly died, still unsure of its chances for full recovery. It was stronger, saner, had regained some of its old fire, but there was a haunted look behind the eyes, the look of one who'd seen how close the end could be and would never be the same again. It was the same look I saw in Lynn's eyes when she thought no one was looking.

Except for missing roof tiles and broken windows, Dean's old family home was intact and ironically worth even more as survivors who'd lost homes looked for replacements. It sold for more than enough to move Lynn and the kids back North near her family. I flew back to Brooklyn where I felt at ease, if not entirely safe; it would be hard to feel safe anywhere for a long time.

When I got home, I took down the panorama of the Klan.

I was tempted to burn it, but that would mean I believed it was part of something supernatural, that it held contaminating magic of its own that could somehow influence others or even me. I was too civilized for that. Then I remembered what Dean had said; it doesn't matter whether you believe in ghosts if they believe in you. The rational part of me wrapped the photograph and donated it to the Museum of Intolerance in Dean's name before I called in the villagers with torches.

No one could tell me if Dean was dead or alive the

night of the party. Water and weather conditions made it impossible. He was dead, case closed; they told Lynn she was lucky to get a body, much less an autopsy. She was still in shock over losing him, too distraught to remember or discuss changes in Dean before the end. I was left to find my own answers. There were none.

I don't know what's harder to live with, that Dean went off the deep end and fell back on the only solid ground he could find or that he'd confessed to being consumed by an ancient hunger. I'll never know which was true, whether he needed a shrink or an exorcist, and I'm not sure I want to know.

I once saw a sign on a pillar in a New York City subway station, WET PAIN, written in bright red block letters on glossy white card stock. Back then I thought it was a joke or mistake, meant to read WET PAINT, but I could be wrong; as much as I don't want to believe it, maybe sometimes a sign that says WET PAIN means exactly that.

The Taken

Tenea Johnson

For all of the construction committee's planning, some details couldn't be replicated exactly. So the barracoons that housed the senatorial sons and daughters had approximately two more square feet of space than those historically built for transatlantic slaves. As more hooded figures were shoved into the cage, Kristen Burke, ignorant of the inaccuracy, felt no gratitude for this small luxury.

She had been the first. First to be stripped down to her thin cotton shirt and silk leggings. First to be branded with ND just below her anklebone. First to have the tape and hood ripped off before they pushed her into the cage.

That was last night or maybe this morning. There were no clocks or natural light in the warehouse. She knew it hadn't been more than a day since the agent— or what she thought was an agent—led her into the idling car that was supposed to take her to her father. When she woke up, cotton-mouthed and head pounding, Senator Burke was not among the men dressed in military black who hustled her through the cold and into the warehouse door. She'd screamed against the tape over her mouth, but by then she was here with grim-faced people who seemed to expect her screams.

Now three women shared the cage with her, shivering and bleary-eyed. She recognized Margaret Eastland from her parents' dinner parties and Bridget Hardy from her mother's campaign commercials. Kristen couldn't place the young blond girl who leaned on her ankle where they had burned her. Though tears slid down her face, Kristen paid the pain no mind.

The warehouse was loud. Gates slid open and closed. Men yelled a language she couldn't understand. Margaret Eastland kept screaming every few minutes, words garbled behind the tape still on her mouth. Somewhere out of sight, metal scraped against metal. Boxes hit floors, and behind all this more voices rose. Kristen couldn't see where they came from, but they never stopped or even paused in their monotonous roar. More than once she thought her ears had started bleeding from all the noise. She would wipe at them spastically, only for her hand to come back clean, save for the sheen of sweat.

She wished Eastland would shut up. Or that Bridget Hardy would speak again. They'd shared a few words when Bridget first arrived. As soon as they dumped her in, she started asking questions. Her blue eyes boring into Kristen's, she'd asked who she was, where had she come from, how long had she been there? Kristen Burke. Manhattan. She didn't know. Two men had scooped Bridget off the street in front of her Upper East Side apartment with the same story that got Kristen off the NYU campus and into a dark sedan. Everyone who was anyone knew Eastland kept a place in

Murray Hill, so they'd probably taken her from there. Kristen would bet on the blond girl too. All Manhattan, all in the last day or two. All senators' daughters.

And sons. Five men filled the second barracoon.

Kristen didn't wonder who'd taken them. It was plain as the brand on her skin: ND, New Dawn. Rumors about the group ricocheted from the news reports to the Senate Floor to conversation over martinis at Saul's Bistro. Of all the groups demanding reparations for slavery, none was more feared than New Dawn. They didn't want educational vouchers or free medical care like the other groups, they wanted everything— land redistribution, financial compensation, and stock in every conglom that had benefited from slavery. And even by 2024, that was all the conglomerations. Worse, New Dawn didn't believe in legislation or picketing or economic sanctions. They believed in results. The one and only press statement New Dawn ever issued said just that: "We believe in results." Those words perplexed those outside political circles. It worried her father's camp. Like Kristen, they knew what it took to get results.

A man in a black mask sat on a low stool outside Kristen's cage. He'd been staring at Margaret Eastland for the last few hours, the hours she'd spent screaming. Now he looked in Kristen's direction. He turned his eyes slowly, as if measuring each inch between them. Kristen's lip quivered, and her shivers turned to jolts as he turned his full attention on her. Like the dozen other men outside the cages, he was dressed in all black, a mesh mask obscuring his features. It was hard to tell his height, but he seemed big holding a long stun stick. He tapped it on the floor every few minutes, sending blue sparks dancing along the concrete.

Kristen tried to look him in the eye, but the mask stopped her. It had an opalescent sheen, making it seem to float in front of his face. The Mask looked her up and down, stopping at her stomach, her breasts, her bent shoulders and sweaty face. The longer he looked, the more her throat tightened, the harder it became to breathe. She tried to distract herself, craning her neck to look into the men's cage, but her skin prickled with the weight of his stare. Kristen turned back, looked down at the scratches on her hands, the dirt under her fingernails. After thirty minutes, she began to understand why Margaret Eastland screamed.

Somewhere inside the building a door slammed. Kristen jumped, jabbing her elbow into one of the bars. The Mask laughed at her, then fell silent, staring up at the landing behind the cages. From this angle, she could see the man beneath the mask, the reverence that smoothed out the tight lines around his mouth. She followed his gaze.

Phillip Tailor, New Dawn's leader, wore no mask; instead he donned a smile. Like the others, he wore black fatigues. In place of the mask, a pair of opaque glasses covered his eyes. A tall man, he towered over the cages, and Kristen felt a spell of vertigo. Tailor nodded acknowledgment at the man guarding Kristen's cage. Leaning gracefully over the railing, he surveyed the busy warehouse floor. Another Mask, much smaller than Tailor, walked up to him. This one spoke in that gibberish language and pointed Tailor toward the back of the building. Before leaving, Tailor nodded once more at the Mask outside Kristen's cage.

Abruptly, Eastland stopped screaming. The Mask returned to his original posture, leaving a trail of blue sparks as he slowly dragged the stun stick back to his side. Eastland slumped against the bars, fingers twitching the last of ten thousand volts from her system. The blond girl scurried farther away from the prone body, pinning Kristen into the corner. Kristen was grateful for the sweat pressed into her skin, grateful for someone to hold on to, for something to come between her and the apparition who scrutinized her, sparking blue intention across the floor.

Their captors were yelling. Still holding the blond girl, Kristen tried to follow one set of gibberish from man to man. The tone suggested commands, but she couldn't be sure. She looked toward the sound of a bodega gate moving. This gate was much bigger and going up. The whole wall behind the barracoons recessed into its upper reaches and let dawn in. She smelled salt water, heard distant traffic, and hoped for a moment. Maybe New Dawn had gotten their ransom. Maybe her father had arrived. Maybe someone would see them and send agents. Maybe . . . maybe.

Her brain stuttered at the sight of the gangplank. She could hardly take in the ship and the open water beyond it. The gangplank was too much. She opened her mouth to scream.

Hours of sitting hadn't slowed the Mask. He lunged with precision, knocking his stool over. The stun stick passed through the barracoon's bars and touched Kristen's shoulder. Still clutching each other, she and the blond girl shared the strong current.

Conscious, but unable to move, Kristen watched as her hand slipped from the tangle of blond hair receding from her grasp. After New Dawn dragged the younger girl out, they pulled at Kristen's ankles. She felt the silk, then her skin, tear against the rough floor. When her head fell from the cage's lip and onto the concrete, she whimpered.

The Mask hovered close to her face, squinting at her. He reached down and pinched her ear. Hard. Her hand jumped. He made a low noise in his throat, snatched her up by her armpits so that they were face-to-face. She heard him exchange a few words with someone. Another set of hands held her from behind, her head resting against a broad chest. Her gaze followed the other women being dragged out of the door and into the half-light—then out of her field of vision.

The man behind the mask peeled it up from the bottom, stopped just above his lips. A translation patch stuck to the mesh's underside. Now the gibberish made sense.

"Say good-bye to home," he said, his voice clear and deep without the conversion.

The hands behind her covered her mouth and lifted her away from the barracoon, toward the ship.

She was trying to remember the diagrams. All her life, she'd flipped past the Black History Month specials, those horrible images somebody should have forgotten by now. But now she wished she could remember. Then at least she would have some idea what the hold looked like. Maybe then she'd know where the blond girl was and where they'd put the men. She could feel flesh, but the heat made it difficult to tell which was hers. The Masks hadn't been back since they'd chained the captives to each other, and then to the ship. And she'd been near unconsciousness then.

Someone coughed. Was that a man's cough or a

woman's? Did it matter? Someone was awake. She tried to use her voice. When she heard it, it sounded like she'd been up for days, high on too much Mystique.

"Bridget?" she pleaded into the dark. "Margaret?"

"Matthew." The voice came from beneath her. "Matt Holleran. From Georgia."

Kristen saw a flash of a gangly redheaded boy with green eyes beaming out from an "Equality is Now!" poster. Senator Holleran and his family had posed for the short-lived campaign that was supposed to help end the call for reparations. She thought back to the faces in the men's cage. There. The one with the dark red beard. Broad-chested, head bent beneath the cage's low ceiling. Matthew Holleran.

"Blake Denning," a voice said below her.

"Harry Anderson," another said.

"Preston Caleb," one said from above.

"Bridget Hardy," the skin on her left said.

A high-pitched whisper from above said, "Margaret Eastland."

"Chuck Lassiter," the skin on her right said.

"Drew Ellison," the last one said.

Captain Tailor watched the infrared images calling out their names. He tapped the screen, then turned down the volume. *Should feed them soon. No, just water*, he corrected himself. He'd been battling how many inaccuracies to allow, trying to find the balance between highlighting their advantages and introducing them to the Middle Passage's suffering, so that they could in turn introduce the white world. Though he and his crew were perpetrating one of the most ambitious experiments in the Rep War campaign, he had to maintain parameters. Already, he worried about the Examples' advantages: a shared language, a smaller group, the faster voyage, and of course, all the moral prerogatives: no rape, no dying, limited physical abuse. But he aimed to get the voting majority into their heads and hopefully their hearts through the body. Identity politics infused with psychological warfare. He knew the formula would get results. He had to remain vigilant if they were to be the right results.

Shireen entered the surveillance room, still talking on her handheld. Moving toward Tailor, she concluded her conversation and slipped the handheld into her bulky jacket.

"Fifteen dead at the Baltimore demonstration, though they're reporting them only as injuries," she said to him. "Over three hundred arrests."

"What about Tuscaloosa and D.C.?" Tailor asked.

She sat down in the chair next to him.

"The Representatives in Tuscaloosa never stopped walking, just got in their transports and bolted. And the PFC postponed the March in D.C." She pulled the rolled-up mesh fabric down to her ears. "It's cold in here."

"Again," he answered to both statements. "How many postponements does that make?"

"Three. This time something about one of the organizer's connections to the Court of International Trade muddying the waters."

He laughed. "Once again, nonviolence proves itself nonviable."

Shireen fell silent. They'd always disagreed on this point. He knew that she believed a happy *median* existed between the extremes; that she'd signed up for this project to protect the Examples, though "Monitor" was her official title, and, on the ship, "First Mate." That title must have rankled her feminist leanings. But that was exactly why Tailor needed her: Shireen didn't say yes unless she meant it.

Tailor walked over to the heart and blood pressure monitors that made up the center wall. He tore off hard copies of the latest readings and filed them away, made sure the digifiles were simultaneously saving and transmitting to the processors stateside.

It felt good to stand; he'd been at the monitors for nearly three hours, making notes for the first draft of his press statement. He stretched his arms toward the ceiling, looked out the window at the crew taking in the fresh night air. Latrell shared a cigarette with Two Tone. Their light jackets flapped in the breeze. Good men, those. They knew enough to ask questions. He wouldn't have to worry about them; they would do the job and take the freedom offered in Ghana, leave all the restrictions on felons behind and live as full men again. His attention to the details was just as much for this New Dawn crew as for the nine below. The voyage would change them just as profoundly.

He turned back to Shireen, who sat, jaw tensed, looking at the surveillance monitors.

"Should we feed them now?" he asked.

"Yes," she answered. "I'll go with Two Tone."

"I'll go with you as well." He retrieved a mask from the top of the monitor banks.

Shireen looked at him quizzically.

"Research," he said to the unspoken question.

Captain Tailor and Shireen collected the stocky man outside. All three pulled their masks down, opalescence shimmering in the moonlight as they walked.

The hold stank. Even with the masks' air filters, a level of the stench still entered Tailor's nose—a sharp unpleasantness that reached past technology to give him the impression of feces, urine, and vomit. It smelled like the Rep War: everything let go after being pent up too long. He knew that smell.

Walking past the containers of food and medicines New Dawn would bring onto the shores of West Africa, they reached the back corner where the nine lay, three by three, in a space designed for two industrial sinks. Shireen added powdered protein to the cornmeal mush and handed it to Two Tone, who did the water and food detail. Captain Tailor stood nearby, taking notes on a legal pad. He stepped closer and hovered near the middle tier. Shireen climbed atop the structure and searched for an ankle to spray with the antibiotic salve. Tailor heard her sigh; she turned and looked at him, her expression unreadable. She told Two Tone to give everyone extra water.

Shireen's words came out in Icelandic. With the trans link in his ear, Two Tone understood well enough. After the training, time in the warehouse setting things up, and the sea, they could both probably speak the strange language without the aid of trans patches. At first, Shireen had questioned Tailor about his "odd choice," but now he was sure she understood: Who could speak Icelandic? Most people couldn't even recognize it.

Kristen dreamed of the sky. Its light gray tones bobbed by, the sun still hidden in dawn's hues: not the sunset sky of her trip to Bali, or the bright blue receding and advancing of her childhood swing, not even the rare red sunrise on the Hudson after a long night of cocktails and conversation. She dreamed of the last sky she saw, bobbing above, as her head bumped on the slats of the pier.

Up on deck, the sky was clearer than Kristen had dreamed it. She kept her eyes on it as she stumbled up and down the small deck. She didn't want to look at the men without their masks. They barked commands in that strange language, though their waving hands made their meaning clear enough. *Here. Go Here. Faster. Faster. Stop. Get Back. Right Now. Do It. Again.*

She didn't want to see the others from the hold, either. If they could just not look at each other, one day they might be able to see one another without the memory. Kristen doubted that "one day" would ever come. Apparently, New Dawn didn't care if she and the others saw their faces. So the men would probably kill them out here on the open sea. They believed in results.

When they went back to the hold, Kristen missed the light.

If left in its grasp too long, the dark crawls over you and molds you into something unrecognizable. Already, Kristen's back had changed shape. Fluid filled her lungs. Her skin had become a separate animal that she tried to fight off. She'd been in the dark for five days.

That night, the crew came down to choose their bed warmers. Tailor picked Kristen.

When the two men who'd brought her up took off the blindfold, Tailor was already seated at a small table, a pitcher of amber-colored liquid at his elbow. The room was small. No more than a cot bolted to the floor, and the table. Tailor took the tail of the chain from one of the crewmen and bid them good night. As soon as they were gone, he pulled the chain roughly, causing her to stumble closer to the cot. Wrapping the chain around the cot leg, he produced a small lock that he secured to the couplings. Next, he wrapped a length around her chest and locked these to the sides of the metal frame. She could move, but only if she wanted to rub metal against her ribs.

Tailor, winded, pulled up a chair and posed a question. "Imagine no one had tended to your brand. How do you think it would look now? How much pain would you be in?"

Kristen didn't answer. Could hardly breathe.

Tailor inclined his head slightly and continued. "Imagine that there were one hundred ninety of you instead of nine. What do you think it would smell like? How many would be dying?"

Silence.

"Imagine that you'd had to walk the fifty miles between where we captured you and the warehouse. How close to death would you have been in your high heels and silk pajamas?"

Rage moved through her. She bucked in the chains, spraining her wrist, bruising her ankles. She called him every name she could think of. Names she didn't know that she knew. She screamed her throat raw and then lay glaring at him, her breath shooting out in short bursts.

Tailor looked at her, smiling a little. Then asked another question.

He went on like that until the sun came up. Just before he called the crewmen to lead her back into the hold he said:

"Now imagine that I had raped you."

The well of tears that had threatened to spill all night came brimming over Kristen's lids. She leaned against the door frame, head bowed, trying to hide her face from him.

"Next time," he said looking at her intently, "if you do what I want, you can have some of the peach juice. It's your favorite, no?"

On the way back to the hold, the crewmen walked a full foot in front of Kristen. They held her chain away from their bodies and looked down at the floor or out at sea. At the entrance, they waited for Kristen to walk through, careful not to touch her.

She was the last one to be brought back to the hold. Eight shadows filled the bank between the ceiling and the floor. They hardly moved and didn't speak, though she could hear one of the men on the top row whimpering. One crewman waited at the entrance, while the other dragged the chain across the planks and locked Kristen back in place. The two left silently, footfalls heavy and slow.

The wood beneath Kristen creaked in time to the waves, but there were no human sounds, not from the crew above or the ones down below. It was as if a spell had been cast over everyone on the ship and now they all lay quietly trying to remember how they'd become so afflicted. Kristen supposed this because she, herself, could think of nothing else.

It was enough that her mind was working again. In the last few days, it had abandoned her for long stretches of time, capable of nothing more than the automatic functions of pumping her heart and breathing. Kristen would wait, ambivalent about the return of her awareness. Gradually, it let her hear the sound of scurrying after a long stretch of silence. When she could feel the cold moisture pooled under her buttocks, she knew awareness had returned. For better or for worse.

Later, she heard the hold door open. Someone above her keened a quick desperate note. She watched as light knifed through the dark, growing larger and brighter. Chains knocked against wood as the captives shifted, trying to curl away.

The door closed. When Kristen's eyes adjusted, four of the crewmen stood at her feet. They'd already unlocked the men on the bottom row; now they worked on her manacles.

Up on deck, the captives huddled near each other. The remnants of their clothes hung at odd angles. All the silk that had once covered Kristen's back was worn away, leaving only deep scratches on her reddened skin. She looked better than most of the other women. The crew kept their distance. No one shouted for dancing or prodded them with the short end of a stun stick. A half dozen crewmen stood against the railing, staring out into the sea. Others dragged fire hoses into the hold to blast out its offal. These were the same men who had hauled the women and two of the men away last night, their shouts louder than the captives' pleas; today, they looked stooped, a little less full.

"Bed warmers, Phillip!" Shireen stood in the middle of the monitor room, arms across her chest, glaring at Captain Tailor.

"It's good to finally hear you call me by my first name, Shireen."

She clenched her teeth until a solid square of tread emerged from the corners of her jaw.

"You watched the monitors all night. Did anything happen?" he asked.

"Hell yes, something happened—you went too far."

"Too far?" Tailor flared with his own anger now; his voice went quiet and steady. "This is *nothing*! A few questions and an uncomfortable night at the foot of someone's bed. Why, Latrell even gave up his bed! Too far? They're not children. They're not dying. This is just a taste of suffering. A taste! They get to go free at the end, Shireen. Their children will be free. Their minds will be free. They won't work a single day. Mark my words, no one will ever deny them their due. Not far enough perhaps, but not *nearly* too far."

Kristen heard Tailor's voice and flinched, jerked her head toward the railing. Two of the male captives stared at her. When Kristen saw how the men looked at her, she knew she had become part of their nightmare. And they would never see her any other way.

That next night, Tailor sent for her. He shackled her to the table, hands pulled down into her lap by a chain looped under the seat, through the back of the chair, and around her waist. Kristen barely resisted. Fatigue had most of her; the rest stared at the camera and tripod pointed at the small cot in the corner of the room. Tailor pushed her up to the table and placed the pitcher of peach juice below her chin. Kristen's nose worked independently of the rest of her, pulling deep breaths of peach into her mouth and chest. Captain Tailor sat down opposite her. He crossed his legs loosely at the ankle.

She eyed the video camera over his shoulder, a hot knot of foreboding forming in her stomach. She wanted to believe the camera had been there the last time but knew it had not. Tailor's last words to her echoed in her memory. Between them, her pain, abject hunger, and the cold gusting around the edge of the door, it was all she could do to stay conscious—never mind sane.

"Kristen—" Captain Tailor looked directly at her, his tone even.

For twenty-two years, Kristen, Senator Burke's daughter, answered when someone called her name. The new Kristen, woman snatched from her native soil, cried when she heard her name for the first time. She made no sound, only shook with her pain. Every other heartbeat, she gasped for breath. Her hands hung loosely in her lap, and her head dropped straight down into her chest.

Captain Tailor reached behind him to turn the camera around. And started his questioning.

Kristen broke before the ship reached the Tropic of Cancer. She told Tailor all the answers to his questions. All the ways her passage differed, bettered. Listed all the things she didn't go through, mentioned the medical care she'd received. Learned his brutal lesson. Tailor had to reload the camera she talked so much. In between answers, she guzzled from a goblet of amber-colored liquid.

Before agents overran the ship and liberated what was left of the senatorial sons and daughters, Tailor threw away his own draft and broadcast Kristen Burke, dirty, ragged, and grateful, as his statement.

Mr. Bones

Christopher Chambers

> "MINSTREL, n. A nigger with a color less than skin
> deep and a humor more than flesh and blood can
> bear."
>
> —Ambrose Bierce, *The Devil's Dictionary*

Nanh-unh, *Mr. Bones*, I hissed inwardly, *I'm not done with your black ass yet!* I plopped him on the stool before his dressing room mirror. I cleared the stink of his whiskey breath from my nostrils. The stink of his words still assaulted my ears.

"Brudder gwine guide me home . . . bright angels gwine biddy me ta come . . ."

I felt my stomach shoot down in my knees when he said that. Oh, I heard him mumble when he was drunk before, or high as a cloud from his Chinaman's pipe, sticky with opium. Yet tonight, he looked like he'd sucked down a cask just to die and spite *me* . . . as if that was possible. And the words? Not his usual liquor-induced grunts or fitful dreamy whining about what he did that night in Tennessee, when I first met him. He was just a child then. Still was, to me. At least I thought so, until tonight, and so I was shivering and pacing and wondering who'd gotten to him. Crazy fool'd ruin it for us! Worse for him, though, if it got ruined. Far damn worse.

I snapped open the gold watch dangling from my vest fob. Quarter past six. I snapped it shut, paced again. Another forty-five minutes to curtain call. Took that long to sober him up, get on his makeup. But I had to know. Shit. *Bright angels biddy me to come . . .*

He stirred. That great brown bald pate swayed toward its reflection in the mirror. He must've felt my eyes boring into him, because his eyes opened, and he reached for a handkerchief to wipe the slobber from his lips.

"Y'all still heya, Scratch?" he wheezed. "Lawd . . . ah ain't neva be rid y'all's taint. . . ."

Better to coax him to get ready for the performance. Easier to root out why he said what he said later. I sighed, and my pulse ratcheted down a bit when I saw him grab his cotton rag and the black greasepaint. One swipe, another. I calmed with each layer of black on his brown face. Red next, for his mouth. Red as new blood on those meaty lips. Slowly, quietly but for a few sniffles and belches and nary a complaint, Mr. Bones came to life in the mirror. Good-bye, Jim Trice. So long, this wanna-wet-my-draws feeling!

You know, white folks loved the red lips. Don't know why—Jim started out back with Zip Coon & Christy's Minstrels with white lips and the audiences hated it. Then we opened at the Beaux-Arts in Cincinnati with the red and a bass-toned chant and song and flip and reel. Lord, did you see those fat, pie-faced sots jump up in their seats, hooting and cheering? That's when Christy fired ol' Zip, tried to get Jim. Mr. Bones. Everyone wanted Mr. Bones. Even Zip came to me for help. Heard he got lynched a few years back, down in Indiana, and then smoked like ham. Poor Zip. Rich Jim, for yes, I, Scratch Jones, stage name "Professor Miscegenation and da Interlocutor," signed Mr. Jim Trice of east ass-bugger Tennessee with Messrs. Feeley & P.T. Barnum for two hundred and fifty dollars a week. Got free accommodations on any Pullman car compliments of Mr. George Pullman the Elder as long as he could use Mr. Bones's likeness in newspaper advertisements, handbills. Couple thousand Negroes working on Pullman sleepers and dining cars, and not one is allowed to sleep or dine on them! But we are. Scratch Jones and Jim Trice. Fine living even for a yellow nigger (or am I red?), and downright heavenly for a country raggamuffin like Jim.

And so I heard my meal ticket croak, "Ah cain't stan' dem electric lights o' Mr. Edison's, Scratch." He started with the white paint. "Ah like de ol' lime footlights . . . dis 'lectricity jus' anudder piece o' man's vanity over Gawd—ain't that right? Vanity."

I kicked over a brass spittoon to catch his last whiskey heave, then passed him my clean handkerchief. "Listen, Jimmy," I said. "You having a sort of dream whilst you were passed out? Partner, you drank like you had a cancer and was trying to kill it."

He shrugged. He's murdering himself with liquor and scaring me white and all he can do is shrug?

I was at his shoulder. "Crying to the angels, Jim?"

He twisted away from me. "Ah open'd da gate," he suddenly whispered. "Ah open'd da gate, an' he say he gwine take car'us . . . me, my mama. Ah open'd da gate . . ."

That he did. "Too late for regrets. We got a show."

Maybe it wasn't anyone getting to him. Maybe it was just nerves. Tonight, the snow was falling like a billion cotton bolls in Buffalo, but Irish Quinn said we'd have a full house nonetheless. The Pinkertons and the cops were already there inspecting the stage, the exits and entrances. President Grover Cleveland himself, escorting his new young wife, would be up in the box draped with red, white, and blue crinoline and festooned with Old Glory. In the other gilded boxes would sit none other than Mr. Jay Gould, Mr. Vanderbilt, and Mr. J. Pierpont Morgan and their respective families. Freezing outside but in the Orpheum, hot as hell itself with the shrieks of delight and applause for *Professor Miscegenation's Darktown Review*. And we'd carry that endorsement across the Atlantic to play before the crowned heads of Europe, from Queen Victoria in London to Czar Alexander in St. Petersburg, Russia, and back again!

Then Mr. Bones'd be free. And plain old Jim Trice could wander back to Tennessee. Dig in the nasty mold that was Fort Pillow before he dies. Angels going to biddy him nowhere!

Little plump white girl with rosy cheeks came in with some cider and some cakes, and I saw Jim eyeing her. Made me feel better but I had to point out that even we couldn't break the law so flagrantly. Wait for the whores at the Ontario Hotel, I counseled. "Reward for a good show." I checked the time again, then told him we needed to get our lines clear.

He nodded. I was only on with him during the Line, wherein I and the rest of the Darktown Cakewalkers would feed him bits and he'd slay the audience. Come the Olio, or second act, there'd be songs and a sketch or two, plus Mr. Bones would do a duet with "Titty Pigeon Pea," a dusky girl named Loretta Sims from North Carolina. Come the third act, it was all Mr.

Bones dancing, singing, clacking on the castanets, and banging his tambourine. Bringing down that curtain. Making the audience happy.

I, as Professor Miscegenation, didn't need to go in blackface. I used white paint with just a hint of jaundice. I prompted Jim to begin the quick rehearsal. "G'head, Mr. Bones—"

"Pardon de integer-rumption, Mr. In-ter-locu-tor," Jim began, aping the white man's language, "but did y'all heya dat anudder mulatto professor did die o' da mos' terrblrifical malefliction?"

"You don't say, Mr. Bones!" I answered, on cue. "Was it Dr. Cliftonwitz Carpetbagger of the prestigious Claflin and Howard and Booker T. Tuskaweegee Culud College? Killed by the Knight Riders?"

He was supposed to mug and bug his eyes and say, "Pob'ly not dem Knight Riders. Pob'ly fom all dem words he had ta spit out he mouff jus' ta say he name!" The liquor was hammering his head no doubt. The dressing room door slammed and I think we both thought it was either Irish Quinn or the chubby, bosomy white girl. If the latter, I'd have her fetch him some seltzer water with a pinch of laudanum for that headache. So Jim mouthed his next lines as best he could. It was supposed to be a malapropism on *Don't count your chickens before they've hatched.* I had to speak the line for him: "Y'all should neva spek-ulate on da amount o' yo' juvenile poultry untilst da proper pro-cess o' ink-u-bation hab t'ough'rly come ta fruit-tit-tion. . . ."

At the door came a woman's voice, but it wasn't the white girl's, or even Loretta Sims's. The voice was clear, crisp, and bit right through me as it recited: "Imagination! Who can sing thy force?" Whereupon that bastard . . . that dullard black bastard Jim Trice . . . found his own voice and in the best King's English he'd ever mustered, replied: "Or who describe the swiftness of thy course?"

It was a Negro woman. Short, slight. Wetness glistened on her cloak and wool cap so she must've snuck in a stage door from the snow outside. There was a whole line of coons outside in the cold, hoping to get an autograph from Mr. Bones, an invite to our after-soiree at the Ontario, or proffering their own invitations for us to grace their juke joints down Niagara or Lackawanna way. But she didn't belong to them. I saw her eyes. Eyes that beamed so sweetly at Jim yet burned at me.

So I cursed at that bitch to leave and hollered for Irish Quinn. Jim mumbled sheepishly about a handbill he saw for some Negro players reciting the work of some long-dead coon wench named Phyllis Wheatley onstage at a nigger church. I thought that was a joke! Colored folk paying to hear poetry? Who was "Phyllis Wheatley"? Nah, they spend their nickels on a shaky tail feather and a Minstrel Line and Mr. Bones! Beloved by niggers and howling whites alike!

Yet now I could feel my blood boil and my face must've turned as red as Mr. Bones's lips, for he surely backed up off that stool. . . .

Get a hold of yourself, Scratch, I said to myself. *No need for Quinn. Handle this quietly.* Maybe it was this bitch who got to Jim, filled him with notions of angels. "You know her, Jim?" I asked. "We only been in Buffalo for two days, partner."

"Oh, he knows me, Mr. Jones," the woman said. "He's always known me. I was there at Fort Pillow, too. Fort Pillow, Tennessee, Mr. Jones."

I felt the chilblains spike down my back to my balls and down my calves.

"When Nathan Bedford Forrest Confederates attacked, 1864, a traitor opened the fort's gate . . . a traitor with the small, trembling hands of a child . . . a traitor who meant no one any evil but did evil nonetheless. And the garrison surrendered . . ." She turned toward Jim and he sank his painted face. ". . . then they killed every colored soldier and every soldier's wife, save for one. Bayoneted every colored child. Save for one."

"You mean two?" I pointed out. "Including you? You said you were there on that horrible day when Forrest murdered all those folks, and you about Jim's age, eh?" Then I got slick. "Listen, miss . . . can we talk outside? I think I may have something for you."

"Your money means nothing," she snapped.

No, cash and coins wasn't what I would offer, but I did get her out of there. I whispered a promise to her.

We left the dressing room, slipped past the scurrying stagehands, the other players slipping into their swallowtail coats and top hats, the orchestra members tuning fiddles, horns, and banjos. My pulse was pounding again, but not in that awful way when Jim sang for angels.

We reached the cold alley lit by a sputtering lamp. The alley turned a dogleg to the street, so everything was hushed but for the gentle hiss of falling snow on the wet cobblestones. Her eyes stabbed straight at me, but mine darted like a fox's. My gaze arched and dipped and swung, and then I indeed locked eyes with her. I smiled. I'd already pulled the stiletto from my trouser pocket. Carried it purely for self-defense, of course—never know what roughnecks you'll met on the road, and I hated guns. . . .

The thin blade slid into her throat as if the flesh was air. Blood gushed in a single stream, even as she toppled, eyes still stabbing me as surely I stabbed her. Not a look of terror or even surprise, though. A few twitches and I knew she was gone.

It was only then that I realized we weren't alone.

An old tramp, trembling in the snow. Moth-eaten wool coat barely covered him. He smelled of urine and the same bad whiskey Jim snorted. Terror in his eyes, all right. I knew what to do. Put the stiletto in his hands. Call for help. And I told him he wouldn't hang for killing a Negro woman. Best scenario for him if he confessed, as he'd be guaranteed a warm cell, three hot meals a day. His hands still grasped that stiletto, yet his tongue was like glue when the Pinkertons and cops came running. Damn shame. I went inside to find Mr. Bones.

You know that fool didn't even ask me about the woman! All the commotion over some ruckus in the stage alley, and he didn't have a clue why! He'd even donned his stovepipe hat and got his spats fastened. Face coal black with red slips and white teeth and white gloves. Ready for curtain call and here I didn't even have my own costume ready. He didn't even look at the white girl come to collect the cider and cakes, and showing him some ankle. She was too stupid herself to even note the murder outside. Hell, I'd take her to the Ontario now, ride her like a mare. But the chilblain sliced again when Jim saw a spot of blood on my face.

"Now, hold on, Jim-buck," I said. "Lemme just tell you—"

He cut me off. "Ah hab some bad spot o' blood on mah face, too, Scratch, when ah wuz a chile, dere at Fort Pillow. Lak she says, dem Rebs come an' Bedfor' Forrest bury colored chiles alibe. Know how dey get in when dey attack, Mr. In-ter-locu-tor?"

"Somebody let 'em in, Mr. Bones. They stormed the walls but they didn't break through until the gate opened. Somebody let them in. For a promise. But past is past and let's move on, eh? We got work to do."

"Yeah-sur. Promise dat he lib. He mama lib. Den a promise dat he be rich an' dem same crackers whut kilt his folk gwine come see he name in dey limelight . . . now Mr. Edison's 'lectric light. An' colored lub him lak de whites. Sing he songs. Buy he choc'late an' matches an' cornmeal flour dat he face be on. An' now de pres'-dent gwine come see'em, too. All fo' o'promise."

I shimmied out of my trousers, and the white girl giggled at the sight of my drawers and garter. I took my baggy pin-striped pants and slipped them on and just let him rant, go off in his fugue. As long as he sang, danced, cakewalked, cooned—no one would care. And that bitch was dead. Yet stupid me, I had to ask.

"Who was she, Jim? Twenty years and we hadn't had one bit of trouble."

He popped a wide melon-eating smile, clicked his castanets. "Ain't tell you a thing. Say I can do better . . . we *all* do better than dese minstrel shows. Teach me a line or two 'bout good things. *Imagination*, by Phyllis Wheatley. Colored men doin' Ot'hello by Mr. Shake-speare. Writin' dey own shows, own music. Mo'dem poems. Ain't Olio songs fo' ig'rant niggahs to prance to. Not 'bout habbin' money!"

Spittle was flying. I couldn't help myself. "She said all this, huh? When—the hotel last night? And where're these handbills about some Negro play, Negro show at some church?"

"Ah's sober now, Scratch. Curtain call soon. President and all dem big white folk be waitin' . . . waitin' on *Mr. Bones*."

Artful, he wasn't. And his story about that woman made no sense. He was hiding something, though. Irish Quinn shooed the white girl out and said we had two minutes to curtain, so what was I to do but trust him?

Fanfare. Chickens and mules down on the farm; cakewalkers prancing in the town. Me, stage right. Him, stage left. We slayed. Act two. The Olio. I was calmer and everything was going better than I'd dreamed. Titty Pigeon Pea and Mr. Bones nailed their final duet, "Darky Sweeties," and even I shed a tear as I wiped off my makeup. Act three. Mr. Bones, alone. Our finale. Hushed crowd as he entered, stage right, tambourine in one hand, clicking "bones" in the other . . .

And then that son of a bitch dropped the tambourine and those bones to his feet.

He took off his hat. That syrupy bass crooned a song I'd never heard. It was about a little boy's nightmare. Blood. Fire. Pain. Shame. And a dream. Redemption.

Oh no. Oh, shit no . . .

More shame, this time aimed at the audience. A black finger pointed at them all, from the middling folk in the cheaper seats to the titans of industry and politics in the upper boxes. And a final song, like a nail dragged across tin. I wailed.

"Brudder gwine guide me home . . . bright angels gwine biddy me ta come . . ."

It was one of the Pinkertons who first saw the revolver. I guess he thought Jim was going to shoot President Cleveland, just like someone else, whom I knew, shot President Garfield some years before over a job the fool didn't get. The agent drew his weapon, got off a round at ol' Jim Trice. But Jim was dead before that bullet struck his liver—Jim having put one in his own head a split second prior.

People rushed the stage, but I backed into the wings, mind spinning, heart exploding with every beat. I could feel a look on my back. A stabbing look, but with pain worse than I'd felt in a long time.

I turned. He was there. The old tramp from the alley.

He stood plain as he did on the third day, when the stone was rolled away from the tomb. He was smiling. And the bitch I killed backed him right up, not a smear of blood on her neck. The tramp had some blood. Oh yes. Where it usually oozed. From his wrists. And there, soaking through his torn socks.

It wasn't fair. What did he care? Why stop me? Why save this piece of vomit who betrayed his own people just to save the bitch that sired him? And kept on betraying and made so much cash holding his people to ridicule—with those very people laughing right along?

My shriek pierced every human ear in the Orpheum. My skin broke from me and liquefied on the floor. My gums bled till my fangs erupted and my guts split open with worms. My tongue became forked and slimy, for this had always been my punishment. I was beautiful once. My songs bested the voices of a thousand million Jim Trices. I sang for God Himself and all my brother and sister angels until I betrayed them like a little boy who opened a fort's gate and let death ride in.

And in a flash of light I was gone. Scratch Jones. Whimpering. Brooding.

Waiting.

Not for long.

Deondré's mother was a nurse and his father was a senior mechanic for a Toyota dealership, and they loved him so much. They lived outside Washington, D.C., in a comfortable little house with cable TV and a PC. But he had to be hard and ran with some boys he shouldn't have. A girl and her date got shot as they stood in line for popcorn at a movie about black women in strip clubs and the thugs who desired them. Deondré went to a state boys' camp, charged as an accessory to the assault. And at that camp, I came to him in a wet dream. I was a honey-hued woman with pendulous breasts and a thick, sweaty backside and pouty mouth.

A promise was made. And Deondré would get his ticket out of that kiddie jail. He would see me later, in the flesh, as Tasha Brown, and I worked for the record label and knew all the right white people. Deondré composed such nasty, hot rhymes when he should have been doing his homework. His syrupy bass was intoxicating and his curses heartfelt. I hooked him up with my producers in Atlanta. Five years later, Deondré's parents forgot their shame, for they moved into a six-thousand-square-foot mansion. *Dirty South Hoes*, their son's debut album, had gone double platinum.

Oh yes, the bookstores big and small alike dropped Zora and Richard and Langston and Walter and Alice, and replaced them with Deondré's new line of pulp novels based on his "life stories." You know—shit that never happened, like the hookers he turned into tricks themselves, and the weak men he turned out in prison (not a state boy's camp).

Girls fainted on *106th & Park* when he appeared as a guest.

His line of athletic and outerwear almost bankrupted North Face.

He sat in skyboxes at two Super Bowls, despite stabbing deaths at his pregame parties each of those years. I slept with star players on the winning football teams and they agreed to endorse his clothing line.

He headlined homecoming at the black college his mother had attended, bragging about gunplay and sex with the cheerleaders and sorority girls. To mollify the college's president, he wrote a check to the school for three million and the music department got a new studio bearing his name.

They wanted him for movies. They wanted him for a sitcom on UPN.

The year he hosted the Video Music Awards he gave MTV its highest ratings in ten years.

He smacked Bill O'Reilly on Fox News. Bill thanked me off-camera for the highest ratings he'd ever had. A promise was a promise, after all.

Fools debate his worth to this day. I never did. From the first time I saw him, so weepy for not stopping his drunk-ass homies from shooting that girl in the multiplex parking lot. Pleading for God to have mercy on him. Well, my eyes glowed red as hot coals with nothing but love for him. And I had to think of a new stage name for him.

By the way, the new CD cover portrayed him just as

in the video for the first track—which I wrote. *Niggas Holla Shoop Shoop Wow.* There he stood, muscles brimming through his white wifebeater. Lips red as new blood. The album was simply self-titled.

Mr. Bones.

Can you hear me laughing, bright angels?

Rip Crew

B. Gordon Doyle

Tonk had an eye for the bitches. And it all started with Tonk.

Once a month, the four of them, the whole crew, would roll out and seriously light it up. Usually, it was the weekend before a full moon, on accounta' Redbone's witchy moms tellin' him back when he was a young'un that a waxing moon favored beginnings.

Redbone was the first to get his license and a ride, so it was his call from jump. After that, it was just habit. Kinda like a ritual. The moon would start to gettin' full, an' the crew would start to grinnin' an' schemin'. . . .

They'd head down to the barbershop, get all cut an' clean, then drag out the fresh junk, the bling an' designer suits an' fake IDs, and step correct. They'd hit Solitaire's or Hardbar or Ascot and tear shit up, flashin' fat knots an' choppin' lines and tossin' drinks at anything with cleavage an' a thong. And it was all good, and straight-up righteous, considering wasn't one of them, not Redbone or Tonk or Lil' B or Young 'Dre even twenty years old.

But back to Tonk. And the bitches.

It was Friday late at the Ascot, an' the niggas was down, sweatin' on the dance floor, chillin' at the bar, when Tonk lamped her comin' out of the ladies' room. Tonk always kept his eye on the ladies' room door, 'cause he knew that sooner or later, every bitch in the house got to come through there.

"Gotta get that perv on, to get some swerve on, yo."

That was Tonk speakin', and Young 'Dre listening.

"Yeah, dog. Uh-huh."

'Dre was distracted; he was watching a low, busty, Latina freakin' redbone under the lights. That nigga could *keep* them light-skinned shorties on the leash. He had game. More fool they.

"*Got* damn. Check this shit out."

'Dre followed the older boy's eyes across the crowded nightclub, and felt his heart thud in his chest.

She was tall, nearly six feet in her heels, with skin the color of honey and cream. Her hair was jet-black, straight and long, hanging down to the hem of the black, laced-up minidress that looked painted on. She wore no jewelry, save for a studded, black leather slave collar around her neck. She was fine-featured, with the generous lips and sculpted cheekbones that other women bled for. And she was looking directly at Tonk.

"Grab this, yo." The older boy passed 'Dre his drink, pulled out a handkerchief, and wiped his hands. "And tell me she ain't lookin' over here."

"Can't." 'Dre watched as the woman moved away from the bathroom door, walking with the haughty confidence that only beauty can bestow. "I'd be lyin'."

"Then I'm about it, nigga." Tonk looked around for a mirror as he smoothed at his eyebrows and goatee, and pulled at his silk tie. "You wit' me?"

Young 'Dre had not taken his eyes off the woman; he watched her as she settled in at the bar, sliding easily onto a bar stool, crossing her legs with slow grace . . .

"Nah, nigga. You needs to check yourself."

. . . and was joined by a man like a mountain. Big, black, and wide, like a mountain.

"Say what?" The older boy stopped preening, incredulous. "Check myself? Where dat bitch get to?"

Tonk searched the room for her, as 'Dre grabbed his shoulders and pointed him to the bar.

"Over there. An' she gots a friend."

The black man at her side was nearly seven feet tall, and weighed at least three hundred pounds. He was bald and clean-shaven, dressed in a fitted tuxedo and was holding a black clutch purse under his arm.

"Don' *go* there, Tonk," 'Dre shouted; the music was suddenly louder. "Just *don't*. That black bastid's big like Shaq."

Tonk was silent. 'Dre could feel the thump of bass in his gut.

"Yo, niggas! Who died?"

Lil' B pushed his way through the throng on the dance floor, with a pretty brown club girl in tow. She was obviously drunk; as he joined them, B held her steady with a hand on the small of her back.

"Whassup, B?" 'Dre asked quickly, trying to ignore the fact that Tonk still hadn't said a word. He could feel it coming.

"Shorty here's whassup, yo. An' there some for y'all back at her table. Plenty plenty. Ain't that right, baby girl?"

"I's my birfday." The girl giggled, smiling at 'Dre. "What's your name? Didn't you go to Banneker?"

Lil' B winked and laughed softly, keeping it mellow;

he was feeling good in his Sean John an' steady pullin' down the shorties, the way it was supposed to be. Friday night. Drink a little, snort a little, freak a little. Maybe even get a little. Good times.

But no . . .

"*Fuck* that big mothafucka!" Tonk exploded. "He ain't shit! Bitch was lookin' right at me."

The girl straightened, looked at Lil' B, and then back toward the dance floor.

"I'ma go check in with my friends," she said, as she pushed away Lil' B's hand. "Your boy needs to chill out or somethin'."

"An' fuck you, too, chicken head. Fuck you an' your—"

"*Tonk!*" Lil' B, never one to lose his cool, was furious. "The fuck's your *issue,* nigga? Yo, 'Dre, you needs to talk to this nigga 'fore I get all *gauche* up in here."

"Shorty over there playin' him. Got his nose open f'real." 'Dre nodded toward the bar. Even as he spoke, the woman peered around her escort and smiled at them. She had eyes like a cat.

Lil' B watched her for a moment, then nodded. "Yeah, at the bar in the black Bao Tranchi. She's like, come hit this ass an' that big nigga's like, don't even think it. Okay." He paused, shrugged. "So, what you wanna do, Tonk? Stand here with your dick in your hand or make that move?"

"I jus' wanna talk to her, B. For a minute. I never seen nothing like her before."

'Dre fought back a chuckle. No doubt. When he first saw her, the sight of her had taken his breath away. But now, well, she *was* fine. Real pretty. Just like a lot of bitches.

He was over it.

Not so, Tonk. He was utterly captivated. And to him, the big man at her side was more than an obstacle. He was a challenge.

Lil' B looked out over the dance floor, shaking his head. "A'ight, nigga. Let's do this. I'ma grab up Redbone an' go out to the ride an' get my shit," Lil' B cocked his thumb and forefinger and placed them over his heart. "'Cause if you goin' over there, you better go strong, y'feel me? I ain't lettin' you go out like no punk."

'Dre felt a chill on the back of his neck. It wasn't fear, but foreboding. Here, amidst the clamor and crowd of the Ascot, a life-and-death decision had been made. He needed to say something, before it all went bad. For good. "B, man. Hol' up. That's the liquor talkin'."

"Nah, Young. This nigga already run off the bitches I hooked up. An' if we ain't gettin' no ass, then *fuggit*, we get a little bloody." Lil' B shrugged his broad shoulders again and tucked his hand into his waistband, signaling to Redbone. The lanky, well-dressed boy pushed off from his partner on the dance floor and moved to B's side.

"Whassup, B?" Redbone clenched his teeth and sneered, going gangster. "We needs to go out to the ride?"

"Word. You niggas sit tight till we get back. We see if that big mothafucka's bulletproof."

The two of them, Redbone and Lil' B, turned and jostled their way through the crowd. Tonk was shaking, and it wasn't from the blow.

The music was pumpin' sinister, like a horror movie sound track. Young 'Dre felt he had to do something. *Anything*. To stop what he knew was coming.

He did something.

'Dre turned, and picked his way slowly across the packed dance floor, fighting to keep his head on straight. He ordered a drink, waited while the bartender took his own sweet time, then walked down the bar until he was only a few feet away from the woman with the cat's eyes and jet-black hair. He took a long, slow sip, moved close enough to smell her perfume. The man mountain leaned forward and whispered to her, then raised a hand to shove him back as 'Dre declared:

"You gonna get somebody *killed* tonight."

She laughed. It was like breaking glass; hard, sharp, and brittle.

"Wait, Julian. Not yet." The woman turned on the bar stool, slowly uncrossing her legs, and placed her hands on her knees. "You are the only man to dare approach me tonight. And you approach me, only to tell me that someone will die? How delightfully . . . *piquant*. Tell me more."

'Dre moved closer, so he wouldn't have to shout. Julian, the big man, raised his hand again and shook his head. 'Dre eyed him warily, set his drink on the bar beside hers, then continued. "My boy over there. He thinks you've been watching him all night."

"Perhaps I have. He has hungry eyes."

"You need to quit playin' him," 'Dre said with rude bravado. "He's about to come over here an' start up some shit. An' your big-ass boyfriend ain't scarin' him."

"Really?" she asked demurely, as she cocked her thumb and forefinger and placed them on her breast. "Not at all? Not even the *teensiest* bit?"

'Dre stepped back. There was no way she could have seen Lil' B give the high sign. Something was wrong here, way wrong.

"Now then," she continued. "Here's what you're going to do. You're going to go back over to your little friend with the hungry eyes, and tell him I'd *love* to speak with him. And then, you're going to leave." She stirred her drink, and smiled. "Quickly now! Before your ... *homeboys* ... return, and my Julian has to disarm them and break them into little pieces. *Teensy* pieces."

'Dre could feel his courage slipping away. Draining away. He picked up his drink and quickly finished it.

"C-can't do that," he stammered, wiping his mouth. "Can't leave a brother behind ..."

"Just so. Julian?"

Quick as light, the big man leaned out and grabbed 'Dre by the lapels, turned, and pinned him against the bar. He stared down at the boy, pulled him close until they were face-to-face, eye-to-eye. 'Dre swung at him, struggled, to no avail; he was like a stuffed doll in the teeth of a pit bull. He tried to yell for help, but before he could gather the breath, he peered into Julian's black eyes and saw ...

A flicker of darkness. A veil lifted, a glimpse ...

The three of them. Redbone and Lil' B and himself, lying in the alley next door to the Ascot. Lying broken in the alley, their limbs twisted at impossible angles. Lying in the alley, sightless eyes peering upward, with a red pool of blood beneath them that ran slowly into the gutter. Slowly. Slowly.

'Dre moaned unintelligibly as Julian dropped him to the floor. A couple at the bar looked down, saw him slumped along the bar rail, shook their heads, and went back to their drinks.

"Now, little one," the woman hissed. "Go do as you're told."

'Dre whimpered and got to his feet, staggered back across the dance floor, bouncing off bodies. He had to warn Tonk, had to tell him . . .

He reached the other side, fell into Tonk's arms. An overwhelming weakness flooded over him like a deluge.

"Nigga, you crazy!" Tonk said admiringly, reaching out to hold 'Dre up. "You got some heart, yo! What she say?"

'Dre tried to answer, but the words wouldn't come. There was something wrong with his head; he felt slow and dim.

"She. She . . . wan . . ." 'Dre slurred, shaking his head, trying to clear it. "Doan!"

"Yeah, man. I see dat. She wavin' me over." Tonk shook him, squinted at him closely. "Damn, yo. You lookin' like you need some air. Go on out an' tell B an' Redbone that it's all good, a'ight? I check you niggas later. Much later."

Tonk slapped him on the back and pushed him toward the stairs. 'Dre stumbled, careened off a table, and fell into a group of revelers who'd just entered the nightclub.

"That's it!" 'Dre heard a voice bellow behind him. "You are done!"

'Dre felt himself seized, pushed up the stairs and out the Ascot's front door. He turned, pleading with the doorman as he was rushed past him, but the words came out wrong. The downstairs bouncer looked over at his coworker, sharing a laugh at 'Dre's expense as he shoved the boy out into the street.

"Say when, rookie."

'Dre staggered back to the curb and slouched down,

his back against a parked car. He could hear the party kids lined up outside the club laughing. Jeering. Yelling.

Yelling. His name.

He raised his chin from his chest, looked up.

Redbone. And Lil' B.

Tonk was still inside. And it all started with Tonk. . . .

'Dre woke to the sound of a car horn, and the stink of vomit. The long light of afternoon filled the room. He was in his own bed, in his uncle's modest brick Colonial on Lincoln Avenue in Takoma Park, Maryland, still wearing his suit pants and shoes. His dress shirt, balled up on the floor by the side of the bed, was the source of the foul smell.

He sat up slowly, then moved to the window of his upstairs room. Outside, double-parked along the curb, with the windows up and speakers blasting Scholly D, Redbone's Toyota Celica sat idling. The car horn sounded again.

'Dre threw open the window and yelled down to the street: "What!!"

The driver's-side door opened in a cloud of reefer smoke. Redbone looked up to 'Dre's window, his hands cupped at his ears.

"What! What!" he mimicked. "It's *Sunday,* nigga, that's *what.* Get you ass up and get down here. We got bid'ness."

"Here, Young." Redbone grinned and passed 'Dre a forty-ounce of Old English 800. "Get ya head right for the ride."

'Dre cracked the bottle and drank deep as the car pulled away from the curb. He'd showered and changed in record time, but was still out of sorts. He needed this bracer, before he started asking the questions that rattled in his head like stones.

"Watch you don' puke again. We run by Popeye's on the way in, get a feed on."

"Nah, I'm good," 'Dre began. "It *can't* be Sunday. . . ."

"Sure you right." Redbone shook his head. "You ain't gettin' it, yo. Shorty dropped a little somethin' in your drink, knocked you outta the game. Then while me an' Lil' B were carryin' your ass back to the ride, she took off with Tonk and that big mofo'."

"Somebody *dosed* me?" 'Dre was angry and confused, trying to remember. "Some *bitch* poisoned me?"

"Nah, man. It weren't all that. Half a roofie. Tonk said she was tryin' to calm your ass down." Redbone paused, lit a Newport. "It was the drink and blow that got you to heavin'. But don' worry none. We gonna get some payback. Wait'll we get down there an' let Tonk tell it."

The two of them drove down Georgia Avenue in silence, as Young 'Dre drank and tried to piece everything together in his mind. It was hopeless; the last thing he could remember was Lil' B and some girl . . .

And nothing. It was as if his memory had been wiped clean.

"Damn, 'Bone. I can't remember shit."

"Fuggit, yo. You got tore up, you puked, we brought your ass home. End of story."

"But I can't remember . . . something happened. That big nigga . . ."

"I said, don' sweat it. Tonk is on this shit. We gonna get ours. Just be cool."

The malt liquor was having the desired affect; Dre sipped, bobbed his head to the music, and surveyed the brownstones and storefronts along Georgia Avenue as they went past Walter Reed, past Howard University, and moved deeper into the city. At Thirteenth Street and Florida Avenue NW, the Celica slowed and Redbone looked around for a parking space. Finding none, he continued down Thirteenth to W Street, turned left, and pulled over in front of some new town houses.

"We here. Kill that bumper an' we out," Redbone said simply. 'Dre complied, as always, deferring to the older boy. The two of them clambered out of the car and crossed back over W Street, then headed up Thirteenth Street half a block before turning into a service alley.

The sight of the alley made 'Dre nervous. Something about an alley . . . "Yo, 'Bone. Th' fuck we goin'?"

"Almost there, Young. Let Tonk tell it. It's his call."

They moved up the alley until they came to the back of an abandoned row house; it seemed someone had attempted reconstruction and repairs, then tired of it. The backyard was fenced off with sagging chain-link and razor wire; there were stacks of soggy Sheetrock and torn tarps and piles of garbage everywhere. Redbone slipped through a hole in the fence, gestured for 'Dre to follow. They climbed up into the house, as there were no stairs.

It was getting dark.

As the two of them picked their way through the accumulated trash and moved to the front of the house, there was the creak of wood from the floor above. A harsh whisper queried from the darkness . . .

"Who'zat!"

"Yo' baby mama," Redbone answered gruffly. "Where my check at?"

"Fuck you, 'Bone," Tonk snapped back. "You got 'Dre wit' you?"

"Yeah. So put your shit away, we comin' up."

Redbone and 'Dre climbed the stairs noisily, and emerged on the second floor. The upstairs area was remarkably clean. All the walls had been knocked down, leaving only the bare support beams in a single, large room. The windows had been boarded up, but the wide cracks between the boards showed dusk outside. Tonk and Lil' B were sitting on a worn wooden bench, passing a bottle of wine back and forth, while Tonk peered through the cracks with a small pair of binoculars. There were two pistols lying on the floor at their feet.

"Tell everybody, why don'cha?" Lil' B said sharply. "'Dre, you back with us?"

"I'm a'ight," 'Dre said. "So, whassup, Tonk? Redbone said you'd gimme the four one one."

"Nothin' to tell, nigga." Tonk waved the boy forward, handed him the binoculars, and pointed to a crack in the boards. "'Cept in a couple hours, we gonna be tearin' up that place over yonder. Upstairs, window on the left."

'Dre raised the field glasses to his eyes, followed Tonk's directions. He saw nothing until his eyes adjusted to the interior shadows in the room across the street. Then he saw her.

Skin the color of honey and cream. Jet-black hair. A lush, ripe body barely covered by the thinnest of white negligees.

'Dre felt a stirring between his legs. More than a stirring. His mouth was dry.

"So, after y'all cleared out, after the bitch dosed you an' shit, she an' that big fuck, Julian, brought me back here for fun an' games. Had a party going on up in there, more freaks an' crazies than I seen anywhere, *ever*," Tonk whispered, as the boy watched her move around the room. Back and forth, in front of the window. "Weird, fucked-up shit. They got a dungeon in the basement, yo. Chains an' shit all on the walls. Mofo's whippin' bitches, burnin' them with hot wax an' cigarettes, piercin' 'em, makin' 'em bleed. She take me into a changin' room, an' while she's puttin' on some kinda robe, I'm s'pose to strip down an' squeeze into this leather jock with studs an' shit. Then she gimme a leash, clip it to her collar. Tells me tonight, she my slave an' do as I please."

Across the street, the woman had slipped out of the negligee and was standing naked at the window, a red gown folded over her arm. She turned, and a man came into view. He was white, of medium build and fully dressed. As 'Dre watched, he shrugged into a black overcoat. The man moved to kiss her; smiling, she turned her face away.

"She got . . ." 'Dre's voice cracked; he swallowed and passed the glasses back to Tonk. "She got somebody up there with her. Not the big one, somebody else."

"He ain't gonna be there long. She got mofo's comin' and goin', day an' night. And that big one, fuck him. He's just her driver. Hired help. I better not see his ass—"

"She a pro, Young," Lil' B broke in. Tonk's antipathy was plain. B passed his partner the bottle and nodded at Redbone, who sat down at the top of the stairs and lit a joint. "Some kinda SNM ho—"

"S *and* M. Sado-Masochism." Redbone coughed

smoke. "Damn, B. You needs to read somethin' 'sides *GQ* sometime. She a dominatrix. Niggas pay her to kick they ass, piss on 'em. All that freaky, evil shit."

'Dre stepped away from the boarded-up window. He looked around the darkened room at each boy in turn. Tonk was edgy and eager, ready to make a move. Lil' B seemed calm, but that was probably the wine; B loved his mellow grape. Redbone was standing aside, distant, smiling like he knew more than he was saying.

"So what? We gonna take turns lampin' an' jerkin' it?"

All three of them laughed aloud at that. 'Dre felt like he'd missed something, but he'd felt like that since he'd wakened to the sound of Redbone's horn.

"Didn't let me finish, yo. Y'see, we been in an' outta here Saturday, Saturday night, Sunday morning. Watchin' *her.*" Tonk sneered angrily, walked over, and snatched the joint from Redbone. He drew deep, held the smoke, relaxed. "Yeah. So I'm down in the basement, but I ain't about puttin' on no sex show, y'feel me? Ain't no fuck puppet for a room full a' freaks. If I want the ass, I *take* the ass. So I tell the bitch to get busy. If they want a show, they can watch her eat every pussy in the place. An' while they all standin' around watchin', I ducked out, had a quick look around upstairs. Bitch had cake up in there, Young. Gold. Silver. Paintin's an' shit. Now, me, I couldn't jack no goods, not wearin' nothin' but a leather jock an' a smile. So I eased back down to the changing room, an' took a peek in her little black purse. . . ."

Tonk reached into his pocket and pulled out a metal ring. Attached to it were three keys, and a tiny gold phallus.

"Are those . . ." 'Dre stopped short, his head spinning.

"Gate. Front door, back door. Tried 'em all 'fore I left up outta there."

"Hello!" Lil' B burst out, slapping his hands together for emphasis. 'Dre jumped at the sound, much to the other boy's amusement.

"Now y'feel me, Young." Tonk turned his eyes toward the house across the street, and it seemed he peered through the very walls. "Now we wait."

Moonlight poured through the holes on the roof. In the distance, the squeal of tires, the howl of a police siren.

"Tha'sit," Tonk said. "Let's roll."

Redbone was snoring softly, his back in the corner, his Eddie Bauer jacket zipped up past his chin. 'Dre and Lil' B were playing out a silent game of blackjack, a buck a hand. 'Dre was seven dollars down, after being up twenty. There were four empty bottles of wine and two dozen Newport butts scattered over the floor.

"C'mon, get that chronic nigga up. Lights out over there." Tonk stood and shook the circulation back into his legs. "Time to do this."

'Dre collected the cards as Lil' B woke Redbone with a light slap on the head. The four of them stretched in silence, not looking at each other.

"A'ight, then. She just turn out all the lights upstairs—" Tonk began.

"By twos. Me an' Tonk. 'Bone an' 'Dre," Lil' B interrupted. "We go first. Y'all count to fifty, then follow. Meet up at the front door. If there's anybody on the street, any cars, *anything*, circle round the block an' come back. Niggas round here don' see or hear shit. Let's don' give 'em a reason."

"Yeah. Like that. 'Cept I get first crack at the bitch. Twenty minutes, and then you niggas can have her. What's left of her," Tonk amended. He tucked one pistol under his sweatshirt, held out the other. "'Bone, you hold this strap. We out."

'Dre and Redbone moved silently down W Street, past the carryout where they'd bought the wine and playing cards, and turned left, onto Twelfth Place. The street was only one block long, terminating at Florida Avenue, just below Cardozo High School. Row houses, identical save for their exterior paint, lined both sides. There were bars on every downstairs window, and gates on every door.

At the far end of the street, almost to Florida Avenue, Tonk and Lil' B stood for a moment, then turned back, moving slowly so they would reach the front door at once with Redbone and 'Dre. The plan worked to perfection. They were all of them through the gate and door, Tonk, then Lil' B and 'Dre, moving across the threshold, in moments.

But not Redbone. He stopped short, looked down, and stepped back from the door. His eyes were wide.

"Nah, man," he whispered, pointing to the floor. *"Shit ain't right."*

The moonlight spilled onto the hallway floor, illuminating a perfect square of white tile with a large red circle at its center. At each corner of the square was a decorative flourish, a trompe l'oeil, painted so it seemed each design was floating above the floor.

"Don' you punk out, nigga," Tonk rasped, his eyes hard. *"You in this!"*

"No! That's a blood circle! It ain't right!" the boy answered, shaking his head frantically, remembering something his mother had told him long ago. He

shoved the pistol into Lil' B's hand. *"I'll be at the car. I'll wait . . ."*

Lil' B pushed Tonk and Young 'Dre deeper into the darkness of the house, and quietly closed the door with Redbone outside. As Tonk bent down and removed his shoes, Lil' B looked at 'Dre, pointed to the door, and slowly mouthed the words "punk-ass bitch."

'Dre was shaking, his guts rumbling in protest. He should have eaten. He should have bounced out with 'Bone. He should never have come here, gotten caught up in this ill-starred sortie. But even as his eyes grew accustomed to the darkness, and Tonk moved silently up the carpeted stairs, he knew it was too late.

Lil' B shifted the pistol to his left hand, reached into his jacket, and pulled out a bundle of pillowcases. He tossed one to 'Dre, who was standing nervously at the bottom of the stairs. The house wasn't big; there was the living room in the front, with two windows facing the street outside, then a single step up into a small dining area that held a large mahogany table set with several chairs. Farther back was a large kitchen, with two doors; one led out to the backyard, the other, set beneath the stairs that Tonk had climbed to the second story, led to the basement.

The living room was a hodgepodge of overstuffed single chairs and serving tables on a wine-colored Persian rug; it appeared to be a reading room, and was dominated by a large bookcase that ran from floor to ceiling, from front windows to dining room. The shelves were crowded with curios, figurines, and books of every size, from tiny pamphlets to great, oversized volumes. On one shelf, in the center of the bookcase, was a display of bottles with several types of liquor.

Lil' B and 'Dre moved quickly to the bookcase, and

snatched the figurines from the shelves. They were made of gold, and showed a mélange of partners—men, women, and animals—in a profusion of sexual positions. Lil' B dropped them into his pillowcase, along with an engraved set of silver bells and an African mask, then gestured 'Dre closer.

"Check downstairs, yo. Grab up anything worth takin'," he whispered, pointing back to the kitchen.

'Dre nodded, moved past the dining table, with its centerpiece of black candles, and through the kitchen. On impulse, he pulled open each kitchen counter drawer as he passed it, noting the contents, not sure what he was looking for. There were ladles and wooden spoons, plastic bags of spices, silverware, knives, and tongs, and in the last drawer, closest to the basement stairs . . .

Dozens of key rings, identical to the set Tonk had shown him. Three keys and a tiny golden phallus. 'Dre felt a thrill along his spine, and waved to Lil' B.

B shook him off, pointed to the basement door.

'Dre acquiesced. He opened the door and felt for a light switch. Finding it, he clicked it on, flooding the stairwell with reddish light. As he moved slowly down the wooden stairs, each step filled him with a sense of *wrongness,* of apprehension, that loosened his bowels and squeezed sweat from his brow. He just wanted to leave this place. . . .

He reached the bottom of the stairs and looked around him. It was as Tonk had said: a dungeon. In the dim red light, he could make out the bare brick walls set with chains and manacles, a pair of stocks, an inverted wooden cross. Several rough wooden benches were scattered throughout, some sporting large metal rings at each end. At the foot of the stairs was a flaking, life-sized painting of a woman standing in a red circle, wrapped in a flowing black robe that looked like wings. She wore a necklace of small skulls, and clutched a small trident in one hand, and a coiled serpent in the other. Beside the painting was a wall display that held whips, scourges, pinchers, and other implements of torture. As 'Dre reached up and touched one of the braided leather whips, he felt his pulse thunder in his head and realized he was hard, his cock bulging full in spite of his fear. Or perhaps, because of it.

He looked over to his left, through a beaded curtain, and saw the changing room; masks and robes and harnesses hung from hooks along the wall, waiting. Now he pushed aside the curtain, stepping deeper into the red-hued darkness . . .

Above him, something hit the floor hard enough to shake the very house. The red lights dimmed, then brightened again. 'Dre stood stock-still, frozen by fear, not knowing what to do, and then . . .

Another sound. Something scraping across the bare dining room floor.

He couldn't wait any longer. 'Dre took the steps two at a time, turned through the doorway into the kitchen . . .

The front door was open.

Lil' B was on the dining table, flat on his back, his knees bent at the table's edge, his arms outstretched, waving helplessly. Above him, holding him down, one hand across Lil' B's mouth, slowly turning the boy's head, something big. Some-*one* big. And black and wide. Like a mountain.

As 'Dre watched, horrified, Julian lowered his mouth to B's exposed neck; 'Dre could hear the muffled screams as the man sank his teeth into the soft folds of Lil' B's throat, worrying his head from side to side like a feeding lion.

The pistol was on the floor, near the table. As B gurgled and died, 'Dre rushed forward and swept it up, sliding a bullet into the chamber and pointing it in a single motion.

"Freak mothafucka!" 'Dre screamed. "Now you dead!"

The big man raised one hand contemptuously, and carved a design into the air with his fingertips; the symbol hung there, glowing, incandescent, then dissipated.

The boy pulled the trigger.

Click.

Again. *Click.*

Now Julian pushed away from B's quivering corpse, and smiled. His teeth were filed to points, with blood and bits of flesh in the corners of his mouth. Without thinking, 'Dre reached back and threw the useless pistol with all his strength; the man ducked aside, and slowly moved toward the terrified boy.

'Dre stumbled back into the kitchen, his legs weak, his heart pounding to burst. Looking around, he grabbed a pan from the stovetop, threw it, then another, and another. Julian slapped them aside; they clanged off the walls like carillons. Desperate, filled with fear, 'Dre searched frantically for something . . .

And then he saw the open drawer. Filled with knives.

He grabbed a handful of cutlery, bloodying his hands on their edges. Screaming, he drew back and heaved them at Julian's face. The man turned his head reflexively, his hands raised in defense. . . .

'Dre threw them at Julian's face, save one. And with that one clenched in his fist, in that instant that Julian's eyes were turned away, 'Dre leapt, and plunged the steel blade into his chest. . . .

'Dre was crying as he climbed the stairs. It took him a long time to reach the second floor. He didn't know how many times he'd stabbed Julian. He'd kept stabbing him until he stopped moving and his hands were soaked past the wrists with black blood and the wooden knife handle had slipped from his fingers. Then he cut his throat.

"*Tonk!* We gotta go, man." 'Dre sniffed, wiped his nose. He could feel the wine in his belly trying to come up. "We gotta go. . . ."

He moved down the hallway to the front bedroom. The bedroom where they'd watched her.

It seemed like hours ago. More than hours. More than a lifetime.

Finally, he stood at the door. Tonk's pants and shoes were in a pile on the floor. 'Dre guessed he'd figured to surprise her in her sleep, gun in his hand, his pants off, hard and ready to hit it. But this house held surprises of its own.

'Dre pushed the door open.

The woman stood naked in the center of the bedroom, and smiled when she saw him. Skin like honey and cream. Tonk was kneeling in front of her, in his sweatshirt and socks, his eyes white, pupils rolled back in his head. She was holding a cell phone in her left hand, the pistol in her right; the barrel was in Tonk's mouth.

"There you are, little one. You're just in time," she cooed softly. "My Julian isn't picking up. Is that him you're wearing?"

"Wait," 'Dre muttered, pleaded. "Please don't . . ."

"You beg for him? This thief? This ravisher? His death should take . . . weeks!" She wet her lips, shuddered. "Here, then, is my mercy. My *sweet* mercy."

She pulled the trigger. The blast blew out the back of Tonk's head, spinning him across the floor, splattering the wall behind him with blood and brains.

'Dre howled like a wounded animal and fell to his knees, as she tossed the cell phone over her shoulder and turned the gun on him. Still smiling, she reached down between her legs, then raised her hand to her lips, slowly licking her fingers. "That was good for me. And you?"

'Dre was sobbing uncontrollably, his mind all but broken by the unceasing horror of this night. He was ready to die now; this hideous world he'd stepped into when he crossed the threshold was no longer his own.

"Do you have questions, little one? Do you want to know the secrets that elude reason, that threaten your very sanity? Do you hunger for . . . darkness?"

"*No!* No more!" he screamed. "Just kill me, just *kill* me . . ."

She circled around to stand at his back. He waited for the bullet to come. His loins afire, he waited. . . .

"Liar. Your flesh betrays you. Now I see you clearly. Your . . . desires. My Julian made a grave mistake. It was you who should have come home with me. And all this would have been avoided." She leaned down, behind him, above him, her naked breasts on the back of his neck, her hands running down his body to his thickened cock, her breath in his ear. "My house in disarray. My protégé, slain by your hand. What am I to do? How can I know if you are worthy of my secrets, my clever, courageous boy? I have so much to teach you. How will you show me your devotion?"

She reached under his chin and tilted his head back. 'Dre could smell her perfume, musky, and forbidden. He sighed, his mouth open, as she kissed the tears from his eyes.

"Let me tell you," she whispered. "Let me tell you how. . . ."

It was nearly dawn.

Redbone was dozing in the car, with the windows rolled up and the radio playing softly. The dashboard lights glowed red.

'Dre didn't bother to wake him; he merely placed the barrel of the pistol against the glass and pulled the trigger three times.

He wiped off the gun and dropped it in the street, turned, and walked back to the house on Twelfth Place. There was so much to do, what with the blood and the bodies and the trash in her second house across the street, where all the crew had watched her. He'd have to clean up, get rid of any evidence that they'd been there. She insisted the upstairs be kept neat. For the other guests who liked to watch.

So much to do, so much to learn. The protective charms and exercises and rituals. The wards that could stop guns from firing, the glamour that could cripple minds. He knew he was in for a long apprenticeship. After all, Julian had been her most dedicated disciple. And 'Dre had killed Julian. Easily.

'Dre looked up at the window as he came up the walk to the front door. She was standing in the waxing light, wearing a black leather harness and domino mask. 'Dre pulled out his new set of keys, stepped through the door, and locked the gate behind him.

Power and Purpose

L.R. Giles

"Karyn?"

She didn't answer. Synthesizer music and a mass choir sang from her television speakers; it had to be her fiftieth time seeing the ad, but it still entranced her just like the first.

"Karyn, you in here?" She heard heavy footfalls in the hallway. Reggie—her best friend—had a key to her place and no problem letting himself in. "I'm coming into your bedroom. I hope you're not naked. Well, I kind of hope you are, but it's awkward saying it out loud."

He stuck his head in.

"Pajamas," he said, "Damn. So much for nakedne—" His attention shifted to the screen. "Is this it?"

"Uh-huh."

"Where—"

Karyn pointed to the right of the screen as the video cut to a group of four. Three men, one woman. "That's her in blue."

"You two look alike."

She glared. "You need to work on your flattery."

"Get naked and I'll retract the statement."

She groaned and raised the volume with her remote control.

"—come be enlightened at this four-day celebration and conference at the grand opening of the new Heavenly Duty Worship Center. Bishop Horace Sinclair invites you to change your life for now and forever—"

Bishop Horace Sinclair, spiritual leader to thousands, perhaps millions when you counted his television ministry. That's who the ad campaign was really for.

Sinclair's Power and Purpose Conference had been in the works for the last two years, set to coincide with the grand opening of his new worship hall, Heavenly Duty. It was a fifty-million-dollar megachurch designed to hold a congregation of thirty thousand. In the spiritual community it was the biggest of big deals. All of the celebrities of gospel, ministry, and evangelism would be in attendance, plus a crowd of eager worshippers that could rival a Super Bowl audience.

And Karyn's mother would be in the midst of it all, utterly enraptured.

Her mom had been a loyal follower of the good bishop for most of Karyn's life. From his original services in high school gyms, to his first church in the suburbs of Portside, Virginia, to now, Jessica Manning was a servant to God first and Horace Sinclair second.

Over the years she'd established a place in the good bishop's inner circle, thus her prominent appearance in the Power and Purpose ads. Her access to church resources—and The Bishop himself—had many of the other church members, particularly the women, dipping into the Envy bucket of the Seven Deadlies.

All despite having a daughter like Karyn.

The ad ended with ticket and contact information, though Karyn was willing to wager there were no more tickets. It was long rumored the conference would sell out. And it wasn't like there was much time left. It started tomorrow.

She clicked the television off and turned to Reggie.

"Well?" he asked.

She raised an eyebrow. "Well what?"

"Are you going?"

Her gaze flitted to the two tickets wedged into the molding over her mirror—front row seats, a gift from Mom. She shrugged.

"I think you should," he said.

"I know what you think. It's easy for you to think that. You didn't grow up with her . . ." She searched for a word powerful enough to construe the years of degradation she suffered at her mother's hands. "Rants. She threw more scriptures in my face than those crazy apocalypse guys on the corners downtown."

"But it's been a while. Things could be different now. I've seen Bishop Sinclair on TV and he focuses strongly on forgiveness. Maybe your mom—"

"Has forgiven me?" Her voice was hot venom. "And what exactly is she forgiving me for, Reggie?"

He raised his hands—one palm out, the other grasping a large, padded manila envelope. "It will never be said that Reggie the Wise does not know when to shut up."

Karyn, angry at Reggie for going where she didn't want to go, but equally mad at herself for being angry at Reggie, hopped off the bed and disappeared into her walk-in closet. It was easier to cool off when she couldn't see anyone, when she couldn't *feel* the waves of emotion wafting off them.

She tugged the day's clothes off hangers. "What's that envelope you're holding?"

"Don't know. I grabbed your mail on the way up."

"Open it."

As she sifted through her denim, she heard the envelope rip. Then, "Speak of the Dev—" Reggie caught himself, and then finished, "It's from your mom."

What now?

She poked her head out and saw him holding a leather-bound Bible and a sheet of paper. "Her note says 'God told me to send you this.'"

Figures.

He opened the Bible's cover, chuckled.

"What?" she asked.

"It's autographed by Horace Sinclair."

Karyn's face twisted. The guy autographed *Bibles?* The cynic in her nearly overloaded; she left that one alone. "Let me see."

Reggie tossed it to her.

Her day immediately took a turn for the worst.

She caught it and felt the warmth immediately. The heat spread from her hands, up her arms, hit her chest, and went supernova through the rest of her body. Reggie and her bedroom blinked away. There were—

—people. Too many people. The aisles are choked, some rush the exits, and others rush the stage. There is already a crowd there, though. They huddle over someone she cannot see.

But she can see the blood.

It drips over the stage's edge.

Crying. So much crying.

In the huddle, she sees her own face. Crow's-feet clutch the corners of her eyes and her mascara is smeared. Karyn doesn't wear makeup and she's yet to

*develop her first wrinkle. This is her mother's face,
horrified.*

*Behind Mom, a banner of ten-foot-tall letters reads,
POWER AND PURPOSE. A sloppy, bright red splatter fills
the o in Power, like a child who hasn't learned to color
inside the lines.*

*All becomes quiet. The crowd at the stage, includ-
ing her mother, turn to her, and stare with pleading
eyes. But she looks past them, to what they concealed
before.*

*A man with a ragged hole in his chest lies motion-
less, gone from this world.*

Horace Sinclair.

The Bible smacked the floor. Karyn leapt backward,
banging her head against the closet door. She became
limp and slid to her butt. Her legs felt like cooked
spaghetti and her breathing was ragged.

Reggie knelt over her but did not touch her. Not yet.
"What did you see?"

"Someone's going to . . ." The images were still
fresh in her mind, still shocking. "Someone's going to
kill Horace Sinclair."

"What?"

Adrenaline flowed through her. She sprang to her
feet and sprinted around Reggie in search of her cell.
Had to call Mom.

In her wake she heard Reggie say, "Why is it never
the winning Lotto numbers?"

The first time it happened, she was eleven years old.

They'd been visiting her grandparents in Stepton, a
small, close-knit community where most folks—at
least on the black side of town—knew Jessica Man-

ning and her daughter, Karyn. It happened in the market when Jessica bumped into an old friend from high school and began to chew the man's ear about her church, Heavenly Duty. Karyn saw his eyes gloss over before he politely excused himself, claiming a forgotten appointment.

Hastily he said, "It was good to see you again, Jessica." He shook Mom's hand, and then turned to Karyn. "And you, too, Little Bear." He patted her head, and she cringed. Not from the odd nickname, but from the pictures flashing suddenly through her mind.

She saw the man on a ladder, trimming branches on a tree. An electrical line was tightroped through the foliage. He did not notice the wire until his trimmers bit into it, and then it was too late.

The man quick-stepped to the checkout line, leaving Karyn nearly in tears.

"Mom, he's in trouble."

Mom's attention was on a leafy head of lettuce. "You got that right, you can tell he don't know Jesus."

"No." And she told her mother what she instinctively knew to be the man's fate if no one interceded on his behalf.

Jessica Manning heard her daughter out, her expression unchanging. When Karyn was done, Jessica nodded. Karyn thought her mother would stop the man before he got away.

Instead she said, "I won't have you making up any more stories."

"No. I'm not making it up. I saw—"

"Only God can see the future, little girl. Now stop this nonsense."

Karyn panicked. She didn't want the man to get hurt and she also knew what her mother said wasn't true.

She'd learned otherwise in Sunday school. "What about prophets, Mom? They can—"

Her mother's palm cut off the words like a severed limb. The slap echoed in the aisles. "Don't you ever try to turn the teachings of the Lord to support lies. Do you hear me?"

Karyn nodded, tears rimming her eyes. She didn't say another word.

The next day, it was her grandpa Tom who gave them the news of Darren Telfair's electrocution while trimming branches off his sycamore tree.

Karyn ran from the breakfast table sobbing, leaving her grandparents perplexed.

Jessica came to her room, a sullen look on her face. Karyn felt horrible for her mother, the guilt she must've felt for not warning Mr. Telfair.

The sympathy for her mother dried up quickly, though.

"See what you've done?" Mom asked.

Karyn's sobs receded.

"We can sometimes speak things into being," Mom said. "That's why it is of the utmost importance to keep our minds focused on God and positivity, just like Bishop Sinclair says. I don't know what made you tell that story yesterday, but . . . " She trailed off, perhaps realizing the lunacy in her logic. "I don't want you to blame yourself. It must have been Darren's time. The Lord works in mysterious ways."

It got no better over the years. As she and her mother grew further apart, the visions grew stronger, clearer.

As an adult, she had more control over her ability. A mere touch wouldn't trigger the visions, not unless the premonition was so horrible her learned defenses could not fend it off. Like now.

She tried to call her mother, but got her voice mail.

"Today is a day that the Lord has made. You have reached the voice mail of Jessica Manning. I'm unable to take your call right now, but if you—"

Karyn clicked End, redialed the number, and let it ring three times. Voice mail, again.

"Damn it."

Reggie hovered over her. She often found comfort in his presence. His bulky girth and fuzzy beard always reminded her of Baloo the Bear from *The Jungle Book*. It was what she loved most about him. But today, there was no comfort to be found.

He fumbled for words. "Are you sure about what you saw?"

Her eyes narrowed, and he dropped his gaze. They'd known each other long enough—been through enough—for him to know her visions were *never* wrong.

She paced the length of the apartment, unsure of what to do next. She'd learned long ago the police weren't an option. She'd be written off as a nut, and if the shooting went down her advance knowledge would propel her to the top of the suspect list. If she could just get a hold of her mother . . . despite their differences Jessica Manning, like Reggie, knew her daughter's visions were always on point.

Mom would make sure Bishop Sinclair was out of harm's way. She valued his life over her own.

Probably even over mine, she thought bitterly.

She shook it off and tried Mom's phone again. No luck.

"Reggie, do you have a suit?"

"Unfortunately. Why?"

"Because, if I can't get my Mom on the phone tonight, we have to figure out a way to save Horace Sinclair."

He nodded slowly. "Okay, again. Suit? Why?"

"You're going to be my date to the Power and Purpose Conference."

The next eighteen hours were a blur of brainstorming, caffeine, and anxiety. Karyn kept touching the autographed Bible, unsure of what she hoped to see. There were no more visions. As far as her extraordinary gifts were concerned, Horace Sinclair would still die before his congregation if she did not act.

It was eight in the morning before she gave in to the inevitable. "Go home and change, Reggie."

By nine-thirty, Reggie was wedged in the passenger seat of her Toyota Prius, looking like a clown-car passenger. "So, what's the plan?"

"I don't know exactly. Talk to security, try to use my mother's name for leverage."

"Sounds like a long shot."

"Maybe not." She turned onto Northwest Boulevard; it would bring them up on the tail end of the new Heavenly Duty Building. "It's early. The conference doesn't start until eleven. Maybe we can make them listen if they're not too concerned with a crowd yet."

"Maybe."

As the blocks and the buildings sailed past them, Karyn couldn't help but notice how dead Portside was this early on a Sunday. All was still; the only movement was the wind through the branches of cypress trees planted in the sidewalk. In a way it was ominous. As if she was already too late, and instead of having the death of Horace Sinclair on her conscience, the demise of the world would be.

Karyn, you will get this right. You're here. There's no

crowd. You'll get to a guard and everything will be all right.

As they crested the last block of squat buildings, the gray shale and regal blue dome of the Heavenly Duty Worship Center floated into view. It was modern architecture at its finest, a bald giant among square trolls. The air-conditioning units alone were the size of Karyn's apartment.

A sigh escaped her. "This is going to work," she whispered.

Then they passed the Heavenly Duty Worship Center and got a look at the front plaza.

"Ho-lee shit." Reggie twisted in his seat and Karyn felt her heart sink as she eased her car to a halt.

There were hundreds—possibly thousands—of worshippers crowding the plaza, bustling and conversing, raising their arms in praise of the Lord. They were joyful, an emotion Karyn could not share.

These people—this crowd—would slow her down, possibly prevent her from doing her job. And, somewhere among them, was a killer who would not be deterred.

"Find a place to park," she said. "I'm going to wade through this, see if I can find someone with security."

Reggie glanced toward the throngs of people. "Are you sure about this?"

She tried to look sure. "I'll be fine."

He was wedged behind the wheel of the tiny car, looking even more awkward than he did in the passenger seat. "How will I find you?"

Karyn held up her cell. "You've got the number."

She rounded the car and sank into the growing crowd of parishioners who looked regal in the morning light. Karyn blended in well. Her enthusiasm for dress-up was only slightly better than Reggie's, but attendance here required a little more than casual attire.

She'd donned her tan linen pantsuit with a white blouse beneath, one of the outfits she kept on reserve for special occasions. Preventing homicide wasn't on her list of possible affairs when she purchased it, but good fashion was prepared for anything, even when people aren't.

Her outfit—and looks in general—was on her mind mainly because it was on the mind of the people—*men*—she passed in an effort to find security. She wasn't a mind reader, not by a long shot. She supposed the ability fell into the empath category, but even that was more glamorous than the reality of it.

Every woman knew when she was being ogled. It was an instinct developed around the same time the body began to mature, making a woman a target for the scrupulous and unscrupulous alike.

For Karyn, it was a million times worse.

With her talent, every unwelcome pair of eyes felt like a featherlight hand pawing her flesh. She was subconsciously aware of every part of her body being assessed as she passed even the subtlest voyeur. Her face, eyes, breasts, stomach, hips, butt, and, more often than she cared to consider, feet (she didn't even own a pair of open-toed shoes) were under review.

She'd learned long ago, when her abilities were in their infancy, that this type of visual molestation was the nature of man. For that reason, she usually avoided crowds. Something else she learned long ago . . . it was rarely any better at church.

With her skin crawling, she forced her way through, suppressing the urge to scream. There were times in the past when she hadn't been so successful. But an outburst here could ruin her chances. *Stay cool, girl.*

Thirty yards ahead, she spotted what she was looking for. He was tall and lithe in a navy-blue blazer with the Heavenly Duty crest on his sleeve. A wire coiled out of his collar to a bud in his ear, Secret Service–style. As she approached, she felt her mind slip into a prayer, her first one in a long time. Please, *God, let this work.*

He caught her in his periphery and faced her. Immediately, she felt him undressing her with his eyes. She ignored the discomfort and went into her spiel. "Excuse me, sir." She eyed the name tag on his left lapel. "Dale?"

He smiled. "What can I help you with, miss?"

"Do you know Jessica Manning?"

"Of course. She's a senior pastor here."

"Good. I'm her daughter. Karyn Manning."

His eyes flickered away, then back to her. She didn't need psychic abilities to read the expression. He was skeptical. "Well, she would've left your tickets at the Will Call table. The doors will open in an hour and you can—"

She dug into her handbag and produced her ticket to prove she wasn't trying to con her way into the conference. "No. I already have my ticket. I just need to know if my mother is here yet. I need to tell her something."

His skepticism shifted to downright suspicion. "I wouldn't have any way to confirm senior staff's arrival. That's not part of my detail. But I do know Miss Manning has a cell phone. I'm sure *her daughter* would have the number."

She felt him shut down, the tunnel of cooperation

contracted to a pinhole. The indirect approach wasn't going to work.

"Excuse me." He turned away.

"Wait."

Dale raised an eyebrow. His expression said, *What now?*

"I'm going to tell you something. I'm not crazy and here." She raised her ticket and tore it in half. "I'm not even going in, so don't think I'm the one who's going to give you trouble. But you're security, and if you choose not to act the consequences will be on you."

"Miss, you're not making any sense."

She leaned close, unwilling to let anyone else hear. "Someone's going to shoot Horace Sinclair. They're going to do it when he goes onstage to open the conference. You have to warn him."

Dale took a step back. His expression was stone.

"Please." Karyn felt the tears coming. "You have to believe me."

"Don't move."

The guard turned away and spoke into a communicator attached to his cuff. Karyn could not hear what was said, but when he faced her, he nodded. "Come with me."

It was her turn for skepticism. "Why? Where are we going?"

"Someone wants to speak to you."

"My mother?"

He shook his head; his face glowed with eerie reverence. "Bishop Sinclair."

Dale ushered her inside Heavenly Duty through the front door. Some onlookers rushed the entrance and were halted by more guards. Curious shouting turned to angry screams. Karyn barely noticed.

She craned her neck, looking around. This place . . . marble-tiled ceilings fifty feet high, gold light fixtures with crystal ornaments, a glass wall overlooking a sunken sanctuary, concession stands, a bookstore, credit union, employment office, full-service restaurant, day care, and, over the entrance to the worship hall, a gargantuan portrait of the good bishop. It was like the Sistine Chapel and Staples Center thrown in a blender.

In Reggie's words, ho-lee shit.

"This way, miss." Dale motioned to an unmarked corridor. She shook off her awe and followed his directions.

The hallway took them to a steel door marked PRIVATE. Dale unclipped his ID badge and passed it over an electronic lock mounted in the wall. It buzzed and a bolt retracted in the frame. The door swung outward, revealing a brightly lit stairway.

Karyn looked to the guard, uncertain.

"It's all right," he said.

They ascended to Heavenly Duty's second floor.

This new level was less religious regal and more like a corporate call center. Gray carpet led through a bay of unmanned cubicles. On the far wall, a series of locked doors barred them from darkened offices. But one office was open and well lit.

"Wait here." Dale entered the office and closed the door.

Karyn was anxious, but relieved. She'd never expected someone to actually listen and take action. Cooperation was so rare when it concerned things yet to pass. To coin her mother's favorite phrase, God was looking out for her.

The door opened. Dale motioned her in as he left, casting furtive glances over his shoulder.

This office resembled the royal décor of the Heavenly Duty's first level. Rich carpet, high ceilings, oil paintings . . . and the patriarch himself. Bishop Sinclair sat staring out of his window, troubled.

He swiveled to face her. Though it had been years since she'd been in his presence, she believed time had taken a greater toll on her than him. He had to be near the half-century mark, but didn't look a day over thirty-five. He wore gold-framed spectacles over hazel eyes, and only a few renegade strands of gray could be seen in his goatee.

He smiled; it was strained. "When he told me Jessica Manning's daughter wanted to see me, I was a bit startled. I hope I don't offend you by saying this, but it's been so long since I last saw you. I'd forgotten about you."

Embarrassed heat seared her cheeks; she hoped her complexion hid her blush. "It has been a while, hasn't it?"

"You've grown into a very beautiful woman. The spitting image of your mother." It was an honest compliment, nothing implied there. It was flattering; and with that, Karyn got a glimpse of how a woman could become enraptured by the compliments of such a powerful man. Somehow, she couldn't convince herself he ever took advantage of the affections of the women in his flock. He was one of the good ones.

And she was going to save his life.

"As happy as I am to see you, Dale gave me some troubling information. He says it came from you."

She swallowed. "Yes. Someone—I think someone—is going to—"

He held up a hand. "Not here." He motioned to the

window, and for the first time she noticed the people on the rooftops of a building in the distance. The people and their cameras.

Bishop Sinclair rose and closed the blinds. "It's funny, there was a time when only movie stars had to worry about paparazzi. Our country is so consumed with celebrity. The saying should be 'In Tabloids We Trust.'"

"Bishop—"

He stopped her again. "There was a newspaper article a few years back, during the time Mayor Peppers was running for his second term. I spoke openly against his policies, so he attempted to discredit me. Things I said in private appeared in the article, out of context. At first, I thought someone in my senior staff was leaking information. We later found out my office had been bugged.

"That was taken into consideration when we designed this building."

The bishop moved to what she assumed was a bare wall. He pressed on the plaster. Some sort of locking mechanism clicked, and a crevice appeared.

It was a door to a hidden room.

"Come," he said. "It's safe to talk in here."

She stepped inside, a little awed by the level of intrigue the bishop's type of celebrity demanded. The room was a scaled-down version of the main office. There was a desk, a small bookshelf, a console of security monitors, and a worktable littered with circuits and tools that smelled of oil. It was an odd setup—the worktable more than the rest—but she supposed it served its purpose. Especially today.

As soon as he closed the door, she vomited the words: "Don't ask me how I know what I'm about to say, but you have to believe there's going to be an attempt on your life. Someone's going to shoot you in front of your congregation if you don't do something."

"Dear Lord." He kneaded his face with stiff fingers. "That's what Dale said. I prayed he'd gotten mixed up."

"It's true. I swear."

He looked at her, sighed, and nodded. "I believe you, child."

At his desk, he scooped up the phone and thumbed a red button on its face. "Mr. Markham, come to the back room, please. Bring Jimmy with you." He placed the receiver back in the cradle.

"Who did you call?"

"Our chief of security."

His statement could've been an introduction, for as soon as he said it, the lock disengaged. A linebacker-sized, blue-eyed behemoth entered the room. His hair was long, platinum and slicked back, a stark contrast to the bishop and the mostly black Heavenly Duty congregation. He looked Nordic—like Thor without the hammer. Mr. Markham, she presumed.

A shorter, frailer blond—the bottle variety—tailed him. Once they were all in, the room felt too tight . . . and hot. Karyn found it difficult to breathe, as if these men didn't just inhale the air, but absorbed it.

The sensation wasn't physical. This was part of her gift. A warning. Something was wrong here.

Mr. Markham sealed the door behind his little buddy, and then focused his gaze on Karyn. "What appears to be the problem, Bishop?"

She glanced at Sinclair. He couldn't even look her in the eye. "She knows, Mr. Markham. I don't know how, but she knows about our plan."

*   *   *

The world tilted. Sinclair's words and her heightened sensitivity to the present danger were almost too much to bear.

She backpedaled, collided with the wall, and used it for support while she forced her breathing to regulate. A fine sheen of sweat plastered her blouse to her chest and back.

Why was it so hot?

Markham spoke: "She does, does she?" His voice was high, squeaky. It made him no less intimidating. He shot the other blond—Jimmy—a look. "Now, how did that happen?"

Jimmy shook his head frantically. "Nuh-uh, wasn't me. Wasn't Jimmy."

Karyn didn't need her powers to realize Jimmy was mentally challenged. What the hell was going on here?

"We should call it off," Sinclair told Markham. "If there's a leak, we shouldn't go through with this."

Markham gave him an easy smile. "Our objective hasn't changed. Think of the good this will do. It's worth the risk."

Karyn found her voice. "What are you talking about? Objectives? The *good?*"

"Karyn." The bishop's eyes begged her to understand. "You've got it all wrong. No one's going to kill me. The bullet's not even real."

"What?"

"It's supposed to be a blank and a . . ."

"A squib," Markham chimed in. "It's what they use in the movies to make gunshots look real." He moved to the worktable and picked up a harness and a bag of what looked like hospital blood. "It's a low-charge explosive and a packet of red corn syrup. Bishop Sinclair's in no danger whatsoever."

Karyn shook her head. What she saw in her vision wasn't corn syrup. In the future place she could smell the copper stench. It was blood and it was real.

"Why?" she asked. "Why this?"

"Forgiveness, Karyn," Sinclair said. "It's all about His message. Our congregation is at its peak. And we're going to only rise higher. But somewhere along the way, His message got lost. It became about being in the 'cool church,' about getting your Heavenly Duty license plate holder. It's about being the Heavenly Duty choir director, or chief financial officer. People have started to look at our church like a country club. The in-crowd belongs to Heavenly Duty, and we don't cotton to nobodies around here."

Sinclair's eyes glistened. "It never should've come to this."

"So you're going to fake an assassination?" she asked. "It's come to that?"

Markham spoke up. "It's not the assassination that makes this special. It's the assassin."

Before she could question him, Jimmy began to bounce up and down like a hyper child. "Point and shoot. *Bam!*"

Karyn could've burned a hole through Sinclair with her gaze. "No. Tell me you don't intend to involve him in this."

Sinclair spoke with his voice and hands, channeling the energy that made him a world-famous speaker. "If you'll let me explain, you'll see why it could only be him."

He continued. "People threaten my life all the time. Most recently, members of the Church of King Christ."

He let that hang and she bit. "That's the Aryan church. It's been in the news a lot lately."

"Right. The officialdom of the church claims no knowledge of the threats, of course. But it's all semantics, now, isn't it? The lines have been drawn. There have been talks of riots, even among my people."

She began to understand Jimmy's bottle-blond locks. If Sinclair wanted it to look like the shooter was connected to an Aryan church, Jimmy needed to look Aryan. She got that, but not what Sinclair hoped to accomplish.

"When we do this, there will be horror and panic . . . Old Testament terror," he said. "The true Christians will be separated from the vengeful charlatans. We'll finally know who's been listening."

Now Karyn was clear, on one thing anyway: Sinclair was insane.

"You're doing this because you want to weed out the lukewarms?" she asked.

"No. So I can save them."

"I thought only Christ saved. Or is that just semantics, too?"

Sinclair's eyes flickered. He concealed the anger quickly. "When I 'survive,' and I *forgive* Jimmy for what he's done, my message will be stronger than ever. My followers will be stronger for it. Don't you see?"

"It won't work," she bluffed. She knew more than any of them it was going to work better than they'd dreamed. "You'll be seen by medics and cops. They'll find the squib."

"You'd be surprised how many of our members are in law enforcement and medicine," he countered.

"What about Jimmy? He's supposed to be ostracized, maybe go to jail, for your ego trip?"

Markham spoke up. "True followers make sacrifices to spread God's Word. Besides, we have strong ties to the legal community, too. Someone in Jimmy's condition will never see trial. This *will* work, miss."

She shook her head, her resolve hardened. "No. It won't. Because I won't let it." She made for the door, but was halted by Markham's manacle-like grip.

The heat in the room went nuclear.

This is not the future. It's the past, gray and grainy like old news footage. Markham's here, talking to men who look like him. They nod, laugh, and over their heads a crucifix hangs and the Lord looks over their deeds with anguished eyes.

Markham shakes the hand of another. In the web between the thumb and forefinger of this other man's hand, there's a swastika.

Fast-forward. Markham tinkers with a rifle. He removes one set of rounds—the blanks—and replaces them with black casings that look like missiles.

Skip. The future's now. While the masses huddle over a dead bishop, Markham watches from a balcony with Jimmy murdered at his feet and a smile on his lips.

Karyn blinked to get her bearings. How long was she out? Seconds? Minutes?

"Is she all right?" Sinclair asked.

Markham watched her carefully. "She's fine now."

"Wait." She went to move and felt her arm snatched backward. A silver cuff chained her to the heavy worktable. The table was bolted to the floor and would not be moved.

To Markham, she said, "What are you—?"

Her eyes drifted past him, to the fifth figure in the room.

She bit back a scream.

A black mass of living shadow hulked over Markham.

The heat from before—it came off the mass in waves. She saw it radiating from the . . . thing. In all her years—all of her visions—she'd never seen anything like it.

Somewhere in the distance, she heard the voice of Luther Vandross, and then realized it was her cell's ring tone.

Markham came closer, as did the blackness. She cringed.

"He's not going to hurt you, Karyn," the bishop assured her. The sad thing was, he actually believed it.

Still, it wasn't Markham she was concerned with. Not anymore.

The murderous Nordic reached into her bag and confiscated her phone, slipping it in his jacket pocket. "I'll deal with you later." Then, to Sinclair: "We need to go." He gathered up the squib harness. Jimmy led the way out, followed by the bishop.

"We'll work something out," Sinclair said.

No, Karyn thought, *you won't.*

He left. Then went the Nordic, and, thank goodness, that shadow.

Before the door closed, trapping her, the shadow twisted in snakelike fashion. The mound at the top— the head—faced her, shooting that unnatural heat her way. Then a horizontal crescent moon appeared, perfectly white pointed teeth flashed. The damned thing was grinning.

Then they were gone.

Reggie hung up his phone. "Where are you, Karyn? Damn it."

"Can I help you, sir?"

He turned, embarrassed. "Um, darn it. This darn phone."

The man he faced was massive. Reggie was no small guy; at six feet two, two hundred and eighty pounds, he dwarfed most people he met. Now he knew how those folks felt.

This security guard was Shaq-sized. His skin was tanned bronze, his hair light brown, with eyes like olives. Reggie could honestly say he was the strangest-looking man he'd ever seen.

"You seem lost, sir. Can I help you with something?"

People milled around, on beelines for Heavenly Duty's open doors. Reggie scanned their faces. "I'm not the one that's lost. I'm looking for my friend, Karyn."

"Karyn Manning?"

"Yeah, how—"

He tapped his earpiece. "I heard her name over the radio. I think she was taken to meet Bishop Sinclair."

A sigh slipped out of Reggie. "Good. That's good."

"I should take you to her," the guard said.

Then something in Reggie flicked on, a sudden need to get to Karyn and get to Karyn now. "Can you do that?"

The guard nodded. "Just stick close."

They began to move through the crowd with odd ease. People stopped short or sped up to clear a direct path for them, yet no one even glanced their way.

They entered the foyer, detoured down a long corridor.

"Hey, I'm Reggie, by the way. I didn't catch your name."

The guard turned, and gave him the warmest smile he'd seen in a long time. "Just call me Michael."

Moments later, they were on a deserted floor. Reggie knew when he was somewhere he wasn't supposed to be. "Don't you think they're in the sanctuary by now?"

Michael did not respond, but opened a door at the end of the floor. Reggie followed and realized this was the bishop's office.

"Mike, no one's here, man."

Again, no response. Instead, the guard approached a bare wall and pressed his hand, fingers splayed, against the plaster. He turned to Reggie and placed a small metal trinket in his palm. "You'll need this."

"What?" He looked past Michael and saw there was a door concealed in the wall. A step closer and there was a familiar voice. "Sinclair, is that you?"

Reggie ran into the hidden room and saw Karyn tugging on a cuff that trapped her wrist to a table. He looked down to the tiny metal in his hand, and understood what it was. A cuff key.

"Karyn." He rushed forward.

"I had another vision, Reggie."

He stopped just shy of her. "Just now?"

"No. It's been a while. You're fine."

Still, he was hesitant. Early on in their relationship, before he understood the nature of her abilities, he'd touched her while she was in the midst of a powerful, ugly vision. That day, they both found out that not only could Karyn see visions of the past and future, but she became a cipher of the visions, for a time.

When Reggie touched her, he saw what she saw.

And his mind couldn't take it.

It was three days before he woke up again, in a hospital with an IV snaking to his arm.

Warily, his hand hovered toward her wrist like she was a hot oven and he was afraid of getting burned. He touched her, snatched his hand back like she was hot, and then touched her again. Nothing. Good. He unlocked her cuff while she filled him in on what was what in Heavenly Duty.

Listening to her tale of Bishop Sinclair's Aryan security chief planning to turn his harebrained scheme against him, he was again reminded of her burden and was secretly glad the ability was hers and not his.

She rubbed her raw wrist. "How did you find me?"

"This guard, Mic—" He turned to introduce his ally and found the entrance to the room empty. He stepped to the door and peered into the equally empty office. "He was right here."

Karyn pushed past him, checked the wall clock. "Sinclair's going on soon."

"What do we need to do?"

"Give me your cell phone."

He handed it over. She said, "Use the desk phone to call the cops."

"And tell them what?"

"I don't know. Tell them you saw a black man with a gun chase a white girl into the church . . . that might get the whole police department plus SWAT down here."

"And what are you going to do?"

"Reggie, I've got a date with a rifleman."

He stiffened. "I'm going with you."

"No. You're not."

"Look what rolling solo has done for you so far.

Should I go ahead and keep the cuff key in case we need it later?"

She touched his hand. "You can't come with me, Reggie. I know what I have to do and you don't want to be there when I do it."

He didn't want to, but they'd been down this road before—if she had a plan, he had to trust her. Before he could relent, she was out the door.

It took twenty minutes to find the entrance to the balcony she'd seen in her vision. She ran into no resistance from security. No surprise there. Markham was the boss on these matters, and since he was the only legitimate threat to Bishop Sinclair, of course he'd want the guards out of the way.

Which leaves me, she thought, a rodent of fear scurrying along her intestines.

She'd told Reggie she knew what she had to do. It was a lie.

The truth: Reggie was her only friend, and she didn't want to risk him in this business. The image of that smiling darkness was fresh in her mind. It was real, as real as any vision she'd ever had. The forces at work here were sinister, indeed. And they were her load to carry.

Creeping through Heavenly Duty's upper level, she kept low and peered across the length of the balcony. It ringed the sanctuary—what some would call nose-bleed seats—currently unfinished and unused.

Moving to the safety rail, she peeked at the illuminated pulpit below. The crowd murmured while a live band accompanied the low voices of a mass choir.

Ahead of them all was the banner and the words from the vision that led her here: POWER AND PURPOSE.

There was movement to her left.

She crouched and backed behind a row of new stadium seats still wrapped in plastic and not yet bolted to the floor.

Jimmy approached the railing with a long duffel bag slung over his shoulder. Karyn didn't need to guess what was in it.

He unloaded the rifle, snapping pieces into place, attaching a scope, and testing the trigger, all while grinning and humming along with the choir. Whatever his disability was, assembling a rifle was not part of it.

Karyn leaned out for another look at the stage. Sinclair wasn't out yet. There was still time.

She pulled out Reggie's cell and dialed the number to the phone Markham took from her. It began to ring and she lowered it from her ear to seek another sound.

Faintly, she picked up the sounds of Luther in the distance.

Jimmy turned from his task to peer in the shadows. "Mr. Markham?"

The Nordic stepped out, one hand digging in his jacket pocket to silence the cell.

"I didn't know you was coming up here," Jimmy said, actually gleeful to see the secret puppet master.

Markham grasped Jimmy's shoulder. "Just wanted to make sure you were all right."

"Right as rain. Ready to do the Lord's work."

Karyn watched, trying to figure her next move. Unfortunately, it wasn't hers to figure.

Behind Markham, the shadows swirled and solidified into a hulking man-shape; it was the thing she'd

seen in Sinclair's office. It drifted toward her quickly;
she had no time to react. There, before her, it hovered,
still radiating heat like a furnace. Then it reversed its
direction, returning to Markham until the two nearly
touched. A second later, it faded like smoke.

As if tapped on the shoulder, Markham turned in her
direction. There was no way he could actually see her,
but she also knew he was aware of her presence, thanks
to his Dark Friend.

"Stay here, Jimmy." Markham approached, his hand
snaking inside his jacket. He reappeared with a large
saw-toothed knife, just out of Jimmy's line of sight.

She stood. She couldn't outrun him and there was
no point in hiding.

"Is your name really Markham?" she said, trying to
buy time. His eyes narrowed, but he didn't answer.
"Are you a member of the Aryan church, or did they
just hire you to kill Bishop Sinclair?"

Markham tensed at her knowledge.

"Hey, lady," Jimmy said, his voice cheery. "That's just
a game. The bishop ain't going to die. God wouldn't let
him."

"God doesn't have anything to do with this, Jimmy.
Right, Mr. Markham?"

He closed the gap between them and his blade
seemed to grow. Karyn rounded the seats she'd used
for cover, keeping them between her and him.

"I don't know who you are, lady, but you picked the
wrong Sunday to show up in church," Markham said.

She kept probing her mind for some sort of saving
grace. She could scream, but she doubted it would even
register over the noise of the increasingly crowded sanctuary. Her only defense at the moment was her mouth.
"You'll be gone when it's over. When the bishop's dead,

when Jimmy's dead. They'll look for Markham and find out he doesn't exist. Wicked, but smart, I'll give you that."

"I don't know who tipped you, but you're not going to stop this," Markham said. "Three bodies are just as simple as two."

With one hand, he grabbed the corner of the loose seats and tossed them aside, removing the barrier between them. He feinted and she scrambled back several steps, her back to Jimmy.

"Mr. Markham? Why you got that knife?" Jimmy asked.

Markham looked over Karyn's shoulder. "Shut your mouth."

"You think he's still going to shoot for you?" Karyn kept backing up, an idea in mind.

"Doesn't matter if he shoots or not. That gun's a Beretta M107. I chose it because it's one of my favorites. I'll do fine without the dummy's assistance."

"Why'd you call me that, Mr. Markham?" Jimmy asked. "I ain't dumb."

"No," Karyn confirmed, sensing his hurt. "You aren't, Jimmy."

"Enough of—"

Markham was cut off by volcanic applause from below.

"Welcome to the First Annual Power and Purpose conference here at Heavenly Duty."

Karyn was startled, not from the whooping and hollering, but by the speaker's voice. She spared a glance over the rail and caught a glimpse of her mother behind the podium.

"The man I'm about to introduce—" Jessica Manning continued, but Karyn's attention shifted.

"Well, it's showtime, lady. Time to exit, stage left."

Markham's mouth became a thin line. He advanced, ready to gut them.

"I ain't no dummy!" Jimmy screamed, almost at random, it seemed.

And Karyn got an idea.

"Jimmy, hold my hand," she said, realizing if this gambit did not work, she'd have no time to regret her error.

Jimmy was obedient and grasped her palm.

For the first time that day, she took control. Instead of a spontaneous vision, she summoned her ability willingly and peered into Jimmy's past. He—

—is an idiot. Stupid son of a bitch. A fucking retard.

Boys surround him after school. This is the past, but it's bright and clear. It's remembered well. Their fists fall, but their words hurt more.

The years shift. The setting changes. The attackers change, but the violence and the taunts remain. And filtered through a troubled mind like Jimmy's, these boys and men are hungry monsters, their sustenance is his anguish. And—

Karyn blinked. That was her gift. The ability to be in both places—the present and Jimmy's mind—at the same time. Markham moved toward them, his knife leading, but his movements were slow, to her anyway.

The blade came at her; she sidestepped easily. Her free hand struck out and grasped Markham's wrist. In that instant she became a circuit, the transmitter of Jimmy's vision.

Markham screamed.

All of Jimmy's torment became part of Markham through her. The visions weren't meant for him, were too much for his mind to grasp. He tried to snatch away, but Karyn held strong. In this manner, she was the mightier one.

"It's my pleasure," Karyn heard her mother say through it all, "to bring you a true man of God. Rise to your feet and welcome Bishop Horace Sinclair."

Applause rose.

Karyn continued pumping her visions into Markham.

His knife clattered as it hit the floor; his free hand flew to his head and tore at his platinum hair, as if to snatch the images out of his skull.

Karyn let him go. Markham writhed and spun, screaming, "I am me. I am me. I ain't no dummy."

He spun over the balcony rail.

There was a mighty racket as his body fell into the bandstands, destroying a set of drums. Karyn peered over the rail at the broken, twisted form that used to be Markham. The applause for Sinclair ceased. Someone screamed.

"Be calm," Sinclair demanded, then, to the television crew: "Kill the cameras."

The red lights atop the cameras did not go off.

"Kill the—"

Sinclair's chest exploded.

Karyn's mother ran to him, shrieking. Sinclair staggered, his expression shocked and numb, viewing the wound over his heart like there was an odd bug on his shirt and not his blood. He looked that way because it wasn't his blood.

The squib had gone off.

Her mother, frantic, touched the blood seeping from the bishop's shirt, rubbed her thumb and forefinger together, then touched the redness to her tongue. She backed away from the bishop, uncertainly.

Confused murmurs rippled through the crowd. Sinclair glared into the balcony, as did his congregation and cameras.

Karyn kept a softly weeping Jimmy behind her, while she glared back, knowing in her heart that she'd done the right thing, saving the bishop's life, even at the possible cost of killing his church.

Police and media filled the Heavenly Duty plaza on separate sides of yellow crime-scene tape. The authorities searched for facts and statements to piece together the crazed events, while reporters were willing to take what they could get from anyone willing to speculate.

Karyn spent four hours answering questions and, by the end of it all, knew she'd be answering questions for weeks to follow.

Finally free to go, she met Reggie in the plaza, wanting nothing more than to see her apartment and bed. Before she got that wish, there was one more piece of business.

Her mother stood in the wash of bright lights with microphones shoved in front of her. Karyn could not hear her statement, but when she turned away from the media piranhas, she was clearly distraught.

"Stay here, Reggie." She left her friend for her mother.

Jessica Manning didn't notice her right away, her gaze focused on the Heavenly Duty Building.

"Mom."

She blinked as if awakened from a trance. "Karyn?"

She opened her arms to hug her mother. Mom stepped back. "Do you hate me that much, Karyn?"

Karyn's arms fell. "I don't—"

"They're saying he's ruined. You know that, don't you? They're saying all sorts of things."

"They? They who? Mom, I saved him."

"When I saw you in the balcony, I knew." Her voice became high; her eyes were spotlights. "I knew it was some of your deviltry that brought this blight on us. You've destroyed a great man today, and you've lost us a lot of souls."

Mom shook her head, disgusted. "I'm sorry I gave birth to you." She spun and disappeared into the crowd.

Karyn couldn't move. Stunned was not a strong enough word.

A heavy hand fell on her shoulder: Reggie. "Did you hear that?" she asked.

He nodded.

"She's completely lost her—" And the rest of the words wouldn't come. The sobs wouldn't let them.

He held her amidst the chaos while she wondered if all heroes cried like this.

On top of the Heavenly Duty dome, two hundred feet in the air, a hulking being with dark, sharp eyes and a security blazer watched the two embrace. Even from that distance, he could see the tears on Karyn's cheeks. He longed to comfort her, but knew this was part of her trials.

An equally huge shadow materialized next to him to view the show. He fought a wave of disgust and prepared to be cordial. Those were the rules after all.

A toothy smile split the shadow's face. "Some day, huh, Michael?"

"Yes, I suppose."

The darkness of the being swirled and receded as it changed into another form. The previously indistinguishable shape formed a long black coat, matching untucked shirt, spit-shined shoes, and coal-colored hair slicked back. Its skin was bronze, its nose hawk-like. It could've been Michael's twin, with one exception. It had no eyes.

"I have to say, it was a master stroke getting the mother to send the prophet that signed Bible. Good work. Tell Him I said so."

"He already knows. I will not be delivering messages from you, Lu."

"No, I guess you wouldn't. I will say, I was surprised to see you working behind the scenes here. I'd have thought this type of mission beneath you."

"I could say the same." Michael glared at his fallen brother, the Morning Star. He never stopped feeling sorrow for the vile creature.

"It's always good to get out and do a little of the old 'go ahead, take a bite.' Besides, it gives the minions a break. They get disgruntled, too."

Michael's eyebrows arched. "Like you once did?"

Lucifer did not answer, and said instead: "I still won. I'd say the outcome here was better than my original plan."

"Of course you would. You're shortsighted."

"This church is destroyed. Without a leader the people will scatter, fall back into their old ways. My ways."

Michael shook his head, and actually chuckled. "Some will, yes. The rest will be strengthened by the pain and loss. They will learn that their faith was misplaced. They shouldn't believe in another man, they should believe in the teachings of Him. As for Sinclair, he was misled, he's human. But his faith is genuine. His students will return, in even greater numbers. And he'll be a better teacher for this. You'll see."

Lucifer nodded and patted Michael on the back with a hot hand. "You have it all figured out, don't you? There's one problem, though. . . ."

"And that is?"

He smiled, and a noticeable hiss escaped his throat. "Sinclair was only a secondary target." His gazed shifted to the courtyard. "I want the prophet."

With that, Lucifer disappeared in an explosion of flame.

Taken aback, a rare thing for him, Michael cast a furtive glance to the tearful woman blessed with The Sight, then unfolded his wings and shot toward the heavens to report the news, praying to the Almighty that it was not too late to protect her.

The Love of a Zombie Is Everlasting

Tish Jackson

Okay, so I'm a zombie. Does that make me a bad person? Don't answer that, reading public. The answer is *no,* it doesn't. I'm just a black woman looking for male companionship like anyone else. I just happen to prefer human flesh to animal flesh. It could be argued that we're all animals, but I have to tell you that there's a special flavor to Bob's Burgers that McDonald's simply doesn't have. Unfortunately, my palate preferences fill a lot of people with revulsion, some with outright hatred. As if vegans are any different with their radical diets! I'm still a person on the inside, for Pete's sake! That is, before I ate him.

My name is Talyna Wright and I wasn't born this way; the world wasn't born this way. Every couple of years, something new comes along on the disease front and changes the world as we know it. This new challenge polarized communities, pitted families against one another, and sent the government into a tizzy. Did I mention it was also man-made? About three years ago, in 2007, a biological agent trapped inside a rhesus monkey escaped from a weapons lab in China, attacking several people before being tranquilized and then euthanized. Those treated for bites and scratches soon returned to their doctors, complaining of serious digestive complications. The smallest fluid transfer spread the disease like wildfire through the hospitals, and sudden irritable digestion syndrome, or SIDS, soon swept the continent and spread like the Black Plague of the Dark Ages. It caused the digestive tract to reject all the usual forms of sustenance, from projectile vomiting to chronic diarrhea reminiscent of dysentery but worse. Within forty-eight hours a body that refused even intravenous fluids got too weak to support its own life systems.

The infected usually passed away in the next forty-eight hours and SIDS had a hundred percent mortality rate. Once SIDS victims succumbed to the disease, everyone thought death was permanent, and they were interred as usual. Some were cremated and saved the horror of waking up six feet under.

But two months after SIDS first appeared (actually, *escaped* would be a better word) the first victims began to appear around nearby graveyards. The original "revitalized" ones were thought to be homeless people with a bad case of rot and an insatiable appetite. However, when a delegate at the embassy recognized a French tourist, an inkling of the truth was leaked to the ever-accurate *National Enquirer,* assuring its absurdity. At first, authorities believed there had been a rash of misdiagnoses, and that these few lucky souls had escaped a fate worse than death. They would soon find out how untrue that was when the examining doctors were killed. So those first victims were unlucky enough to be the guinea pigs of the medical commu-

Tish Jackson

nity, and were subjected to all kinds of experimentation and/or dissections; once dead they could not be killed again by conventional methods. Modern doctors refused to entertain the idea that zombies could really exist, until a former Department of Defense scientist came forward and announced that she'd been part of a secret trial that hastened the putrefaction process while creating unstoppable soldiers; their appetites were a troublesome by-product. Apparently, the Chinese were trying to beat the U.S. to the punch when the virus escaped from a secret lab in Beijing. Alas, before her story could be documented, the scientist was killed in a freak accident two days later; evidently a gun she didn't own accidentally went off and shot her in the head. You know how it is when folks tell government secrets.

Anyway, the U.N. doctors went to work off her statement and gave their guinea pigs a little putrid flesh, and the zombies liked it just fine. Their previously irritable digestive systems took the nourishment like ambrosia. The scientists also noticed that the buried victims tended to roam near their own grave sites. They seemed to be territorially connected to their original resting places. New victims of SIDS that hadn't died were given bits of flesh and blood to ingest, and though they were able to digest it, it sped up the zombification process and forced them to die sooner. The bottom line—just like in all the movies, one bite condemned you to a radically altered lifestyle that included a lot of raw meat.

Now, to be fair, not all the zombies were raving lunatics; some were lucid and simply trying to live their new lives without getting set afire on the way home from work. There was a movement going on to stop the extreme violence against the zombie population, since it was possible to bring people back with most of their faculties. If their rabid appetites were treated with processed meat, they were distinguishable from regular humans only by the faint smell of decomposing flesh. Plenty of people sympathized with the zombies' cause (mostly relatives of the newly Revitalized, unwilling to let go of their loved one) and were petitioning the government to protect our new citizens. Before my transformation, I was an ardent supporter, signing a petition here or there from not liking to see people tortured and killed whether they were dead or alive, but I hadn't started marching in the streets for the zombies just yet.

Two months before my wedding date, a nonterritorial zombie attacked me in my home.

At the time, I was engaged to a wonderful man, Ralan Johnson. A little under six feet, with solemn brown eyes and generous mouth, Ralan was the most beautiful black man I ever had the pleasure to fall in love with. He was honest and idealistic, gentle with my idiosyncrasies and as passionate about his politics as I was. We'd met at an Urban League meeting and the attraction was immediate. We were both Bay Area natives living in Vallejo with similar interests and compatible work schedules—it was destiny. After six months of serious dating and no infidelities (a feat in itself in this day and age) we moved in together and lived like that for four idyllic years before we decided to seal the deal and get married. With AIDS and SIDS out there, we both felt safer ensconced in our little love nest off Lake Herman Road. It was isolated but we were farther away from the ruckus in town. With the zombie population holding demonstrations to fight for equal rights as former humans, walking down the street could become a life-changing ordeal. So we cooked or ordered in, and worked from home. I was an editorial columnist for *DJ Dynasty,* the largest black media publication on the West Coast, so I needed only my laptop to get paid. Ralan was a research assistant for Meatco, the leader in packaging recycled flesh for zombie consumption, a booming business. It may sound disgusting, but it cut down on zombie maulings considerably. Ralan worked via computer most days, analyzing the decomposition rates of new and used flesh. On the rare occasions he did have to go into the office, a car and bodyguard were sent to escort him to and fro. As Murphy's Law would have it, though, I turned out to be the susceptible one and I never even left the house.

A rogue zombie broke into our apartment one afternoon when Ralan was at work. An emaciated, half-eaten dead woman climbed into the bathroom window and jumped me as I was using the bathroom. Now, I'm not a small woman: at five six and a hundred seventy pounds, I will get down with an aggressor. But the circumstances were a little awkward, as I was using the bathroom at the time when she slammed through the door. I jumped up off the toilet and backed into the tub, looking for possible escape routes. I saw that she'd been buried, because her death raiment was still hanging off her body in tatters and her eyes were crazed and hungry. I was thinking about using the shower curtain to wrap her up in as I ran around her, but that only works in the movies. I attempted to pull the curtain off the rod, and of course it got stuck, and while I tried to recreate movie magic, the zombie caught me by my braids and bit a large chunk out of my neck. That little bit of sustenance occupied her enough for me to run past her then, but the damage had been done.

The authorities came and took her away, and sent a doctor to patch me up. Ralan came home immediately after my frantic call, and the look on his face was tragic. His gaze was stuck to the bandage on my neck, and his inability to meet my eyes made my heart sink. What can you say when your lover has just received a death sentence? The doctor gave me an antibiotic that would give me an extra week before dying, the best modern science could do at the moment, and left us instructions on how to keep me as comfortable as possible during the transition. I have to give Ralan a little credit, he stayed with me as I regurgitated my very life onto the floor and held me even after I turned cold. However, he made it clear that once I died, our relationship would be over.

"I'm going to miss you so much, Talyna," he cried to me one evening as I crept closer to death.

"I know, I know. But you can come see me any time you want. It doesn't have to be over, Ralan."

The look on his face clearly showed how he felt about that statement. No matter what my arguments were or protestations of love, my fiancé could not see a future between us after my revitalization—the PC term. It was known by then that zombies could function in society if routed through the death process correctly, but were still considered beyond the normal range of emotions. Which I can personally tell you is not true! I was definitely feeling the pain of my lover's loss before he was even gone as I entered the zombie state. Ralan's family encouraged him to place me in the

Revitalize Museum, a kind of apartment complex for zombies, two weeks before my scheduled demise to "help start the grieving process." How rude is that? It was obvious to me that they were trying to set the scene for my eventual replacement and I wouldn't be surprised if they already had someone in mind. I believed that as long as we were careful, Ralan and I could still be together; keep lots of Meatco packets around and stay away from the rogues equals smooth sailing. Okay, maybe I was a little forward in my thinking, but if my heartache then was any indication, my love for Ralan was more than strong enough to survive the grave.

However, getting through to Ralan was one thing; convincing his parents was quite another. Near the end, I became so weak from the vomiting and diarrhea that I was immobile. As Ralan tended to me as best he could—while keeping all his appendages away from my mouth—his parents would argue their point over my inert body.

"There is no way I'm letting my only son marry a *zombie!*" Pete Johnson, Ralan's father, would say. "Can you imagine what people at the club would say?" Our happiness obviously came second to the opinion of his club cronies. Mrs. Johnson was more concerned with the possible aesthetics of future grandchildren. In her defense, the image of a half-rotten, flesh-eating infant attacking one's tit with gusto was a little scary. But I still couldn't stand her.

"Mr. and Mrs. Johnson, Ralan and I could adopt children if the natural results worry you so much," I said.

All I got was a derisive snort in my direction, so I tried again.

"We really believe this is not an insurmountable obstacle! As long as I die correctly, I'll still be human and feel human, just in a different way. Why don't you believe that?"

Ralan's mom said, "Ralan, tell her that zombies are not human, zombies are dead and this family does not practice necrophilia! We won't have it." She stopped talking to me after I got sick and would communicate with me only through a third person, as if she could catch my disease through conversation.

"Ralan, please tell your mother that I'm not dead yet! She can speak to me directly!" I said. My anger gave me enough strength to sit up, only to see Ralan's mother turn her back to me. Ralan's father didn't have any problems disparaging me face-to-face, which was about the only time he stood up to his wife in any regard. I tried to plead with him anyway to get his support.

"Pete Johnson, this is racist rhetoric that you're spouting and you should be ashamed of yourself. I am being discriminated against because of a disease! That I had no control over contracting! If it was my skin color or sexuality you objected to, you could be sued. I know you're not *that* concerned with public opinion that you would begrudge your only son love and happiness."

His father looked me straight in the eye and said, "My dear, that's exactly what I object to—because he is my only son and I do want him to be happy. From my point of view, your attempt to bind Ralan to you even after death is just selfish! How can you want to take away his chance for a normal life?" His eyes beseeched me to see his side, and I was momentarily floored. Was

I being selfish by insisting we could work it out? I thought it was just everlasting love.

"Ralan?" I lay back and looked at him, hoping for reassurance or at least acknowledgment that I wasn't way off base. What I got was an agonized expression and lack of eye contact. Instead of a declaration of love or some willingness to at least try and work it out, I was begged for forgiveness and got a hand squeeze.

"Oh, honey, I'm so sorry, please please forgive me, I want to, I really do, I want to be with you forever. God forgive me, but . . ." Yes. I got the "but." The signal that all is not right with the world, the death knell of every relationship, the one-word way to say I don't want you anymore. The fact that my almost husband had caved in to popular thought crashed my will and I had to squeeze my eyes shut so I didn't have to look at his weak ass.

The day I died, I wanted only Ralan to be present. Since he was siding with everyone else, I was still a little disgusted with him, but I couldn't imagine not being with him. Of course, I banned his parents, who were only too glad to stay away those last couple of days. They did insist that their son wear surgical scrubs and a mask when he visited. To his credit, he took them off when he came inside. Since the day he'd finally told me we would not be together after I died, I refused to discuss my afterlife plans with him and tried to get used to the idea of being alone and craving human meat. The latter was easy to prepare for; I had a whole room of the apartment stocked with Meatco products that Ralan had gotten with his employee discount from work. I was dying in my own house, so I would be territorially tied to a safe place. Ralan had already moved his things back to his parents' house and was amenable to letting me stay here—after all, as a regular human he could get any place he wanted.

We didn't talk much. I was almost too weak for conversation by that point. Ralan took advantage of that and rambled on about past memories and how he was going to miss me; it was obvious that he was only too glad not to be asked any hard questions. I wanted to call him a lying leading-me-on bastard, but tears pricked my eyes at the thought of never cussing him out again. The thoughts I'd had of the two of us making civil rights history, proving that zombies can be loving productive members of society and don't have to eat their loved ones, were very hard to let go of. I wondered if I would have the strength to do those things without Ralan by my side, and I shuddered. Would I let the loss of love turn me into a monster?

Ralan saw me shivering and responded by laying another blanket atop me. "You look cold, honey."

When I could feel the final veil starting to descend over my vision, I panicked a little and grabbed Ralan's hand to get his attention. I gave him the prearranged signal and drew my finger across my throat to say it was coming, and Ralan started to sob. I sighed and asked, "Are you going to stay until it's over?"

"Yes, Talyna, I promise I'll be here."

"Ralan, I don't know how to live without you!"

"Shh, you'll be fine, I swear. You're the strongest person I know."

"Can I come see you after? At least one time?" I could see his hesitation and wondered if he was think-

ing of me, his dying fiancée, or what his parents would
say. "Just to say good-bye. I won't hurt anyone, Ralan,
you know that."

"I know you won't. I'll come by here, okay? Two
weeks from today, I'll come just to make sure you're all
right. Okay?"

I was so grateful at his words I could only cry knowing I would see him once more. Then that old Trickster
came and took my life away, leaving me with a huge
hole in my heart and an inimical darkness all around me.

I don't remember waking exactly, I remember only
eating. When my faculties began to work once more, I
was surrounded by several dozen empty Meatco packages that looked as if they'd been opened in a hurry.
About a tenth of the stockpile Ralan had arranged for
me had been decimated. Apparently the hunger is so
strong it brings on a fugue state and the body blindly
attempts to feed itself whatever is at hand. I shudder to
think what might have happened if I hadn't prepared
properly; I can easily imagine breaking out of the
apartment and attacking unsuspecting innocents in a
frenzy. The need was so strong!

After finishing the half-consumed flesh I woke up
with, I set about straightening up the food room, dis-
posing of empty containers and gobbets of meat strewn
around the place. I then showered and changed, stopping to look at my new self in the mirror. My chocolate
skin had an ashy gray tinge to it, like death had laid a
light covering of itself over my pores. My eyes had
sunken in just a tiny bit, but my hair and nails had
grown a couple of inches during the transition. The
new growth in front of my braids was probably three

inches longer than it was before, and if things were different, I would've been doing the happy dance. But now I stared at the familiar face looking back at me, so very different but still the same. Looking into my eyes, I still saw some intelligence and empathy, which was reassuring, but I also fancied I saw a flicker of madness, a promise to do absolutely anything to satisfy that psychotic hunger—for flesh. The burning hunger that filled my whole body forced me to devour another helping of processed human flesh every couple of minutes, provided by my friend and yours, Meatco Packaging Plant. And Ralan. Contacting him was still very important to me, but calling his parents' phone number up from my memory was impossible. I guess the Revitalized don't do numbers, because I couldn't remember a single one. Which was fine with me; I didn't want to take the chance that they might answer instead of Ralan, and I knew that would open a whole new can of worms. So I made myself presentable, packed a bag full of my new favorite snacks, grabbed the door key (to make sure no other zombies came by and hit the jackpot), and stepped outside for the first time in my new incarnation.

I really didn't mean to eat Ralan's parents. I purposely brought an alternative source of food so I wouldn't even be tempted. I even waited until I saw them leave the house so I could be alone with Ralan. Munching on a Meatco packet, I watched them walk down the block before I walked up the stoop and turned the doorknob. I was ecstatic to see Ralan standing in the foyer as if he were waiting for me. I *wasn't* happy to see all the packing boxes full of his things around me, though. Ralan appeared to be frozen at the sight of me standing in the doorway. Maybe I came back to life a little too early, which of course was what the boxes were all about. It was obvious even to a zombie.

"Ralan, I'm back. I came to see you like I promised."

Ralan didn't move, stuck in some emotion that would not allow him to speak.

"Ralan, what's going on? Are your parents moving away?" I looked into the box nearest me because I sensed the worst sort of betrayal. And yes, the box was filled with knickknacks belonging to Ralan—his Meharry sweatshirt that I loved to borrow, a picture of the two of us on the beach in Monterey Bay before the world erupted in disease and it was still safe to go out . . . I wondered briefly if this box was going or staying.

I stepped toward Ralan, who still hadn't said anything but was suddenly able to move and quickly scrambled backward on unsteady legs, tripping over boxes to land on his gluteus maximus. Seeing his things packed away could not eclipse the pain I felt when Ralan almost broke his legs to get away from me.

"What is this?" I grabbed a poncho that I'd bought him last year and threw it at him. Instead of answering me, my previous pillar of strength sat on his ass and began to cry. I tore through the box, filled with remnants of our former life. I pulled out the picture of us in Texas and threw it at his head.

"Ralan, you were going to leave me, weren't you? You promised—*promised!* You said you were going to come see me at least once. Do you know how scary this is for me? And you were just going to leave me alone to—to live dead!" I cried bitterly, but no more than Ralan did, covering his face and sobbing loudly. However, his tears did not move me in the slightest.

I grabbed around for my bag of Meatco supplies because anger was bubbling up inside me and I needed to be masticating madly on something. As I looked around the room frantically to see where I'd laid it down, I understood how even cognizant zombies accidentally ate loved ones. I was so monumentally mad that I feared for Ralan's safety. The fact that he just sat on the floor crying like a lamb asking to be slaughtered didn't help matters. Seeing my bag lying in the archway, I started for the door, wanting to get away from him before I could not control myself anymore and bad things happened. Unfortunately, Ralan's parents got there first.

Looking back, I can just imagine what the Johnsons were thinking when they saw me in their house. *The dreaded zombie scourge had ARISEN, found them, and there was going to be hell to pay!* Mr. Johnson had a roll of masking tape in his hands from the store, so I guess they had run out before they could finish packing. Mrs. Johnson was empty-handed, but her face wasn't empty, it was full of disgust—nose wrinkled up and lips pulled back in an unattractive grimace as if she smelled something unbearable. Maybe she did, though I was pretty sure I'd taken a shower before I left. However, Mrs. Johnson didn't get a chance to harangue me like she did constantly when I was dying. The previously uncontrolled anger I had experienced watching Ralan boo-hoo over his own betrayal broke loose from the feeble hold that had held it in check. I growled, "You!" and leaped on her. I jumped right onto her face and chomped on her nose and boy, did it taste good! I ignored Mr. Johnson's attempts to pull me off his wife and continued chewing on her face, oblivious of Ralan's piercing screams. I held my hands on both sides of Mrs. Johnson's face and tried to pull her nose off to swallow what was left, so I could start somewhere else. I do remember pushing her against the front door to close it and seeing her terrified eyes, broadcasting fear, pain, and yes, revulsion. I don't remember snapping her neck, only that she eventually stopped struggling and I started to eat her in earnest.

I awoke chewing on Mr. Johnson's testicles. Ralan was trussed up on the floor with masking tape, hogstyle. His mouth was also taped shut and above that, his frightened eyes still leaked and seemed to beseech me for . . . for what? I would never eat Ralan. His folks had asked for it for months, though. I swallowed the tasty morsel Mr. Johnson had unwittingly supplied and looked around. Mrs. Johnson's body lay in front of the door, wedging it shut so even if someone had tried to open the door they couldn't have. Her nose was indeed gone, as were her eyes and throat. I don't know which got eaten first, but for her sake, I hoped it was the eyes. She was a bitch.

I assumed there was a struggle, because the room was a mess; upended boxes were everywhere and the belongings of the Johnson family were scattered all around me. Anything fragile had been broken and I wondered why no one had come over to find out what the hell was happening at the Johnsons'. Lucky for me no one did; I'd have been carried off to the containment asylums for rogue zombies straightaway. I was aware that my lack of discovery could change at any moment and began to take steps to get out of there ASAP.

I turned to Mr. Johnson, who in addition to having no balls was wearing a red necktie minus the neck part.

He obviously would not be making the Great Escape with me. Getting his manhood chomped on was pretty appropriate, considering he never had the balls to stand up to his wife. I still liked him, though, and don't really know why I attacked him. Probably because he was trying to save his wife. He should have looked at it as a favor.

That left Ralan, whom I was taking with me. I wasn't up for conversation with him at that point, so I left him all taped up. I mean, what can you really say when you just ate a man's parents? Not much, believe me. I really wanted to take Mr. and Mrs. Johnson to the graveyard and let them turn there, forever dooming them to the life they so abhorred, but I didn't have time to be dragging their asses all across town and whatnot. I kind of don't want to say what I *did* stay and do, but I moved Ralan to the back door, where he couldn't see into the living room area. But the reality is that Meatco packets are a bit like soy milk—just not as good as the real thing. I wouldn't have known what I was missing if Ralan had kept his promise to me. I never would have tasted . . . well, tasted his parents. After that, Meatco was a poor substitute. Who would have thought that those two racist assholes would taste so good? Okay, basically I just took some of Lois and Pete Johnson with us. Just think of it as preserving their memory; as I eat them, they kind of live on inside me, right? Ralan never has to know.

I took Ralan back to our apartment. That was actually the only place I could take him since I was territorially linked there by death. He was still taped up, as I didn't think he was ready to be released yet. After the first day, I did take the tape off his mouth, but he refused to speak to me. His anger was understandable but I was angry with him, too! If he had stood up to his parents from the get-go, the tragedy of them getting what they deserved would have been avoided altogether. After the third day, Ralan did talk but only to tell me that he would never forgive me after what I'd done. *He* would never forgive *me?* Boy, did that ever piss me off! I was kind of glad this whole situation occurred so I could see how flaky he really was. I mean, what if we had gotten married? He probably would have pulled a similar stunt. So much for unconditional love.

However, I did decide to give him another chance. I was planning to love him for life, and technically I was still alive. And I still thought it could work between us. Ralan, of course, took some convincing, but I tried using a little sex to get his mind going in the right direction. After all, he said he couldn't forgive me, not that he didn't love me. Full-blown sex was out of the question since I'd have to unbind Ralan for that, but the truth was that if you give any man head—under any circumstances—he tends to listen. I did get a little too excited during the maneuver, and accidentally gave him a little nip. But basically, I was as good as ever. I wasn't even a little bit hungry. Ralan started showing symptoms a couple of days later, vomiting the food I tried to give him and complaining of stomach cramps. It wasn't on purpose, I swear, but wasn't it funny how things worked out? I thought it could only bring us closer together, really! I made him as comfortable as I could, and would, of course, be right there for him. At least he'd have someone with him when he awakened, which was more than I had.

I tried to feed him a Meatco packet yesterday, but he was still refusing meat. I knew that would change soon enough. I figured once he's weak enough, it would be safe to loosen his bonds without him trying to escape, so we could get ready for his change. I was a little worried about our food supply running low; it was supposed to feed only one zombie. I knew we could get around that, though, we'd just have to go out every now and then to replenish our stock. And of course, I still had my secret stash, courtesy of Ralan's parents.

Gosh, it would be so nice to have someone with me who totally understood what I was feeling! I just couldn't wait.

Ghostwriter

Brandon Massey

"How's the new book coming along, honey?" Andrew had been reaching for the bowl of tortilla chips, anticipating dipping a fresh chip in the dish of spicy salsa, his mouth watering in expectation. Danita's question made his mouth go dry.

"The book?" He drummed the table. "It's coming along okay, I guess."

Danita's brow creased—the same look he imagined she gave her clients at the law firm when they tossed a lie her way. Frowning, she folded her arms on the table, leaned forward.

"What page are you on?" she asked.

He cleared his throat. "Well, lately, I've been doing some outlining, working out some of the fuzzy story elements. You know how I write. I need to have a clear sense of direction before I move forward."

"You've been outlining for a long time. Your deadline is only three months away."

"I know my deadline, Danita. You don't have to remind me."

"Right, but like you said, I know how you write. You always do several drafts before you're finished, and you haven't even completed a first draft yet. I'm worried about you."

Andrew idly stirred his sweet tea. Her concern both touched and annoyed him. For many years, he'd longed for a relationship with a woman like Danita. She was smart, ambitious, loving, pretty. She admired his talent for spinning tales and supported his writing career not for the money and fame it brought him, but because she understood that writing was his labor of love. She wanted him to do well, and he loved her for it.

But sometimes, he wanted her to back off and let him be a neurotic writer—with all the loopy work habits, unpredictable creative impulses, and paralyzing bouts of angst that came with it.

"It's fine," he said. "The book is coming to me slowly. It works that way sometimes."

Danita's lips curled. She didn't believe him; worse, he didn't believe himself.

The book was not coming to him slowly—it was not coming to him at all. His second novel was like a head-strong dog that refused to be either cajoled or punished into obedience. The more he pressed and teased, the more it resisted. It was maddening.

It hadn't been that way with his first novel, *Ghost-writer*. He'd written *Ghostwriter* in a frenzy, burning through five hundred pages in only four months. And it was good, damn good. The first agent he queried wanted it; the first publisher they sent it to bought it, plunking down a six-figure advance that enabled him to quit his day job as a programmer. Books by black authors were hot, and industry people were calling him "the African-American Stephen King," a derivative label that he despised, yet tolerated because it gave the marketing people an effective handle. Film rights were sold for three hundred thousand; lucrative foreign rights sales to eleven countries followed soon after. The book had been flying off the shelves since it hit stores five months ago. Readers were clamoring for the next book. His editor was ready for the next book. So was his agent. Add his girlfriend to the list, too.

But no one was as ready for the next book as he was—and he couldn't write it. Writer's block, which he had long believed was a myth made up by wannabe authors who'd never finish anything, had fallen like a brick onto his hands, rendering them numb and useless. Each morning, he sat at his brand-new computer, a bright and painfully blank screen staring back at him, and after an hour of fitful typing and story outlining that led nowhere, he'd log on to the Internet and spend the rest of the day surfing the Web under an alias so none of his online writer buddies could ask him what he was doing, and shouldn't he be working on the next book . . . ?

"Did you hear me, Drew?"

He blinked. "Sorry, I spaced out. What did you say?"

"I said, you need inspiration. Something to get your creative juices flowing."

"Maybe I could start drinking. It's worked for some writers." He chuckled.

She didn't laugh. In the past, she would've found humor in such a joke. He wondered if she was actually worried he just might take up the bottle to loosen his creative muscles.

"Why don't you immerse yourself in a place that fits the stuff you write about?" she said. "Somewhere scary."

"Like your parents' house?"

That time, she did laugh. "Oh, you got jokes now, do you? No, silly, I mean, you write about ghosts, haunted houses, stuff like that. Why not go somewhere creepy?"

"Like a haunted house?"

Her eyes widened. "The cemetery. At night!"

Andrew laughed, then shook his head. "I know which one you're talking about. Girl, you're crazy."

"It's the perfect place," she said. "And it's so close. You wouldn't even need to drive—"

"Ain't no way in hell I'm walking around a grave-yard at night, Danita."

She grinned. "See? That's why I know it would in-spire you—because the very idea scares you. It'll put you in the mind-set you need to write your book."

"Uh-huh, right. You're a better lawyer than you are a psychologist."

"Make jokes if you want, you know I'm right," she said. "Go to the cemetery for one night, Drew. I know it'll help you beat your writer's block. I can feel it."

"I'll think about it," he said, which was his way of signaling that it was time to change the subject. Danita and her crazy ideas. Why in the hell would he want to creep around a graveyard at night? What would be next—visiting haunted houses? Participating in séances? Simply because he wrote about such things didn't mean he wanted to experience them firsthand. He didn't need to. His own imagination, nourished over the years with a steady diet of horror flicks, nov-els, and the nightly news, supplied all the inspiration he needed.

But what had his imagination done for him lately? he had to ask himself. He had been fiddling with the novel for ten fruitless months, the deadline thundering toward him like a freight train. He could request an extension, but an extra three months would mean nothing if he didn't defeat his block. He knew he had to do something drastic to rekindle his creative spark.

By the time they finished lunch, Andrew had reluctantly decided that Danita was right. He would visit the cemetery. Tonight.

After his agent sold movie rights to *Ghostwriter,* Andrew moved out of his apartment in Atlanta and purchased a stylish, two-bedroom condo in the suburb of Marietta, northwest of the big city. The condominium was located next to Magnolia Memorial Cemetery. He hadn't minded because the condo was great and he got an awesome deal. Besides, he found it oddly fitting for a horror writer to live next to a cemetery; death, his favorite subject matter, was right next door. In fact, the town newspaper had mentioned it when they interviewed him: LOCAL HORROR WRITER FINDS INSPIRATION IN HIS BACKYARD.

What few people knew was that he'd never so much as set foot in the cemetery. Why should he? Using the cemetery's proximity to his home as a PR ploy was clever; but the thought of walking amongst the graves, especially at night, scared the hell out of him.

He couldn't explain his fear; it was a primitive dread that seemed to be biologically hard-wired into him, the same way irrational fears of the dark, enclosed spaces, and the number thirteen affected some people. Was there an official, psychological term for graveyard phobia?

An hour before midnight, after spending yet another evening meandering at his keyboard, Andrew stood beside his Range Rover. He wore a light jacket and gripped a yellow utility flashlight. In front of him lay the deep, dark forest. Beyond the woods, the cemetery awaited.

Andrew shivered, but his chill had nothing to do with the cool March breeze that swept across the parking lot.

A pale, full moon gazed down at him. His mind, so attuned to the ominous meanings of full moons, night-blackened forests, and graveyards, churned out a carnival of nightmarish images: hulking werewolves creeping through the forest; rotted corpses struggling out of the earth; phantoms drifting like smoke across headstones . . .

"Okay, cut it out," he said to himself. "Go in there, walk around for a few minutes, and come home. Save the macabre imagery for the book."

He exhaled. Then, heart thrumming, he entered the forest.

Viewed from the lighted parking lot, the woods had appeared to be dark. But when Andrew actually stepped into the forest, it seemed much darker, as if light could not penetrate the area.

He resisted his compulsion to flick on the flashlight. Artificial light would ruin the mood. The whole point of this exercise was to help him tap into the spirit of the night, if there was such a thing. He carried the flashlight for an emergency.

What kind of emergency, Andrew? Like being chased by a headless corpse, for example?

He shook off the absurd thought and crept through the undergrowth, grass crunching beneath his boots. Leaves brushed his face, and twigs probed him like fingers, the darkness alive with the sounds of nocturnal creatures.

The cemetery lay ahead, bathed in soft moonlight and shrouded in mist.

As he stepped out of the woods, a length of barbed wire snagged his jeans.

"Shit." Stepping back, he tore the denim loose from the wire. *There goes a pair of good jeans.* He noticed, concealed in the shrubbery at the edge of the forest, a low, barbed-wire fence that seemed to run the entire length of the woods on this side. Was it there to keep the forest-dwelling creatures out of the cemetery? Or . . . was it there to keep something in the graveyard *out* of the forest and the world beyond?

He laughed at himself. Danita had been right. This little jaunt was filling his head with all kinds of strange ideas.

He leapt over the fence and into the cemetery. Fog enveloped the area. He noted, on his left, a huge mound of dirt, like a man-made hill. Ahead, he saw countless graves, most marked by footstones on which stood metallic tubes filled with sprays of flowers. The funeral home lay in the distance, barely visible through the mist.

Silence had cloaked the night. He could hear his heart pounding.

"All right," he said to himself. "Walk around for a few, soak up some atmosphere, then go home. That's all I need to do."

He started forward. The churning fog seemed to thicken around him as he moved. He was tempted to turn on the flashlight, but he decided against it. Certainly, a caretaker patrolled the grounds at night. A light shining in the darkness would be a dead giveaway.

He could imagine how he'd explain why he was there. "Well, I'm a horror writer, mister. I came here seeking inspiration for my novel. My name is Andrew Graves. Graves is roaming the graveyard, you know? Pretty funny, huh—"

Wrapped in mist and his own thoughts, Andrew didn't see the dark pit yawning in front of him. He walked into emptiness and fell, screaming—all the way to the bottom of a freshly dug grave.

"Hey, are you okay down there?"

Lying on his side on the hard, damp earth, his head spinning, Andrew thought he was hearing things. It was a young woman's voice—soft, musical, soothing. Like something out of a dream.

"Hello?" she called again. "If you're conscious, please say something."

"I'm here," he said, shakily. He sat up, winced as pain bolted through his shoulder. He didn't think he had broken any bones, and though his shoulder ached, he knew that it wasn't dislocated. He'd dislocated his shoulder when playing high school football, and this pain was not nearly as bad as that had been.

He looked up. The woman's face, a featureless black oval, peered down at him.

"Can you stand?" she asked. "Give me your hands and I'll help you climb out of there."

"Okay." Who was this woman? The caretaker?

He stuffed the flashlight into his jacket pocket and struggled to his feet. The hole was six feet deep; the top a couple of inches above his head.

The woman's hands seemed to float toward him through the mist, as if they belonged to a disembodied spirit. His heart stalled . . . and when he moved closer, he saw, clearly, that her hands were ordinary flesh. His imagination was running away with him.

He grasped her hands—her soft, warm skin sending an unexpected thrill through him—and she pulled him up. He worried that he'd be too heavy for her, but she tugged him upward with ease.

She was a few inches shorter than him, slender, wrapped in a knee-length, silvery jacket. Her dark hair flowed to her shoulders. In the darkness, he couldn't see much of her face.

"Thanks," he said. "I don't know how I fell in there. I guess I wasn't paying attention to where I was going."

She shook a cigarette out of a pack and struck a match. When she brought the flame near her face, his breath caught in his throat.

She was absolutely gorgeous. She looked like a black porcelian doll, her features too perfect to be real.

Maybe she's not real. Maybe I hit my head when I fell and I'm really lying in the grave unconscious, dreaming up all of this.

Seemingly unaware of his admiration, no doubt accustomed to causing hearts to stutter, the woman slowly took a draw from her cigarette. "I wasn't going to ask you how you fell in there. I was going to ask you what you're doing here."

"Why?" he asked. "Do you work here? Are you going to throw me out?"

She laughed—a low, throaty chuckle. "I asked first."

"So you did," he said. He motioned behind him. "I live in a condo near here. I'm a writer and . . . uh, well, I guess I was looking for some inspiration."

"Why would you of all people need to visit a cemetery for inspiration? Andrew Graves, the most exciting new horror writer of the decade?"

She laughed at the surprise on his face, and then took his hand.

"Come with me, sweetie," she said. "We've got some things to talk about."

Okay, this could be the plotline for a story, he thought. *A horror writer crippled with writer's block wanders into a nearby graveyard seeking inspiration. He foolishly walks into an empty grave, and is rescued by a beautiful woman who thinks he's brilliant.*

But then what happens?

Feeling like a hapless character in one of his own tales, Andrew followed her.

A dozen yards away, a black granite sarcophagus stood about six feet high. The woman climbed on top and invited him to join her. There, as if in the midst of a picnic, she'd spread a blanket on which stood a bottle of Merlot, a wine glass, a leather-bound notebook, and a shiny Waterford pen.

Her name was Alexandria, and she didn't work at the cemetery. She was a writer, she said, and the solitude of a graveyard, at night, stimulated her creativity.

Andrew realized that many writers were eccentric, but he had never heard of a writer regarding a cemetery as the ideal place in which to write. It was strange as hell.

He would've made up an excuse to leave, but he stayed for three reasons: one, she claimed to be a huge fan of his, and he needed an ego boost. Two—he felt an instant and profound chemistry with her that had nothing to do with her good looks. Three—well, she *was* heart-achingly beautiful. He made his living with words, and he could not describe the startling impact her beauty had on him. Although he loved his girlfriend, when he looked at Alexandria he found it hard to remember what Danita even looked like.

He'd never been under a magic spell, but it must feel exactly like this.

"I've read your novel three times," Alexandria said. "You're so talented, amazingly so. Why would you need to come here for inspiration? That sort of thing is reserved for amateurs like me." She laughed, took another drag of her cigarette.

Ordinarily, he didn't like to be around smoke, but her smoking didn't bother him. In a way, it added to her appeal, as though she were a film star from decades ago when famous actresses smoked and it was considered glamorous, sexy. Alexandria had an air of grace and sophistication that recalled those fabled silver screen goddesses.

And she'd read his book three times! Now, that was flattering—after completing the book, he hadn't wanted to read it even once.

"The first novel came very easily," he said. "Maybe too easily. I got spoiled. Writing this second book is like being thrown in a tub of cold water—having to face the reality that writing isn't always easy. It's work."

"You're damn right it's work." She tapped her leatherbound notebook. "I've been working on this novel for two years, and I'm nowhere near done."

"What's the title?" he said.

"A Midnight Haunting," she said. "It's a ghost story,

and a love story, all wrapped up into one wondrous, Gothic tale."

"Sounds interesting. I'd like to read it when you finish."

"*If* I ever finish. When I'm most frustrated with it, I think of hiring a ghostwriter to complete it for me. I simply want to be done with it! But I doubt I could ever do that. A ghostwriter would have to be completely filled with my spirit to do any justice to the story. Know what I mean?"

"Definitely. Our work can be so close to us, so personal, that we have to write it ourselves."

Her eyes were dreamy, her voice a whisper. "My only wish is to complete the novel before I die—and if I die before I'm done, then I'd want to have my ghostwriter finish the tale. But I like to think that I have a full life ahead of me, and that I have plenty of time. I don't have a real deadline like you have."

When she saw him frown, she giggled and said, "Oh, sorry. I'm sure you didn't want to be reminded."

"That's okay." He sighed, looking around. Although fog rolled across the gravestones, and the night was as dark as ever, the graveyard did not seem quite as forbidding as before. "You know, I've never hung out at a cemetery. How long do you usually stay here?"

"Until I'm ready to leave." She refilled her wineglass. "I didn't bring another glass since I wasn't expecting company. Would you like some?"

"Sure." She was a relative stranger to him, and here they were drinking from the same glass. He and Danita had not drunk out of the same cup until after they had been dating for a month, at least.

He sipped the wine. It was dry, yet smooth. Delicious warmth spread across his chest. As he reeled in the drink's potency, Alexandria unloosened the belt straps of her jacket and shrugged out of the garment.

Andrew almost dropped the glass.

She wore a black lace slip that barely reached past the top of her thighs. Her cleavage swelled out, adorned with a tiny silver crucifix that glittered in the moonlight.

Although the night was cool, probably fifty degrees, Alexandria raised her head to the sky and stretched languorously, as though luxuriating in the moon rays.

"I love night in the cemetery," she said. "To be here with you, my favorite writer, in my special place, is like a dream."

"Is there a caretaker here?" he said. "Someone who might . . . see us?"

"You don't need to worry," she said. "It's only us, and the dead." She laughed.

He laughed, too, much harder and longer than he should have. He felt drunk—intoxicated by the wine and by this bizarre, fabulous woman.

They talked long into the night about books, movies, traveling, their families, and countless other subjects. She was fiercely intelligent and shared deep insights that challenged him, moved him. She laughed at his dry wit, and she amused him with her comedic timing.

When their conversation finally dipped into a lull, Alexandria slid closer, pressed her body against his. She took the wine from him and ran her tongue across where his lips had touched the glass.

"You inspire me," she whispered. She placed her hand against his thigh, squeezed. "I want to be your inspiration, too, my brilliant writer."

He closed his hand over hers, brought her slender fingers to his lips, and kissed them.

"You already are," he said.

Sometime later that night—Andrew had lost all track of time—he made his way back home. He stumbled through the door, exhausted, yet excited, his nerves jangling. What an incredible night. It had been beyond anything within his ability to imagine.

Now he needed to write. He had to write. This very minute.

Trembling, he raced to his office and switched on the computer. It began to go through its boot-up cycle. He drummed the desk impatiently.

This wasn't right. He couldn't do this on a machine. That was the problem with this book. It demanded to be handwritten—a purer method of writing.

He found a spiral notebook in the desk drawer.

His Mont Blanc pen, which Danita had given him as a Christmas gift, was in a case on his desk.

With paper and pen in hand, he rushed to the glass dinette table. He uncapped the pen and tore open the notebook.

He wrote nonstop until dawn.

"Drew, you look like you need some rest," Danita said. "Your eyes are bloodshot."

They were at Danita's town house, reclining on the living room sofa. They'd ordered a pizza and were watching a movie; some sappy chick flick that Danita had insisted on renting. Although Andrew's eyes were on the screen, he saw only mental images of the story he was writing—and breathtaking visions of Alexandria.

Danita tapped his shoulder. "Did you hear me? You've been zoning out all evening. Are you okay?"

He glanced at his watch. Nine-thirty. He had a date that evening. At midnight. In the cemetery.

"Drew!"

He looked at Danita. "What?"

"What's wrong with you? You aren't yourself."

"The book is coming to me. Finally. I was up all night, spent most of the day on it, too. I don't even remember whether I slept or not. The book is blocking out everything." Everything except Alexandria, that is.

"I see," she said carefully. "So, did you take my advice and visit the cemetery?"

"Not yet." He looked away. The cemetery would remain his secret. "The book hit me last night and has been flowing ever since. I've never felt a flow like this. This is unreal."

"Hmm." Her eyes held a trace of suspicion, and then she sighed, her suspicion giving way to resignation. "This is what I get for dating a writer. Occasional weird moods and temporary obsession. But I love you anyway." She leaned forward and kissed him.

He quickly broke off the kiss and stood up. "Danita, I've gotta go."

"To write?"

He nodded fervently. "It's taking me over, calling to me. I don't know how else to explain it. I'm . . . under a spell."

"I won't pretend that I understand, Drew," she said. "Because I don't. But go handle your business."

Driving back to his home, he swung into the parking

lot of Tom's Beverage Depot. He bought five bottles of Merlot—the same French label he and Alexandria had shared.

He also bought a carton of Newport cigarettes. Her favorite.

At midnight, they found each other at their special meeting place: the empty grave he had fallen into the first night they met.

"I missed you," Alexandria said, pulling him into her embrace. He wound his fingers through her silky hair. He could hold her forever. He never wanted to leave her. She inspired him. She excited him. She understood him. She loved him.

Before meeting Alexandria, if anyone had asked him whether it was possible to fall in love within minutes of meeting someone, he would've called that person a hopelessly romantic fool.

Now he knew better.

Wrapped in each other's arms, they went to their spot on the big granite tomb.

Later, when he returned home, his creative batteries more powerfully charged than ever, he scribbled in his notebook for twelve hours straight.

For five consecutive days, the book was Andrew's world, and Alexandria was his sun.

They met each night at midnight, always in the cemetery, always at the same location. Once they embraced, time spun out like spools of thread, became meaningless. They drank wine, talked, made love, drank wine, talked, made love . . .

Within five days, he had filled the notebook's five hundred pages with words. The novel was done.

He couldn't wait to tell Alexandria.

A few minutes before midnight, he dashed out of his condo and into the woods. He followed the path that he had created during his previous trips, and then jumped over the barbed-wire fence and wandered into the cemetery.

It was midnight when he arrived at the grave, their meeting spot. But Alexandria wasn't there. Odd. She was always on time.

He also noticed that the hole was no longer empty. It had been filled, a gravestone embedded at the head, and a wreath of bright flowers placed atop it.

Well, it was about time someone was buried there. He could've broken his neck when he'd fallen into it on that first night.

Out of curiosity, he flicked on his flashlight. He focused the beam on the headstone.

Reading it, he was seized by such shock that he dropped the flashlight.

"No," he said, in a choked voice. He bent to retrieve the flashlight—and crashed to his knees.

"No, no, no, no, no." Like a blind man, he crawled across the grass, fumbling for the light. He grabbed it, shone it on the inscription.

Alexandria Bentley
Beloved Daughter. Gifted Writer.
January 18, 1976–March 5, 2006

Hot tears scalded his skin. Had to think. This would've been the sixth night he had spent with Alexandria. They had first met around midnight of March 7 . . . two days after she had died. . . .

"Impossible," he said. He fought to stand. Staggering, he went to the black granite monument on which they had spent so many hours. He peered over the top of it.

The surface was bare. There was no blanket, no wine, no cigarette ash.

He had touched her, kissed her, loved her. Here. Right. Here.

"Impossible!" he shouted.

He ran out of the cemetery.

Danita was knocking at the door of his condo when he ran out of the forest.

"Where are you coming from?" she yelled. "Jesus, Drew, I've been worried sick about you. You haven't returned my calls, you've been acting distant, I haven't seen you in days. What's going on?"

He didn't answer, just unlocked the door and brushed past her.

Danita slammed the door. "Damn it, Drew, talk to . . . what have you been doing in here?" She gasped, looking around the living room.

Blinking, he scratched his head—and saw what had been invisible to him for days. Wineglasses and bottles of Merlot littering the coffee table. Empty packs of Newport cigarettes scattered everywhere. Saucers, bowls, and cups brimming with ashes and cigarette butts.

"I don't . . . know." He was groggy and disoriented, as if he had awakened only minutes ago from a deep slumber. "I've been writing a novel. Done with it now." He grabbed the spiral notebook off the dinette table and handed it to her.

Confused and anxious, Danita opened the notebook.

"What is this?" she asked, flipping through the pages. "What the hell is this?" She turned back to the first page, smacked it, and shoved it toward him.

He looked at it.

A Midnight Haunting
A Novel by Alexandria Bentley

"Oh, Jesus," he said, and fell onto the sofa.

Alexandria's words, spoken during their fateful first meeting, came to him:

I think of hiring a ghostwriter to complete it for me . . . A ghostwriter would have to be completely filled with my spirit to do any justice to the story . . . My only wish is to complete the novel before I die— and if I die before I'm done, then I'd want to have my ghostwriter finish the tale. . . .

"Drew?" Danita said. She stepped toward him hesitantly.

He stared at the title page. Then he lowered his face to the pages and wept, his tears mingling with the ink . . . running in black streams down the paper.

ABOUT THE CONTRIBUTORS

Tananarive Due is the national best-selling author of *Joplin's Ghost*, *The Good House*, and many other acclaimed novels. She lives in Southern California.

Wrath James White is a former world-class heavyweight kickboxer, a professional kickboxing and mixed martial arts trainer, bodybuilder, distance runner, performance artist, and former street brawler, who is now known for creating some of the most disturbing works of fiction in print.

He is the author of *Succulent Prey*, a novel of extreme erotic horror, the acclaimed short story collection *The Book of a Thousand Sins*, and the novella *His Pain,* published in 2006 by Delirium Books. Wrath is also the coauthor of *Teratologist,* cowritten with the king of extreme horror, Edward Lee, and *Poisoning Eros*, cowritten with Monica J. O'Rourke.

Anthony Beal is a thirty-one-year-old lunatic whose passions include aged tequila, Cajun food done right, and writing erotic horror fiction and poetry. A passionate fan of Poe, Brite, and Lovecraft, Anthony enjoys pressing his sweaty body against liquor lounge wallflowers and is believed to exist in more than one universe. It is said that he possesses the uncanny ability to distinguish between people closest to him sheerly by the taste of their sweat. When he isn't baptizing nude nuns with flavored oils, Anthony enjoys collecting skulls, maintaining his Web presence, www.anthonybeal.net, and achieving states of spiritual transcendence through inebriation

Lexi Davis's imagination runs wild . . . sort of like a starving cat at a sushi bar. But this is a good thing when she channels it into writing fresh, fun paranormal stories.

A UCLA English graduate and native Californian, Lexi is fascinated by the supernatural realm. First she wrote horror but quit after scaring herself and running out of the room. She abandoned hard-edged horror and opted to write wickedly entertaining stories showcasing her humorous voice and witty dialogue. This landed her a multibook deal with Pocket Books. Her debut novel, *Pretty Evil*, was nominated for Best First Novel by *The Romantic Times*.

Randy Walker is a former lawyer turned writer. "To Get Bread and Butter" is his first major publication. He resides in Mississippi, where he is at work on several novels and short stories.

Dameon Edwards is a native of Gastonia, North Carolina. He currently resides in Greensboro, North Carolina. "Dream Girl" is his first professional writing credit. He is currently working on his first horror novel.

He is a graduate of the Ohio State University in Columbus, Ohio, and obtained a master's degree in public administration. He is also an alum of HBCU's Voorhees College in Denmark, South Carolina, with a B.S. in political science and Mary Holmes College in West Point, Missouri, with an A.S. in social science.

His literary influences are James Baldwin, Richard Wright, Lloyd Alexander, Stephen King, Dean Koontz, Steven Barnes, Octavia Butler, John Ridley, Omar Tyree, Noire, Peter David, Richard Laymon, Frank Miller, Mark Waid, and Keith R.A. DeCandido.

Chesya Burke has been writing professionally for several years. Her work has appeared in *The African American National Biography*, published by Harvard University and Oxford University Press, and in a variety of distinguished magazines and anthologies, such as *Dark Dreams I* and *II, Would That It Were*, and many more. Chesya received the 2003 Twilight Tales Award for fiction and an honorable mention in *The Year's Best Fantasy and Science Fiction: 18th Annual Edition*.

She lives in the suburbs of Atlanta, with her husband, four daughters, three dogs, two cats, and a fish called Michael.

Robert Fleming, a former award-winning reporter at the *New York Daily News*, is the author of *The Wisdom of the Elders, The African American Writer's Handbook, Havoc After Dark, Fever in the Blood,* and the editor of the collections *After Hours* and *Intimacy*. His poetry, fiction, and essays have appeared in numerous periodicals and books, such as *Brotherman, Up-South, Gumbo, Sacred Fire, Gumbo, Brown Sugar, Dark Matter, Proverbs for the People,* and *Dark Dreams*. He lives in New York City.

Born in Port Chester, New York, **Rickey Windell George** recalls having written horror since the tender age of five. Now internationally published, he is best known for his unique blending of no-holds-barred carnage and over-the-top sexuality.

George's work has been seen in a host of publications, including *Dark Dreams I* and *II*, *Fantasies, Blasphemy, Chimera World #1, Scared Naked Magazine,* and *Peepshow Magazine*. He is also the author of the 2005 collection *Sex & Slaughter & Self-Discovery*.

Lawana James-Holland, in her words: *For York, member of Lewis & Clark's Corps of Discovery, 1803–1806.*

"History is about more than dates and places. It is about interaction, choices, and life." This is her third appearance in the *Dark Dreams* anthology series. Lawana lives with her husband in the Washington, D.C., area. Please visit her Web site at www.ellenkay.com/lawana.html for more info.

Michael Boatman's stories have appeared in *Red Scream* and *Horror Garage* magazines, and in the anthologies *Sages and Swords; Revenant: A Horror Anthology; Badass Horror; Daikaiju II! Return of the Giant Monster Tales!,* and *Voices from the Other Side: Dark Dreams II*. As an actor, he's best known for his role as Carter on ABC's *Spin City,* and for the HBO comedy *ARLI$$,* in which he played Stanley Babson. He is at work on his third novel, and developing a horror/comedy feature film at Stan Winston Studios in Hollywood. He lives in New York with his wife and four children.

Maurice Broaddus is a lay leader at the Dwelling Place Church, a scientist, and a writer. He's been published in dozens of markets, including *Weird Tales Magazine* and *Dark Dreams II* and *DeathGrip: Exit Laughing* anthologies.

His sole goal is to be a big enough name to be able to snub people at conventions. In preparation for this, he often practices speaking of himself in the third person.

Terence Taylor is an award-winning children's television writer who lives in Brooklyn, where he now writes speculative fiction for adults. His previous stories appeared in *Dark Dreams I* and *II*, and he recently completed his first novel, *Bite Marks*, which he hopes will see publication soon. For more about Terence and his work, visit his Web site at www.terencetaylor.com.

Tenea Johnson was blessed to be born a Johnson, "the latest survivors in a long line of the constantly strong." She has learned to coax the stories from congas, djembes, and jazz guitars. Together, they created fusions: storytelling to music. So far the Knitting Factory, Dixon Place, the Public Theater, and others have opened their doors to the form. Recently, she started an independent label, Counterpoise Records, to amp her signal. Her fiction, fusions, poetry, essays, and interviews have appeared in *African Voices*, *Arise*, *Humanities in the South*, *Infinite Matrix*, *Contemporary American Women Poets,* and *Necrologue*. You can reach her at latestsurvivor@hotmail.com.

Christopher Chambers is the author of three Angela Bivens mysteries, *Sympathy for the Devil, A*

Prayer for Deliverance, and *Official Mischief,* the last of which has been optioned to USA Networks. His historical novel, *Yella Patsy's Boys,* noted in the *Federal Register* by the U.S. Senate, comes in 2008. He has written short stories featured in major literary magazines. He is also coauthor of two graphic-adventure collections: *The Darker Mask* and *The Green Hornet & Kato Return.* He is a veteran of the *Dark Dreams* series. Mr. Chambers resides in Washington, D.C.

B. Gordon Doyle, in his own words:
Born and raised in the Empire State,
The son of the son of a preacher.
A dark horse, a falling star.
The last of the Dunbar Apache.

Knave of ravens, reluctant magician.
Out of the blue and bold as love,
I go walking after midnight along
The moonlight mile.

L.R. Giles is a Virginia native whose work has appeared in *Dark Dreams I* and *II.* His serial novella "Necromance" was featured at www.awarenessmagazine.net and his full-length novels *The Darkness Kept* and *See/Saw* are currently seeking homes. Check out more of his work at www.lrgiles.com.

Tish Jackson has been writing since elementary school, usually creating stories of suspense or horror to terrify her family and friends. She is also an avid poet and was a regular on the poetry circuit in the Bay Area and Las Vegas. She has written for several Web sites as an editorial columnist, and currently runs a Web log,

"Really Smart Talk," where she participates in the monthly "Radical Women of Color Carnival." However, Ms. Jackson has decided to focus more on the creepy aspects of literature, as those seem to be the most satisfying. This will be her first published horror story.

Brandon Massey was born June 9, 1973, and grew up in Zion, Illinois. He is the author of the supernatural thriller novels *The Other Brother*, *Within the Shadows*, *Dark Corner*, and *Thunderland*; a collection of short fiction, *Twisted Tales*; and editor of *Dark Dreams: A Collection of Horror and Suspense by Black Writers* and *Voices from the Other Side: Dark Dreams II*.

Mr. Massey currently lives near Atlanta, Georgia, with his wife and their two dogs. Visit his Web site at www.brandonmassey.com for the latest news on his forthcoming books.

Grab the Hottest Fiction
from
Dafina Books